VACATION
STORIES

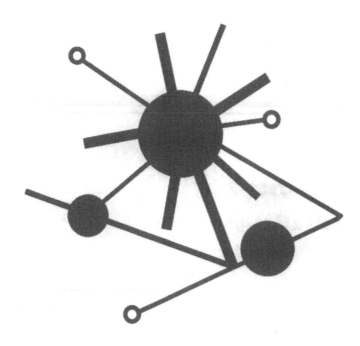

VACATION STORIES

FIVE SCIENCE FICTION TALES

Santiago Ramón y Cajal

Translated from the Spanish
by Laura Otis

University of Illinois Press
Urbana and Chicago

First Illinois paperback, 2006
© 2001 by the
Board of Trustees of the
University of Illinois

∞ This book is printed on
acid-free paper.
Library of Congress
Cataloging-in-Publication Data
Ramón y Cajal, Santiago, 1852–1934.
[Cuentos de vacaciones: Narraciones
seudocientíficas. English]
Vacation stories : five science fiction
tales /Santiago Ramón y Cajal ;
translated from the Spanish
by Laura Otis.
p.   cm.
Includes bibliographical references.
ISBN 0-252-02655-1 (alk. paper)
1. Science fiction, Spanish.
I. Otis, Laura, 1961– .
II. Title.
PQ6633.A63C813   2001
863'.62—dc21   00-011587

PAPERBACK ISBN 978-0-252-0-7355-7

University of Illinois Press
1325 South Oak Street
Champaign, IL 61820-6903
www.press.uillinois.edu

CONTENTS

Figure 1. Santiago Ramón y Cajal, in *Les Prix Nobel* (1906). Courtesy of Ulrike Burgdorf, Max Planck Institut für Wissenschaftsgeschichte, and the library of the Technische Universität, Berlin.

INTRODUCTION

Laura Otis

In 1905, a collection of five *Vacation Stories* appeared. Its author called himself "Dr. Bacteria." Dealing with scientific ethics, biological warfare, and the social responsibilities of scientists, the *Vacation Stories* challenged people's assumptions about the way science worked. What is more, they challenged the political system, organized religion, and social class privileges. The author of these stories was Santiago Ramón y Cajal (1852–1934), who a year later would win the Nobel Prize for medicine.

Originally, there were twelve *Vacation Stories*. Cajal wrote them early in his career, but he waited nearly twenty years to publish them. According to Cajal, the stories were unoriginal and stylistically defective. More probably, he feared that these "anti-religious, anti-establishment" tales would jeopardize his scientific funding (O'Connor 100). Cajal waited to publish them until his scientific reputation was well established, and he never circulated them generally, showing them only to trusted friends. If these are the five stories he chose to publish, we can only wonder what the other seven were like. Sadly, we will never know, since they were lost in Madrid during the Spanish Civil War (Tzitsikas 29).

Cajal as Scientist

Cajal won his Nobel Prize for showing that neurons were independent cells, disproving the prevailing hypothesis that they formed a physically continuous net. He shared it with Italian anatomist Camillo Golgi, who favored the nerve net idea but whose staining techniques allowed Cajal to see individual cells. Cajal's vision of dynamic, freely branching neurons gave rise to our current understanding of the nervous system. His beautiful, intricate drawings of neurons are so striking—and so accurate—that they are still used in neuroscience textbooks today.

Originally, though, the "Father of Neurobiology" did not want to be a scientist. He wanted to be an artist.

Born in the village of Petilla de Aragón, Cajal grew up in Navarre, one of the poorest, most rural regions of a country not known for scientific achievement. In the 1870s and 1880s, however, when Cajal was studying medicine, Spain was by no means a scientific backwater. Many gifted microscopists and bacteriologists were investigating the causes of disease, but Spanish scientists lacked the international connections and support systems of those in Germany or France.

Cajal's father had escaped poverty by walking to Barcelona, over two hundred miles through mountainous country. There he fulfilled his dream to become a surgeon, surviving as best he could while taking his courses. A man of invincible will, he was determined to make his son a physician, which at that time was a more prestigious occupation than that of surgeon. Unfortunately, though, his unruly son wanted only to ramble and draw.

From his youngest days, Cajal loved nature. He regarded school as a prison and preferred spending his time outdoors. During particularly boring classes, he made elaborate drawings in the margins. His favorite subjects for sketches were terrible battles between warriors—later, between different kinds of cells. Frustrated, his father took away his paper and pencils and apprenticed him to a cobbler. After one dangerous prank, he had him imprisoned for three days. It was no use, however. Cajal continued to draw, and he continued to hate school.

As a young man, Cajal studied at Catholic schools in Jaca, then in Huesca, but he always felt he was wasting his time. Education in his day meant rote memorization, an absorption process motivated largely by fear. Believing that "la letra con sangre entra" (learning comes only with blood), the teachers beat their slow or unwilling learners. A visual thinker, Cajal learned best through observation; he could never remember words dissociated from things. For him, walks along the Aragón river were much more enlightening than the abstract language he was forced to memorize. He still had no interest in medicine.

In anatomy, though, Cajal found ways to combine his exploratory instincts and artistic talent. His father, who had himself become a physician after having become a surgeon, won a post as a medical laboratory assistant at the University of Zaragoza, and in 1868 the father and son began dissecting cadavers. During the same year, Cajal discovered photography, which would interest him for the rest of his life. Once science and medicine became a visual experience, Cajal found himself fascinated by the human body. His anatomical drawings pleased his father so much that he attempted to publish them. Cajal began studying medicine in earnest and was licensed to practice five years later, in 1873.

Gradually, Cajal's fascination with the way the body worked inspired new interests in everything. In medical school, he was especially intrigued by Rudolf Virchow's depiction of the cell as an independent being. He was deeply impressed by the evolutionary theories of Jean Baptiste Lamarck, Herbert Spencer, Charles Darwin, T. H. Huxley, and Ernst Haeckel, and he explored the philosophical works of Immanuel

Kant, Johann Gottlieb Fichte, George Berkeley, and David Hume (López Piñero 13). He mistrusted metaphysics, however, especially Friedrich Hegel's ideas, since this kind of thinking seemed divorced from physical experience.

Cajal would have to wait before he could pursue his new interests, however. At the time, there was a mandatory draft, and the young doctor was sent first to the Carlist campaign, then to Cuba. Since 1833, the conservative Carlists had disputed the succession to the Spanish throne, contending that King Ferdinand VII's daughter, Isabella II, had no right to it because she was a woman. During the nineteenth century, the Carlists staged several armed uprisings, waging all-out war when the question of succession arose again in 1868. In the same year, Cuban nationalists attacked their Spanish colonizers, demanding independence. Cajal was sent to both campaigns as a military doctor, with the rank of captain. In Cuba, he was placed in charge of two hundred patients suffering from malaria and dysentery and almost died of malaria himself (Tzitsikas 9).

When the emaciated Cajal returned from the war in Cuba, he would face even greater trials: it was time to look for an academic job. When Cajal came back to Zaragoza in 1876, he immediately resumed his anatomical studies. In 1877, while working in Maestre de San Juan's laboratory in Madrid, he discovered microscopy and was deeply inspired by the new world it revealed. From 1877 onward, he looked for a job that would let him explore the body microscopically.

Candidates for university professorships today visit their campuses in separate, carefully orchestrated interviews; in Spain, in 1876, they confronted one another directly in *oposiciones,* grueling contests that were part examination, part debate. During these contests, the candidates often attacked each other, so that the ones with the best rhetorical skills often emerged triumphant. Twice Cajal entered *oposiciones,* and twice he failed, once for a job in Granada, once in Zaragoza (Tzitsikas 9). Like Juan Fernández, the pessimistic protagonist of his fourth *Vacation Story,* Cajal grew embittered, feeling he was being judged not on his scientific knowledge but on his ability to play with words. Finally, in 1879, he won a post as an assistant professor in Zaragoza. While teaching anatomy and helping his father at the hospital, he studied histology and set up his own microscopy lab.

Once he was able to study cells for himself, Cajal quickly won respect as a histologist. In 1883, he won a chair of anatomy in Valencia; and in 1887, a chair of histology in Barcelona. In 1892, he was appointed professor of histology and pathological anatomy in Madrid, a position he would hold for the next thirty years.

In the 1880s, when Cajal established himself as a scientist, most microscopists were concerned about microbes. Within one decade, German bacteriologist Robert Koch had identified the microorganisms that caused anthrax (1876), tuberculosis (1882), and cholera (1884), and French bacteriologist Louis Pasteur—who had preceded Koch in attributing diseases to microbes—developed vaccines for anthrax (1881) and rabies (1885). Considering how quickly infectious diseases were being attributed to microorganisms, it seemed likely that someday all of them might be explained—and cured—through microscopic studies. In Cajal's fourth *Vacation Story,* for instance, Juan Fernández refers to the "still unknown germs of cancer."

It was one thing to identify a causative microorganism, though, and quite another to develop a cure. To some degree, knowing that germs caused diseases made life much more frightening, since there were few ways to fight them once they had infected the body. During 1885–86, while Cajal was writing the *Vacation Stories,* a cholera epidemic broke out in northern Spain close to Valencia, where he was living. The Spanish bacteriologist Ferrán was trying to develop a vaccine for the cholera bacillus identified by Koch, and Cajal joined other Spanish microscopists in testing Ferrán's sera.

During the same years, Cajal developed a strong interest in hypnosis, which was then the subject of vigorous medical debates. Some scientists, led by French neurologist Jean Martin Charcot, maintained that only neurotics could be hypnotized, and that hypnosis was essentially a pathological state. Others, following French psychologist Hippolyte Bernheim, contended that anyone could be hypnotized, and that the power of suggestion underlay most social interactions. As a physician, Cajal was particularly interested in the use of hypnosis to relieve pain, and he published an article on the use of hypnosis in childbirth. Just as bacteriology presented the body as vulnerable, Bernheim's theory of suggestibility presented the mind as vulnerable. While writing the *Vacation Stories,* Cajal was following two branches of research stressing people's openness to invasive microbes and ideas.

Cajal turned his attention to the nervous system only after the cholera epidemic had waned, but by 1888, he was already convinced that neurons were individual cells. Since 1871, when German anatomist Josef von Gerlach had described nets of tangled cell branches, most neuroscientists had accepted that nerve cells merged. Among these scientists was Camillo Golgi, who had developed a new staining technique. When Golgi applied his potassium dichromate and silver nitrate solutions to neural tissues, only a few cells would absorb it, but they would transport it to all of their branches so that they were revealed in the exquisite detail of a tree in winter. Neuroanatomists still use Golgi's stain and, to this day, they cannot explain why only some cells absorb it. In the 1880s, it revealed extraordinarily complex snarls of cell processes. Were they the cross-links of a net, or the free branches of closely associated individuals?

Confronting complex tangles under their microscopes, neuroanatomists could either keep perfecting their stains, year after year, and try to resolve individual cells, or they could give up the quest and decide that there were no individual cells to see. Unbeknownst to Cajal, two scientists had already challenged the nerve net hypothesis: Wilhelm His, who studied neural development, and August Forel, who studied neural degeneration. The definitive evidence, however, could come only from clear pictures of distinctly bounded nerve endings. Cajal, a brilliant technician, provided this evidence with his studies of the bird retina and cerebellum in 1888–89. In 1891, German anatomist Wilhelm

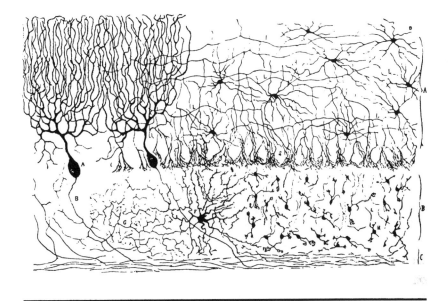

Figure 2. From "The Structure of the Nerve Centers of Birds" (1888)

Waldeyer coined the term "neuron," and by the end of that year, most scientists had accepted that neurons were independent cells.

Vision was thus central to Cajal's work, both in its subject matter and in its techniques. The most essential quality of a scientist, he maintained, was the ability to see clearly. According to Cajal, Golgi was actually *seeing* separate cells, but he believed he was seeing a net because he fell victim to suggestion. While everyone saw the same snarls of cells, it took a special kind of vision to picture them as interwoven individuals. Unlike others, Cajal persisted in his attempts to resolve them partly because he thought the brain needed independent cells in order to work. Only where there were freely terminating individuals could neurons make new connections, and if the nervous system was not dynamic, how could people learn and change their ways of thinking?

Considering his fascination with vision, it is not surprising that Cajal has become as famous for his ideas about science as for his descriptions of neurons. In 1897, he published *Advice for a Young Investigator* (*Reglas y consejos sobre la investigación científica*), originally entitled *A Tonic for the Will* (*Los tónicos de la voluntad*). While intended for aspiring Spanish scientists, it has inspired researchers everywhere. In *Advice for a Young Investigator,* Cajal urged everyone to become "the sculptor of his own brain"—a feat that was possible because of the cerebral dynamism he was demonstrating through his laboratory work. Believing that through individual willpower, anything was possible, he contended that if he could make himself a good scientist, surely anyone could. There was no such thing as a "scientific type"; in science, there was room for everyone. The one essential quality was mental independence, the ability to resist suggestions and see things for oneself.

Cajal as Artist

According to French philosopher Henri Bergson, Cajal first *saw* the truth, then confirmed it experimentally (Marañón 53). Cajal never trusted an idea that couldn't be represented visually, and he thought that words lost their meaning once they were cut off from visual images. The problem of seeing is as essential to art as to science, and Cajal's creative writing, like his scientific drawing, calls attention to the many aspects of vision.

Cajal always knew that he had an inclination for painting, and he believed that drawing taught people to observe the world more closely. In *Advice for a Young Investigator,* he cites comparative anatomist Georges Cuvier, who claimed that without the art of design, natural history and anatomy would have been impossible. According to Cuvier, people needed to understand their own artistic conventions and ways of representing the world before they could start comparing the forms of animals. To see reality as it was, they needed to know what seeing meant.

The challenge of seeing the world just as it is has figured as prominently in literature as it has in science. In Spain, it is best represented by don Quixote, the idealistic knight who believed enchanters were preventing him from perceiving the world's true appearance. Statues of don Quixote have graced many lab benches, and Cajal himself has been called the don Quixote of the microscope. What has received less attention is the way Cajal has "disenchanted" the world through his literature. With his tremendous talent for "painting verbal pictures," Cajal allows readers to see what he sees (Pratt 1993, 14). When people read his stories, they look through the microscope with him (Benítez 28).

Literature was always an important part of Cajal's life. He went regularly to Madrid's book fairs, and he owned more than ten thousand volumes in the humanities (Lewy Rodríguez 16). The *Vacation Stories* were by no means the only fiction he wrote. While studying for his bachelor's degree, he created an adventure novel patterned after Daniel DeFoe's *Robinson Crusoe.* Later, in medical school, he wrote a second one about an explorer who traveled to Jupiter and ended up inside the body of a gigantic being. This biological novel, as Cajal called it, showed readers the body from a microbe's perspective and featured terrible battles between white blood cells and invasive parasites. Both were richly illustrated, but, sadly, both have been lost. Cajal believed the second one disappeared while he was serving in the army.

As literature, the *Vacation Stories* have more in common with these early adventure novels than with his epigrammatic later works. His autobiography—like *Advice for a Young Investigator,* designed to inspire future scientists—appeared in 1901 and sold quite well. Two other works, *Café Conversations* (1921) and *The World from an Eighty-Year-Old's Point of View* (1934) offer astute observations and witty advice about how to survive in society. They reflect his many years of participation in *tertulias,* groups of friends who meet regularly in cafés to discuss political or artistic issues.

As a fiction writer, Cajal owes the most to Jules Verne, whose best-loved novels were appearing just as Cajal developed his passionate interest in medicine. With his vivid descriptions, Verne took his readers to unknown worlds, and it is easy to see why his intensely visual style would have appealed to the artistic medical student. Cajal mentions *Five Weeks in a Balloon* (1863), *From the Earth to the Moon* (1865), and *Around the World in Eighty Days* (1873) as sources of inspiration. To complement his novels of exploration, Cajal believed, Verne needed an adventure about the body, so finally he wrote it himself.

While he was consciously trying to imitate Verne's science fiction, Cajal also re-created some of the classics of Spanish literature. In his first *Vacation Story* he uses the title—and to some degree, the plot—of Pedro Calderón de la Barca's play, *For a Secret Offense, Secret Revenge* (*A secreto agravio, secreta venganza*) (1635). In this play, a man suspects his wife of adultery, and rather than confronting her and her potential lover, he concocts a covert scheme to dishonor him. Cajal's first story owes even more to another of Calderón's plays, *The Healer of His Own Honor* (*El médico de su honra*) (1635), in which a man has his innocent wife bled to death because he suspects her of being unfaithful.

Cajal openly acknowledged his debt to Miguel de Cervantes, and his second *Vacation Story,* "The Fabricator of Honor," recalls one of Cervantes's one-act plays. In this farce, *The Miraculous Altar* (*El retablo de las maravillas*), two con artists set up a table in a small country town, telling the inhabitants that miracles take place upon it, but only Christians of legitimate birth can see them. Naturally, no one admits that he cannot see the elusive miracles. One can understand why the play would have appealed to Cajal, who fought social suggestions that altered people's vision of reality.

Besides drawing on Verne and classical Spanish writers, Cajal owes a great deal to his contemporaries, the Generation of 1898: Azorín, Pío Baroja, and Miguel de Unamuno (Granjel 227). Although Cajal wrote the *Vacation Stories* in 1885–86, he edited them extensively in 1905, so that they could be associated with this literary movement. Like Cajal, its writers focused on individual willpower as a means to regenerate Spain. Alarmed by Spain's loss of its last colonies to the United States in 1898, they lamented their country's slow cultural decay since the mid-seventeenth century and called for political and educational reform. As can be seen in the *Vacation Stories,* particularly the last one, Cajal supported their views that Spaniards needed to study other European cultures but, at the same time, to look inward and learn what made Spain unique.

Whatever Cajal may owe to other creative writers or scientists, his vision is still his own. Like all science and fiction, his *Vacation Stories* allow readers to see things in a new way, inviting them into a world where microbes threaten, but the scientists studying them may be more dangerous still. The loss of his two early novels and seven of the twelve stories is a great tragedy, not just for literature but for science. If Cajal was right, new ways of seeing mean new ideas, and he offered these in his fiction as well as his scientific writing.

Cajal's Incorrect Politics

Cajal may well have suppressed the remaining seven stories for political reasons. In his politics, he was "notoriously left-wing" (Perrín 193). Over the course of his career, he contributed many articles to the liberal journals *El liberal* and *El imparcial* (Lewy Rodríguez 18). A socialist, he regarded himself as a worker and criticized aristocrats who "lived parasitically off the memory of their ancestors" (Perrín 201, 207). When he moved to Madrid in 1892, he chose the working-class neighborhood of Cuatro Caminos because it was the place he felt most comfortable living in. As a scientist, he was never highly paid, and he—and his wife and six children—could probably not have afforded to live anywhere else. Cajal was infuriated by references to Spanish workers' laziness, attributing their low achievements to poverty and ignorance. Having risen from poverty himself, he confessed that "without wanting to, I always discern, on every coin I receive, the sweaty, weather-beaten face of the peasant who definitely pays for our academic and scientific luxuries" (Lewy Rodríguez 21).

While statements like this might have disturbed officials enough to cut off his funding, had they been known, Cajal's left-wing views were combined with beliefs that are hard to reconcile with liberalism today.

As a Spaniard, he was intensely patriotic and considered patriotism one of the most essential qualities for a scientist. Cajal's devotion to his country, moreover, did not stop at the Atlantic and Mediterranean coasts. A dedicated imperialist, he saw science as the key to recovering Spain's lost empire. Like many bacteriologists of his day, he believed that scientists should form a colonial vanguard, attacking the microbes that prevented Europeans from settling in Africa. While such ideas are repugnant today, they were common at the time. Arthur Conan Doyle, another doctor who wrote fiction, ran for parliament as a Liberal Imperialist.

The views on race and gender expressed in the *Vacation Stories* are even more disturbing. Jaime Miralta's long anti-Semitic harangue in "The Natural Man and the Artificial Man" attacks Jews for their lack of patriotism, and many other remarks—sometimes presented by narrators as accepted truths—link general attitudes to particular peoples. An author's view, of course, must not be confused with his character's, and I have found no other anti-Semitic passages in any of Cajal's writing. There are, however, numerous generalizations about race. One must keep in mind that in 1905, race science was a scientifically respected field, an accepted division of anthropology. Among its practitioners were Jewish anthropologists who sought to define their "race" and culture in relation to those of other peoples. Unfortunately, when Miralta refers to the Jews' inherent materialism or women's capriciousness, he is echoing the views of respected authorities.

Cajal's negative depictions of women are also typical for his time. The *Vacation Stories* present women as vain, undisciplined, emotional, and dangerous because of their vulnerability to suggestion. As a whole, the stories are thoroughly misogynistic, reflecting Cajal's own view that a woman is a "necessary evil," a backpack that weighs you down in battle but comes in handy once the fighting is done. In the stories, particularly "A Secret Offense" and "The Accursed House," women are depicted favorably only when they yield to men's superior reason and will.

Judging past writers by present standards, however, has never been a fruitful task. It is important to note that sexism and racism extended to gifted scientists in 1905, and were not restricted to marginal groups, but it is pointless to attack a writer a hundred years after the fact for voicing views generally accepted in his culture.

Instead, we can celebrate Cajal's unique vision, his image of the brain as a dynamic system full of endless possibilities. Cajal's pictures of independent neurons have inspired generations of scientists to "sculpt their own brains." Hopefully, his stories will do the same for all readers.

A Note on the Translation

It has been a great challenge to turn Cajal's nineteenth-century Spanish into twenty-first-century English. Cajal wrote the *Vacation Stories* in the language educated readers of his time would have expected: long, convoluted sentences that sometimes continue for half a page. His level of diction is very high, providing the right tone for his dry humor. Since he is writing for scientific friends, he uses technical terms employed in contemporary journals. Finally Spanish, a wonderfully rich language, offers many words that have no English equivalent, or that are dimmed considerably when replaced with a more general English term.

As a translator, I have done my best to retain Cajal's humor, high tone, and inspirational insights. At the same time, I have tried to make his writing more accessible to modern readers by dividing his long sentences into shorter ones and splicing out a few "that is"s and "in sums"s. Where bacteriological or optical terms require some explanation, I have added footnotes, as I have for words like *tertulia* and *oposiciones,* which cannot be rendered into English.

The information in these notes has been taken in part from the *Enciclopedia Universal Ilustrada Europeo-Americana* (Madrid: Espasa Calpe, 1958), *The New Encyclopedia Britannica* (Chicago: Encyclopedia Britannica, Inc., 1995), *The Oxford English Dictionary* (Oxford: Clarendon, 1989), *Stedman's Medical Dictionary* (Baltimore: Williams and Wilkins, 1995), and Thomas Brock's *Robert Koch* and Arthur Conan Doyle's *History of Spiritualism,* as given in the bibliography.

Acknowledgments

I am deeply grateful to all those who have assisted me with this translation. I owe my greatest appreciation to my loyal friend, Francisco LaRubia Prado, who for fourteen years has not just helped me to appreciate the Spanish language and culture but has enhanced my appreciation of life in general. Without his help, I could never have deciphered Cajal's text. I'd also like to thank my colleagues at Hofstra, Antonio Cao, who explained a few puzzling idiomatic expressions, and George Greaney and Pellegrino d'Acierno, who helped with the Latin and Italian. At the Max Planck Institute, Cornelius Borck, Jean-Paul Gaudillière, Michael Hagner, and Henning Schmidgen provided valuable input on the German and French phrases. I am indebted to Mary Gaylord and Tony Cascardi for informing me about the Golden Age plays that inspired these stories, and to my friend Dale Pratt for his perceptive readings of Cajal's works. I thank Sander Gilman and Bill Regier, whose unflagging support have kept me going this past year. I dedicate this translation to all the neuroscientists studying our plastic, dynamic brains—especially my teachers Mike Stryker and Hugh Wilson, who, like Cajal, have shown me new ways to see.

PREFACE

Many years ago (I think it was in '85 or '86), I wrote a collection of twelve fables or semi-philosophical, pseudoscientific tales that I never dared take to press, both for the oddness of their ideas and the laxity and carelessness of their style. Today, encouraged by the affirmative judgment of some renowned literary scholars, I am hurrying to publish them, though not without retouching their form and updating the scientific data on which they are based.

If the educated public likes these literary trifles, the present collection will be followed by another that will complete the dozen stories. If, on the other hand—as one may expect—my scientific sermons and stale lyricism do not find favor in their eyes, the rest of these compositions will sleep the slumber of all failed artistic works, which must be far deeper than the so-called *sleep of oblivion.*

The subtitle, *Five Science Fiction Tales,*[1] means that these stories are based on reasonable facts or hypotheses from the biological sciences and modern psychology. Consequently, it would be good (but not indispensable) for the reader who wants to understand the characters' words and ideas in these simple fables to have some familiarity with natural philosophy and general biology, even if it is very rudimentary.

About the foundation and genesis of the book I have little to say. The rather extravagant speeches that grace it represent the unbosoming or dynamic compensation of a spirit exhausted by twenty-five years of discipline and scientific work. They are the stretches and capers of a restless imagination impatiently champing at the bit in the horse-powered pump of teaching. Regarded this way, these narratives are like the joyous, playful café tales with which a gloomy, lachrymose elegiac poet releases his bile, or the laments of the *cante jondo,* a sentimental compensation used by the expansive, lively, bantering Andalusians. But then, they are the exclusive work of a few wheels in the cerebral mechanism, or in other words, the motor discharge of some neglected fallow fields in the brain. It is hardly necessary to dwell on their clumsiness, inconsistency, and deficiency of style.

Five stories have been included in this volume. In the first, which opens the way under the emblem "For a Secret Offense, Secret Revenge," the author intends simply to entertain. At the same time, he hopes to expose some striking traits in the curious psychology of scientists, which is essentially amoral and profoundly egotistical (there are exceptions, of course). The second and fourth offer rather ordinary, respectable philosophical and scientific theses, though in a form far too declamatory and diffuse. The third, entitled "The Accursed House," contains a transparent symbol of the ills and remedies of our fatherland (pardon me, you leaders of literary naturalism!). If we can believe those who have read it, it is the least offensive one in the col-

1. Cajal's original subtitle was *Narraciones seudocientíficas* (*Pseudoscientific Narratives*). I have changed it to *Five Science Fiction Tales* because "pseudoscientific" has much stronger negative connotations today than it did in 1905 and creates a false impression about the nature of the stories.

lection. Finally, the last one, labeled "The Natural Man and the Artificial Man," is a critical, pedagogical study I have recently composed about the routines, weakening, and decay of national education.

A word of warning to the suspicious and malicious before I close. The characters in our stories sometimes expound and proclaim the most exaggerated, contradictory systems of thought, and as one may presume, they are liable to considerable inconsistency, ignorance, and naïveté. This results from our desire that the protagonists be more like real men than symbols, and that they offer the passions, defects, and limitations of real flesh-and-blood people. Of course, the author does not accept responsibility for any of the preposterous ideas defended by these characters, not even when he fails to disguise his sympathy for the moral figure of Jaime (last story) and don José ("The Accursed House").

VACATION
STORIES

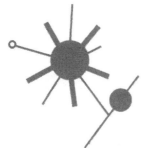

FOR A SECRET OFFENSE,
SECRET REVENGE

Dr. Max v. Forschung, Professor Ordinarius at the University of Würzburg, *Geheimrath,* member of the *Phys. und Med. Gesellschaft,*[1] fortunate author of brilliant physiological and bacteriological discoveries, lived as happily as scientists can live who are disquieted and kept awake at night by the devouring fever of investigation and the desire to emulate glorious reputations. At fifty, he was tall, lean, and red-haired, with green eyes full of goodness. He had thin lips that expressed irony and formed simple, precise words, for he was accustomed to conveying the truth without veils or rhetorical artifices. Seen in profile, he exhibited one of those long, hammer-shaped

1. In German, *Forschung* means research. At the time this story was written, Professor Ordinarius was the highest academic rank for a professor at a German university. *Geheimrath* was an honorary title bestowed by the government on outstanding academic scholars.

heads that seem expressly made to beat obstinately on the facts until they emit some sparks of light. Slightly bent in the shoulders and thin in the arms and legs, he looked like a grapevine in winter. Like the vine, he offered a dry, harsh exterior, but when the warmth of thought came upon him, he produced beautiful, savory fruits. In sum, our scientist was gawky and plain enough—without actually being deformed or physically repugnant—that he did not make love, which for most men is the perennial preoccupation in life.

Forschung now found himself in the season of true scientific productivity. Every six months he discovered a pathogenic microbe, and on those rare occasions when he found nothing new, he knew how to demonstrate point for point that the microbes described by rival bacteriologists were miserable discredited or false bacilli, and therefore incapable of playing any pathogenic role in man or animals. Needless to say, such an attitude did not please the great master's adversaries, who would have preferred to find deadly germs capable of bringing desolation on half of humanity.

For half a century, Forschung had remained celibate because he had had no time to make women fall in love with him, nor had it entered into his calculations to complicate his life with the care of a wife and children. Undoubtedly, he would have remained single forever—and probably quite happy—if that rogue Cupid, scheming stealthily against Minerva, had not inoculated him with the terrible toxin of love.

Miss Emma Sanderson, a twenty-four-year-old American, fresh, blonde, appetizing, and a doctor of philosophy and medicine from the University of Berlin to boot, was the one charged by destiny to awaken the rather drowsy impulses toward the preservation of the species in that naive scientist.

Let us excuse this fifty-year-old lover. In his place, who would not have done the same? When life is half over, laboratories grow so cold, and friends so self-centered! Besides, there were extenuating circumstances. In addition to being an orphan (which no one can deny is an excellent condition), and possessing a healthy, sparkling, captivating beauty, the aforementioned Emma had the truly diabolical impulse to make herself the professor's private assistant. Perhaps her goal—this is what was said, at least—was to study and gain a command of Forschung's precious methods of investigation, so that she could later export them to the free, Saxon land of America.

How else could it have ended? Forschung passionately longed to acquaint himself with a new field about which he had only vague, very outdated information. For her part, Emma ended up persuading herself that it was no mean bargain to become the wife of a prince of science, a *Geheimrath* who earned 50,000 marks a year and used the aristocratic *von* in front of his glorious name . . . And so, leaving preambles and prudishness aside, she accepted the scientist's hand.

Let us be impartial. Let us admit, with generosity, that the bold American was far from being a vulgar gold digger. In two years of daily scientific cohabitation and intimate spiritual communion, Emma fell in love with—or at least believed herself to have fallen in love with—the prestigious master. Glory fascinates enlightened, cultivated spirits, and the pleasant doctor, who had perfumed incubators and autoclaves, microscopes and swan-neck flasks with her beauty, came to feel an affection for that microbial Eden, where the lofty *fiat lux* of scientific creation had so often sounded.

One must admit—and we say it with envy—that the protagonist of this story succeeded in this rare opportunity granted by fortune. What a great stroke of luck to unite, in a single body, wife and helper, spiritual and sensual confidante, shrewd counselor, capable of understanding the shudderings of the soul (in those agonizing times when the microscope seems like a dark well and the incubator, a Pandora's box), and faithful, rapid executor of experimental intuitions! But let us not distract ourselves from the matter at hand.

Once married, the couple took great care to avoid the horrid vulgarity—and who could blame them?—of spending their honeymoon in Paris or Switzerland, like any other ordinary bourgeois newlyweds. They likewise rejected the *commis voyageur,* which provides tickets à *moitié prix*[2] for a honeymoon trip. On the contrary, they decided to exploit the enthusiastic ardor of their first months together to carry out an interesting, fruitful scientific exploration. And so, equipped with their instruments, they traversed Greece and Egypt, Syria and Persia, and had the good fortune to discover and cultivate several virulent microbes. Among them was one undocumented bacillus responsible for the severe dermatosis one encounters in sleepy eastern villages.

When they returned, they continued their investigations of the new parasite's etiology with even greater eagerness and fervor, if such a thing is possible. They discovered a serum that successfully counteracted its effects, and they published a long, luminous report, illustrated with splendid chromolithographs, in the *Zeitschrift für Hygiene und Bakteriologie.*[3]

Just about the time that this interesting communication appeared, Forschung's brave, gallant collaborator brought to light another microbe, that is to say, a strong, beautiful baby boy, incubated under the fiery sun of Palestine . . . Needless to say, this new sprout received the name of Max; and the microbe, *bacillus Sandersoni,* in honor of the winsome assistant.

Dr. Forschung had achieved his highest aspirations. Four things now bore his name: a pathogenic microbe (not to be confused with the recently discovered one), a son, an attractive woman, and a street in the city's new district, the elegant *Forschungstrasse,* lined with thick-topped linden trees just like the renowned *Unter den Linden* in Berlin.

Who could ask for more? To have people who envied him? There were dozens. Ferocious enemies? There was no shortage. His glory lacked nothing . . . except for misfortune. And the good scientist came to know it . . . Yes, he suffered the same disappointment in love as any vulgar, prosaic philistine abandoned by his hysterical, uncomprehending wife.

2. à *moitié prix,* half-price
3. As of 1886, there was a *Zeitschrift für Hygiene,* founded by Robert Koch and Carl von Flügge.

He came to roar with jealousy and desperation just like any novice in love . . . But let us not anticipate events or change the order of narration.

Three years after his expedition to the East, the scientist fell into a deep depression. He became involved in scientific polemics full of acrimony and personal attacks, initiated by insolent challengers who could not pardon him for having relegated their mediocre minds to the background. Profound meditation and persistent experiments to gain control over the intoxicating state of things had undermined his health and embittered his character. The devouring fever for new truth, the desire to discover some decisive fact that would redeem his theory and crush his enemies, gradually became an agonizing obsession. In comparison to that, what did other feelings matter? And so, as is wont to happen, the fire in his mind stole all the fuel from the burnt offerings of love.

One must recognize that when one is fifty-three years old and has a pretty young wife, devoting oneself excessively to science can be a little dangerous . . . At great expense, Forschung learned this sad truth. But let us recount the facts in an orderly fashion.

Gradually, our scientist began to notice that the loving feeling of his home had changed for him. The thing is that, in the face of the doctor's indifference, Emma had reacted in her own way. Her impetuous flights of feeling had given way to a coolness and reserve that deeply disturbed the scientist. A certain disquieting conjecture was appearing, then disappearing in his mind—weak and hesitant at first; then, more emphatic and colorful; and at last, agonizingly strong, painfully shaking the most intimate fibers of his being.

In vain he tried to cast it aside. His efforts, though, only helped the empty shade to fill his surroundings with accusations, to coagulate into human flesh and acquire a vibrant reality. Finally, as if fantasy and reason had finished their creative work, and his will, now tamed, had entirely adapted itself to the distressing vision, he exclaimed bitterly:

"There's no doubt about it! Some man has cast a shadow over my wife's soul . . . And this man can be none other than Mosser, my romantic, scatter-brained assistant . . ."

Doctor Heinrich Mosser, *Privatdozent*[4] at the university and laboratory assistant to Professor Forschung, was the very epitome of the southern type so admired by the pale, prudish daughters of the north. A very tall man with a bizarre countenance, he had lusterless, dark skin and an aquiline nose. His huge, enflaming, fascinating black eyes offered the attraction of an abyss and the provocation of an irresistible don Juan. With its shadowy, mysterious depths, his entire swarthy, arrogant figure seemed expressly made to set off the bright, rosy highlights of blond, Saxon flesh. To complete this portrait, let us mention his head of curly, jet-black hair, an excellent decorative frame for an impeccable bust. His curled, pointed, well-trimmed beard gave his face some indefinable priestly, majestic air reminiscent of those proud, correct, solemn heads of Assyrian rulers on the bas-reliefs of Nineveh. Without a doubt, Mosser must have been known among his friends down at the *brasserie* as *the Terrible Ashurbanipal.*

Perhaps time, which dissolves all things, and scientific worries, which are the best product of afflicted souls, would finally have erased that disquieting conjecture from Forschung's mind. But Providence, which likes to disguise itself as random chance, brought the infamous traitor to light . . . Who was responsible for this? In the laboratory, who else could it be but *the terrible microscope?*

One day, working alone in his laboratory, the doctor spied something on the opaline crystal that underlay his preparations and brought them into focus. Much to his astonishment, he saw two long hairs: one, straight and blond; the other, curly and black, entwined in an intimate, passionate embrace . . .

The fact in itself, of course, was hardly worthy of note. Every day that laboratory was visited by students sporting hairs of many different colors. The surprising, disconcerting thing for poor Forschung was

---

4. A *Privatdozent* is a lecturer at a university, a teacher or laboratory assistant who does not have a permanent position on the faculty.

that, when viewed under the microscope, the black hair had exactly the dimensions, color, and length of his assistant Mosser's, while the blond one perfectly matched the splendid gold filaments of Emma's crown. If any doubt remained as to the origin of these fibers, a micro-chemical analysis resolved it. The dark one revealed a few minuscule droplets of bergamot, Mosser's favorite shaving lotion. On the blond one, he could see traces of essence of oregano, Emma's perfume of choice. Both compounds could be found in the laboratory, where, as is known, they are used to prepare histological sections.

But what astounded the unhappy scientist was the accusing posture, the intimate relationship of those two hairs. Bitter, overwhelming suspicions passed through Forschung's mind, shaking him with terrible fits of trembling! Now there could be no doubt! The entwining and wriggling of those two microscopic organs was more than symbolic. In reality, it represented the faithful image of other, macroscopic entwining and wriggling, which the doctor could not even imagine without feeling his heart pound with rage!

"Good God!" exclaimed poor Forschung, once his agitated nerves had calmed themselves a little. "To what depths of intimacy and criminal abandon can those disloyal heads and bodies have sunk, that their hairs have entwined themselves so inextricably?"

Assuming a facial expression somewhere between bitterness and irony, in which there glittered a sparkle of the scientist's inquisitive passion, he added:

"Now, here's a deep, psycho-physiological problem that I must resolve without losing an instant. My outraged honor demands it. The continual attacks on my scientific work also require it, for the paralysis of my research would bring my unjust adversaries the greatest possible satisfaction . . . Anything is better than living shrouded in darkness . . . anything, even disillusionment with love and trust. And I shall avenge myself secretly, avoiding the scandal and taunts of the world at large . . . I will do it through original scientific procedures, which will remain unknown even to their victims . . ."

As one can see, even in Forschung's fits of indignation, the investigator predominated over the husband. The idea of stooping to vulgarity, of avenging this outrage to his marital honor according to the muscular formula of stone-age man—of falling back on violent motor reactions that he shared with all other animals—infinitely pained his self-love.

A scientist, you see, has an eminently aristocratic mind. Those who know him only by his works—poor, innocent souls—believe that he labors for the good of humanity! Such is not the case: he works for his own pride! The investigator loves progress . . . the progress that he brings about himself. When the press notes the appearance of a new truth triumphing over distance, pain or death, the world prostrates itself before the genius, intoning clamorous hosannas. Only the men in laboratories applaud coldly, mutedly, . . . taking care to play down the value or originality of the invention, if they are not—as is also often the case—maintaining their sepulchral silence.

Yet still, if we disregard the private, egotistical driving force that moves the investigative spirit and focus exclusively on the social impact of each discovery, the scientist's claim to altruism is affirmed. His inventions really do benefit humanity. The apparent contradiction dissolves when we remember that in science, as in love, the protagonist is deceived by Nature. By virtue of an irremediable illusion, the scientist and lover believe—as far as their own respective functions are concerned—that they are working *pro domo sua,*[5] when in reality, they are only working for the good and glory of the species. Oh, what supreme inventions, what powerful forces for progress are imbecilic pride and the vain desire for glory!

But, leaving aside all cumbersome digressions, let us again take up the thread of our tale. When we left off, the aggrieved Forschung was doubting his wife's loyalty. Deeply disturbed by his feverish imagination (the renowned imagination of the scientist), he was beginning to take these images of the lewdest, most criminal pleasures for reality.

5. *pro domo sua,* for their own sake

Yet with all of this happening, one must confess that the jealous husband had nothing but glimmers and inklings . . . no decisive proof of Emma's dishonesty. Finally he came to recognize this and conceded that, before carrying out his terrible premeditated vengeance, it was absolutely necessary to convert these vague signs into flagrant, accusing proof.

Unfortunately, scrupulous new explorations of the laboratory furniture yielded data of great importance.

One day, when Forschung was using a magnifying glass to examine the chaise longue in the library adjacent to the lab, he discovered new pairs of accusing hairs and other highly significant tokens. Silken threads from Emma's blouse were consorting intimately with woolen filaments from his assistant's gray suit. What is more, one could detect unusual depressions, molds, and chaffings in the couch's stuffing, suggesting how that weary piece of furniture had creaked in time to the spirited movements of passion it had contained. What desecration! To dishonor that comfortable divan whose soft, cool velvet had so often soothed the scientist's agitation when, after interminable hours of mental fatigue, he had anxiously sought—in the refuge of meditation—an explanation for unexpected results in the day's experiments!

Eager to know the whole truth, our scientist decided to persist with his investigations, but to carry them out without arousing the suspicions of the happy lovers. Like microbes cultivated on a slide, they swam and refreshed themselves prettily, far from realizing they were the target of persistent observation.

To obtain the critical evidence, he set up four Marey receptors[6] under the feet of the aforementioned piece of furniture so that they were

6. French naturalist and photographer Etienne-Jules Marey (1830–1904) developed new technologies for the systematic study of motions. He is best known for his series of photographs analyzing complex movements like walking. The device described here is based on German physiologist Hermann von Helmholtz's myograph, which charted the time courses of muscle contractions. Working on the same principle as modern seismographs, Helmholtz's and Marey's apparatuses used rolling cylinders of paper to plot changes in position over time.

hidden by the carpet. These were linked via rubber tubes to a receiving device he had installed inside a cabinet. Operated by electricity, the mechanism was rigged in such a way that it could only be activated when two people whose combined weight exceeded 225 pounds settled onto the couch. With things arranged in this fashion, he waited tranquilly, like a camouflaged hunter, to take a shot at the turtledoves. Soon they would be denounced, personally and unwittingly, by the writing of the machine.

Several days passed, and the smoky paper remained untouched. But, ah! One night, when Forschung had just returned from the Royal Academy of Physical and Natural Sciences where he had delivered a lengthy paper, he saw, with growing amazement, that two people had been resting on that piece of furniture . . . or, rather, more accurately, that they had not modestly limited themselves to resting . . .

Stupefied, the good man studied the long, graphic printout, as eloquent and explicit as any scientific document. Instead of accusing the traitors in vague, general terms, it marked out, with cruel pleasure, every phase of the repugnant crime. The graphic record began with subtle inflections, but minutes later, the curves seemed to have been seized by a sudden fit of illness, exhibiting great mountains and valleys. The rhythm then assumed an unwonted liveliness, which became a gradual crescendo until, at last, the allegro movement came—a bold, extremely high, and valiantly sustained plateau. After a magnificent pause, the inscription came to an end, returning languidly and meekly to its primitive state of repose . . . to the straight line, perhaps, of disillusion and fatigue . . .

Now there could be no room for doubt! His ungrateful wife, the one who claimed to be in love with the scientist, the one who had vowed to devote her life to enhancing the glorious investigator's precious existence, had forgotten her sense of decency and sullied the immaculate honor of the prince of science! Ah! Such an outrage called for revenge . . . terrible revenge!

2

During the period in which these events took place, heated debates were occurring at medical congresses and scientific academies about whether tuberculosis was transmissible from animals to man. It was an important question, for only its definitive solution would prove the legitimacy or inappropriateness of certain prophylactic measures. Opinions were divided. Certain scientists, headed by the illustrious Koch, declared themselves *pluralists* and contended that the human tuberculosis bacillus cannot be transmitted to various mammals, particularly the cow.[7] Other bacteriologists, Forschung among them, maintained with equal obstinacy that the tuberculosis microbe found in the ox, the rabbit, the guinea pig, in short, in most domestic animals, was always capable—when its virulence was artificially enhanced—of provoking genuine pulmonary tuberculosis in the human species.

To support their respective theories, both contingents cited illuminating and apparently irrefutable experimental results. The controversy continued, however, for no one had ever attempted the one decisive experiment: the production of tuberculosis in a healthy human being by inoculating him with microbes taken from other animals. Naturally, respectable feelings of humanity and scientific morality prohibited the performance of such a rash, radical experiment.

Now that the reader is acquainted with these facts, he will undoubtedly guess what the rancorous Forschung's intentions were: to turn the

7. When Cajal wrote this story in the mid-1880s, German bacteriologist Robert Koch (1843–1910) believed that the bovine tuberculosis bacillus could produce tuberculosis in humans. By the time Cajal was editing the story for publication in 1905, however, Koch was creating considerable controversy by claiming that the bovine bacillus could not give people tuberculosis. Koch, who had discovered the tuberculosis bacillus in 1882, was then the most highly respected bacteriologist in the world, and his opinion carried a great deal of weight. If he were correct, governments and dairy industries would be wasting the money they had invested in programs to pasteurize milk. There is a slight biographical similarity between Forschung and Koch in that Koch left his wife in 1891 for a beautiful actress thirty years his junior. When Cajal wrote the story in 1885–86, he could not have known this was going to happen, but the scandal was well known by 1905.

unwitting lovers into guinea pigs, into animal vili. But the crafty doctor planned his experiment in such a way that, without ever compromising his scientific aims, it would constitute irrefutable, accusing proof of the adulterers' guilt. Here is the ingenious way he carried out his Machiavellian plan.

Most evenings, when they had finished their work in the laboratory, the assistant Mosser would write out and affix the labels to the preparations and test tubes. To avoid confusion, he always performed this task himself. Very well: one night the professor gathered up all the unused labels and amused himself by dexterously covering the gummy sides with a certain gelatin solution spiked with the finest hint of crystal and some extremely virulent bovine tuberculosis germs . . . Then, with the cool patience of a fisherman, he awaited the results of that terrible experiment.

He didn't have very long to wait . . . Twenty days after the bait was laid, Forschung had the keen satisfaction (as a man of science, naturally) of spotting some tiny papules on Mosser's lips and the tip of his tongue that looked like signs of incipient tuberculosis. Deceived by the lesion's smallness and painlessness, the unfortunate assistant had paid it no heed. In the giddiness brought on by the joy of conquering an important scientific truth—the transmission of bovine tuberculosis to man—Forschung was tempted to examine the inflammatory nodule microscopically, to see whether it contained Koch's bacillus. But realizing how imprudent such a test would have been, he decided to forego it, restricting his role to that of a mere clinical observer. To prevent new, accidental inoculations from complicating the results and perhaps warning the inattentive youth of his condition, Forschung destroyed all the contaminated labels, replacing them with harmless ones.

Twenty days of mortal anxiety passed by, during which Forschung stealthily observed his wife's mouth and lips. He was already beginning to regret the evil act he had committed against his assistant when one morning he spotted a painful-looking eruption upon Emma's labial commisure. When the doctor analyzed it in secret, it turned out to be a genuine, quite typical tubercle. To top off this powerful evidence, the Ziehl-Neelsen staining technique[8] revealed the presence of numerous specimens of Koch's tuberculosis microbe.

At last, the unknown had become completely clear! It was easy enough now to retrace the steps of that experiment. The germ had first attached itself to Mosser's lips, from which, borne on the wings of a kiss, or, more probably, on those of an endless, noisy string of sinful explosions, it had moved on to Emma's sweet, savory mouth. What a terrible pity the uninformed woman had not pre-inspected the mouth she had longed to kiss! But just try to get a woman in the throes of flaming passion to use disinfectants and take the precaution of *microscopically scanning* the object of her desires!

It happened, therefore, that Dr. Forschung achieved admirable success as a scientist, but as a husband . . . At any rate, he was terribly well avenged, and, besides, he had performed an unforgettable service to bacteriology. Confirming his theoretical predictions, he had produced the first decisive proof that tuberculosis could be transmitted from animals to man. Hygienic and medical journals would sing the praises of his new contribution to science, and his adversaries, the pluralists, would learn a hard lesson. One more triumph would be added to his already incalculably long list of titles, merits, services, and discoveries . . .

To tell the truth, though, the memory of that outrage perpetrated against his conjugal honor was still keeping him up at night. He was no longer in love . . . or so he thought. Now indifferent to beauty's bewitching spells, he sacrificed himself only upon the majestic altar of science. Besides, he had resolved to distance himself quite definite-

8. In the early 1880s, German physicians Franz Ziehl (1857–1926) and Friedrich Neelsen improved the staining technique that Robert Koch had developed to visualize the tuberculosis bacillus when they introduced carbolic acid and fuchsin. The Ziehl-Neelsen stain has been used by bacteriologists ever since.

ly from his idol, once so beautiful and adorable, but now rendered ugly by disease . . . With all this happening—we repeat—he was not at all happy . . .

Why? It is hard to explain. Infamy does not exist, cannot exist when—as in the case at hand—the dishonor and punishment elude the scandalous response of the outside world . . .

Ah, but the scientist remained a man! In human consciousness, as in the heavens, stars seem to keep shining even after they have been extinguished for some time. In other words, the consequences of moral feelings persist even after they have been rejected by reason. By virtue of this psychological mechanism, a highly unusual affective phenomenon can be explained: Forschung was keenly aware of the comic, grotesque figure he cut. By some doubling of his inner being, part of his personality seemed to have been converted into a spectator, who slyly regarded the other as it suffered in the pillory of ridicule.

In any case, even supposing that the doctor's skeptical philosophy had immunized him against the effects of "what they would say," two painful, open wounds would have continued to bleed: the anger of his offended self-love and the collapse of his dreams of happiness.

3

Three months after the aforementioned events, our scientist was vegetating in the depths of loneliness and withdrawal. In his hatred of the human family, he had separated himself even from his innocent son, little Max. At present, the boy was being raised by one of the doctor's sisters, Anna Forschung, who was married to a professor of philosophy. As for Emma and Mosser, they had been removed—under the advisement of the faculty and with Forschung's approval—to a well-known sanitarium in the Tyrolian Alps for those suffering from tuberculosis.

There, in sight of eternal snows, under a splendidly blue summer sky, the two lovers languished, increasingly emaciated by fever, insomnia, and terrible sweats. In spite of this, though, they were relatively happy. At long last, they dwelt under the same roof—though in different wards—and on the days when they could leave their quarters and go out into the corridor or gallery, they had not just the consolation of seeing one another but the sweet satisfaction of talking about their troubles and comforting their aching hearts.

A young person in pain is optimistic: he believes neither in misfortune nor in death. But among all optimists, the tubercular stands out as the least realistic. Prostrate and powerless on his bed, he plans excursions in the mountain heights. Incapable of stirring, he fancies himself an athlete. As he struggles with death, he dreams of love . . . In no chronic, terminal disease does merciful Nature act with more exquisite consideration. Only in the sad death of the consumptive does the figure of Fate appear veiled and embellished in the triumphal robes of Hymen!

Such was the case, above all, with the unfortunate Mosser. At times he grew worse, and he judged himself near convalescence. Any change, tiny as it might be, struck him as a good omen. One tranquil night, there was a slight remission of his fever. When he stopped spitting blood, it was as though a ray of sun gladdened the atmosphere, bringing a fleeting flush to his waxen cheeks. This slight alleviation of his condition was enough to make the overencouraged young man forget his terrible illness and dream up the sweetest, rosiest illusions about his future. He gratified himself, above all during his loving exchanges with Emma, by giving his fantasy free reign. He dreamed of fleeing with his graceful lover to the free, open-minded land of North America. There, far from the Old World, liberated from the autocracy of egotistical, disagreeable old scientists, they would devote themselves wholeheartedly to the unspeakable joy of love, creating a peaceful, happy home. Not even material matters concerned him . . . Emma still possessed some property in her own country, and, besides, with all the scientific connections he had made while working in Forschung's laboratory, it would not be hard to find a job as professor at some American university—maybe in Boston, the Yankee Athens, home of Harvard University, the best of the best . . .

The congenial Emma, whose beauty had assumed a spiritual quality under the fever's harsh chiseling, consented sweetly to Mosser's encouraging plans. To tell the truth, though, she conceded without much enthusiasm, like one who reserves the right to change her mind. In reality, she did not share her lover's pleasant hopes. A vague disquietude and an indefinable sadness were restraining her soul, cutting short the flight of her golden dreams. The idea of abandoning her son forever, her own flesh and blood, and openly betraying the good, generous scientist whose glorious name she bore made her quake with terror. Besides, could there really be any hope of a definite cure? When she regarded herself daily in the old mirror, she saw—disheartened—that the fever had made her eyes sink, clouding them with blue shadows, and that the roses in her lips had been changed into lilies. To be sure, she had been feeling better and regaining strength for the past two or three weeks, but ah, how slowly!

One morning in September, after a night of dreadful insomnia and persistent, fatiguing fits of coughing, Mosser met his lover in the gallery. Instinctively, they moved toward the balustrade, and, joining their burning hands, they looked outward toward the grandiose panorama of the Alps.

It was nine o'clock in the morning. The brilliant, golden sun was rising majestically over the horizon, warming the atmosphere and inviting the grasses and flowers to raise themselves. Struck obliquely by the yellow rays, the *glaciers* glowed with ivory tones, while the snow's deepest folds, out of the sun's reach, reflected the blue tones of the sky. In the distance, they could hear the dull rumble of rushing streams and the low thunder of waterfalls. From much closer up, from the foot of the hill on which the sanitarium stood, came the sound of the woodsman's ax, whose dull, rhythmic blows made the forest tremble and evoked distant echoes from the huge boulders. Along a nearby path came an oxcart driven by a robust villager, his neck and arms freely exposed to the air. Glowing golden under the sun's fire, his muscles shone with metallic gleams like those of a bronze statue. Behind him flowed a picturesque troop of fresh, happy girls, bearing heavy pails of milk. Last of all, down on the right, at the base of the trail that led up to the icy regions, a group of climbers were preparing their gear, ready to hurl themselves into the conquest of the silent, gigantic, majestic peaks under their eternal coat of immaculate snow . . .

By way of contrast, that pulsing of abundant red blood, that rumbling of potent life, of vibrant human energy, produced a painful, melancholy impression in Mosser's spirit. As for Emma, a dark sadness clouded her face. Her shining eyes, like sapphires in a bed of amethyst, wandered indecisively and languidly about, now regarding the cheerful scenes of the pleasant landscape; now the face of the depressed, brooding Mosser . . . Suddenly, as if prompted by a thought she had had for some time, she exclaimed:

"Ah, Mosser, how wicked we are! It would have been so much better just to have stifled this criminal passion that has brought us such unhappiness! Don't you think maybe this suffering is a punishment from God?"

"Emma, my love, you're talking nonsense! You call this a punishment, this lucky accident that has brought us together? Of course the illness has crippled our bodies, but hasn't it freed our souls? Don't you find comfort and strength in the sweet confidences of our hearts, in the free growth of our desires and hopes?"

"Yes, but our freedom is such a sad thing . . . the freedom to live in pain!"

And wrinkling her brow, as though she were trying to banish an obsessive thought, she added:

"Mosser, there is something I want to confess. For some time now, I've been tormented by a cruel suspicion. I have a feeling my husband has found out about our love and, seeing us mortally wounded, has left us to our sad fate . . ."

"What! Do you really think so? What's the basis of your suspicion?"

"Two very eloquent, significant facts: his strange indifference toward me, which dates to a period just after our own love began, and his odd willingness to let you accompany me to this sanitarium, something truly incomprehensible in a suspicious, jealous husband."

"But allow me, my darling Emma, to tell you that both of these facts prove exactly the opposite. Remember that four months ago, when we were both sick, and I less so than you, I begged him to let me go with you to this place so that I could watch out for your health and notify him about the progress of your cure. Forschung not only consented to my request; he warmly thanked me for my good deed. This trust of his, doesn't it clearly show he was unaware of our feelings?"

"Maybe . . . I want to believe you . . . At any rate, you must agree that his silence and absence for more than three months are quite strange. Doesn't such conduct seem odd to you in a man who is apparently in love with his wife?"

"You put it very well: 'apparently' . . . Although it may hurt your self-love as a divine, adorable woman, permit me to tell you that men bottled up in scientific investigations never love anything but science. Given the choice between a beauty and a microbe, they opt for the latter. For them, a woman represents—at the most—a fleeting, disturbing episode that occurred in their youth. Their passion for glory allows no rival sentiments. Tell me: if I were eagerly pursuing that elusive aura of celebrity, would I be intoxicating myself now with the perfume of your breath? Would I be basking in the light of your eyes and basing my happiness on explorations of your most secret ideas and feelings?"

Seeing his darling Emma a bit more resigned, he continued:

"I find your husband's conduct very natural, given his fervent love of glory and progress. Surely you're not forgetting that the distinguished Dr. Funcke, director of this sanitarium, is a great friend and admirer of Forschung, who not only sends Funcke patients, but sera, vaccines, and tuberculin extracts to try out as cures for various chronic infections. In my understanding, this was your husband's main motive for sending us to this famous establishment, where we are being treated—one must confess—with the exquisite care . . . due to the relatives of an illustrious scientist . . ."

• • •

An unpleasant silence, broken only occasionally by painful fits of coughing, followed this conversation. Seeing that the veil of dark sadness had once again clouded his beloved's eyes, Mosser seized one of her hands, and, covering it with feverish kisses, he added:

"Don't be afraid, little girl. Our illness, these terrible symptoms that have so weakened us, is subsiding. We are going to recover our health and strength—don't you doubt it. Calm yourself, my darling, and know that, no matter how things turn out, I'll be responsible for your safety and your happiness . . ."

Believing that he had guessed the cause of his lover's distressing sadness, he continued, giving his words a tone of heartening confidence:

"Don't worry about your son. On the day of your joyful emancipation—and it is not far off—you're going to get him back . . . Your good-hearted husband is so generous, so indulgent, so knowledgeable about all human failings, that . . ."

• • •

Just at that moment, a chambermaid brought in the mail, leaving some daily papers and scientific journals on the table. Mosser was going through them almost mechanically when, glancing through a scientific article, he suddenly turned pale and was seized by the greatest anxiety. As he continued reading, he was choked by a sudden inability to breathe. His heart pounded violently. Finally, when he could contain himself no longer, he burst into the following exclamations, which were interrupted by harsh, rattling gasps:

"The scoundrel! The murderer! The miserable wretch!"

Poor Emma shook with terror to see her friend so enraged. Summoning her strength, she found the presence of mind to pull the journal from his hands and read the following passage, in a voice that was wet with tears and tremulous from sobbing:

"'I declare myself,' wrote Dr. Forschung with arrogant self-assurance, 'a convinced unitarian in the matter of the etiology of tuberculosis. In my view, all of the bacilli associated with this terrible disease have the same origin and belong to the same botanical species. The differences they exhibit in terms of virulence and preferences for certain animals are easily effaced when the microbe in question is submitted to special procedures of cultivation and growth. Thanks to my new culture technique, the avian tuberculosis bacillus, the piscine, the bovine, that of the tortoise, etc., can all become pathogenic in man, in whom they produce the most severe infections.

"'We had already offered irrefutable proof of this with our old experiments in which animals were inoculated with the human bacillus. Definitive, decisive evidence was still lacking, however, for the transmissibility of the bovine tuberculosis bacillus to man. Motives of a very high moral order detained us as we stood eagerly on the threshold of truth.

"'By a sheer stroke of luck, random chance has come to our aid, offering the proof we have so long desired. In one of those inevitable slips that can occur even in the best-ordered laboratory, a small quantity of pure bovine tuberculosis culture was accidentally spilled onto a box of labels. This culture was so virulent that a fraction of a drop killed a guinea pig by septicemia in just a few days—that is, by inducing the most rapid form of tuberculosis, in which no tubercles are produced (the Yersin type).[9] An ox, a dog, and a goat, inoculated in the same fashion, succumbed in less than eight days.

"'Unfortunately, the unlucky young man in charge of affixing the labels was completely unaware that the contamination had occurred and continued, as he always had, to moisten the gummy side with the tip of his tongue. Fifteen days after the aforementioned accident, a genuine miliary tubercle appeared on his swollen lips. Thanks to the invincible virulence of the germ, this tubercle was quickly followed by submaxillary tubercular infarcts and a metastasis to the lung. Less than

9. French bacteriologist Alexandre Yersin (1863–1943) is best known for his discovery, in 1894, of the bacteria that cause bubonic plague.

a month after the accidental infection, another, very similar lesion appeared on the lips and mouth of the laboratory assistant's unfortunate wife, who, despite my expressed prohibitions, could not restrain herself from dangerous outbursts of conjugal love.

"'Needless to say, we have assured ourselves of the nature of the illness, taking the appropriate measures to analyze the pathological products, which were teeming with Koch's tuberculosis bacillus.

"'At the present time, both patients are under observation at an accredited Swiss sanitarium. From recent reports, we can say that the tuberculosis has gradually become widespread, particularly in the male, giving rise to severe metastases in the lung, liver, and spleen. All indications point toward a fatal outcome, despite the very reasonable treatment and exquisite care lavished upon them by the distinguished Dr. F., who is overseeing their cure (at my expense, naturally, since I must not forget that the patients contracted their illness in my own laboratory). It is my hope that very shortly, the autopsy results from the more serious of the two cases, that of the male, will show that . . .'"

When Emma reached this point, the unfortunate Mosser lost the relative composure with which he had been listening to this dreadful account. Enraged, he crushed the journal in his clenched fists, as Emma, who had turned deathly pale, fell to the floor in a dead faint. Utterly desperate, with the gestures of a raving lunatic, the lover burst into violent insults and imprecations.

"This is abominable, unheard of!" he cried. "Oh, you miserable wretch! So, you're waiting for our autopsy results? You're making a mistake! The one who'll be autopsied is you! I'm setting off this very day to find you, and you'll see how, despite your specially grown microbes, I have more than enough energy left to strangle you with my own hands! . . ."

The heart-rending scene that later ensued between the two lovers is among those that defy the pen . . . one of those that show the pallor and insufficiency of emotional language. But then, when faced with profound suffering, we tend to maintain a certain reserve . . . Let us respect this custom.

Poor, hapless lovers! They, who had so innocently counted on Forschung's pardon or compliance! And to avenge himself in such a low, underhand way, displaying cold-heartedness a thousand times more abominable than the violence of wrath! How vile, to take advantage of infidelity, almost to provoke it, in order to convert one's wife and friend into miserable experimental animals!

4

Eaten away by his terrible infection, poor Mosser never carried out his dreadful plans for revenge. That very night he was attacked by a fit of coughing in which he spat up a copious amount of blood. For days afterward, he suffered from labored breathing so agonizing and severe and a fever so intense that Dr. Funcke lost all hope of saving him.

Shortly thereafter, the unhappy lover died in the sad loneliness of his own ward. Confined to her bed by a flare-up of her own illness, his poor, one-time friend had not even the consolation of watching over him and hearing her beloved draw his last breath! On the other hand, even if her health had allowed her to pay Mosser these last, compassionate tributes of friendship and gratitude, the strict rules of the sanitarium, which forbade any kind of sexual promiscuity on the wards, would have made it impossible. In her soul, Mosser was beginning to be more than a husband, but to the rest of the world, he was only a stranger . . .

Two more months passed by. Winter was coming, which in those lonely alpine heights meant the appearance of heavy snows. With the arrival of the winter cold, Emma recovered some of her strength, which had been almost completely sapped by the terrible crisis she had undergone. A faint carmine colored her cheeks, and in her blue eyes, moistened by tears of sincere repentance, there shone for the first time a ray of hope. Little by little, the painful vibrations died away, and the natural calm of her spirit was reborn, which proved as favorable for restoring bodily health as for producing a clear vision of past events.

With the serenity in her heart came a sense of justice. When she looked back at her memory's happy images through the shadows of recent events, she realized that her recollection of Forschung was progressively losing its bloody tints and melodramatic gestures, growing ever gentler and more human. At the same time, the image of romantic, impetuous Mosser was fading little by little, steadily distancing itself from the vibrant present until it seemed like an idle dream that was about to melt away.

Filled with the benevolence that precedes repentance, Emma finally came to forgive her husband's cruel vengeance, so coldly planned and so mercilessly executed.

"What if, in the end, he was right after all?" she asked in one of her soliloquies. "Of course he acted maliciously, but wasn't the offense malicious as well? Certainly Forschung's rage and the punishment he devised were out of all proportion with the crime, considering that I didn't just blindly abandon myself to my lover's whims . . . At any rate, he should have conducted himself more prudently, demanding an explanation on my part, and maybe . . . But let's be honest: my heart was no longer his, and, sooner or later, the infectious passion of that fiery man, who bewitched me with his looks and drove me mad with his caressing voice, would have led me to dishonor and scandal . . ."

Emma was telling the truth. In reality, she was less guilty than she appeared.

Her feeling toward Mosser was a sensual urge, one of the outer skin, without roots in the heart or the mind. It was a simple effect of suggestion—fiery and overwhelming, if you will—but in the end fleeting, like all results of suggestions. Because of this, as soon as the hypnotist disappeared, the enchantment ended. In the presence of Mosser, who was beautiful with a lion's beauty, bursting with youth and strength, she would feel her senses grow faint and her will grow dim. But as soon as she lost sight of the irresistible seducer, her reason would recover its strength, imposing itself on her overexcited nerves. Despite these eclipses of her will, despite this idyllic love duet which she had sung so lustily for half a year, this straying wife never actually sullied her conjugal honor, at least not in the way that common morality gauges faults. Certainly there had been forbidden pleasures, outbursts of affection that were more or less sensual, effusions that had aroused her husband's suspicions and brought on the entire drama. But—let us repeat—she had never crossed the Rubicon of honor. For all her impressionability, Emma—like a good American—was far too calculating and prudent to yield herself without reserve and risk losing, perhaps forever, an excellent, enviable moral and economic position.

Besides—why not say it?—in some of her Homeric struggles between desire and duty, a soft, maternal feeling came to her aid, detaining her when she was on the verge of making the ultimate concession. Just before she had begun her intimacy with Mosser, Emma had discovered that she was again expecting . . . and she trembled with fear at the thought that one day the consequences of a mother's errors would fall on an innocent child's head.

Ah! If only Forschung had had youth and beauty as well as genius and glory, how happy Emma would have been! What a joy it would have been, to have felt her intelligence and her senses, her vanity and her pride, satisfied all at once! Unluckily, however, such good fortune tends to be an unattainable chimera. Glory, wealth, and social considerations almost always entail an equivalent expenditure of youth and strength. To desire simultaneously, in a single man, the precious, exquisite gifts that Nature usually grants to different individuals, or at the most, to different phases in one individual's life, is to pretend that the seed sown in the earth does not destroy its protective cotyledons or expend its vital energy as it grows into a proud stem and a beautiful, fragrant flower.

5

The letter that Forschung received from his wife two months after Mosser's death was a great relief to his heart, a moving confession of bitter disillusionment and sincere repentance. Maternal love stood out as its central, predominant feeling. Emma wanted to see her husband to beg for his forgiveness, but above all, she was longing to embrace her own child again, to purify and warm herself in the Jordan of youthful innocence and deep, everlasting love . . .

The letter ended by declaring that the senses and force of youth had played a greater role in the wife's flirtation than the true impulses of her heart.

"Only the weakest, crudest part of my soul," she told him, "was on the point of yielding. The best part of it, the love and veneration for an illustrious scientist, the worship of his immaculate name, the gratitude and affection one feels for a husband and father, remained completely intact. If I have sinned in any way, I have been thoroughly punished. I am being perfectly honest with you. Love until death, can that be feigned?"

If any reader has had the patience to stay with us up to this point, he will surely say: "these men of science are proud and cold; they have the souls of Inquisitors or paid assassins. They console themselves by torturing innocent laboratory animals because they can't satisfy their terrible curiosity by experimenting on the palpitating flesh of their neighbors . . ."

But this is a profound error! Just a quick glance through scientists' works should be enough to assure one that they have exquisitely sensitive hearts, more sensitive than those of other men. If they didn't enjoy the greatest impressionability, how would they be able to discover new truths? If they weren't touchy and punctilious about questions of priority, would they still pursue glory? How many of them, unjustly hated by the sensitive old maids of the Societies for the Prevention of Cruelty to Animals (the third sex, according to Ferrero),[10] pass sleepless nights after they have performed bloody, emotionally exhausting vivisections!

10. Guglielmo Ferrero (1871–1942), criminologist Cesare Lombroso's son-in-law, collaborated with Lombroso in his studies of prostitution and female criminality. Ferrero was particularly interested in female sexual deviance.

When it came to wounds to his dignity, Forschung was extremely touchy. It was precisely because of this hypersensitivity of his honor that he had avenged himself and had felt his wife's disloyalty so bitterly. But now, filled with generous indulgence, he was about to forget his resentment.

In truth, things had changed considerably. There is nothing like death to simplify matters of honor. The only one capable of revealing their conjugal mishap had been permanently silenced. In his heart, the scientist gradually felt his old love for Emma starting to bloom again, and he deeply regretted her distressing moral position. He also knew, from his friend Funcke's frequent reports, about her marked improvement. He was confident of a complete recovery, or at least of a temporary amelioration that would allow them to try some heroic measures. Here again, as we shall see, he had his plan.

Forschung answered Emma's submissive letter by writing, more or less: "My dear, somewhat estranged wife: I excuse your weaknesses, for which I realize I was partly responsible. I forgot that the brain is a center for reflection; and the will, a radiometer that fancies itself free because it doesn't see the light. I should have cared more for your impressions and divided my sensibility more equitably between my two idols: between science and you—or, to put it better, between you and science—to the extent of committing an occasional infidelity to the latter in order to avoid the reprisals of the former. Your blue eyes meant something more to me than the eyepieces of a microscope, and your eyelashes deserved more eager, attentive observation than all the bacilli and spirilli in my culture dishes.

"But in the end, things can still be set right. A wonderful discovery I have just made assures me of your definitive cure. You will live, then, and enjoy robust health and happiness so that you may serve as joint testimony to the sovereign power of science and the sincerity of your repentance. Ah, I almost forgot to tell you: within a few days your son and I will be arriving at the sanitarium."

6

And in effect, one morning in February the doctor did indeed arrive, accompanied by the charming young Max, and the reader can well imagine the scene that unfolded. Poor Emma had the ineffable pleasure of clasping her innocent child in her arms and receiving from his father the most moving, undeniable attestations of forgiveness. Deeply touched, masking a few furtive tears, Forschung extended his pity so far as to plant a passionate kiss on his wife's faded, entreating lips . . .

"What are you doing?" cried Emma in dismay. "Have you forgotten how infectious my disease is?"

"Don't be afraid; I know these microbes very well, and I know how to hold them in check. As I told you in my letter, I've brought you an antituberculin serum of whose efficacy I am completely assured. It's a therapeutic secret I have not yet divulged . . . Here you were imagining that your husband had abandoned you, and you were as wrong as you possibly could be. From the very moment you contracted the disease, I suspected that your guilt was perhaps not so great as appearances might lead one to believe. I thought that maybe your excessive nervousness, and the vehemence and sensuality of the false Romeo, had affected you overwhelmingly, without—of course—completely capturing your heart. I also believed that no matter how closely your faint will may have complied, I had no right to inflict capital punishment on the guilty parties. At the most, I could carry out a harsh demonstration that, despite its outrageous principles, would benefit and instruct all humanity.

"Only in war is it permissible to kill; only in the hard-fought battle for free science, in the honor and best interest of the human race, is it right to sacrifice some propitiatory victim. These considerations, along with the grave turn that your illness was taking (something I had not expected), incited me to work feverishly to find a rational, therapeutic method that could successfully fight either the microbe or the action of its toxins. Your love and my intense desire to save you increased my strength and gave me the clear-sightedness necessary to hit the mark.

"At first, the tubercular rabbits treated with this antibacterial, antitoxic serum experienced only fleeting relief from their symptoms. But then, once I modified the procedure for preparing the remedy, most of them held on. In the end, through sheer trial and error and interminable experiments, I obtained a product that abruptly halts the course of the disease in experimental animals (including large-sized ones), killing the bacilli and promoting a full recovery.

"I have it right here," he said, showing Emma a sealed tube in which his precious elixir, a viscous, amber-colored liquid, shone in the lamplight.

"In order to give you the necessary concentration and dose, I have had to sacrifice thirty goats and ten horses. The remedy costs dear, but your health and my happiness are well worth this small sacrifice! What a great pity that poor thoughtless, presumptuous Mosser succumbed before I made this redeeming discovery!"

Poor Emma, transfigured by emotion and bliss, could only respond: "Ah, my dear Max, how good you are!"

7

Thanks to Forschung's serum, within a month and a half Emma was able to leave the sanitarium completely cured.

A trip to Italy with her husband, who was ever more deeply in love with his better half, strengthened Emma's constitution, bringing back the innocent, unreserved joy of other times as it restored the freshness of color and fullness of her face. It was a second honeymoon, reminding them of that unforgettable one they had enjoyed among palms and sycamores under the burning oriental sun.

That journey was like a sponge, wiping away painful memories and preparing the couple for a fruitful new existence. Once the tranquillity of his home had been restored, Forschung devoted himself with growing enthusiasm to the tasks of teaching and research. To make their happiness complete, Emma gave birth to a beautiful baby girl, free from any dreadful tubercular taint and sporting Forschung's reddish hair and yellow-green eyes. Those little red hairs reassured the scientist as much as the others had once tormented him.

But the lucky investigator knew too much about the failings of the human heart and the psychology of his wife, whose impressionability and susceptibility to suggestion he still feared, to leave himself open to any future mishaps. For prudence's sake, Emma stopped working in the laboratory, where she had been alternating with the students and assistants. She was now fully occupied with the tasks and responsibilities of their home and the care and education of their children, sweet, maternal duties that she would not have exchanged for all the Mossers in the world. When she was free, she diligently helped the scientist, straightening up his library, sketching and photographing his microscopic preparations, consulting texts and monographs to simplify the vast bibliographical searches that Forschung's publications demanded, and handling his correspondence. This incessant activity, united with contempt for the doubtful pleasures of vanity, removed from her soul all traces of sickly, dangerous romanticism. Maternal love, an indispensable moral derivative, extinguished the fire of her senses, which no longer thrilled to the subjugating looks of arrogant Lovelaces.[11]

In spite of this, we repeat, Forschung did not suffer from any illusions. The physical contrast between the husband and wife was growing more marked with each passing day. The rough battle of science had consumed the scientist's vigor, so that when he looked at himself in the mirror, he discovered sadly that gray hairs—those ashes of thought!—

11. Lovelace is the complex villain of Samuel Richardson's novel, *Clarissa* (1748). A highly attractive, smooth-talking man, Lovelace begins pursuing Clarissa after first courting her older sister. When her family refuses to let Clarissa marry him, he persuades her to run away to London with him and sets her up in a brothel. Clarissa, however, resists all his physical advances. When he finally drugs and rapes her, she loses her sanity.

had made his temples deplorably white. The crown of his bald head, shiny and smooth, seemed to have been licked clean by the endless waves of ideas.

The handsome Emma, on the other hand, was resisting the action of time and its abrasion, which creates waves of pain in even the strongest, most stoic natures. She maintained her beauty to an admirable degree and seemed to have grown even more graceful and seductive. The sweet tranquillity of her heart, the greatest form of comfort, had given her eyes the brilliance and fine outlines that one normally sees only in children. Her hair, which had been excessively pale, now shone with a rich, succulent, golden bister tone, which set off the immaculate whiteness of her skin quite marvelously.

This divergent evolution of the couple's exterior morphology became a source of profound worry to Forschung. With each passing day, he felt more dissonant and ridiculous when considerations of health or laws of courtesy required that he accompany his wife on her walks and visits.

"Oh!" thought the scientist to himself, "if only I could discover a serum that would rejuvenate me like Faust, or at least slow my decay and let me wait peacefully for my beloved Emma's sweet, gradual decline."

"But unfortunately," he added, "the potion that gives long life, the discovery of the marvelous, vivifying Fountain of Youth, is a crazy chimera. What a beautiful dream! And how insistent it becomes when one is on the threshold of old age, exactly that time when Nature should—out of pity, at least—instill man with a desire for inertia, a humble resignation to death and oblivion. There's nothing to it! To travel, when one is nearing the sea of death, back up the impetuous river of time until one is close to its mountain source! To stand on the banks of the roaring river of youth, before the gayest, most flowery gardens and the most luminous, seductive views! What sublime madness!

"But unluckily for all those Fausts, life is a function of matter and time. It is a mere mechanism, and like industrial machines, is subject to irreparable wear and tear. Our mastery, more nominal than real, of that marvelous steed Clavileño[12] whom we ride across a heaven of illusions and hopes is really only a simple ability to regulate the motor's velocity, so that it consumes the energy allotted to us at birth more or less rapidly. The idle man conserves his fuel, believing that he will live longer, but he tends to live less fully because his slowness of movement allows the machine to rust. The coal, or let's say the grease, overloads and stupefies the heart empty of sentiments and the brain empty of ideas. The scientist, the artist, the hero, the worker, force the machine to function at full steam and exhaust the coal supply before the natural end of the journey . . . if they don't run off the tracks first into the arid fields of neurasthenia and *surmenage* or the terrifying abyss of madness. Only the temperate man, the one who runs at normal velocity without squandering the fuel supply, will reach old age without breakdowns, arriving at the natural terminus of his existence . . .

"But," continued Forschung, through whose mind these thoughts were rapidly passing, "given that in the order of physiological processes, it's easier to run forward than to stop or regress, why (in my own particular case), instead of dreaming of the absurdity of matching my wife's appearance, don't I try to make her match mine? We've rejected the elixir of long life as Utopian, but would we do the same with a serum that causes aging?

"One illustrious scientist has considered it possible that we will discover substances which can arrest the decay of the brain, whose cells— in his view—fall victim to the insatiable voracity of phagocytes and connective elements. Now there's a therapy that strikes me as quite problematic, a realistic hypothesis based on a false supposition. But

12. Clavileño is a legendary flying horse described in *Don Quixote*. In Cervantes's novel, don Quixote's mischievous hosts convince him that he must ride Clavileño through the heavens in order to remove a curse on some young women who have suddenly found their faces covered with beards. They explain that Clavileño appears to be a wooden hobbyhorse because the knight is under the influence of enchanters. The hosts then blindfold don Quixote and Sancho, and they mount the powerful steed. After a long, uncomfortable ride, both seem to believe that they have flown.

what if this conjecture of Metchnikoff,[13] the scientist in question, were taken seriously? What if it were based on real facts, that is, on the existence, within young nerve and muscle cells, of negative chemotactic substances that hold the phagocytes in check? If such were the case, there would be nothing wrong, as far as I can see, with inferring that in aging tissues there are other excitatory materials that attract the phagocytes in a positive sense, provoking the action that ruins and destroys our noble organs . . ."

When he had reached this point, the scientist brusquely interrupted his reflections, exclaiming:

"Let's understand each other! I'd like to find an aging serum, but one that would age people only on the outside, superficially, preserving the noble organs and some of the graceful wheels of the vital machinery. I want a serum, in sum, that would mature my wife's dangerous beauty ever so slightly, adding a few gray strands to her splendid head of hair; discreetly molding a few gentle lines into the firm, pearly skin of her face; softening the fineness and elegance of her figure with a few extra pounds; imposing on her whole outward physical appearance the flavor and color of an overripe, slightly cloying fruit . . ."

• • •

All the wonders of civilization were once mere fantasies of dreamers. But sometimes a stubborn, solidly constructed mind thinks so deeply about a problem that a poet's dream is converted into an actual fact, into a powerful, vivid industrial creation which produces great wealth as well as intellectual and moral fruits.

And so it was with Forschung's odd fantasy. At first he dismissed it as an unrealizable chimera, but then he stopped for a while to think

13. Russian biologist Elie Metchnikoff (1845–1916) won the Nobel Prize for medicine in 1908 for discovering phagocytosis. He was one of the first scientists to describe cell-mediated immunity. Cajal was particularly intrigued by phagocytes and leucocytes, mobile cells that engulf and destroy bacteria and other invasive particles in complex organisms. To Cajal, the independence and dynamism of leucocytes suggested the individuality of all cells, and he often used leucocytes in a metaphoric way to describe the plasticity of cells in the nervous system.

about it. Once he was deeply absorbed in the analysis, he realized that while the discovery of a decadence serum would be no simple task, it represented a problem which in principle might be approached.

Encouraged by this initial result, he took the question into the laboratory. He analyzed the chemical and morphological composition of old people's skin; he determined the proximate causes of baldness, gray hair, fat deposits, the atrophy of the glands, and the weakened elasticity of the face that causes wrinkles. And so, working in secret, our scientist who played the dice of chemistry with such skill discovered a compound very similar to that found in the organs of hundred-year-old men. From the skin and internal tissues of senile dogs and aged, feeble cats and horses, he extracted a substance that, in small doses, caused the cutaneous glands to atrophy, the hair to lose its color, and the skin to wrinkle.

The first tests of this serum were conducted at a charity asylum on twenty incorrigible, syphilitic prostitutes. The results were brilliant. Fifteen days after subcutaneous injection with this stupendous liquor, girls of eighteen to twenty-five were converted into matrons of forty-five. In the process, they were completely reformed, for there is no greater teacher of morality than the loss of beauty. But what pleased Forschung the most was that the remedy acted in a purely local, very restricted way, with only minor diffusion along the bodily surface around the cutaneous region where the inoculation had occurred.

Seniline—as the scientist baptized his new serum—possessed undeniable *antitegumentary* properties, that is to say, it withered the skin and its accessory parts, respecting the strength and integrity of the internal organs.

Certain now of the physiological effects of *seniline,* the far-seeing husband shared his prodigious discovery with his better half, explaining the painful sacrifice he felt was prudent to impose upon her beauty in order to guarantee the future peace and happiness of their home. The pliable Emma, who in the end was a woman and eager to please, at first risked a few timid protests, but as these were badly received, she resigned herself to the experiment. Beforehand Forschung calmed her, reassuring her that the *maturing process* involved only an insignificant area of the organism, to be specific, the face and the hair. People who took it, by their own reports, added only five or six Januarys to their twenty-eight Aprils, at the very most.

So that they would be free to carry out the transmutation, the couple went on a pleasure trip. In order to create a better illusion for his audience, a cinematographer alters photographic images during instantaneous eclipses of an electric light. In just the same manner Forschung, who hoped to hide the rather violent transition between Emma's two phases of youth and maturity, extinguished the lamp of curiosity by disappearing from Würzburg and spending an extended period in England and the United States.

Months afterward, when the couple returned from their journey, Forschung's friends and acquaintances suffered an acute attack of curiosity. They saw the husband and wife, but they could not believe their own eyes. The ease of hotel life, the invigorating influence of fresh air, and the mental repose had rejuvenated Forschung. Emma's beauty, on the other hand, had visibly decayed, assuming the ruddy tones and amplitude of visible surface characteristic of one whose sun is setting. What had happened?

No one knew, but people dreamed up the most unlikely explanations. Many began to think that the doctor's companion was really the elder sister of the unhappy wife, who must have died during that long, unfortunate trip. Without a doubt, the unscrupulous Forschung must have married or *come to an arrangement* with his sister-in-law, without respecting the dead woman's memory or maintaining the mandatory period of mourning . . . These scientific geniuses were so odd!

And in truth, this absurd tale, which the scientist never tried to cut short, seemed to have all the qualities of verisimilitude. The unhappy Emma did look exactly like her elder sister, a rather crumpled, faded version of her former self. She consoled herself about her transformation, however, by observing her husband's increasing passion and vigor. There was also the innocent love of her children, to whose up-bringing she devoted any tenderness that Forschung's heart had been unable to soak up. Freed at last from any sort of nuisance or domestic care, the lucky scientist could now dedicate himself entirely to perfecting his marvelous discoveries.

8

Before I finish telling this tale, I must satisfy a legitimate curiosity on the part of the reader, who, if he has even a slight passion for industry, will be itching to know about the scientific and commercial fate of the renowned *seniline*. A priori, it would seem that a panacea for youth would be a poor business venture. One cannot even think of seeking consumers for this product among capricious coquettes of sixteen years, or cartilaginous old maids of forty-five. Nor would one expect to find buyers among gleeful, frivolous old men with dyed beards and toupees, artifices against which, of course, the aging elixir is absolutely useless.

But we must not judge things by mere impressions. We have thus requested information from Dr. Forschung himself (of whom we are fervent admirers) about the economic future of this odd remedy.

Here are some of the most revealing paragraphs from his extremely interesting reply:

"I believed at first," writes Forschung, "that seniline, apart from the particular case for which it was originally conceived, would constitute a mere scientific curiosity, one of those many organic compounds ending in '-*ine*' that are discovered by chemical analysis and which, for lack of industrial applicability, sleep the sleep of the just on the dusty shelves of pharmaceutical plants. Fortunately, we were wrong. The new *seniline* has a splendid future. To avoid confusion, this new derivative should be called *antifreniatine,* since it has been modified by the addition of an extract from senile brains and the remains of some antitegumentary compounds.

"At the present time, when injected intravenously into delinquents and lunatics by a commission of forensic doctors, it has produced some very surprising psychical effects. To be specific, it has proved to be an all-powerful moderator of criminal impulses and a marvelous sedative of the will. In raving madmen, five drops a week make the use of a straight jacket unnecessary, and in either ailing or healthy men, two drops a day cause the most complete paralysis of the will. In reality, the new product works by aging one's nerve centers, that is to say, by creating the mental inertia, slowness of memory, emotional frigidity and hatred of anything new that are characteristic of extreme old age. All of this occurs without compromising the muscles or visceral organs, which maintain their youthful state.

"But there is more. Some individualistic sociologists, concerned about the growing threat of socialism and anarchy, have undertaken experiments (with the appropriate reserve, of course) in which they have inoculated members of the impoverished classes with the new seniline, and these experiments have produced most encouraging results. No less intriguing are the recent successes of German missionaries in Central Africa. According to a letter from Reverend Schaffer, which I have here before me, the said panacea is a powerful aid to evangelism because it notably weakens the rudimentary critical faculties of black tribesmen and deadens the ardor and fanaticism of Mohammedan dervishes.

"In view of these results, you will not be at all surprised by some information that I will now reveal to you in secret. By way of their respective embassies in Berlin, some politicians from those nations a certain British statistician has designated *moribund* have requested that I supply them, in all haste, with large quantities of *antifreniatine.* They want to conduct experiments, on a grand scale, to test potential chemical pacifiers for their more restless spirits. They claim, and perhaps they are correct, that the said product is an irreplaceable tool for their governments, for it can curb the rebelliousness of the hungry masses, tame people's dangerous capacity for original thought, and wipe out their people's excessive desire for philosophical and political novelties once and for all.

"Thanks, therefore, to the inexhaustible markets constituted by the aforementioned peoples, I expect to make millions and win glory that will never fade. Here you can see that Emma's painful sacrifice, a thousand times greater and more heroic than that of the legendary Iphigenia, will have been as useful for my family's prosperity as for the final peace and sedation of the more unfortunate part of mankind."

My God! Is it true that Spanish statesmen have entrusted the social order to the redeeming effects of seniline? There are some highly revealing signs of this final eviction of our national soul . . .

If these suspicions are confirmed, and such a vaccination becomes obligatory, let us all prepare ourselves to conquer the heavens, after abandoning the earth to the watchful enemies of our race. Let us all *senilize* ourselves . . . in whose cartilaginous brains there already exist such distressingly high levels of *mysticines, decadentines,* and *misoneines,* the sad legacy of barbaric times and the mental laziness of five centuries!

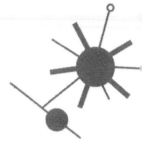

THE FABRICATOR
OF HONOR

Dr. Alejandro Mirahonda, a Spaniard educated in Germany
and France, held an M.D. and a Ph.D. from the University
of Leipzig and was the favorite disciple of those learned doctors of hypnotism, Bernheim and Forel.[1] On returning to his
own country, he requested and obtained the right to practice medicine in the historic, turbulent, and discredited city
of Villabronca, where he proposed to exercize his profession

1. French psychologist Hippolyte Bernheim (1840–1919) headed one of the two
prominent schools of hypnotism in the 1880s, maintaining that anyone could
be hypnotized and that hypnosis was the result of suggestion. Swiss psychiatrist
Auguste Forel (1848–1931), who ran the prestigious Burghölzli mental hospital
in Zurich, hoped to use suggestion therapeutically and agreed with Bernheim
that it was a widespread phenomenon in society. Bernheim's older, more prominent opponent, French neurologist Jean Martin Charcot (1835–93), believed
that hypnosis was a pathological phenomenon occurring only in neurotics. For
reasons that will soon become apparent, Mirahonda shares Bernheim's view.

and develop an idea that had been crawling around in his brain for some time.

But before describing the deeds of this prestigious personage, we must first introduce him to our readers.

Let us begin by declaring that there are some missions so lofty and solemn, they cannot be realized in any physique. The surgeon who desires fame must have something of the athlete, the warrior, and the inquisitor. The obstetrician must have just the right hands—soft, tapered, and effeminate, a Lilliputian stature, and an unctuous, pleasing personality. And the alienist who hopes to implant suggestions will surely fail if he lacks the solemn *coram vobis*[2] of a prophet or the beard and gigantic eyes of a Byzantine Christ.

Fortunately, in Dr. Alejandro Mirahonda, profession and physiognomy were marvelously matched. He was very tall, with a large, hairy head housing neural batteries of vast capacity and tension. He had the tempestuous beard of an angry apostle, and his enormous, deep, black eyes with an irresistible, searching gaze had pupils that seemed to emit clouds of magnetic effluvia. His eyebrows were long, thick, mobile, and serpentine, apparently endowed with a life of their own. One might say that when he frowned, with an expression of supreme authority, they caught the interlocutor up in their folds, fascinating him and rendering him impotent. Besides this, he had a very substantial voice famous for its roars, but he knew just how to manage it, transforming it, according to the situation, into the gentlest, sweetest, and most caressing music. In contrast to his brows, his fleshy, well-proportioned lips were normally immobile, so that the expression of his eyes and the lightning flashes of his thought had an even greater effect and he could assume the august, mysterious silence of the statue of Apollo at Delphi.

Let us add to these physical attributes his exciting, colorful language, which flowed effortlessly from some inexhaustible deposit in his memory, and his invincible iron will . . . And then you will have some idea

2. *coram vobis,* a powerful physical presence

of the enormous power that Mirahonda exerted over his friends, relatives, and patients.

For him, to impose ideas or suppress existing ones in docile minds was child's play. With very little effort, he could create negative and positive hallucinations, metamorphoses and dissociations of the personality, and all sorts of sensory and motor phenomena not just in hysterical people but even in sane, alert individuals. All of the wonderful miracles attributed to saints and magnetizers were for him a mere game. To enact them, all he needed was one impetuous look or a simple verbal command.

During the first months of his stay in Villabronca, he dedicated himself exclusively to paving the way for the wonderful experiment he had been contemplating. He offered his medical services to the inhabitants for practically nothing. With his wife—a splendid German blonde whom he had subjugated forever with a single look—he attended all of the social gatherings and soirées. He joined both of the town's clubs (both that of the bourgeois and that of the workers) and contributed with great generosity to local collections for the needy. Through science, affability, and affected simplicity, he so completely captured the admiration and sympathy of his neighbors that they could not imagine why a man of such merit and extraordinary talent had condescended to live in such a remote, rustic place.

As is wont to happen with all great illuminati, the resonant, adoring voice of the women stood out in that concerto of congeniality. The presence of such a proud, virile specimen of the *human animal* aroused and enchanted them. As Madame Necker de Saussure[3] asserts, woman "possesses a *self-concept* weaker than a man's," a *self* that senses its own feebleness and instinctively seeks the force of willpower and strength. In compliance, no doubt, with some far-seeing mandate of nature, the truly feminine female trembles with pleasure and feels herself deliciously enslaved when she inhales the aura

3. Swiss intellectual Albertine Adrienne Necker de Saussure (1766–1841) wrote about women's education in her highly influential book, *Progressive Education* (1828–38).

of a virile, triumphant tyrant, the epitome of energy and intelligence, the *man's man* . . .

In some fiery wives and shameless Magdalenes, the restrained, respectful admiration of an honest woman gave way to tones that were hardly decorous and attitudes that were outright provocative . . . One of the most daring, one of the ones who took the most liberties with the doctor was the registrar's wife, a charming brunette who was withering away and dying of boredom among papers and manuscripts. But our scientist, faithful to his principle that the fascinator must never himself be *fascinated,* or else risk losing all his prestige, shut his eyes and ears to this threatening wave of sinful love. Besides, let us say to his credit that he was already too much in love with sweet Röschen Baumgarten, that beautiful, graceful daughter of the North, who also happened to be a wealthy heiress. In a fit of passion, she had laid her beauty and millions at the feet of that fiery son of the South, so as to avoid the slightest hint of a reproach from her better half.

It is hardly necessary to say how strong his professional reputation was. Very quickly, word of his marvelous cures escaped the city's limits and spread throughout the entire province. His house resembled a church in a jubilee year, and his reputation as an infallible diagnostician ran so high that it was considered an egregious blunder or an unpardonable fault to die without having heard the sentence from his own lips.

But don't think that his sphere of influence was restricted to hygiene and pathology. As a talented, thoroughly educated man who had traveled extensively and read even more, he aspired to be, and rapidly became, his neighbors' confidant and obligatory adviser. In accordance with his premeditated plan, he offered a series of lectures at the club. These were accompanied by demonstrations and covered several subjects that promised to interest a predominantly agricultural and industrial town: domestic and common hygiene, the diseases of plants, pauperism and the problem of the worker, charitable institutions and savings banks, chemical fertilizers, the cattle industry, etc. Besides captivating the audience with the fine craftsmanship of an impeccable structure filled with felicitous images, these lectures displayed his marvelous erudition and his extraordinary yet practical spirit.

Since Mirahonda acquired such authority, it is no surprise that the mayor and the judge, the farmer and the worker, all rushed to him demanding illumination. They accepted his advice willingly, for our hero knew how to convince people of things without making them feel humiliated. To each one, he generously offered that portion of science and reason that was his due, skillfully avoiding any references to bad dealings or obvious ethical or intentional faults. Instead, he would attribute the injury to random chance, acts of God, the particular circumstances, or the unconscious. Equally impressed by his knowledge and his appearance, the townspeople called him the Christ.

As one can see, a golden legend took shape around that singular, extraordinary man, a legend worthy of the happy days of the apostles—which just goes to show, by the way, that despite all the brilliant achievements of science, a great portion of contemporary society still lives in the shadowy, simpleminded age when people talked about gods, were terrorized by demons, and believed they could perform miracles.

2

Villabronca was far from a model of peaceful, temperate towns. From day to day, the disorder and lewdness spread, especially now that the city—enriched by an influx of wealthy immigrants—had become primarily industrial. Despite the priest's sermons and the mayor's vigorous proclamations, the rising tide of robberies, fights, drunkenness, depravity, and contempt for authority was sorely distressing. Alcoholism played havoc among the workers. Not even the creation of a small corps of Guardians of Public Order or an increased contingent of the Civil Guard could head off this public immorality.

Clearly, things could not go on in this fashion. Representatives of the ruling classes met at the club, respected fathers of families who were justly alarmed by the growing disorder. Moved by the best possible intentions, each one proposed his own solution. The discussion was long and heated . . . But the individualists dragged in the sacred right of *Habeus Corpus,* and the equally sacred right to drink . . . and in the end, they could agree upon nothing.

Meanwhile, Mirahonda was rubbing his hands with glee. The moment for his psychological experiment was approaching . . . and he had to prepare the dice as quickly as he could.

One day, he gathered the town's leading citizens at the club and announced, in a voice breaking with emotion, that he had just discovered—as the result of a fortunate laboratory accident—a serum with marvelous powers.

"This serum," declared the doctor, "or rather antitoxin, has the singular property of tempering the activity of nervous centers where the antisocial passions reside: idleness, rebelliousness, lasciviousness, criminal instincts, etc. At the same time, it markedly heightens and vivifies one's images of virtue and shuts down all tempting evocations of vice . . .

"Permit me to tell you, in brief, about the results of some experiments recently performed on man and animals with the aforementioned serum. A single drop of this wonderful liquor transformed a vicious wolf into a loyal, gentle, submissive dog. With half of this dose, a starving eagle was made to abhor meat, and a cat to forget its eternal hatred of mice . . .

"In man, greater doses are necessary to produce lasting psychological transmutations. Although the experiments conducted in this field have concerned only a limited number of people and types of passion, the results have been so astounding that I cannot resist the temptation to describe them.

"When five cubic centimeters were injected under the skin of an alcoholic, the patient lost all fondness for fermented beverages. The same quantity, when applied, respectively, to a professional pickpocket and a certain renowned bully, completely eliminated their criminal impulses and converted them into harmless, temperate individuals within just a few days. With similar treatment, a morphine addict and a nymphomaniac have come to forget their odious habits.

"In view of these eloquent facts, which grow more numerous and convincing with each passing day, I hope that you will not dismiss as chimerical a dream that I have long cherished, a dream that has inspired persistent, extremely arduous research. By strictly material, uncoercive means, I hope to realize an ethical purification of the human race, converting vicious individuals and criminals into decent, upright, utterly correct citizens. I am firmly convinced that a sufficient dose of my *anti-passion serum,* injected under the cranial skin, will transform the most hardened criminal into an impeccable man."

And so, *incontinenti,* the learned doctor proceeded with his demonstrations, for he knew all too well that strong minds are not persuaded by more or less truthful tales, but only by irrefutable proof *de visu,* which cannot fail to be accepted.[4] He signaled to his assistants, who led the people and animals who had undergone these experiments out of an adjacent chamber. To the astonishment of the audience, which until then had been cold and a bit skeptical, Mirahonda's claims were fully substantiated.

Now there could be no doubt! The wonderful anti-passion serum had made carnivorous animals lose their bloodthirsty instincts, and the men had been transfigured as though a flash of faith had illuminated and uplifted their souls! The proof was all the more brilliant and overwhelming since the people who had undergone the treatment— an alcoholic, a smoker, a gambler, and a brawler—were very well known to the people present. When the audience was convinced, by accounts from the respective friends and families, of the reality of these psychological transformations; when they saw the subjects reject liquor, tobacco, and cards with expressions of horror; when they learned from

4. *Incontinenti,* "immediately" or "unable to restrain himself any further"; *de visu,* "visual" or "that can be seen."

the factory foremen that these regenerated delinquents had not missed a single day of work in the past month . . . , they burst into enthusiastic, deafening applause that resounded through the room, filling the illustrious speaker with intimate satisfaction.

The next day, when it came time for his consultations, our doctor found that his practice had doubled. Those who were physically ill had been joined by those who were morally ill. Hysterical women in love with their servants; wayward, incorrigible boys; drunken, quarrelsome husbands; depraved, nocturnal profligates; idle, womanizing students, etc., had been dragged in almost by force by their respective families. In an endless procession, they filed in to submit themselves to the famous *moral vaccine.*

Within two months of that unforgettable lecture, the enthusiasm and support of Villabronca's leaders had reached such a point that the civic administration en masse, under the advisement of the judge, the registrar, the club president, the schoolmaster, and the surgeon, declared—in a celebrated proclamation—that the new vaccine must be obligatory for all persons between twelve and sixty years of age, regardless of sex or social condition. Undoubtedly, those far-seeing councillors believed that the old had already been thoroughly vaccinated by their debility, and the young, by their innocence.

At first, as one may presume, the council's arrangements to save the town ran into some serious difficulties. Those accustomed to vice, particularly those who engaged in it only sporadically—those who enjoyed having a good time once in a while, that is—protested indignantly. In noisy harangues, they declared the new measures contrary to the citizen's most sacred rights and an offense to Villabronca's immaculate dignity. They kept arguing that the council's plan involved the assumption—unjust in every respect—of a collective immorality, and that it failed to distinguish integrity from libertinage; respect for the law, from the violation of people's rights.

This delicate question was taken up in the columns of the only local periodical, a weekly paper called the *Villabronca Cymbal.* It was published, collectively, by the entertainment manager at the club, an approved highway contractor, an officer who had been retired for refusing to go overseas, two law students who had been indefinitely suspended, and an incompetent lawyer with no cases. These individuals—the *intellectuals,* as they called themselves—discussed the well-handled question of the preventive measure's legitimacy from various points of view, at first in moderate ways; later, with sectarian fervor. This campaign, undertaken or inspired by rascals and incorrigible libertines, coincided with a subsidy granted to the *Cymbal* by the owners of gambling houses, taverns, and brothels, whose industries feared—not without reason—a considerable drop in their shameful businesses if Mirahonda's projects went ahead.

As for the proletarians, they found themselves divided. The majority decided in favor of the new moral treatment, swayed by the doctor's authority and generous altruism and above all by the domineering voice of their women (which Mirahonda had taken great care to win for his own cause). But some bad apples, impassioned anarchists, roundly rejected the serum, fearing, no doubt, that the medicine would deaden the proletariat's rage against the hated bourgeoisie. In times of strikes, it would soften the workers' resolve. It would defer, in sum, the triumphant day of the great social revolution—which according to them was quite near.

But the one who fought the new psychological panacea with the greatest arrogance and jealousy was their spiritual leader. In sermons crammed with Latin phrases, passages from the Holy Fathers, and maxims of moral philosophy, he tried to show that the doctor's famous experiments were the devil's own snares and temptations, comparable, at bottom, to the experiments of magnetizers and spiritualists. He added that even in the hypothetical case in which Lucifer had nothing to do with such unusual phenomena, it was still undeniably true that the serum worked directly, selectively on the mysterious sources of free will. Consequently, it narrowed the channel of moral liberty, making civic responsibility and the value or unworthiness of one's actions almost illusory.

But we, who devote ourselves to the cult of truth, must say that the real, unconfessed reason for this sacerdotal ill will was that the fervent man felt humiliated and annoyed to see some upstart quack, ignorant of theology and sacred texts, brazenly intruding upon his spiritual domains. The new doctor threatened to usurp one of the highest, most important functions of the priest's august ministry: the purification of consciences and the correction of vices and sins.

Luckily, the doctor was exquisitely courteous. Full of tolerance and affability, he put his arguments to everyone in a friendly way, with the result that he won the support of the town councillors and patriarchs and inspired an almost religious fervor in the women. This, along with the brilliant demonstrative quality of his experiments, gradually appeased the irritated souls and silenced the more meticulous consciences. Besides, Mirahonda knew everything there was to know about certain matters. When he donated a substantial sum to the *Villabronca Cymbal*, its shameless intellectual publishers moved lock, stock, and barrel to the other side. Subsequently, they converted themselves into sounding boards echoing the doctor's achievements and became the most effective supporters of his regenerative campaigns. He also made—sotto voce—a donation of several thousand pesetas to the local Anarchist Committee, designated as a generous contribution to the *strike fund*. Nor did he neglect the church, to which he left a hefty bequest for Masses and charities, specifying that the jealous pastor was to have absolute control of its investment and distribution. If these and other clever maneuvers did not entirely win over the recalcitrants, they succeeded at least in keeping them quiet, which was good enough for Mirahonda.

3

The day of the great experiment had finally arrived. During the morning, the doctor's wife and assistants prepared the mise-en-scène with diligent care. They set up the table with the antiseptic instruments, the Pravaz syringes,[5] and the mysterious flask containing the magic potion. They positioned a Chinese screen that was there to protect the arms of extremely modest women from any profane looks, and they laid out some bandages and other curative measures that would be of assistance in the unlikely event of a slight hemorrhage or excessive irritation.

Nothing escaped the foresight of Mirahonda. To strengthen the suggestive effect of the psychological experiment, he had requested and won the right to perform the inoculations in the salon of the town hall, under the supervision of the mayor, the priest, and the most distinguished citizens. Since there is no better way to inspire the will than to gladden the stomach a little, he saw to it that a certain highly esteemed caterer from Madrid, who had been summoned expressly for that purpose, laid out a beautifully served, quite splendid lunch in the secretary's offices just adjacent to the vaccination room. Finally, to make the intermissions more pleasant, he had hired the hospice's brass band, instructing them to play grave, solemn, monotonous, and soporiferous pieces . . .

But before discussing the results of this unforgettable moral vaccination, we must clear up some doubts that will most certainly have been assailing the reader's mind. To dissipate them completely, let us reproduce an important dialogue which occurred over lunch between the eminent doctor and his affectionate, somewhat distrustful wife, just minutes before the regenerative injections began.

"I am pleased, extremely satisfied with my work," said Mirahonda, stroking his apostolic, tempestuous beard. "Today, at last, after two years of abundant sowing and constant tillage, we are going to bring in the harvest . . ."

"You certainly have good reason to be glad. I, too, in my own way

5. French physician Charles Gabriel Pravaz (1791–1853) developed the first modern hypodermic syringe in 1853. Pravaz's syringes were made of silver and could deliver up to one cubic centimeter of fluid.

am a collaborator in your momentous project, and I'm feeling very lucky. I'm happy because you are, but I also have a very private, personal reason to rejoice . . ."

"I can guess it! Oh, you women! You're always the same! To come to me now with some little tale of jealousy, to tear me from the heaven of my scientific triumphs! For you fervent worshipers of the individual, the particular, what are humanity, science, and glory itself, compared to the petty satisfactions of vanity and self-love?"

"You're wrong. I love glory, too, but—don't you know it!—my greatest glory is you. Your image in my soul is so great, I can hardly even picture humanity. Besides, my feeling complements your intelligence. You are the centrifugal force; I, the centripetal. Thanks to me, your supreme mental faculties, which would unleash themselves as mad altruism if they were set free, are directed toward our home and applied to the wholesome, selfish goal of our mutual preservation and happiness . . . What you so disdainfully call the miserable satisfaction of vanity and self-love is only the joy of preserving your own love . . . How dare you scorn this egotism!"

"My darling Röschen, allow me to tell you, in light of your own personal point of view, that this intimate fruition to which you refer—which certainly seems very close to some savory kind of revenge—would be justified if this afternoon's glorious experiment were interrupting some pleasures or sinful debilities. But have you, by chance, any reproach to make against your husband?"

"No. I'm only afraid for the future . . . Pardon my jealousy—I understand that it's making me look ridiculous . . . horribly disagreeable, but there's nothing I can do about it. I'm going to be honest with you. How can I be sure that one of these fiery dark beauties who swoon with love in your presence isn't finally going to capture your fancy and rob me of your love? What about the registrar's wife, who fakes fits of hysterics so that she can see you every day, and who has never missed any of your lectures, to which she listens in a state of mystic ecstasy?"

"Calm yourself, little girl," replied the doctor sweetly, lovingly taking one of Röschen's hands. "This will never happen, as you very well know. Only two great passions burn in me: my passions for glory, and for you. There's no fuel left in my heart or my brain for a third . . . But let's talk of something else . . . Let's think about the magnificent event that's about to unfold. Haven't we prepared the bait skillfully? There's no doubt about it—the whole town is going to bite."

"You're right. One must admit, you've been far-seeing and obstinate, and you haven't budged an inch on a single issue concerning your plan. But you must let me ask you a question. I don't understand how Mirahonda, hypnotist extraordinaire, president of the Leipzig Society for Psychical Studies, the successful inventor of efficacious new methods of animal magnetism, a man so capable of planting suggestions that he can produce all kinds of nervous phenomena in completely healthy individuals, in the waking state . . . I cannot fathom, I repeat, why in this particular case you have renounced your usual methods and resorted to simple fraud."

"My dear, are you forgetting that the moral experiment in which we are now engaged is an extraordinary one, infinitely more difficult than those trivial cases of individual hypnosis for therapeutic ends? You already know my philosophical and pedagogical ideas perfectly well. I've said a thousand times that if the human brain were to develop in an austere psychological environment, highly charged with authority, instead of this tepid, shaky, frivolous moral atmosphere formed by the blurry, contradictory suggestions of parents, teachers, and friends, then all the troubles tormenting the miserable human race (idleness and vice, cowardice and cruelty, egotism and crime) would rapidly diminish. If the definitive modeling of the cerebral centers were carried out in an autocratic way by skillful, energetic hypnotists charged with the double duty of removing the rust of heredity and habit, and imposing ideas and feelings suited to the ends of civilization and society . . . then we could take a giant step toward our species' physical and moral redemption.

"In order to achieve this brilliant result, it would be necessary for energetic, iron-willed professors to induce, from the time of childhood, an atrophy of the cerebral centers responsible for the antisocial instincts we share with the lowest animals, and a compensatory hypertrophy of the inhibitory centers and the organs that evoke images of virtue and duty . . . Love of one's country to the point of self-sacrifice, passion for science and truth to the point of madness, an inclination toward virtue to the point of martyrdom—these are the suggestions that will lead to the formation of the perfect, thoroughly modern man, the precious fruit of scientific education, invincible in war and peace, the compassionate civilizer of inferior races and glorious examiner of all arcane matters . . .

"Now that the educational phase is over, we must act, restricting ourselves to inhibiting people's baser instincts. Admittedly, our present experiment represents only a very small trial in this grandiose system of human transformation. But even so, its results will be necessary for the development of hypno-pedagogical theory and will constitute the first surveyor's stake along this fruitful, luminous path . . ."

"But you've gotten so carried away in all your generous enthusiasm, you still haven't explained to me the principle on which you've based your new procedure for reeducating the will."

"You're right . . . I forgot. It's a very simple thing. Now, listen well. In a group of a hundred people, selected at random, only fourteen or sixteen will be capable of being hypnotized and suffering, by way of suggestion, amnesias, paralyses, contractions, emotional transformations, hallucinations, etc. A very prestigious hypnotist, who knows how to strike deeply at the public's imagination, can increase this figure to twenty-four, maybe even thirty. But despite all his efforts, he'll still be left with the remaining seventy percent: inattentive, open-minded, refractory to any belief in miracles, and, therefore, immune to suggestion.

"Very well, then, in a large population like that of Villabronca, when dealing with a collective process of suggestion that does not involve personal rapport, one would expect the number of refractory individuals to be very much greater. And to ensure the success of our enterprise, it will be crucial to conquer the strong minds, the ones that boast they believe only in God or science. It will therefore be necessary to remove any idea of traumaturgic or magnetic action from these rebellious minds, for this would immediately awaken their critical sense. Instead, we must skillfully conceal suggestion under the cape of saintliness and genius. In this way, they'll accept the imposition, because they'll never realize that it is one. And the innocent public will fall victim to the singular illusion that the scientist or saint is responsible for a phenomenon created by its own imagination.

"And now I come to the justification of this fraud, which has so excited your curiosity. Among the various ways of sugarcoating the suggestive pill and lulling the critical sense to sleep, there is none so effective as associating the suggestion with the banal act of taking some medicine or swallowing some therapeutic serum. If the doctor's scientific prestige is very great, the subject's reasoning faculty is thrown off the scent. Obeying a natural, logical impulse, he immediately classifies the mysterious phenomenon as one of those with which he is familiar. In the present case, our *esprit fort* knows that there are antitoxic sera against diphtheria, tetanus, etc. So how can we fail to persuade him that there is an anti-passion serum, especially when he has seen people dramatically cured with just a few drops of it right before his very own eyes?

"From this one can infer that the most effective aid to the mental orthopedist is the common people's crass ignorance about the sovereign power of suggestion. They know nothing about the multiple ways in which it can be disguised, and they fail to see the deplorable facility with which the best constructed brain uncritically accepts any absurd dogma imposed by talent, saintliness, or genius."

"According to this theory, even the best organized, calmest, most reflective minds would be vulnerable to the power of suggestion?"

"No doubt about it! But only if the hypnotist knows how to conceal himself behind the man of science and provoke phenomena that fall outside the circle of natural facts with which *elite* minds are familiar. Luckily, this is not at all hard. Raised with the erroneous doctrine of free will, we almost all believe that our religious, philosophical, and political convictions represent logical constructions erected by reason. But really, as is well known, they are the fruits of undemonstrated, unconscious suggestions imposed by religious, pedagogical, and political figures . . .

"But, little girl, with these digressions, we are forgetting our obligations . . . It's two o'clock . . . Let us make haste . . ."

4

The operation—if one may call it that—took place at the appointed hour, in the best possible order.

With great suspense in the audience, the session opened with a brief, discreet address from the mayor. This was followed by an extremely eloquent, ardent, utterly subjugating speech from Mirahonda. Casting aside all modesty and affectations of delicacy as inappropriate to his evangelical mission, he declared that he had been inspired by God in his portentous discovery of the anti-passion vaccine; the Lord Himself had called upon him to redeem the human species from its physical and moral degradation. The brass band then played a solemn march filled with peaceful, melancholic cadences, and finally the vaccination took place. In deference to local laws of courtesy, it began with those who had aristocratic blood, talent, or money.

In an atmosphere of the most religious abstraction, the operation was conducted without incident. The first day, Mirahonda inoculated a little more than a third of the population of both sexes in the municipal district. On those that followed, he injected the rest, except for about a ninth or a tenth of them, who used illness or absence as an excuse to escape the sedative effects of the aforementioned serum so that they could maintain a monopoly over vices and petty crimes.

Submissive and docile, those of the fair sex who were of marriageable age rushed noisily to the *communion table of virtue*. On this altar of concord, they sacrificed the intimate satisfactions of vanity and the refined pleasures of coquetry and flirtation so that peace might reign in their homes. Somewhat less enthusiastic were the frivolous wives. From the nervous trembling with which they received the syringe, you could easily guess their repugnance at knowing that their fickle, capricious hearts were about to be enchained, perhaps forever.

Even the naughty, provocative wife of the registrar, who, as we have already indicated, had had the misfortune to annoy and arouse the jealousy of Madame de Mirahonda, yielded her rosy skin to the secular arm of science. In truth, however, she did it very reluctantly. If it had been up to her, she would gladly have remained on the sidelines, but her stern husband, highly suspicious of his better half's fervent enthusiasm for the famous doctor, would not hear of it.

In the group of bustling vaccinators, the handsome figure of Madame de Mirahonda stood out, her blond hair covered by a dazzling white cap; her supple figure wrapped in an elegant, antiseptic duster. It was she who was in charge of administering the serum to the most distinguished, prudish wives and single ladies. In accordance with a wise, far-seeing interpretation of Mirahonda's designs, she varied the quantity of the precious liquor . . . apparently, in proportion to the clients' physical robustness, but actually, according to the dangers of their feminine attractions. Needless to say, the lively wife of the registrar received a double dose, much to her husband's great joy.

Faithful to his method, our doctor reinforced the suggestive influence by extolling the marvelous virtues of the vaccine. With tones of profound conviction, he promised everyone that it would create an inhibition, an inalterable repose, of all impulses provoked by the passions, without hindering anyone from enjoying the most robust health or the free satisfaction of salutary instincts. He told them that it would cause a definitive renunciation of all tempting ideas. From here onward, in sum, they were going to ignore every immoral, criminal, or anti-Christian stimulus.

In each individual case, he knew how to vary the suggestive formula according to the history and predominant passions of the client. From time to time, apparently by accident, a group of *mansos*—that is to say, of people who had already been regenerated—passed casually through the lines of candidates for virtue. With contrite gestures and seraphic expressions, they underscored the doctor's commanding eloquence and helped to make up the minds of the mistrustful and irresolute.

The experiment turned out to be just what was needed. A veritable hurricane of virtue thrilled the Villabroncans' hearts, penetrating even the most secret dens of iniquity and vice. It was a sublime madness, not unlike the fervor that had made men die for the cross centuries before. On all sides, loafers and profligates, drunks and gamblers began to emerge, apparently moved by a spirit of sincere remorse. No one wanted to be known as incorrigibly vicious.

The final scene on the last day was tremendously moving. A group of lovely sinners, caught up in the general contagion, advanced resolutely toward the dais. Though their smooth skin was still colored with rouge and scented with the pungent perfumes of the night before, they offered it up to the redeeming syringe of science . . . Down in the amazed, applauding crowd, the people could hardly believe their eyes!

5

The results of the moral vaccine were wonderful, surpassing even the most optimistic calculations. Criminality entirely ceased. All vices, greed, and dishonesty seemed to have disappeared forever. The taverns, once a breeding ground for drunks and a boiling cauldron of disputes, now seemed like peaceful, wholesome refectories where workers could find nourishing food and light refreshments. Feverishly, eagerly, as though fighting a heated battle for their well-being, people labored in the fields, workshops, and factories. In their homes, order and economy reigned, along with their natural fruits, health, happiness, and artistic inspiration. Gambling dens and brothels were shut up tight. Never had the plume of smoke from the factory risen up closer to heaven, nor had the sublime hymn to vivifying work resounded more deafeningly, sung by dynamos and locomotives in grave, majestic tones.

No less momentous was their progress in the realm of feelings. Love was purified. Their homes, once cold due to the absence of fathers and the selfishness of children, were transformed into deliciously warm nests where honesty and fidelity fluttered their wings and looked upward toward heaven. The Golden Age was returning to that decrepit, exhausted land, bringing not the empty-headed, crude simplicity of primitive man but the bitter, knowing, fruitful experience of the prodigal son!

6

Three more months of that memorable experiment had now passed by. The local authorities, like the police, were delighted with the tranquillity that let them sleep so soundly at night.

But even with all this, in the midst of all this calm and good fortune, there were brooding, fastidious minds that seemed uneasy about the future. This Octavian peace was frightening them. They feared that the inhabitants of Villabronca had been transformed into automata, into moral machines, incapable of feeling the stimulus of sin, but equally unresponsive to the great impulses of generosity and patriotism.

Not long after this, life began to feel utterly monotonous and dull. Some students and soldiers, who had just arrived from Madrid when the dog days began, bitterly deplored the desolating lack of public muscle. In vain they pleaded for favors—more or less illicit—from single and married women. How they missed that gracious old coquetry, so rich with sweet promises and delicious dangers!

Faithful now to their sacred vows, the pretty young married women were more seductive than ever, thanks to the irresistible attraction of modesty. They maddened the unvaccinated rich men and libertines whose only profession and reason for existence had always been gallantry. Once gossip was abolished from their nightly conversations, there remained only ennui. In the summer theater, the operettas lulled a few feeble old men to sleep, the lone devotees of Thalia and Terpsichore. In the cafés, all pleasure in conversation ceased, for the envy and backbiting between cliques and literary groups had vanished. They saw then how difficult it is to make anyone laugh without giving offense. It became clear that those who were considered witty and funny were really just shameless: when they could no longer draw blood, they made everyone yawn with drowsiness . . .

• • •

Two more months passed by. Gradually, complaints timidly ventured by malcontents became brazen protests. Day by day, the cloud of irritation was accumulating an electrical charge that threatened to explode in a noisy flash.

The men of order, or, to put it better, the men who made their living off of the public order, began to twitter about a state of things that, according to them, threatened to upset the foundations of society and make their stomachs rumble. The political bosses, republican as well as monarchist, lamented the indifference of the masses. Filled with dread, they foresaw ominous days in which they, the town's paternal, far-seeing chiefs, would have to work for a living. Without vices or wicked passions, with health, economy, and hard work—what did the Villabroncans care about redeeming political creeds or infallible sociological panaceas?

Still, until that point, the complaints and gossip had not extended to the press or the pulpit. As you will recall, the parish priest had declined the vaccine, deigning only to authorize the vaccination with his presence. Not surprisingly, it was he who initiated the public protest, creating great noise and scandal in a fierce sermon against hypnotic suggestion, fulminating with terrible accusations against the doctor. In truth, he had good reason to be indignant, seeing how the religious fervor of his parishioners had cooled and how, from day to day, the sacraments and ceremonies of his cult were less and less well observed. According to him, this distressing decline called for godly bequests and those generous, time-honored donations earmarked for the adornment of altars and the splendor and dignity of religious festivals. Once again it was confirmed that the public only remembers Saint Barbara when it thunders. Why ask God for things that hard work and sobriety were already providing? Furthermore, the new excess of weddings did not compensate for the decrease in funerals and other more remunerative religious functions. If things continued in this fashion, a sad time would soon come when the human flock, emancipated from all dogma, would learn to live without a pastor . . .

Although the priest was not exactly aware of the psychological mechanisms underlying his hate, there can be no doubt that that saintly man thoroughly detested the audacious revolutionary, Mirahonda. Certainly the distressing ruin of his religious revenues accounted in part for this aversion, but at the same time, there were other, much deeper causes. Maybe the secret voice of instinct was telling him that the exotic doctor was an apostle in a rival religion and had come to rob him, in the name of who knew what rights of profane science, of the monopoly he held over people's consciences.

His instincts did not deceive him. Ah, if the priest had only read the psychological and hypnological journals! If he had only known Mirahonda's works, published in *Archives* and *Centralblatts,* what extremes of indignation would he not have reached in his excommunications! For that very same Mirahonda was the author of a renowned book, *La Suggestion religieuse et politique,* in which he presented priests as suggesters of absurd dogmas and crude fetishistic practices. To impose these suggestions, he argued, they used the terror of hell, the ecstasy of glory, the ostentation of their cult, the mysterious darkness of the church, the soporific monotony of their rites, and the languid chords of the organ, among other tools.

According to our doctor's theory, religious suggestion worked, first, by creating a deep impression of a dogmatic formula in the brain; and second, by causing all the adjacent associative pathways to atrophy, precisely those used by the critical sense. For Mirahonda, philosophi-

cal religious dogma was like a hermetic canton of ideas, completely isolated from any principles of reason or experimental data. It was like an
erratic block of stone, dragged to a plain by some colossal, prehistoric
glacier, which bears no relationship to the mineralogical or geological
systems of the surrounding country. According to the aforementioned
reformer, a teacher's main goal should be to purge the cerebral convo-
lutions of these gigantic monoliths that interrupt the course of thought
and sterilize our effort to reflect.

But let us return to our noisy, fickle parishioners, whose discontent
was not lessening, though for reasons much cruder and more mun-
dane. Some petty lawyers the doctor had forgotten to pay off raised a
great public outcry over the fact that in an entire year, there had not
been one single swindle in the municipality, not one mysterious ho-
micide, not one miserable case with which to earn their bread. Utterly disconsolate, wishing that a plague might fall on Mirahonda, the
congressional representative of their district made the rounds of the
eating houses and taverns, factories and fields. As usual, he was not
sparing in his promises: a suppression of the draft, an abolition of the
tax on consumer goods, the construction of who knew how many
bridges, roads, and dams . . . But nobody paid any attention to him.
It was horrible!

The purveyors of luxury goods fearfully noted a steady decline in
their revenues. Jewelry stores and silk shops were being ruined before
one's very eyes. Once the road to ruin for married and single ladies was
barred, who needed to buy bangles, rings, and pendants? Without the
cult of envy and vanity, what good were feathers, ribbons, and silks?

Like screechy high notes, the bitter voices of the libertines stood out
in that chorus of malcontents, for they were disconsolate on seeing
themselves condemned to a temperate barracks life in all the luxuriance of their youth. Their forced abstinences were all the more painful in that the priests of Aphrodite had abandoned their cult, taking
refuge in the holy, regenerative religion of work.

Among the impenitent corrupters of this sort, two particularly distinguished themselves. The first was a captain from the army reserve, who was vainly trying to revive the love the feather-brained wife of the syndic had once given him. The other was a certain heir to an entailed estate, a sensual, degraded fop who went crazy when he saw himself disdained by unhappy wives, over whom he had once fearlessly exercised the delicious, historic *droit de seigneur.*

Who would have thought it? Even the most rigid people, those of the highest moral probity, felt uneasy, almost humiliated to see themselves suddenly deprived of the veneration and respect that sin renders virtue. In a town of saints, what could honor be worth? Finally, even the schoolmaster and the judge, who had once been the staunchest supporters of Mirahonda and the greatest advocates of his highly celebrated pedagogical experiment, were won over by the seditious agitators.

7

After a year and a half of the experiment, the clamor of the exploiters extended itself to the neutral masses. Possibly the serum's effects on everyone had begun to wear off. Maybe bankruptcy could accomplish more than virtue, and their stomachs had finally conquered their brains. At any rate, the insubordination became general. In the silent cloud that hovered threateningly over the doctor's head, violent insults began to rumble, and there were lightning flashes of rage.

To avoid possible violence, the authorities took the matter into their own hands. There was a great meeting at the town hall; opinions were exchanged, and accounts of attempted offenses were heard. In the end, their respect for science and Mirahonda's prestige imposed certain measures of moderation. They decided to appoint a committee to ask the doctor, in the name of the town and its council, to dissolve that painful enchantment, that distressing paralysis. As a people, they were now dead to sin, but they would beg him to restore the full enjoyment of their own free wills and, consequently, the free exercise and development of their evil instincts.

This request was to be accompanied by a petition in language not at all bureaucratic. It ended with the following paragraphs full of warm sincerity:

"Show some compassion. Remove these odious blinders from our souls that have let us see nothing but the straight, dusty path of duty. Put a little charm and lasciviousness back into our women's sleepy eyes. Make life pleasant again, brightening it with envy and jealousy, vanity and arrogance, insolence and crime.

"Give us back pain, the stimulus of science and spur of progress. Light up this gray, silent limbo where the boredom is enervating us. Give us a spark of Lucifer's spirit, a gust of God's breath.

"This way, we will see to it that virtue has a price; and religion, a following. Above all, we will see to it that our unhappy prodigals have lots of nourishment and well-being. We will fatten them like mushrooms on our own decay, letting them exploit the ignorance, excesses, and madness of the human flock . . ."

Faced with this uniformity of opinion, recognizing from their states of mind that a second vaccination would be impossible, Mirahonda yielded. And he yielded without sorrow, almost with delight. For he presumed that if the past experiment had been interesting, the new one—the act of contra-suggestion, that is—would be even more so. Suddenly, without any transitional phase, he was going to loosen all the controls that their consciences had been imposing for more than a year.

And so, determined to carry his psychical experiment through to the end, he called a meeting of the town's most prominent men and addressed them as follows:

"In deference to your request, in sight of the fact that—contrary to all expectations—order, health, and virtue are presently intolerable to you, I am going to radically suspend the effects of my anti-passion serum, which have already been slightly weakened in some excessively ardent temperaments. Just now, a most fortunate opportunity has permitted me to discover a certain substance, the *passional contra-antitoxin.* This new serum completely neutralizes the active principle of the

aforementioned remedy, returning the brain to the exact same anatomical and physiological conditions as those in minds that have never
been vaccinated."

And presenting them with a flask full of a transparent liquor, he
added, with a tone of the most profound certitude:

"Here is that precious elixir. Anyone who drinks even one cubic centimeter of it will regain his original personality and feelings within ten
minutes.

"But before giving you this mysterious potion that vivifies the passions, I must make a moral prediction that is not at all pleasing. The
old ethical antitoxin or panacea did not destroy the encephalic centers where the soul evokes sinful images and anticipates the tempting
fruits of forbidden pleasures. It simply rendered these unhealthy representations and desires ineffectual, no more than that. It merely disabled the nervous pathways that connect regions where antisocial sins
are evoked with the motor centers that carry them out.

"Pathways like these, which in the Villabroncans have been blocked
due to long inaction, will now be clear, wide open, and anxious for
vindication and revenge . . .

"You thus have reason to fear that the accumulated charge of unsatisfied appetites, of images of quite reprehensible acts that have been
held in check, will suddenly achieve a state of such tension that it will
be powerful enough to break down all the barriers erected in your consciences by dignity, religion, and law . . .

"By warning you that your passions will probably run riot, I relieve
my professional conscience of a great burden. And I reciprocate loy-
ally with the noble confidence that all of you—patricians and proletarians, powerful and humble, so full of fervor and enthusiasm—will
let me subject you to the effects of the regenerative moral vaccine.

"All of you who exercise authority should prepare yourselves, without delay, for these so-called *government measures*. Augment and discipline your police force, which has grown weak and rusty through pro-

longed inaction. Perhaps with this foresight you will still be able to guarantee public tranquillity, domestic honor, and respect for the law.

"But if, as I suspect, you are unable to reestablish the normal course of life, a disquieting doubt will vanish from my conscience. I owe you something . . . something that I have still not repaid. I must restore the losses of all those social professions that, by some sad, implacable fate, base their well-being on vice, disorder, and crime. Fortunately, the coming unruliness will let me repay this sacred debt with interest . . . May God will that you do not rue this choice!"

Immediately following this discourse, the doctor's assistants placed some long-necked vessels full of a mysterious liquor on the great tables. As has been described, one needed to drink only half a cup[6] of it to feel his mind cleansed of any moralizing suggestion.

It is hardly necessary to say that all those in attendance, including the mayor, were deaf to the doctor's mournful prophecies. Rushing thirstily toward the flasks, they greedily savored that passional potion that permitted the prickling sweetness of forbidden fruit. The flasks were quickly emptied, and they had to bring out more. But as the demand for the *liquor of evil* grew from moment to moment, they finally had to set up a sort of shop or branch office in the main square, which was guarded by sentries. In an interminable procession, the devotees of Bacchus, Venus, and Mercury lined up before it. The women rushed in in great flocks, jostling one another. You can just imagine how, in their thirst for sin, the registrar's wife, the syndic's wife, and many other distinguished women of leisure ignored the recommended dose, emptying not just cups but entire pitchers.

Fortunately, this miraculous medicine turned out to be quite economical, for it was just plain water! Thanks to the guards, there were no disturbances or abuses, for they strictly regulated people's turns in the impatient, interminable queue . . .

---

6. The required dose has suddenly increased dramatically. Half a cup is about 125 cubic centimeters.

8

As Mirahonda had foreseen, they soon came to know the sad consequences of their imprudent contra-suggestion. Having been restrained for a year, their passions exploded violently. Vice displayed itself with unheard-of shamelessness and effrontery. For a month, the inhabitants of Villabronca lived an all-out bacchanal. Vertiginously, the clock of their passion ran onward, simultaneously sounding the hour of their fall in all of their flaccid wills.

So that you may form some notion of the prevailing laxness and licentiousness, let us cite some examples. The syndic's wife, who for a year had been deaf to the captain's tempting suggestions, now abandoned herself to immodesty with such boldness that the intrigue was rapidly discovered and the innocent husband had to lock his inconstant mate in a convent for repentant women. Giddy with love and impatience, the frivolous wife of the registrar wrote Mirahonda a hot, voluptuous letter asking him for a date. With widespread surprise they learned that the priest's housekeeper, a fresh, robust village girl, had run off with the sexton. To prepare for their elopement and provide for them once they had escaped, he had cleaned out the collection boxes in a single hour, selling the oil from the lamps and stealing the priceless jewels he had coveted for so long.

Usurers ran through the streets as though chased by the devil, proposing unbelievable deals to everyone they met. Respectable single women were accosted in broad daylight by bands of libertines, who were maddened and carried away by lust. One coquette changed her outfit and hat seven times in one week, squandering a fortune on lotions, flowers, jewelry, and ribbons. In the taverns, which were now open all night, the drunks and brawlers simply swarmed. In just three days there were four murders, ten serious injuries, and a countless number of attacks on private property.

All the frustrations of love, all the debts of hate, vanity, envy, and even political passion were liquidated in a single moment. Scandalized, the honorable people fled the poisoned city in a confused throng . . .

9

Every day, the madness that had taken hold of Villabronca was growing more aggressive and threatening. Fearing serious unpleasantness, Dr. Mirahonda left the town at full gallop, taking only his wife, once he had saved his most important scientific instruments.

Months afterward, when he had regained his calm, the learned doctor submitted a paper to the *Zeitschrift für Hypnotismus*.[7] In its conclusion, he offered the following interesting statements:

"In summary: the possibility of reeducating people by means of suggestion is a firmly established fact. Once a doctor learns how to wield the high prestige of science and appeal to people's generous compassion, his imperative command will suspend or weaken the action of sinful stimuli, granting reason an easy, decisive victory in all conflicts of conscience. We are certain that, had it been possible to repeat the vaccination, had it been possible to renew the suggestive action every two or three months so that its effect on the most rebellious wills was vigorously reinforced, then our success would have been permanent and total.

"For this reason, I would not regard the achievement of a mental orthopedics capable of correcting cerebral aberrations as an irrealizable utopia. On the contrary, I believe it is possible that once certain prejudices are dispelled, physiology—aided by some of the methods of psycho-physical hypnology and scientific pedagogy—will either eliminate our antisocial impulses or reduce them to a bare minimum, inaugurating an era of peace and relative well-being.

"Still, I find it impossible to conceal a tormenting doubt that assails me. My experiments demonstrate that it is possible to abolish delinquency and instill resignation to poverty, hard work, and strong social

7. The *Zeitschrift für Hypnotismus* was an actual journal founded by Auguste Forel in 1892.

discipline, without any struggles or protests. But is such a state of things conducive to progress? Can we be sure that the goal of the human race is to vegetate indefinitely in peace and mediocrity? Wouldn't perfectly smooth, harmonious social relations eventually create a species that is static and routinish, lymphatic and senseless, surfeited with precedents and formulas, utterly incapable of the vibrant struggles needed to build a civilization? Wouldn't the suppression of evil perhaps be the greatest evil of all?

"A little pain and social misery seem indispensable. They moderate character, sharpen the mind, root out softness, and create heroism and greatness of soul. In sum, they improve the human race both morally and physically.

"Injustice, too, can work to our advantage. It has been the modeling tool of progressive political institutions. Without the cruelty and injustice of the powerful, man would never have advanced beyond the tribal period or the natural stage. Even the greatest crimes in history have served the cause of progress. Everyone knows that the foundation of the glorious, civilizing Roman Republic owes itself to the lasciviousness of a king. The maddening abuses and unjust privileges of the French nobility brought us the emancipation of the people and the recognition of the rights of man. Without the popes' artistic madness and immoral trade in indulgences, would Protestantism have arisen, or freethinking, the fruitful father of the philosophical, literary, and scientific renaissance? Isn't it possible that the Inquisition's bonfires lit up the human conscience? In a word: would the hero, the saint, and the scientist, the most exquisite flowers of the human will, open their calyces without the piercing spectacle of poverty, in the gray, lukewarm environment of peace, luxury, and abundance?

"Everything points to the fact that pain, poverty, and injustice are the inexorable laws of life, intimate forces that progressively drive the spirit to ascend to ideal heights. One must presume that the struggle between social classes will continue for centuries, even when the people have been sufficiently illuminated by charity and science to regulate their *production* and *birth rate* in a wiser, more prudent way. Until today, these two extremely important social functions have been left to random chance and have thus been responsible, as is well known, for at least half of all poverty, transgressions, and crimes.

"According to what I have just outlined, as my experiment with social hypnosis has confirmed, the suppression of injustice and crime is not conducive to human progress. What role should science play, then, in the rigorous struggle to which humanity is condemned?

"It is the duty of science to temper this rigorous battle, to humanize it so that the blood and pain disappear forever. The location of the struggle is going to change. From the streets and fields, it will move to the factory, to the scientist's laboratory, and the sociologist's study. Certainly civilization will never completely prevent the strong from trampling the weak, but it will ensure that the assassin of the future is so impersonal and uncoercive, so sweet and exquisitely merciful, that his victim will receive the coup de grace with a gesture of supreme resignation. Even more than that: he will receive it with the sublime pride of a hero or a saint, because he will know that his personal, irremediable sacrifice will create a higher level of altruism, prosperity, and culture for his species or race.

"Even now, in the remote blue distance of the future, I can see a semidivine humanity whose sovereign reason, indifferent to any sort of lowly concupiscence, gravitates toward truth with the same natural impassivity of a heavenly body moving toward the sun . . .

"When these enlightened days arrive, when executioners and victims recognize themselves as harmonious organs functioning within a single living whole, then semisuggestion itself, which is practiced today in its philosophical, political, and religious modalities, will disappear forever. For then, purified and sublimated by science, the human race will have discovered how to eliminate weak, savage, or unhinged minds, and it will understand that *goodness* is a function of *truth* . . . It will know that egotism and delinquency are lamentable errors . . . Humanity will see, in sum, that the small degree of happiness man is allowed to enjoy on this earth is the fruit of his single-minded commitment to the dominion of life and the glorious conquest of the spirit.

"But in the meantime, until these remote ideals can be realized, while three-quarters of all men are poor, savage, foolish, and ignorant, the semisuggestions of authority, religion, and discipline are indispensable for restraining and pacifying those who lack good brains or good fortunes. This is the commandment of Nature, who, ever attentive to her primordial evolutionary ends, hates all disorder. Forced to choose between the lesser of two evils, she prefers tyrannical organization to liberating anarchy; conservative, invigorating cruelty to indulgent, relaxing mercy.

"In summary: as long as the human animal remains so varied and shares its passions with the lowest members of the animal kingdom, then political and moral suggestion will be necessary so that disorder does not hamper progress. But this suggestion must not be so weak that it cannot restrain and control those who are poor in spirit and savage in their lack of will. At the same time, it must not be so strong and imperious (as a hypnotic suggestion would be) that it impairs or compromises the ethical and intellectual personalities of those who drive civilization."

THE ACCURSED HOUSE

"Read this letter," said Inés to her father, radiant with jubilation. "It's just come from my cousin Julián in America. How wonderful! We'll have him here with us in less than a month, and he's coming back rich in goods and experiences, just as you wanted . . ."

Moved by his daughter's joy, Inés's progenitor picked up the letter, pulled on his spectacles, and read:

"My unforgettable cousin: Just as I told you, my business ventures are flying along at full sail. They're going so well that I believe I've now entered the envied flock of the bourgeoisie, and as I'm not at all ambitious, I've decided to return to my native land.

"Toward the end of June, I'll arrive in New York via railway from San Francisco. After that, I'll board a steamer, the *Bour-*

gogne. I'll reach Le Havre on the ninth or tenth of July, and after spending a few days in Paris, I'll have the supreme delight of seeing you again. If, as I presume, you still feel as you did last year, I will throw the fruits of my labor at your feet, a paltry two hundred thousand duros.[1] Please take them from my hand, for they are yours. Only your memory could have instilled me with the health and activity necessary to earn them and the frugality and virtue required to save them.

"I fervently long to be at your side. Embrace my aunt and uncle for me. Your cousin, *Julián.*"

This letter from Inés's fiancé clearly satisfied don Tomás, who was known throughout the region for his honor and noble lineage. He received a regular inheritance from an entailed estate and possessed an emblazoned ancestral mansion in Rivalta.

So proud was he of his daughter's beauty and talent that one can excuse his determination to marry her to a worthy man. He sought one who was discreet and upright and had sufficient means to guarantee the preservation of that historic mansion, offering future increases and prosperity.

In truth, that gentleman from Rivalta had good reason to be satisfied with his daughter. Thanks to an exquisite education, he had prepared her admirably for life, instructing her in science and art, without pedantry; in morality and religion, without superstition; in virtue and dignity, without pride; and in kindness and tenderness, without hysterics or prudery.

Don Tomás was not unfamiliar with his nephew Julián's merits, for the fellow was an excellent young doctor. He had mentored and encouraged him a great deal in his career, that is to say, before his emigration to Mexico. But in those days he had found him too skeptical, with tendencies toward socialism. Above all, he had lacked the financial means worthy of Inés's high merits.

Although it was not necessarily true that republican America would break Julián's democratic, materialist convictions, don Tomás knew

1. A duro is five pesetas.

very well—as one skilled and experienced in the vicissitudes of political life—that revolutionary, antireligious virulence settles considerably under the ballast of four million pesetas. At the very least, it is
reduced to the most inane, inoffensive platonism.

As far as Inés was concerned, as we have already said, she cared only—
with all of her soul—about celebrating her fiancé's forthcoming arrival. For she loved him passionately as a man, without giving a thought
to his philosophy or even his millions.

The young heart rarely chooses freely. Lovingly, the virgin ground
accepts the first seed the wind offers it and devotes all the energy it has
robbed from the sun and surroundings to its expansion and flowering.
Such was the case with Inés. She fell so deeply in love with her cousin
because he had the opportunity to show himself to her heart in those
critical, mysterious moments in which a girl becomes a woman. In
these moments, the feminine soul suddenly feels like a lonely orphan.
Driven by a far-seeing instinct, it looks restlessly about for the strong,
intelligent companion who will serve as guide and shelter in its moments of debility, who will become its confidant and share its amorous
dreams!

Although many years had passed since that lovely sentimental dawn,
how could she forget that faithful, affectionate friend of her young
childhood and adolescence, the one with whom she had roamed
meadows and beaches, building a common foundation of illusions and
hopes? . . . How could she forget the gallant partner with whom she
had danced so often beside the church towers on saints' days, during
those luminous summers the student had dedicated to the pleasant
warmth of home and the comforting life in the open air! Finally, how
could she not cherish, in the reliquary of her memory, the burning tears
with which Julián had taken his leave of his beloved cousin, once his
education was complete and he was ready to embark for America! . . .

But let us say something about Inés, the protagonist of this truthful tale. Don Tomás's daughter belonged to that privileged caste of
calm, well-balanced women, healthy and robust in body and soul like

the strong women described in the Gospels. In her, the tender, compassionate, most exquisitely feminine instincts of woman were combined with an energetic will, serious character, and heroic aptitude for self-sacrifice in a wonderfully harmonious union.

A superficial glance at her exterior quickly revealed this admirable balance of moral qualities. She had a broad, clear forehead, a classic nose, elegant eyebrows drawn with an energetic stroke, and big, blue eyes with a subjugating look. Her graceful yet free and easy walk might perhaps have given her an overly masculine air, but the charming, artistically accentuated curves of youth, the softness and whiteness of her skin, the roundness of her throat, the smallness of her hands and feet, and the sweetness and enchantment of her voice had imprinted the stamp of the most seductive, pleasant femininity on that eurythmic goddess's body.

Everything in her spoke of that interior beauty so highly praised by the poets, which is merely the expression of a wise, harmonically constructed feminine brain. As the Andalusians say, an angel seemed to beat his golden wings in her long eyelashes, peeping out through the luminous windows of her pupils, speaking in the waves of fire from her lips, and giving a gentle measure to the rhythm of her heart.

As Julián knew, females of this type are a safe port for man in the tempests of life. Tender and energetic at once, they are so strong and intelligent that the sun of reason rapidly dissipates any vapors of caprice or nervousness. In times of doubt and anxiety, they give him redeeming counsel, and they create the Providence of home, where order, discipline, and love reign everlasting.

As one may presume, Inés's position as a *professional beauty*—in the honest, honorable sense the Yankees give to that phrase—created quite a few conflicts for her parents. Thanks to her great discretion, however, these were satisfactorily resolved. She politely rejected all suitors greedy for her beauty, displaying at some times a distinct inclination toward celibacy and independence; at others, a fervent vocation for the cloister. When one man, full of passion or audacity, courted her a little too insistently, she would summon all of her strength. Settling matters in the simplest way, she would tell him:

"Sir, I am very grateful for your favors, but I love a man who is far away, and as long as my fiancé lives, I am resolved to be completely faithful to him."

Thanks to this admirable formality, to this perfect lack of coquetry, Julián could rest easily until his long-deferred happiness arrived.

Well, as we were saying, from the time that Inés received that celebrated epistle, she felt herself suffused with the most intimate joy. Still, at times, she trembled with emotion. The very excess of happiness was causing her pain, and during the silent nights, her sleepless imagination painted tragic visions and desolating scenes. When these gloomy presentiments fled like dark bats at the break of dawn, they left a dismal stain in the depths of her consciousness, lending melancholic tones to the most joyous sensations of life . . .

"My God!" she exclaimed at times, "will he have a safe passage? The voyage is so long and dangerous!"

But yielding to a religious feeling, in which women so often find fuel for their optimism, she would say to herself,

"How mistrustful I am! I will pray to the Virgin to bring Julián back safe and sound."

And she prayed fervently . . . and felt her confidence and faith in the future being reborn. For Inés still lived in that happy, ingenuous age in which rain and fair weather seem to represent, respectively, the tears and the joy of a compassionate Father who lives in Heaven, from whence he governs the affairs of the world with love, wisdom, and foresight . . .

2

But fortune, always envious of good people's luck, was to put our amorous lovers' plans to severe tests. Through telegrams from the Fabra Agency, which were later expanded by newspaper reports, the poor girl learned that the *Bourgogne,* in which Julián was returning, had undergone a terrible collision with a merchant steamer. More than half of the passengers had perished in this dreadful catastrophe. As for the survivors, who had been picked up by a German transatlantic vessel, they would be arriving at Cherbourg any day . . .

Terrible anxiety devoured unhappy Inés, who saw all of her beautiful dreams of love and happiness dissipated in an instant. Like a carrier pigeon brutally wounded in its triumphal ascent to the skies, the poor young girl's hope fell victim to the well-directed blow of fatality.

But the law of sentimental responses, the redeeming Providence of man, soon came into play, bringing consoling images to her mind. Under their soothing influence, the loving girl went back to dreaming up her warm, soft nest of fleeting illusion.

"No!" she thought, submitting to the invincible optimism of youth. "Julián has not perished . . . My heart tells me so, and its presentiments have never been wrong. The Virgin promised me, and she can't deceive me . . ."

Luckily, a telegram arrived from Le Havre to relieve her painful anxiety. Julián had been rescued, but his entire fortune, which he had been carrying in gold and banknotes, was now at the bottom of the sea.

• • •

It is impossible to describe the effusion of joy Inés experienced some days later when she saw Julián arrive safe and sound, a handsome young man tanned by the sea air and more in love and devoted than ever! . . . Needless to say, the *American* was cordially received and fêted in Inés's house, for since the death of Julián's mother years ago, her parents had become his closest relatives.

It was then that the noble qualities and goodness of Inés's soul expressed themselves most eloquently. When she had thought her fiancé was rich, her innocent joy had sometimes been clouded by a certain troubled feeling, for she had worried that people, even Julián himself, would presume she had ulterior motives. Besides, money opens so many doors! Could she be absolutely sure that she had no rivals? But now, seeing her fiancé without means, she considered herself completely happy. In her desire to console Julián, she made a special pledge not just to surrender herself more than ever to his will, but to proclaim her love proudly, persuading the world of the depth and permanence of her feelings.

With all this going on, our winning repatriate saw very quickly that his situation in his uncle's house was changing from day to day. Once Inés's father ascertained that since the shipwreck, Julián's whole fortune consisted of his desire to work and a few thousand duros accidentally saved from disaster, he began to act cold and ceremonious in Julián's presence. Still, his inner core of nobility and kindness remained stronger than the greed of an ambitious father, and it prevented him from prohibiting the young man's relations with Inés. But his wife, who was much firmer and more severe, took the disagreeable step required under the circumstances. Asking her prospective son-in-law to leave the house, she notified her daughter that from henceforth, she must cease regarding Julián as her fiancé.

Julián fell into a deep depression.

"Once again," he told himself, "I must struggle against adversity and take up the task of making my fortune. I need to get rich, and I need to get rich right away! . . . But how does one prosper so rapidly? Emigrate again? . . . Impossible! To defer the happiness I've been longing for for another eight or ten years would practically rule it out completely. I'm already thirty-eight, seven years older than Inés, and love, which is by nature impatient, is no friend to old people. What am I going to do? . . ."

3

One beautiful afternoon in April, still troubled by these gloomy preoccupations, Julián was walking mechanically along the winding coastal road that links Rivalta with Villaencumbrada, the regional capital. The spring, coming somewhat late to that foggy climate, was starting to break the monotony of the dark green woods and meadows with flowery patches of diverse brilliant hues. Each side of the road was bordered with hanging garlands: the yellow flowers of spiny gorse, the pink and white petals of daisies, and the purple calyces of irises, all trembling from the impulses of the gentle breeze. From a high, nearby wood came a silent cry of rising sap and a warm, perfumed breath that suggested the joy of being alive. A thin, bluish vapor, like a veil of hymen woven from microscopic germs, was floating in the hollows, hiding the plants' and animals' sublime, mysterious acts of conjugation from the sun's rays. On the left was the boiling sea, restless as a bitch in heat, from whose bottomless breasts, bulging with fertile protoplasm, millions of lives eager for light and oxygen were springing to earth in time to a harsh, grave nuptial hymn. The sky, transparent and pure after long days of mournful rain, allowed one to see the steep mountains of a nearby range against a deep, blue background. There in the remote distance, one could make out the bold, scalloped silhouette of the white peaks of Europe . . .

This contrast between the sad decline of his soul and the joyous awakening of nature; between the melancholy widowhood of his heart and the boisterous weddings of flowers, birds, and insects, gave Julián's thoughts a color of infinite sadness . . .

"Surely," he said to himself, "man is condemned never to harmonize with the symphony of the world. He is forced to live in perpetual conflict with the most imperious commands of nature, from which he seems to persist in distancing himself . . . Ah, how far we are from that blissful time when people, free from prejudice and conventionality, enjoyed the liberty to love one another like the birds in the branches and the flowers in the meadows! . . . What happy days those were when society, crude and simple, had never heard of the social parasite, the bill of exchange, overwork, and above all the dark terror of poverty, responsible for so many crimes and acts of injustice . . . Those were the days, when the human ant, content with everyday toil, had still not invented the imbecilic art of painful, laborious hoarding during the summer of life, only to die of exhaustion and sickness before winter ever comes! . . .

But Julián was not a man to be easily discouraged. Made for great enterprises, he had irrevocable faith in miracles of will.

And so reason, momentarily confused by emotion, mastered the dominions of feeling, implacably sweeping away all depressing, melancholic images. In a fit of optimistic enthusiasm, the inspired youth exclaimed:

"Away with melancholy, the heroism of cowards! Let's follow the example of Nature. She, too, has her Gospels, preached by flowers and insects, plants and animals, but we're so inattentive, we never stop for a single instant to hear their august, eloquent precepts. In that insuperable desire of germ cells to fuse two existences in the burning kiss of conception . . . ; in that perpetual, harsh battle for light, food, and oxygen, she tells us that in this world there are only two serious, transcendental realities worthy of interest to strong spirits: *to struggle to live, and to live to love. Let us struggle,* then, with powerful energy, and *let us love* with great strength, for Nature, our mother, wants it that way . . ."

• • •

Absorbed in these thoughts, Julián had dropped below the horizon of the village without realizing it and had come almost within sight of Villaencumbrada. While making his way down a gentle slope that descended toward the sea, not far from a small, colorful estuary, he spotted a magnificent villa, or rather an aristocratic palace, erected on a fine hill. In its environs, separated by extensive orchards and meadows, he could see various accessory buildings: small huts for farm equipment, a cider press, granaries and haylofts, hothouses and shaded shelters . . . everything, in sum, that a rich colonist, a lover of *confort* and plenty, could desire if he wanted to maintain an isolated, regulated, independent existence. Over the surrounding hills, in an interminable expanse, he could see arable fields and pastures, apple and chestnut groves, all belonging to the luxurious villa, as one could tell from the line of colossal eucalyptus trees that separated the estate from the neighboring property.

But what most called his attention was that this luxurious palace, though almost new, seemed to be completely abandoned. The rust on the gate, the weeds on the garden walks, the dust on the window-panes—many of them broken, and the neglect of the fruit trees—which were growing at their pleasure, parasitically invading paths and avenues, indicated that no owner, tenant, or caretaker lived on that estate.

His curiosity aroused, not seeing a living soul anywhere around him, Julián hastened to a nearby field where a villager was busily mowing hay and asked him the reason for this strange abandonment.

"What? Don't you know anything?" responded the laborer with an amazed expression. "That's the *Accursed House,* so called because all the people who've ever lived in it have died or gotten very sick within a year. Many people say that it's bewitched and that there are blood stains coming out of the walls in its salons and passages, which are haunted by goblins and souls in pain . . . They also say that at night, the tower windows are lit up by reddish flames, and the chapel bells toll a death knell all by themselves, as though invisible hands were pulling the rope . . ."

"But this is absurd! What? . . . A ghost story, in the twentieth century? Are you out of your mind?"

"Sir, I don't know whether this business about the witches is true, but as a resident of these parts, I can assure you that I've seen one very strange thing with my own eyes. You should know, sir, that the bad luck comes not just to the people who risk living in the house, but even to the cows, sheep, and horses grazing in their pastures. As soon as they taste the poisoned grass, all the livestock die helplessly. And I can also say that in wet weather, the mossy garden paths are covered with red spots that look just like blood. During big storms, the stream that comes from that property flows red, as though evil spirits had fought a battle on its banks . . ."

Intrigued by the incredible story he had just heard, Julián asked people in the neighboring villages for more precise, detailed information. Contrary to what he had expected, the reports he gathered essentially confirmed the first villager's account, with the addition of some valuable facts that offered our protagonist a ray of light and hope.

Here is the history of that strange *Accursed House.* It was built, ten or twelve years ago, by a heretic or Protestant millionaire. He might have been English or German—no one knows which. Probably sick with malaria, he had come from the Antilles to the sweet, salubrious climate of the Cantabrian coast in search of health. But a year and a half after construction was complete, just as the pasturelands and cornfields were starting to yield substantial profits, he suddenly died, as did two of his sons shortly thereafter. Terrified, the widow and the rest of her family—some of whom had also suffered from that strange sickness—sold the property at a considerable loss and left the country.

After that, a rich Latin American bought it, a carefree individual who planned to increase its value and paid no heed to mournful predictions. He added new lands and buildings, creating a model agricultural and cattle-raising colony. But when the recently installed cider press, the butter and cheese works, and the abundant livestock, fields, and fruit trees had reached a state of lucrative, full-scale production, a dreadful epidemic suddenly broke out which almost entirely emptied the stables and folds. Within a short time, the owner and two of his daughters perished. The disconsolate widow, the sole survivor of that unfortunate family, fled the *Accursed House* in terror. As a result of this catastrophe, she found no buyer or tenant for a full three years.

At last, eager to rid herself of this dangerous property at any price, the aforementioned widow yielded it—for a tenth of its value—to a certain impenitent freethinker, an *esprit fort* who laughed at sprites and goblins, ghosts, and *jettaturas.*[2] But to his misfortune, the bad luck

2. *esprit fort,* freethinker; *jettatura,* from Italian, *iettatura,* the evil eye

continued full force. A month after moving in, the brave skeptic lost a child and fell gravely ill himself. Needless to say, he escaped from that baneful palace, taking with him those few cows and horses not destroyed by the epidemic. Since then, the splendid property had been completely deserted and abandoned.

As one may presume, popular superstition had embroidered dark, ominous legends on that background of tragic realities. In the eyes of the ignorant, fanatical villagers, that estate, founded by a Protestant dog, was accursed by God. It now served as a dwelling place for witches and demons, who celebrated mournful rites and macabre dances therein. There was no shortage of old women who swore that on more than one occasion, they had seen sinister lights shining in the tower windows, while from the solitary rooms of the empty palace they could hear plaintive groans and the hideous sounds of chains . . .

It is not surprising that popular imagination would create these unbelievable tales when the very priest of Rivalta, to whose parish the mysterious house belonged, confirmed people's absurd inventions. For Mosén Cándido, the cause of the misfortunes that had occurred in the *Accursed House* was divine wrath, which had been justly aroused against the people. Under the pretext of tolerating other beliefs, they had allowed an execrable schismatic, an incarnate enemy of the Holy Mother Church, to make his home in that Christian district and build a palace and chapel without showing the least respect for the venerable cult of the Virgin. In vain the surgeon, a discreet and tolerant man, and some other reasonable people repeatedly challenged the priest's bias, reminding him that not just men (including some faithful Catholics) had succumbed to the *Accursed House,* but also sheep and cows. The priest refused to admit defeat, however. On the contrary, he gathered new strength, citing Jehovah's terrible threats to the Hebrews: "But that city shall be anathema to Jehovah, it, and *all the things* that are in it . . . With the edge of the sword, they destroyed everything that there was in that city, twelve thousand men and women, young and old, even the oxen, asses, and sheep . . . Then Joshua ruled over all the regions of the mountains and plains . . . and over all of their kings, so that nothing remained; *everything that had life,* he killed, just as Jehovah, the God of Israel, had commanded it . . ."[3]

4

When Inés's brave fiancé learned the *Accursed House*'s sinister history in minute detail, he saw the heavens open up before him, as they say.

"What luck!" he exclaimed to himself. "If only I could make myself the owner of that property! Ah!" he thought, "In those abandoned woods and pastures, in that stately mansion inhabited by bats and owls, lies the way to reclaiming wealth and happiness!"

Seized by the greatest impatience, Julián sought out the estate's owner without losing an instant. By chance, he found her right there in Villaencumbrada, and after some brief discussion and haggling, he closed the bargain at 1,500 pesetas. Once the papers were drawn up a few days later, our protagonist took possession of an estate that was worth more than 70,000 duros but which, as we have already said, was bringing its owner nothing but fears and regrets.

Days later, Julián was exploring the terrain and magnificent dominion of which he had just become legitimate master, thanks to the people's terror and ignorance. Taking a fistful of earth in his hand, he exclaimed, in a fit of ardent enthusiasm:

"Poor people! They think, deluded creatures, that you are death, when really you are life and prosperity! Even more: you are Inés, the happiness I have desired, the ideal I have pursued!"

But before proceeding, I owe the reader an introduction to Julián. The proper order and clarity of this story require it; this tale's uncommon merits demand it imperiously.

If the reader has imagined that because our protagonist was an expatriate, he belonged to that great rabble of ordinary, barely adequate doctors—like the *Artistas para la Habana,* who go to practice in countries

3. These sentences appear to be taken loosely from Joshua 11:12–15.

devastated by dysentery and vomiting—he couldn't be more wrong. Julián, a brilliant student who monopolized all the prizes and grants, had undergone his medical training in Madrid. Thanks to the encouragement and opportunities that an impecunious—but talented, hardworking, and serious—man finds in the capital city, his studies had cost his family practically nothing. His mother, the poor, ailing widow of an Asturian surgeon, was thus able to save enough money to make her old age bearable, for it was now growing very near.

Once Julián's training was complete, he had moved to Rivalta with the goal of establishing himself in the municipality and fulfilling his lifelong dream of marrying Inés. But the ambition of don Tomás, who, as we have said, wanted a millionaire son-in-law, along with Julián's own desire to save his heart's beloved from disappointments and worries, had finally obliged him to emigrate.

On the recommendation of some successful business friends in Mexico, he had settled in the city of Montezuma where, thanks to his knowledge, he had obtained a post at the public charity hospital. Within three years, he had become the most sought-after doctor and one of the most influential, highly regarded people in town.

A tireless reader, conscientious observer, and modern spirit, Julián was never satisfied with a mere symptomological exploration of his patients. He adjusted his diagnostic and prognostic aim more delicately, making frequent use of the microscope and chemistry lab. Contrary to the usual habit of the southern races, who insist on solving all problems in life by talking about them, our doctor set up a magnificent laboratory in his house for bacteriological, histological, and chemical analysis. In his library, he collected the world's most important scientific journals, and he devoted himself fervently to profound, luminous studies of the etiology of infectious diseases in tropical climates. The savory fruits of this intense labor were solid medical knowledge and scientific prestige so high and undisputed that in Mexico, our doctor passed as a supreme authority on hygiene and pathological matters.

With his strong will and clear, practical intellect, Julián saw from the first what was wrong with the *Accursed House*. The misfortunes to which the abandoned estate owed its dark reputation were a simple consequence of the natural conditions of the terrain and environment, easy to eliminate with a little bit of science and goodwill. As far as the sprites and goblins were concerned, the plaintive moans and sinister lights, the whole mournful, demoniacal, spiritualist legend was constructed around the positive fact of the estate's unhealthiness, so that they were not even worth a serious thought. They represented merely the hallucinations of cowards, hysterics, and superstitious people . . . the eternal, unthinking creators and sustainers of religions and prophets.

5

Julián's decision to buy the *Accursed House* fell on the town like a bomb. It created dreadful consternation in poor Inés, in whose troubled imagination her fiancé was now threatened by a shipwreck crueler than the one he had undergone.

In vain, the young man's friends tried to dissuade him from what they regarded as veritable suicide. Even don Tomás condemned Julián's behavior, which seemed like a reckless challenge to fate, a bold defiance of divine Providence.

Since it was impossible to speak with Julián, poor, tender-hearted Inés—the unknowing cause of his atrocious decision—hastened to write to the rash young man. She tried her best to shake the certainty of his unyielding passion and the invincible firmness of his mind.

"For God's sake, Julián," her letter concluded, "do not tempt fate. Trust me: I will wait for you unfalteringly until better days dawn for us. If worse comes to worse, remember that I am of age and mistress of my own will. As you know, I have never wanted riches or things to feed my vanity: you have always been enough for me. Although I consider myself a good daughter, keep in mind that for your happiness, which is also mine, I would face even my beloved parents' indignation.

So finally, if you care at all for my peace of mind, please don't move into the *Accursed House* or enter its harmful domains."

Julián wasted no time in answering his aggrieved fiancée. From his momentous epistle, suffused with the perfume of passion and suggestive because of an accent of truth that prevailed throughout, we shall transcribe only a few paragraphs. These should interest readers not just because of their scientific content, but because of their ability to clear up some obscure points in our story:

"You must convince yourself—for I have irrefutable proof of it—that the owners or tenants of the *Accursed House* were innocent victims, some of intermittent fevers; the others, of typhoid. My friend the town surgeon, who cared for many of the sick people, has described their symptoms to me and confirmed my diagnosis.

"Very well, then: from my studies of the terrain, I've learned that some puddles near the estuary are responsible for the tragic end of the malaria victims. They are a breeding ground for certain mosquitoes, the terrible *Anopheles claviger,* whose bites introduce the malaria parasite into the bloodstream. Given that malaria is extremely rare in these parts, the source of the infection, purely local, created here, was almost certainly imported by the English family that had just come from the Antilles—you know—the ones who built the *Accursed House.*

"In the none-too-distant past, the mechanism of this kind of importation was an impenetrable mystery. Today, though, thanks to the work of Ross, above all of Grassi and other illustrious scientists from the Italian school, we know that a carrier of malaria who comes to a healthful district can infect the local mosquitoes. If the conditions of the surrounding environment are favorable (if there are persistent puddles, an abundance of *Anopheles,* sufficient heat, etc.), this importation will form a perennial source of malaria.[4]

4. Malaria is caused by a protozoan parasite of the genus *Plasmodium.* It is transmitted to people by mosquitoes of the genus *Anopheles.* In 1897–98 Sir Ronald Ross (1857–1932) proved that the disease was spread to birds by mosquitoes, and he described the life cycle of the parasite. In 1898, Giovanni Battista Grassi (1854–1925), Amico Bignami (1862–1929), and Giuseppe Bastianelli (1862–1959) showed how the parasite developed in people.

"As far as the typhoid epidemic is concerned, there's no doubt that it was also provoked by conditions of the terrain. Among the water sources in this area, which I have analyzed bacteriologically, is an artificial spring of which the tenants of this property made almost exclusive use. It contains the terrible typhoid bacillus and the *Bacillus coli communis,* along with some other, less important microbes. I can show you completely convincing cultures of them all. The spring I mentioned is fed by clay pipes from a small brook. During the rainy season, all the filth from the mountain villages washes into it, and as a result, it's contaminated with every sort of pathogenic bacteria.[5]

"And the cattle, you will ask, did they die of malaria or typhoid fever as well? No; the cows, horses, and sheep succumbed to *splenic fever* or *anthrax,* a disease they contracted by grazing in a contaminated pasture. According to information I've gathered, some animals who died of the earlier epidemic were buried there. When I tried out the topsoil of that pasture on some rabbits, they died with the most characteristic symptoms of splenic or carbuncular fever.[6]

"So now you know the causal conditions—which are purely physical—of the misfortunes that occurred at the *Accursed House.* Neither God nor the devil has had any hand in them—only the microbe, an

5. Typhoid fever is caused by bacteria which are today known as *Salmonella typhi.* It is spread through food or water infected with these bacteria, often when unclean water is used to wash food. If untreated, it is fatal in 25 percent of cases. In Cajal's day the bacteria were known, but there were no antibiotics with which to treat the disease. *Bacillus coli communis* was the name used in Cajal's day for *Escherichia coli,* bacteria that live in human intestines. The presence of *E. coli* indicates that water is contaminated with fecal matter.

6. Anthrax is a disease of sheep and cattle caused by a rodlike bacterium. Before germ theory became generally accepted, it was known as splenic or carbuncular fever. In the early 1860s, French scientist Casimir Davaine (1812–82), inspired by Louis Pasteur's (1822–95) studies of fermentation, had shown that anthrax could be transmitted through the blood of an infected animal. Robert Koch identified the *Bacillus anthracis* in 1876, systematically studying the bacteria's life cycle. Koch's work confirmed what the French scientists had suspected for some time: that the bacillus could survive as a spore in an open field, reinfecting cattle that ingested it. Louis Pasteur, who had associated the disease with an infectious microbe before Koch began his studies, was the first to develop an anthrax vaccine. In a dramatic demonstration at Pouilly le Fort in 1881, scientists inoculated forty-eight sheep with the anthrax bacillus. The twenty-four that had been previously vaccinated lived, but the control animals developed anthrax and died.

invisible demon much more real and dangerous than all the evil entities dreamed up by naive human ignorance and superstitious fear.

"Knowing the causes, we can eliminate the effects. Luckily, these causes can be easily and cheaply removed, thanks to the favorable disposition of the land and the inexhaustible resources of science. According to reliable calculations, the complete disinfection of the estate will take only three months of work and about three thousand pesetas. And the enterprise will be well worth it.

"Once I've cleansed *Villa Inés* (for that's what I'm thinking of calling it in the future) of the monstrous microbes that have converted it into a kind of Dantesque inferno, I have no doubt that the building and the lands, appraised at their very lowest value, will be worth 100,000 duros. With these, and with the vivifying support of your love, I hope to smooth your parents' troubled brows and soften their hard hearts.

"As for the witches and gnomes, who according to the common folk inhabit these mysterious rooms: if they don't fly away like dazzled owls before the shining sun of knowledge, they'll be dissolved by the magic spell of a fairy whom you know, whom I am planning to make queen of this magical place."

It is a condition of the beloved to believe blindly in the mental superiority of her lover, to find an irrefutable logic in the flattering arguments of his loving desire. In accordance with this well-known psychological law, Inés, who was neither fanatical nor sanctimonious, acquired great confidence in Julián's science and wisdom. To be truthful, though, her faith never ran so high that it completely banished all feelings of disquietude or uneasiness. If her reason were a balance, one would say that the pan of religious superstition, of the cult of miracles, was so lightly loaded that the counterweight of a logical, cogent argument made her faith incline toward the side of truth. Unfortunately, though, the scale of judgment rests upon the heart. With all its emotional tremblings, the pans wobble so much that at certain moments, it seems as though the superstitious one has gained the day.

When the turbid sediment of religious tradition is stirred by emotion, it floats upward into consciousness, obscuring and mastering the will. In one of those moments, fearing a thousand misfortunes, Inés wrote back to her lover. Among other things, she told him:

"Everything you tell me is true. I believe it. I have to believe it. You are wise and confident in your science. But before you finish off the invisible enemies that surround you and watch you, what if you have an accident and get sick? I'm terrified to think that you might fall in this battle and end up lying there all alone in your dark house, abandoned by God and men! Clean up the estate, fine and good. Take all the far-seeing measures your good judgment suggests to you. But if you love living in this world, don't sleep in the *Accursed House!* . . . Only under this condition can you relieve the painful anxiety to which you're subjecting me . . .

"You tell me that the microbes of today are the devils of yesterday. But doesn't God govern the microbes? Can you really be sure that, in all the catastrophes of the *Accursed House,* those germs—which are as visible to their Creator as they are invisible to us—were not the agents of divine Providence? You're good; there's no doubt about that, but believe me, I could live much more easily if you'd let your sharp mind and beautiful heart be illuminated by the pure, redeeming flame of faith."

6

Luckily, the weather and season favored Julián's plans. A stubborn drought, unusual in those mountains, allowed him to put his sanitizing plans into effect, and they continued without mishap throughout the summer months. Assisted by a brigade of Galician and Castillian workers (those from his own region stubbornly refused to work on the estate), he began by opening channels to the swampy puddles near the estuary. He dug up and burned the skeletons of cattle who had died of anthrax, and he scorched the topsoil from the infected pasture, where the spores of the *Bacillus anthracis* were teeming. He poured kerosene and other antiseptic substances into the still water of the brook and the small puddles that resisted drainage, destroying the developing larvae of *Anopheles claviger,* the insidious mosquito that carries the *Plasmodium malariae.*

From a nearby hill flowed a stream whose waters, when analyzed, proved wonderfully potable and free from microbes. Seeing that they were being strewn uselessly down the hillside, Julián conducted them through iron pipes to a tank in the garden where, besides feeding an elegant, decorative fountain, they drove an artistic waterwheel.

After that, the new owner cleaned up the palace rooms. He set up a bacteriological laboratory in the tower and repaired the broken panes on the windows, hothouses, and entryways. He plugged up leaks; he furnished some of the rooms modestly, but with good taste. He bought some cows and horses that grazed avidly on those thickets and virgin lands untouched by scythe or plow. He pruned the apple trees, and then, at last, planted his arable fields.

Along with the mold and fungi, the famous *blood spots* vanished forever. As Julián had expected, they turned out to be colonies of *Micrococcus prodigiossus,* harmless bacteria that produce a bright red pigment and are responsible, in hermitages and sanctuaries, for an infinite number of stupendous miracles.

Meanwhile, the town of Rivalta was astonished by Julián's audacity and was burning up with curiosity to learn how his perilous adventure would end.

The priest was deeply dismayed. In the homes of neo-Catholics and extremely pious people, the most fearful predictions were offered. On the other hand, the town's scarce, scattered liberals, headed by the surgeon, bet boldly on Julián's health and served as the enthusiastic heralds of his good fortune. Thanks above all to the tireless activity and optimism of don José—as the surgeon was called—Julián's friends and relatives calmed down a bit, especially tenderhearted Inés, whose mind, enervated by the silent struggle within her, sorely needed encouragement and hope.

In this way, the entire summer passed by. All through it, our hero worked tirelessly on the conquest and sanitation of *Villa Inés*'s extensive holdings. With amazement, the people saw that Julián did not get sick. On the contrary, he gained weight and flourished in that life of fresh air and constant activity. His workers and livestock did not suffer any accidents or mishaps either.

Despite all this, the superstitious people who believed in witches and devils still refused to declare themselves conquered. They had no doubt about the nearness and inevitability of the catastrophe, some predicting it in the fall; others, at the end of the year.

September and October passed by, the preeminent months for malaria in other regions, but the colonists stayed healthier than healthy; the cattle, fatter than fat! Of typhoid fever there was not a trace. Winter came, with its inevitable cortege of snows, storms, and frosts. The lands were washed; the brooks were cleansed of germs and filth; and from the pools and marshes, even the cadavers of the mosquitoes disappeared. Under these conditions, to doubt the healthfulness of *Villa Inés* would have been the height of pusillanimity. After reassuring his fiancée, Julián did not hesitate for a moment to take up permanent residence in the palace, where he occupied several rooms facing south, with splendid views of the sea.

Since emotions in the town still continued to run high, no one was willing to work for him as a servant. That winter he had to accept the domestic and culinary services of a Galician laborer, who through his work as a helper and kitchen assistant had acquired some understanding of sundry matters, including the care of clothing and shoes. Later, when spring came, he had the good fortune to hire an old peasant woman as a cook and maid. She was as deaf as a post and because of this physical defect knew nothing of the house's ominous legend.

• • •

In this way, the first year passed by quite pleasantly. From an economic perspective, the second year looked even better than the first. Seeing that the gloomy auguries were not being fulfilled and that Julián's project was flying along at full sail, workers began to come to him from nearby towns. Thanks to these reinforcements, he was able to expand the areas of cultivation, mow the fields completely, harvest the apples and corn, and finally increase his herds, whose multiplication seemed almost miraculous.

In addition, he began to run some small industries on the side, such as making cheese and cider and milling grains, since he had been provided with a ruined waterwheel and mill. He even started planning a magnificent electrical plant powered by turbine, whose construction he left for the future.

7

The third year of that magnificent agricultural and cattle-raising colony's development opened under the most favorable auspices. By chance, though, Julián suffered an accident that renewed people's dreadful predictions and filled the guardians of the sacristy with great boastfulness and professional satisfaction. While Julián was riding through the hills adjacent to his property, the mettlesome, skittish colt on which he was mounted suddenly reared, forcefully throwing its unprepared rider. The fall fractured his clavicle and caused some contusions. Limping painfully, the beaten, battered rider made his way back to *Villa Inés,* where he examined the injured site and reassured himself it was only a simple fracture.

With the greatest haste, they sent for the surgeon, don José, who set the bone skillfully and wrapped it in the appropriate protective bandage. But the injured man, who was burning up with desire to continue his agricultural work, saw himself faced with a month of absolute rest.

There was really nothing unusual about what had happened, but still, even such a common, ordinary mishap was enough to unleash the tongues of the Rivalta gossips. They exaggerated the facts and sent out dreadful horoscopes in all directions. As one may well presume, the distorted description of the incident soon reached Inés's ears. Believing her lover was near death, she was seized by the most terrible desolation. Luckily, reports from don José and a reassuring letter from Julián brought some calm and comfort to the distressed young woman's mind, though they were not powerful enough to ease her disturbing apprehensions and fancies entirely.

What pained her above all else was the sad situation of the injured man, an orphan deprived of maternal tenderness and now attended by awkward, mercenary hands. All alone in his dark, imposing manor house, he must certainly have lacked the exquisite, affectionate little attentions that only wives and mothers can give. Ah! If only she were not held back by the tyranny of *what they would say,* with what compassionate enthusiasm would she not fly to her beloved's side, making herself his voluntary, self-denying nurse! . . .

In this manner, fifteen days passed by, which to poor Inés—fainting with impatience—seemed like centuries. During those deadly two weeks, she received no news of her fiancé, nor could she speak with don José, who was away from Rivalta at the time. Piercing, tormenting anxiety was consuming her . . . In her mind, where her old, faded worries were reawakening, sad thoughts and tragic visions flew about like dark birds of ill omen.

"Has he suffered a relapse?" she asked herself. "Did he and don José really tell me the whole truth? Has there been some grave, unforeseen complication? What has become of him? I want to know . . . I've got to know, and I will . . ."

To respect that immoderate passion for originality that troubles us all, I should keep silent here about a generous, selfless resolution on our heroine's part. A thousand times, poets and novelists have attributed it to the various protagonists of their fables. But the right to tell the truth, which is far greater than any literary consideration, obliges me to recount the incident without protective veils, describing an outburst of passion that should exalt and ennoble our winsome, loving Inés's moral character.

Without further preambles, then, let us say that once she had suffered twenty days without any news of the man she loved, this courageous young woman, whose tears and patience were exhausted, cast aside vain scruples and one night secretly left her father's home. As she tremblingly crossed the threshold, she hesitated for an instant, but drawing strength from her inexhaustible reservoir of passion, she stepped determinedly out into the street. She left the town by the sea gate, where the road to Villaencumbrada began. Minutes later, guided by the uncertain light of the moon, she left the highway and ventured bravely onto narrow paths shadowed by gigantic chestnut trees. At last, when she had come quite close to her lover's lonely residence, she found the energy—with a supreme effort—to silence the tempestuous beating of her heart. Valiantly, she rang at the entrance gate of *Villa Inés*.

Despite the advanced hour (it was one in the morning), she saw light in her fiancé's rooms, and she even thought that she spotted him through the windows . . . At once she heard the creaking of doors and the weary, labored step of the old housekeeper. After opening the gate and showering the visitor with exquisite attentions, she conducted her *incontinenti* to the workroom of Julián, who was then awake and apparently absorbed in deep scientific reflections . . . But in reality, he was awaiting Inés, whose burning impatience he knew well and whose imminent visit he had been expecting . . .

Trembling with delight, full of health and strength and with his arm still in its sling, that rogue Julián advanced to receive his idol, Inés. Seeing her lover so fine and jubilant, she almost fainted with joy.

In that moment, she was overwhelmingly beautiful. The folds of her thin, damp dress discreetly and modestly revealed her statuesque, captivating curves. With her face flushed from emotion, her golden hair in artistic disorder, her lithe figure, and her majestic gait, she looked like a supernatural apparition, the spirit of love, who was coming to bring her solitary, suffering lover health and happiness . . .

"Are you really all right, Julián?" asked Inés tremblingly.

"Better than ever, now that I have the pleasure of seeing you."

"Ah! What a great weight you're taking from my heart! You ingrate! Why didn't you write to me? What bitter days you've made me spend! I always knew you were strong, domineering, and stubborn . . . but I never knew that you were also cruel! . . ."

"Inés, my darling, please forgive this simple ruse. I was longing to see you up close, to put your love to the test . . . to see up to what point this love, which to me is more precious than life itself, could overpower frivolous social conventions, those dull, ordinary restrictions imposed on women by what we call a good education . . . Selfish creature that I am, I wanted to offer my senses—which have grown overexcited in this monastic confinement—the luxurious feast of beholding your beauty. I wanted to see you standing against the mysterious background of the night, illuminating the dark loneliness of my retreat, which from today forth will be permeated by your breath and perfumed and ennobled by your spirit . . .

"I forgive you," replied Inés, transfigured by joy and looking at her fiancé with the sweetest delight. "But for God's sake, from now on, don't use such heartless means . . . I got out of my house only by taking advantage of my parents' deep sleep, and I've got to be back before dawn . . . What terrors tormented me on that dangerous walk! With every step, I thought I was going to run into people I knew, or, worse, that I was going to run into those dreadful ghosts—the people, you know, who used to live in this wretched mansion. Only my overwhelming desire to see you could have given me the courage to come this far . . ."

"Inés, my love! . . . Calm yourself, and come sit down here by my side . . . Don't worry about getting back . . . Before dawn, I myself will accompany you as far as town . . . And don't be afraid that the walk will be bad for my health. I'm almost cured, and the night air won't do me any harm."

And so the tender love duet continued toward its *crescendo* . . . A double, contrasting flow of ideas and feelings stilled by absence and oppressed by distance now placed these souls, thirsty for love, in communication with one another. Better said, it placed them in sublime conjugation.

To describe our lovers' effusions in minute detail would be a task beyond our means. The dictionary of emotion is poorer than that of ideas. We lack symbols for the innumerable rhythms, spasms, and palpitations of muscles, entrails, and nerves. Above all, we lack a way to describe those intimate tremblings of the nerve cells which, on receiving vibrations from a lover's eyes, sparkle with inspiration like a bunch of marine organisms and phosphorescent glowworms shaken by the powerful propeller of a ship.

Certainly in books of mysticism, in those admirable treatises of Fray Luis de Granada, Santa Teresa, and San Juan de la Cruz, we would find a whole range of sentimental language, if not faithful and complete, then at least rich enough to express the sublime, superhuman ecstasy of flesh exalted by love. But alas! This fiery language, the only kind worthy of our heroes' passion, exceeds the power of our feeble, inexpert pen. And so, since we are doctors—though modest ones—permit us to use the dull, colorless style of physiological descriptions, for it is the only style that we know.

It is a well-known fact that the rhetoric of love proceeds in an expressive, emotional progression, running from mere verbal allegations with suggestive tendencies to the insuperable, sovereign eloquence of gestures and touches.

Unconsciously obeying this law, the lovers began their exchange, repeating a thousand times the greatness, intimacy, and endurance of their respective passions. But before long they sensed the inadequacy of human words, those subtle vibrations that carry abstract symbols and are good only for evoking the crudest, most material aspects of ideas and feelings. Spurred onward, then, by an invincible dialectical impulse, they renounced words and fell back on the magnetic effluvia of looks; above all, on violent, passionate communications with their hands.

In this tactile language, which man shares with the insects and living things closest to the natural state, they now found greater eloquence. The intermittent tremblings of their muscles marked the growing vehemence of their senses. Along with the heat communicated between them, they could feel intimate effluvia, intoxicating auras that penetrated to the very depths of their vitals . . .

But in time the expressiveness of touches, too, was exhausted. The thick epidermis of their hands still kept their souls too far apart. More intimate contact was urgently needed, a true intermeshing of the nerves across their thinnest, most diaphanous membranes. With each minute, the organic anxiety and restlessness increased. In that forced separation of flesh exasperated by love, there was something almost like the boiling of fertile protoplasm, the dull clamoring of virgin cells for activity, irresistible centrifugal impulses . . . One might say that all these living units, blindly attracted by their counterparts of the opposite sex, were fighting to rush right up against the skin, to peep out through the eyes and ears, and finally to leap, madly and frenetically, across the abyss of space and fuse in an eternal kiss with their sister cells.

Amidst this cellular tumult, the clamor of the inflamed cardiac muscle fibers stood out. As their rhythm accelerated vertiginously, they pounded against their cage of flesh and bone with such unaccustomed fury that it seemed they longed to build a common home in the lover's hot breast. Even the brain, normally so temperate in its habits, was beating impatiently at the temples and would undoubtedly have discharged all of its accumulated electricity in one great explosion, had certain austere, subjugating images of virtue and honor not put a halt to these sinful outbursts.

Soon after that, the organic tension and malaise grew even greater, and the infinite hunger for expression reached its peak. But there was then a redeeming pause, calm, august, and solemn, during which the members of the living hive became convinced of the impossibility of personally embracing their counterparts beyond the intervening air. Prudently, then, they appointed the labial cells to carry out their amorous, collective desire. At last the brain, faithful servant of that community, considered the established antecedents and laws for analogous cases and ordered the body's muscles to execute the salvational act to which they had agreed . . .

Submissive and obedient, the respective labial cells approached one another . . . And suddenly the sound of a round, magnificent kiss filled the room . . . a kiss as loud as a thunderbolt, and like a thunderbolt, a resolver of threatening, opposing energies . . .

This frenzy of love was followed by a soft, sweet, inexpressible calm. At last, the two bodies and souls had expressed themselves! And that decisive, indisputable demonstration had been made through an absolutely persuasive argument, that of touch: the universal, infallible language of life. Only pressure and contact really put substances in each other's presence. The intimate intertwining of nerves brings a true harmony of feeling and hot, deep palpitations of the flesh . . .

Now, not without certain reservations, we shall describe an unforeseen episode which will surely amaze the reader.

At the very instant in which the august nocturnal silence was brutally disrupted by that thundering, epic kiss—the synthesis of all those cellular kisses—a dazzling, purple flash suddenly rent the room's atmosphere, bathing the handsome pair in opaline sparkles. Extending outward through the open windows, it illuminated woods, hamlets, and mountains with pale, mysterious reflections.

Tragic terror jolted poor Inés's nerves. Astonished, her great, open eyes peered into Julián's while he, without seeming the least bit disturbed, continued to cover his lover's adorable hands with burning kisses . . .

"What was that?" exclaimed the terrified young girl, feeling the cold breath of the supernatural down her back.

"Don't be afraid, little girl!" replied Julián hastily, feeling a bit sorry about the joke. "The powerful light you just saw wasn't the flames of hell, but the torch of science . . . Forgive me for taking you by surprise, and don't hold it against me that my mad fantasy has dared profane the solemn moment of our heartfelt outburst by taking an innocent photograph by the light of a magnesium lamp."

Imprinting one more passionate kiss on the lips of Inés—who was gradually coming out of her abstracted state—he continued:

"Don't you know that I'm also a photographer? When your bewitching face—all lit up with emotion—approached my hungry lips, you looked so divine, so radiant with passion and beauty, that I couldn't resist the temptation to transcribe that scene of tenderness and bliss. In time, it will be a delight for my memory and a consolation in my old age. If a cold wave of pessimism penetrates my heart some day, looking at this portrait will give me moral support and reconcile me to life and humanity.[7]

"My God, the things you think of! And the worst of it," added Inés with a tone of indulgent irony, "is that I still have to thank you for that shock. Your photographic impulse seems so exquisitely gallant and spiritual to me! . . ."

"Come with me, little girl," replied Julián, "to the darkroom . . . We'll develop this film . . . and you'll know the supreme pleasure of witnessing a true act of creation, . . . the formation of a being who is progressively revealed from the chaos of gelatin just as the first man must have arisen from the sublime *Fiat Lux* of the Creator."

Seizing the young woman's hand—for she had now calmed down quite considerably—he led her to the darkroom, where he readied the solutions necessary to develop the image.

While our pleasant young lovers develop their virginal film in silver bromide (*honi soit qui mal y pense*),[8] permit the author to indulge in a lyrico-biological digression.

• • •

7. To cut short the lay reader's astonishment at these photographic matters, we will state that the photographic objective, wide open and prepared in advance, was focused on the entire area in which the scene took place, and that Julián lit the magnesium powder by means of an electric current (Cajal).

8. *honi soit qui mal y pense*, a French expression meaning, "a person who thinks bad thoughts about others only reveals his own badness."

(Oh, Mother Nature, creator of life, which you push ever onward with the gentle goad of love, toward remote and unknown shores! How horribly slandered you are! Those who make a profession of admiring you, those who base their happiness on counting the innumerable stars adorning your mantle, on scrutinizing the mysterious, invisible threads from which your body is woven, can only fall at your feet, overcome with fervent enthusiasm, overwhelmed by your profound wisdom! . . . How blind and unjust are those who, without having extended their gaze to the harmonic wholeness of your works, call you cruel because you have placed the sleep of death at the end of feeble, tremulous old age! They never imagine that, thanks to the fleeting nature of individual existence, species prosper, types vary, and progress is promoted.

Absolute bliss is an irrealizable chimera, for to live is to desire . . . to hunger for things outside of oneself. Our appetites are indispensable for the renovation of matter and form. Knowing this, you were so compassionate that you compensated for hunger with satiety; for pain, with forgetfulness; and for death, with love . . .

I am certain that if your power were not limited, if the inertia of matter and inevitable cosmic laws had not thwarted your kind intentions, you would have generously granted life the divine gift of immortality. No doubt, some accursed fate put an end to your paternal longings! But as a just compensation, to avenge yourself against adverse destiny, you gave us love . . . the perfume of life, the guarantee of the survival of the species, the agent of peace and concord among men . . .

But since, despite your infinite goodness, love is the delicate flower of a single day, a swift meteor that flashes out for an instant at the zenith of its form and power, you still knew how to make the rest of life bearable, beautifying adolescence with the sweet hope of loving, and ennobling old age with the memory of having loved . . .

By creating love, oh Soul of Nature! you have justified our existence and consoled us as we face our own death.

But what am I saying! The only people who die are those who do not love! *Non omnis moriar.*[9] In his harsh battle against implacable destructive forces, our merciful deity preserved the immortality of the germ cells, which was granted as a precious benefit of love.[10]

Poor egotists! What a sad lot awaits you! You're a decrepit stock from a past without a future, and destiny will bring you total annihilation. Your remains will wander eternally through the darkness of oblivion, like the fragments of some burnt-out asteroid!

So let us banish all gloomy, pessimistic thoughts. And let us live out our love, for to love is to endure, to conquer the tyranny of time. To love is to rescue something that does not belong to us, along with that imperishable part of our own being: the sacred inheritance of millions of extinguished lives, the fertile germ of a future and maybe better humanity . . .

To love . . . is something greater and more magnificent than just possessing a woman . . . It means entering into spiritual communion with an entire race. In a woman's innards live and palpitate millions of ancestors, all trembling with desire for resurrection. From the remote confines of History, they seem to greet us and beg for our help. Love is a funerary rite.

Let us approach our beloved, then, as a sacred temple . . . Let us re-

9. *Non omnis moriar,* Not all shall die.

10. I presume my readers know the common doctrine of the potential immortality of the germ or seminal cells, as opposed to the perishable character of the somatic cells, those that constitute the rest of the body. I refer to the ideas of Weismann, Hertwig, etc., about the pre-existence of complete or incomplete representations of our series of ancestors in the ovule's nucleus, according to physico-chemical mechanisms still unknown to us. Thanks to this theory, we can explain not just children's resemblance to their parents, but atavism, the reproduction of morphological types that lived in remote ages (Cajal). By the end of the nineteenth century, most scientists believed in evolution, but most favored Jean Baptiste Lamarck's inheritance of acquired characters over Darwin's natural selection as the mechanism by which evolution took place. German biologist August Weismann (1834–1914) took a harder line against Lamarck's idea than Darwin ever did himself, arguing that germ cells were uninfluenced by an organism's experiences and habits and could change only through recombination or randomly occurring mutations. In the early 1880s, in his widely acclaimed essays on heredity, Weismann proposed that living things were mortal, but the germ plasm they carried was "immortal" because it was always passed on intact. German embryologist Oskar Hertwig (1849–1922) studied the role of the cell nucleus in hereditary transmission and was the first person to show that conception depended on the merging of the egg's and sperm's nuclei (translator).

ceive her kisses with the intimate abstraction and fiery zeal with which we exalt God in our prayers . . . Let us remember that through a woman's eyes, we are regarded by the trembling souls of the dead! . . .

Praised be love that ennobles and vivifies us! Hosanna to merciful Nature, who grants us the sovereign gift of creation and resurrection, if only for a moment!)

8

The next day in Rivalta, deep emotion reigned.

Some fishwives had been returning to the town very early in the morning, after selling sardines in Villaencumbrada and the neighboring villages. When they passed close to *Villa Inés,* much to their horror and astonishment, they saw a terrible flash that filled the palace rooms with fire and lit up the sea, hills, and surrounding fields with sinister reflections. Simultaneously, there was a dreadful clap of thunder, and the sharp scent of sulfur, a favorite aroma of devils, seemed to spread through the atmosphere . . .

Speechless with amazement, the villagers stopped in their tracks, hoping, undoubtedly, that the *Accursed House*—shaken by legions of demons—would explode into pieces and bury its foolish inhabitants. Their terror reached its peak when they saw a red light like a glowing coal emerging from the palace tower. Minutes later, they spied two phantoms wrapped in sheets, who passed quietly through the garden gate and were soon lost in the intricate pathways of a nearby chestnut grove.

News of this frightful episode ran swiftly through the town, and for a month it was the obligatory gossip of old women and idlers. The most absurd, opposing commentaries were made. Still, the prevailing opinion was that Julián's days were numbered, unless the imprudent young man had made some sort of pact with the devil . . . This was what came of unbridled ambition and the absence of religion.

The priest, above all, felt as though he were bathing in rose water when he saw his mournful predictions at least partly confirmed. Undoubtedly, these ominous signs foretold the coming catastrophe, the fierce punishment Providence was preparing for the bold skeptic who dared to defy God's righteous choleric rage . . .

"Don't you see, my daughter?" asked Inés's innocent, superstitious mother. "And here you were thinking that with Julián's science and foresight, he had averted the danger! No. Our priest is right: in that unfortunate house, the angel of darkness reigns, and everyone who inhabits it or has anything to do with its inhabitants will die a terrible death."

This time, though, the mournful legends of witches and ghosts did not disturb the beautiful young girl in the least. She knew very well what to believe . . .

Although the mysterious event was a general concern, nowhere was it discussed more heatedly or debated with greater vehemence than in the back room of the Rivalta apothecary shop.

Almost every night, a pleasant, peaceful, never-ending discussion[11] was held there among a group of friends that included don José, the surgeon; *Allan Kardec,* the spiritualist; Ramascón, an old warship captain and distinguished naturalist; two rich Latin Americans; don Timoteo, an old Carlist;[12] and some cannery owners.

We will faithfully recount part of the heated polemic that took place in those days between *Allan Kardec,* don Timoteo, don José, and Ramascón.

ALLAN KARDEC (*a nickname given according to Asturian custom*): [13] Really, I tell you, you're way behind the times when it comes to spiritual manifestations. You should know that men of science as illustrious and

11. The Spanish word Cajal uses here, *tertulia,* has no English equivalent. It means a group of friends who meet every day in the same place to discuss political, social, or artistic issues.

12. The Carlists were a conservative, strongly clerical political group organized in the late 1820s. When King Ferdinand VII died in 1833, they supported his younger brother, don Carlos, as heir to the throne, arguing that Ferdinand's daughter, Isabel, had no right to it because she was a woman. Even after Isabel was crowned, they maintained their position, sometimes resorting to armed violence. In 1872–76, they fought a costly war against the government. In 1900–1902, not long before Cajal published this story, there was another Carlist uprising.

13. Allan Kardec (Hippolyte Leon Denizard Rivail, 1804–69) was an actual person, the main disseminator of spiritualist ideas in France. Spiritualism is the belief that the souls of the dead can communicate with the living. Kardec founded several spiritualist societies and journals and is best known for his work *The Spirits' Book* (1856).

distinguished as William Crookes, the discoverer of thallium; Wallace, the emulator of Darwin and co-author of the principle of natural selection; the famous astronomers, Flammarion and Zoellner; the bacteriologist P. Gibier; and even that selfsame materialist, Lombroso, have confirmed the existence of supernatural forces through rigorous experimental procedures.[14] They've demonstrated, for instance, that certain people called *mediums* possess the marvelous property of provoking *levitations, apports,*[15] *trances,* apparitions of deceased or absent people, momentary disincarnations, possessions, and stupendous adivinations and predictions, all through communication with the dead . . .

As far as the present matter is concerned, there can be absolutely no doubt. Just yesterday a renowned, learned man, *the spirit of the illustrious Jovellanos,* summoned by a medium speaking and writing in our Circle, gave us all the necessary explanations . . . You should know that the *Accursed House* was and still is a favorite refuge for a phalanx of old disincarnate spirits, reinforced, perhaps, by a few souls of the people who died in that villa . . . The sinister sounds, the mysterious lights, the appearances of ghosts and spectral shades, which dissolve like vapor and pass effortlessly through walls and roofs, are all caused by the physical manifestations of these deceased individuals, among whom those of the lower moral order undoubtedly predominate . . .

14. British physicist Sir William Crookes (1832–1919) studied cathode rays and discovered the element thallium in 1861. He was passionately interested in spiritualism and saw his work with psychic energy as a continuation of his studies in physics. British naturalist Alfred Russell Wallace (1823–1913), who independently came up with Darwin's natural selection hypothesis, visited a medium in 1873 and wrote that "every branch of philosophy must suffer until [spiritualist phenomena] are honestly and seriously investigated." French astronomer Camille Flammarion (1842–1925) wrote many highly acclaimed popular books on science, including *The Plurality of Inhabited Worlds* (1861). He also wrote on parapsychology, including one study of haunted houses. German astrophysicist Johann Zoellner (1834–82) met Crookes in 1875 and became an enthusiastic advocate of spiritualism. He believed that through his studies of parapsychology, he was exploring a "transcendental world." French microbiologist Paul Gibier (1851–1900) studied yellow fever, cholera, and rabies and published many books on spiritualism and parapsychology. Italian criminologist Cesare Lombroso (1835–1909) opposed spiritualism for much of his career but became "converted" in 1891 after examining medium Eusapia Palladino (1854–1918).

15. Apports are the sudden materializations of objects that have been summoned spiritually.

DON JOSÉ: Never! To think that *Villa Inés* is a branch office of hell, and that despite five centuries of civilization and stupendous progress, all the terrors, worries, and dark legends of the Middle Ages are still with us! What insanity!

ALLAN KARDEC: I will prove to you that the intervention of spirits is an actual fact . . .

RAMASCÓN (in a bantering tone): My God, Allan, leave off with your goblins and ghost stories! . . . You spiritualists still haven't even demonstrated the existence of the soul . . . Wake up! The spirits are leaving us . . . Science has already proved some time ago that what you call a *soul* is nothing more than a complex chemical reaction of *proteids*. Death is simply the final cessation of that reaction. Only savages want to explore a rifle barrel after the shot has gone off to see if there's a spirit inside . . .

ALLAN KARDEC (interrupting): Thanks!

RAMASCÓN: In other times, naturalists believed that the voluntary movements with which infusoria[16] seek and devour their prey were directed by a soul. Now these motor reactions, which are apparently intentional, are known to be mere effects of *chemotaxis* and variations of the *surface tension* of the protoplasm . . . The same will happen, believe me, with the human *psyche* . . .

ALLAN KARDEC: Ramascón, are you forgetting that man is not an infusorium?

RAMASCÓN: What could be more of an infusorium than a colony of infusoria?

ALLAN: But . . .

DON JOSÉ (interrupting): Let's leave this and return to the matter at hand. What I wanted to say is that even if the spiritualistic theory were right, it still wouldn't fully explain the phenomena at *Villa Inés*. In order for them to be carried out, you would need a powerful, most exceptional *medium*. You would need a *medium* who specialized in materializations, like David Home, Katy King, or in our day, Mr. Schlade or

16. Infusoria are protozoans that feed on decaying organic matter.

Eusapia Palladino, that famous, shrewd Neapolitan woman so mistreated by the scientists.[17] Now then, who is the permanent *medium* at *Villa Inés?*

ALLAN KARDEC: The thing is perfectly clear . . . The powerful, though unconscious, *medium* is Julián himself. At the expense of his vast nervous energies, lowly spirits longing for fleshly pleasures and anxious to communicate with the living are being nourished and materialized. To accomplish this, they are robbing Julián of his *fluid* during the night and devoting themselves to every sort of ploy for attention, from the noise and yammering of the goblin *frappeur*[18] to the showiest, most shocking phenomena of apports and materializations. All of this would come to a rapid halt if the inhabitant of *Villa Inés* would make up his mind to open a frank, faithful correspondence with those beyond the grave and call some enlightened souls, of a higher moral order, to his aid against the despoiling multitude of mischievous spirits . . .

DON JOSÉ: What a lot of nonsense! Who ever told you that Julián is a *medium?* And even if he were one without knowing it, why would spirits entertain themselves by slamming doors, playing ghosts, and making artificial fires in the house of a man who neither believes in apparitions nor pays the least attention to them?

ALLAN KARDEC: Let's take it one step at a time, don José. In the first place, you should know that the dead cease to be men with vices and

17. Scottish-American medium Daniel Douglas Home (1833–86) was famous for his ability to levitate. He described himself as a "passive instrument" and felt he had a "mission" to demonstrate people's immortality. Katy King was a spirit or alter ego who came to William Crookes's subject Florence Cook in spiritualistic trances. In 1874, Crookes published a paper arguing that King and Cook were two different women. The famous medium Henry Slade was known for his ability to record spiritual messages on slates—while sitting many feet away, without touching the chalk. Cajal has made slight errors with Home's and Slade's names. Eusapia Palladino, a poor, illiterate Neapolitan woman, was the first medium to be systematically studied by prominent scientists. Palladino could purportedly levitate, move objects without contact, raise tables, and create rapping sounds. Her examiners tried to see whether she could produce the same effects when her hands and feet were restrained. Among the scientists who examined her were French psychologist Charles Richet (1850–1913), the discoverer of anaphylactic shock; physicist Maria Curie (1867–1934), and Cesare Lombroso. These trials were still going on when "The Accursed House" appeared.

18. A goblin *frappeur* is a poltergeist.

passions, virtues and frivolities, but not because they've cast off their material garb. There are good spirits who console us in our times of tribulation, encourage us on the rough road of duty, and lend us inspiration and energy to triumph in our respective fields of work or our scientific and literary endeavors. At the same time, there are wicked, perverse, frivolous spirits who delight in mortifying us or suggesting sensual urges and low, sinful thoughts. Nor should it surprise you that the dead want to communicate with the living, for the act of disincarnation does not break those bonds of love and interest that link past with present humanity. On the contrary, it tightens them, making them more spiritual and sublime.

In the second place, I don't deny your skepticism about Julián. I am so far from denying it, that I find the exact cause of this persistent summoning of the spirits in your obstinate materialism, in your bold, frank rejection of the supernatural order. Despite our learned doctor's celebrated science, I believe he is languishing from a bitter, unexamined pain that frequently occurs in us older men: the melancholy fear of death, the indefinable, penetrating sadness caused by the impending certainty of not being. This disillusionment of exiled kings and fallen gods . . . this vague, infinite malaise that increases with the loneliness of old age and the proximity of life's terrible dénouement . . . these have not gone unnoticed by the few noble spirits evoked at *Villa Inés* (among whom are Julián's deceased parents). Burning with kind compassion for this poor lost child, they have resolved to enlighten his reason with sublime truths from beyond the grave . . . with inspiring, vivifying doctrines of the immortality of the spirit and the plurality of existences and worlds.

DON JOSÉ: You are eloquent, truly inspiring . . . What a shame all these beautiful thoughts aren't true! We've talked about spiritualist doctrines more than enough times without discussing their foundations. Without reminding you one more time that beautiful literary themes and fine, honorable intentions have never constituted philosophical proofs, let me inform you that all the surprising phenomena that have occurred at *Villa Inés,* including the most recent ones, can be explained perfectly well by natural causes. You can be sure—and I have this from Julián himself—that the mysterious light of the past night, along with that terrible noise that so frightened the fishwives, was merely the effect of a magnesium flash, visible from far off. A bit whimsical and eccentric in his ways, the owner of *Villa Inés* often makes use of it to take photographs in his laboratory . . . As for the sinister-looking red flame in the tower that people took for the glow of hell, it was only the red light of a lamp that photographers use to illuminate the darkroom while they're developing their plates . . . As far as the old misfortunes are concerned, I'm sick of repeating that they arose from natural conditions, some temporary and all modifiable. The English family, who imported the malaria, died from its effects; the other colonists died or fell ill from typhoid fever; and the cattle succumbed to anthrax or cowpox. As for the noises, lights, ghosts, goblins, etc., all that is merely the hallucinatory work of superstitious fear and the insane belief in the immortality of the spirit . . .

RAMASCÓN (slyly, seeing the spiritualist a little confused): It seems to me, don Allan, that you've turned rather *spherical,* like a chloroformized *amoeba* that retracts its pseudopods and suspends its movements.[19]

ALLAN KARDEC (thinking it over a little and changing his tactics): Don't you mock me! This is a very serious matter! I was going to tell you that . . . if the manifestations at *Villa Inés* were unique, unprecedented miracles in our chronicles of the marvelous, I myself would join you and seek their explanation in purely natural laws. But analogous events have been recorded, with the greatest guarantees of exactitude, in modern treatises on spiritualism. Just read, for instance, what they

19. Like other late nineteenth-century neuroscientists, Cajal liked to compare nerve cells to amoebae to show neurons' dynamism and plasticity. Like mobile, independent cells, he believed, neurons could grow and send out new "pseudopods" in different directions in response to environmental demands. Inactive neurons would withdraw their extensions and lapse into a torporous, unengaged state. To maintain one's mental connections, it was essential to keep neurons active.

say about that magnificent, redeeming religion created in 1847 by the Fox family in Hydesville (North America). You should learn, too, about the prodigious acts of Home and Katy King in Dr. Crookes's laboratory, and the stupendous experiments of Asakow, Zöllner, and P. Gibier . . .[20] After that, just you dare to doubt the supernatural character of some of the episodes that have unfolded at the *Accursed House!*

DON JOSÉ: A superb argument! According to your singular logic, just because we've occasionally committed the error of attributing the hallucinations, tricks, and fraudulent acts of living men (and how lively they were!) to the inhabitants of another world, we're forced to make the same absurd interpretation every time we encounter analogous phenomena. My God! Isn't it much more natural and reasonable to think exactly the opposite? Given that the spiritualists are wrong in the case at hand, isn't it very likely that they've also been wrong in similar situations, this multitude of illustrious scientists who—as far as I'm concerned—outside of the special fields in which they've made their names, are as capable of deluding themselves and *putting their foot in it* as any ordinary man?

RAMASCÓN: You said it, don José! Speaking of great scientists making mistakes, I remember that some years ago, when I was in London, I was able to see all these stupendous spectral phenomena described by Crookes executed by skillful illusionists in a theater. When I talked the matter over with physiologists and naturalists, I learned that Crookes, with his ingenuous spiritualism, had been deceived by a great number of bamboozlers. Let's not forget that the scientist, whose brain is adapted energetically, exclusively for a particular type of mental work, tends to be a child in everything else . . .

DON TIMOTEO: With your permission, I'd like to put my two cents into this conversation. As far as I can see, without prejudging the char-

20. Throughout 1847–48, the Fox family, who lived near Rochester, New York, were disturbed by loud rapping noises in their house. When they discovered they could control the noises by snapping their fingers, they began to believe these sounds were communications from the dead. In front of witnesses, the Foxes would ask questions, and the spirits would "answer" with specific numbers of raps.

acter of the facts, it's undeniable that *Villa Inés* has been a theater for supernatural displays, at least in the past. The noises and groans heard by an infinite number of people; the bloody spots on the walls and walkways that I myself have seen; the spontaneous tolling of the bell; and, finally, the sad, overwhelming misfortunes that have occurred on that property (misfortunes that are all the more strange considering that they harm only the inhabitants of that evil place), can only be thoroughly understood with recourse to invisible intelligences.

But with your permission, I will submit to you that both theories, the physical and the spiritual, seem absurd and unacceptable to me. The physical hypothesis seems insufficient and inadmissible because if you take it literally, as the materialists so often do, it has grave consequences for the field of biblical exegesis and the principle of historical criticism. It denies all the miracles and the many cases (recorded in the Holy Scriptures and the saints' confessions) of communication between men and superior intelligences like Jehovah, the angels and archangels, the seraphim, and, finally, the demons, tireless tempters of the human race and inventors of every kind of superstitious cult. The authority of our holy books and the magnificent structure of our sacred religion are based on exactly such instances of divine or angelic inspiration, miraculous celestial apparitions, and demoniacal possessions, all witnessed by fervent though unlearned multitudes . . .

But I also consider the spiritualist hypothesis unfounded since besides all this, it violates that sound, well-known logical maxim, "don't multiply your entities unless you need to." Come now, friend Allan! Just think of the rich hierarchy of spiritual creatures we possess, all of which can influence human conduct. We're overwhelmed with proof that Satan and other evil spirits can—with divine permission—suggest wicked thoughts and torment and penetrate the bodies of women, to whom they lend the abilities to talk in tongues, exert supernatural forces, and work extraordinary miracles. With all this, why the devil do you need your souls of the dead, your *mediums* and *perispirits,* and all your ridiculous concepts of metempsychosis and the plurality of worlds?[21]

ALLAN KARDEC: One step at a time, don Timoteo. Who ever told you that spiritualistic phenomena are the work of the devil?

DON TIMOTEO: I would be right in saying so, even if the Holy Church hadn't told me so first.

ALLAN KARDEC: Well, with all due respect, I submit to you that the Church is wrong from time to time . . . There are a thousand reasons to favor the spiritualistic interpretation of possession, apparitions, the movements of tables, and all kinds of *apports*. One is the very testimony of the spirits evoked. They often declare themselves to be relatives or friends of the people present, and they expose details of their intimate lives which, being known only to the family, absolutely guarantee their identity. Another is that in their written and oral communications, they reveal exactly the character, passions, even the failings and worries of human beings, whose talent and knowledge they have never surpassed. Finally, and most convincingly in my book, is the exalted, altruistic moral doctrine conveyed by these spiritual manifestations. It is the very same one proclaimed in the Holy Gospels, though cleansed of some errors and low superstitions with which human mud has defaced and bastardized Jesus's sublime maxims.

Ah! If you only had the patience and tolerance to attend our family gatherings and hear our possessed *mediums* eloquently defending the unity and wisdom of God! If you could hear them passionately calling for charity and brotherly love, exalting and ennobling humanity and purity of heart, and loudly proclaiming the dogma of slow, ultraterrestrial atonement and remuneration for our acts . . . I very much doubt that you, with all your proud, fervent orthodoxy, would dare attribute such lofty, consoling doctrines to the spirit of Satan!

DON TIMOTEO: So you think I mustn't dare, eh? No, of course not. You think the devil is so stupid that on the first impulse, he's going to

21. Metempsychosis is the movement of the soul to another body after death.

show you his visiting card and innocently confess all his iniquitous plans! *Latet anguis in herba*[22] . . . It's precisely in those displays of pseudo-Christianity . . . ; in that hypocritically fervent cult of the divinity; in that subtle, underhanded way you slip propositions into the dogma that are heretical in every respect, all under the pretext of obeying and fulfilling the purest, most exalted evangelical maxims . . . that's where I see the black claws of Satan . . .

RAMASCÓN: May I say something terrible?

DON JOSÉ: Speak freely—if it's coming from you, no one will take it amiss.

RAMASCÓN: All right . . . Well, what I was going to say is that if disincarnate souls retain the ignorance, passions, and defects of living people, then even the slowest person can deduce that the real perpetrators of the noises, the written and oral communications, the phenomena of possession, etc., . . . are the deluded *mediums* themselves, acting under the force of autosuggestion. It seems to me that spiritualists are like dogs who start barking in front of mirrors, never realizing that they're barking at themselves . . .

ALLAN KARDEC (a little annoyed): The things you think of! . . .

DON TIMOTEO: Well, all joking aside—to pick up the thread of our conversation—let me explain my position on the moral *relativism* of deists, spiritualists, and philosophers. In my humble opinion, this rebirth of spirituality and Christian virtues in the bosoms of societies separated for some time from the holy community is neither the work of philosophy nor the imposition of experience. It's merely the distant echo of religious truth, which is still vibrating in our souls despite a century and a half of skepticism and destructive criticism. Certainly the icy breath of science and free philosophical speculation have cooled the volcano of faith, but the solfatara[23] is still active. This constant smoking of the semi-obstructed crater, these fissures that perpetually move the earth, this endless longing for mysteries that drives us, what are they

22. *Latet anguis in herba,* "A snake lies hidden in the grass," from Vergil, Eclogue 3.93.
23. A solfatara is a vent to a volcano that allows sulfurous gases to escape.

but clear signals that the eruption is coming and the flame of faith, more splendid than ever, will soon crown the peak of human consciousness?

DON JOSÉ: Good for you, don Timoteo! . . . The saddest thing is, you're right! . . . The germ of the immortality of the soul, injected into humanity centuries ago, is still endlessly regrowing in our minds, despite the implacable purges of experimental science . . .

RAMASCÓN: Yes, it's true! The idea of the soul is a tenacious parasite that makes us all miserable wretches. Ah! If only it were just an inoffensive microbe or a symbiotic guest! . . . For you know very well that in Nature there are some very useful symbiotic associations, like the well-known one between algae and lichens, or the ones between the hydra and its chloroplasts, or the roots of leguminous plants and nitrogen-fixing bacilli (*Bacillus radicola*). But unfortunately, the spiritual bacillus—like all other microbes incubated by metaphysics—enjoys a powerful toxicity. They're good only for their skillful, proficient cultivators . . .

Luckily this mental microbe has been considerably attenuated by the scientific sun, like the *Bacillus anthracis* in the presence of light . . . There was a time when its ptomaines[24] drove humanity mad, producing the hallucination of metaphysics in the intellectual order, and the dreaded religious wars and iniquities of the Inquisition in the moral one . . . But we still have to fear a return of the old virulence. Even now, in moments of discouragement or fatigue, it crawls painfully around in our minds, evoking tragic visions, submerging us in dark terrors, and paralyzing our plows in their furrows and our microscopes in our laboratories . . .

Ah! If I could only take matters into my own hands, I'd stop the infection soon enough, implacably sweeping the deceivers out of the lecture halls. I'd be like Ptolemy Philadelphus, whom they say forbade the teaching of the immortality of the spirit in his lands because he found it troubling and pernicious. According to Cicero, this doctrine

24. Ptomaines are amine compounds produced by rotting organic matter. Many are poisonous.

was invented by a certain idler . . . one Pherecydes of Syria. The world's religions should erect a colossal pyramid to his everlasting memory— they could make it out of the bones and ashes of all the innumerable victims of faith, from Iphigenia down to Servet.[25]

DON TIMOTEO: These are all just errors and prejudices!

DON JOSÉ: I'm not going to go as far as Ramascón . . . I think that belief in supernatural agents is a lamentable error, and I agree that humanity has often been numbed and poisoned by dogma. But a feeling of charity and tolerance stronger than reason keeps me from embracing radical, counterproductive acts and prohibitions. Though I won't add my voice to this intolerant chorus, I think now and have always thought that illusion and error can be as respectable as truth. Like Lange,[26] I believe that mysticism and dreams are cerebral fruits as natural and legitimate as science and art. Far be it from me to rob man of the comforting myths and heartening legends in which he finds relief from pain, strength and constancy for hard work, and resignation and valor to face death. Rather than yielding to that criminal temptation, I would lock up all the philosophical and critical books that might draw simple people away from divine Jesus, the invincible master of morality, as Renan affirms . . .[27] If it were up to me, I'd put all those books away in libraries, for the exclusive use of strong minds and cultivated intellects.

For I see with sorrow that the glorious day is still far off when reason, freed from revelation and sentiment, will quench its devouring

25. Ptolemy II, "Philadelphus" (308-246 B.C.), king of Egypt (285-46 B.C.), strongly encouraged the study of the science. Pherecydes of Syros (c. 550 B.C.) is said to have introduced the ideas of metempsychosis and the immortality of the soul to Greek culture. Aristotle criticized Pherecydes's work, claiming he mixed philosophy with myth. In Greek drama and mythology, Iphigenia was the daughter of Agamemnon and Clytemnestra, king and queen of Mycenae. Agamemnon sacrificed her to the goddess Artemis in order to free the becalmed Achaean fleet. Spanish physician Miguel Servet (1511-53) was declared a heretic by both Protestants and Catholics for his new interpretation of the Trinity. In Geneva, Calvinists tried Servet for heresy, then burned him to death.

26. German neo-Kantian philosopher Friedrich Albert Lange (1828-75) strongly opposed materialistic thinking.

27. French historian and philosopher Ernest Renan (1823-92) wrote the controversial *Life of Jesus* (1863) which presented Christ's life as a popular myth created by imagination.

thirst for light and truth solely in the pure, inexhaustible streams of science. Yes! . . . Despite the magnificent conquests of astronomy, geology, chemistry, and biology, the universe is still an impenetrable enigma. As long as this dark secret is not cleared up; as long as biology, science of sciences, keeps illuminating the murky problems of heredity and the evolution of protoplasm, without freeing the human race from deformity, debility, and degeneration; as long as experimental psychology and physiology fail to control our instinctive tendencies, reining in our unrealizable desires, shutting down our unhealthy mysticism, and creating love and resignation in the face of death, then our positive religions will live on and will continue to subjugate our consciousness. They satisfy overpowering appetites, atavistic and primitive, perhaps, but natural and dominant in most men.

RAMASCÓN: You're a fine champion of progress! According to you, we should just stand around and do nothing . . . just let the black wave of fanaticism drown reason and roll right over science . . . abandon our children in the dark cavern of faith so that they come out like the *Proteus anguinis*,[28] without any eyes or understanding of the world, useless in the vibrant, ever more rigorous battles for life!

I'm tolerant, too, but only with tolerant people. I also proclaim people's right to foolishness, but only if we also preserve people's right to the truth. The Church hates the truth, and it claims and will always claim the odious privilege to dull and deform our children's brains so that they will never discover this . . .

The cowardly resignation that you advocate, I don't see a basis for it anywhere. I look at Nature, and I don't see compassion, only a bloody struggle. High or low, intellectual or vegetable, life tolerates only inoffensive companions and parasites. Against macroscopic or microscopic enemies it wages war without quarter. Should man, the sum and compendium of everything great—and even more so of everything small, of the snares, stratagems, and egotism of the living world—should man ever grant pardons?

28. *Proteus anguinis* is a small, snakelike amphibian.

Life is death, Claude Bernard has said.[29] Every idea that arises in our consciousness and longs intensely to live finds itself obliged to destroy. Believers kill, not for the pleasure of killing, but to give life and glory to their beliefs. Scrape the cortex of a believer, and a savage will appear; scratch some more, and a tiger will spring out. Finally, you'll come to the real neural substance, and the terrible *Sphex* will appear, the insect that paralyzes the ganglia of its prey, delivering it unarmed, living and palpitating—sometimes for months at a time—to the voracity of its progeny.[30]

No, don José, you're wrong! To resign yourself is to die . . . to kill is to conquer . . . to progress. Like the microbe that causes the grippe, the exquisite flower of civilization thrives only on soil that has been fertilized with blood. So let's declare war on the clerical *Sphex!* Down with the convents, breeding grounds for *Trypanosomes,* the cause of the *sleeping sickness* to which our weakly Spanish youth has fallen victim![31]

DON TIMOTEO (interrupting): My God, what horrors! You're a fanatic!

ALLAN KARDEC: You're an inquisitor for the other side . . . the lay side, a thousand times worse than the religious one!

DON JOSÉ (with a relaxed, tranquil air): Ramascón! You really got a load off your mind! You can tell an old sailor a mile away! . . . You've got all the fierceness and relentlessness of the sea in your soul! But the ship of faith is still too strong and well-run for you . . . Intolerance toward powerful people is innocence and stupidity, not courage. Since you like to take your examples from the field of zoology, you should

---

29. French physiologist Claude Bernard (1813–78) viewed life as a dynamic interplay between internal and external forces. His predecessor, anatomist Xavier Bichat (1771–1802), had defined life as "that which resists death." For Bernard, life and death were always intimately related as the body struggled to maintain its internal environment in the face of an ever-changing external one.

30. I am referring to the hymenopterus (*fam. Fossoria*), the *Sphex flavipennis,* which, like other species in its family, nourishes its larvae by bringing them caterpillars and adult insects it has poisoned and paralyzed by jabbing its stinger into their neural ganglia (Cajal).

31. I mean the flagellate protozoan that lives in the blood and cephalorachidian fluid of black people in Central and West Africa, provoking the deadly *sleeping sickness*. The species alluded to here is the *Trypanosoma Castellani* (Cajal).

take inspiration from the admirable patience of the galápagos tortoise and the protective displays of the porcupine, not from the spirit and bravery of the lion.

By saying this, I'm not trying to suggest that science should just stand by and do nothing while the day of its reign is just dawning. On the contrary, I think it has a great mission to accomplish. That mission consists of spreading knowledge of our weakness in order to gather the fruits of tolerance. It means demonstrating the fragility and imperfection of the human brain, which is receptive to all kinds of suggestions. It means teaching that man is not a degraded, fallen angel, but a regenerate, noble simian who dreams of becoming an angel and wants to lose his fangs of cruelty and claws of fanaticism. Science must broaden the sphere of the known at the expense of the unknown, a dark region where theogonies erect their heavens and raise up their gods. Science must reclaim the dominions of morality and philosophy for reason, showing by example that virtue is the exquisite fruit of a learned, well-balanced spirit, not a privilege granted by some religious sect. Gently and gradually (after chloroformization, if necessary) science will remove the spine of dogmatism. In the end, it will *humanize men,* as the Chinese define the goal of education.

It will be a long, interminable task, you say . . . Certainly it will be long, but not as long as you think. Through a thousand different signs I can see the coming secularization of our consciences. I only fear that our positive religions will disappear from people's hearts before science has progressed sufficiently to replace them.

DON TIMOTEO (in an indignant tone): No, that's not true! The ship of faith may be battered by contrary winds, tossed by waves of impiety and heresy, but in the end it always arrives gloriously at the desired port, altogether intact! God has proclaimed it to us in the Apocalypse: "times will come when the land will consist of one sole flock with one sole pastor."[32] The Church is imperishable because it's the work of God.

32. John 10:16 "There shall be one fold and one shepherd."

When men's wickedness and the devil's wiles oppose the divine will, they will always be dashed to pieces.

DON JOSÉ: Still, despite all these consoling prophecies, religion keeps getting weaker, and everything indicates that it's very near death . . . When the time comes, it won't be the textbook of some baccalaureate that kills it, as Zola contends, someone denouncing the Bible's ignorance and errors about the mechanisms of life and the world. What will kill it will be men's individual experiences, a thousand times more destructive than all the scientific books or ruthless criticism of Voltaire, Strauss, and Renan.[33] Only individual experience shows us Nature's imperfection, injustice, and impassivity in all of their terrible nakedness.

What will destroy religion, above all, is this new field of biology we have so greatly scorned. Quietly, without any sectarian shouting, it has suppressed the devil, converting miracles into hallucinations and revealing the neurosis of holiness and mysticism. When it finishes tilling the unknown lands of the brain, it will be well on the way to determining the physico-chemical conditions of emotion and thought, illusion and error, anthropomorphic feeling, and that incurable delusion that we reflect the divine.

But let's not talk about the future; let's attend to the present. The work of today should be one of illustration and tolerance. I think it was Victor Hugo who said that he who understands all, pardons all. Let's try to understand, then, so that we can forgive, and let's try to forgive so that we can love . . .

THE APOTHECARY: Gentlemen! . . . It's getting late . . . and we've talked enough nonsense for one evening. Let's all go home to bed . . .

---

33. French novelist Émile Zola (1840–1902) felt that human behavior could be explained by hereditary and environmental influences. A strong advocate of experimental medicine, he did not believe in a "soul" and strongly resisted traditional religious ideas. Voltaire (François-Marie Arquet, 1694–1778) was imprisoned for a year in 1717, then exiled from France in 1726 for criticizing organized religion. German philosopher and theologian David Friedrich Strauss (1808–74) called the gospels "historical myth." In *The Life of Jesus Critically Examined* (1835–36), he argued that writers two hundred years after Christ's death created the idea of his divinity to fulfill their own needs.

Sadly the polemicists filed out, each one with his creed entirely intact and his hands to his head to dispel his intense headache . . . For despite our lofty, spiritual nature, thinking hurts . . .

The next day, as though nothing had happened, the doctor returned to his patients; the spiritualist, to his fish (he was a canner); Ramascón, to his algae and infusoria; and don Timoteo, to his lawsuits. No one remembered his hatred or thought about the existence of the soul for God knows how long.

Unfortunately for the cause of truth, *homo sapiens* only philosophizes in his spare time. He is still too low on the intellectual scale, too utterly dominated by the reflexes of his stomach. Thought in his brain is a bird of passage, an irritating guest who interrupts the endless traffic of interest and greed.

9

And so a few more days passed by.

Little by little, people's worries and misgivings about *Villa Inés* were disappearing. Reality asserted itself. Even some people whose ignorance and prejudices had prevented them from seeing clearly began to doubt the mournful predictions, watching Julián grow stronger, braver, and more enterprising every day, surrounded by a lively crowd of servants, shepherds, and journeymen.

As though the blessing of heaven had fallen upon his house, our protagonist's prosperity kept increasing. Each year they had to widen the granaries to hold the growing harvests; and the corrals and folds, to shelter the teeming flocks. The corn, barley, wheat, and bean harvest measured in the thousands of bushels. In the pastures, it was a pleasure to see hundreds of tender, newborn lambs frolicking about, and colts and calves running around noisily. In good weather, the old cider press full of roomy barrels and the adjoining esplanade—reserved, according to the custom of that region, for games of skittles—became the favorite meeting place of all the drinkers in the district. They were the first to start joking about the dire omens, refusing to believe that the devil could set up shop on an estate that made the best cider in the country.

Before long, the fruits of Julián's teachings spread far beyond his ranch's borders. Seeing the brilliant results he had achieved with sanitation and cattle-raising, the wiser, more learned local villagers pooled their modest capital and combined their efforts to channel and purify the drinking water, set up water mills and hydroelectric plants, drain the marshes, and fight animal epidemics and diseases of plants.

Julián, the selfless apostle of science, generously offered advice and every kind of support for these regenerative campaigns. His teachings combined theory with practice. He would begin by summing up the status of a scientific question in the simplest, clearest, most graphic way possible. He would then take his pupils—rustic villagers, for the most part—into the laboratory, where he would teach them the function and use of hygienic instruments. Under the microscope, he would show them the terrible parasites of men, animals, and plants, teaching them the most practical means of recognizing, destroying, growing, and preventing the growth of these deadly, pernicious germs.

The beautiful fruits of this admirable good citizenship were the health and prosperity of the entire district. Typhoid fever, malaria, and anthrax disappeared from that part of the country, as did foot-and-mouth disease, the "red disease" of pigs, etc. To places that the sanitation campaign could not reach, Julián sent lifesaving sera and vaccines produced at *Villa Inés* and sold at negligible prices. To carry out the more complex, delicate work, he trained and paid two excellent young doctors, who took charge of the bacteriological laboratory and the production of sera.

Finally, to crown his happiness and good fortune, that torrent from a deep, rocky bed—which according to popular legend flowed red like blood during storms—put Julián on the scent of a very rich vein of a ferruginous mineral. Once the metal-bearing soil had been analyzed and several test pits had revealed an inexhaustible abundance of the deposits, a mining society was formed to explore the area. Needless to say, as principal shareholder, our hero was named director and manager and given substantial powers.

At first, so as not to drain their capital too much, they set up mineral washes and crushing machines driven by the old waterwheel, which they reinforced and converted into a powerful, elevated flume. Sometime later, when their collective capital had reached a respectable figure, they installed blast furnaces and adjoining machine shops.

The fields, once so lonely and poisoned by the effluvia of death, were quickly covered with a noisy, active colony of engineers, foremen, and workers, happy people who looked upon their glorious employer as a second God.

After five or six years of work, Julián's capital surpassed five million pesetas, not counting the value of his lands, woods, fields, livestock, and workshops. Before he reached the frontiers of old age, the brave doctor not only developed the most prestigious corporation in the financial world. He became the indisputable lord of the land: the compassionate, paternal enlightened despot; the scientific, patriotic boss that our ignorant, fanatical, helpless villagers so desperately need.

10

But what about don Tomás and tenderhearted Inés? the reader will ask. He is puzzled, no doubt, by our silence about the winning, fascinating protagonist of this truthful tale.

It is easy to guess. Once Julián had passed through the Calvary of the first three years; once he had used his industriousness and intelligence to set the vast estate of *Villa Inés* in motion; once the first splendid profits promised future security and prosperity, rich old don Tomas's feelings toward his nephew changed radically. Yielding to the evidence, he gladly accepted the restorer of *Villa Inés* as a man of strong will, noble talent, spotless honor, and pure industriousness.

United with good fortune, these qualities allowed one to forget Julián's revolutionary impulses and dogmatic radicalism, which are after all just harmless, platonic convictions. For, always respectful of other people's ideas, Julián never acted like a propagandist or aspired to become the leader of some sect.

Moreover, as a loving father, don Tomás could not fail to see that his daughter's passion was far from waning—it was growing steadily. Given this young girl's constancy and fortitude, he knew he would never be able to avoid the ensuing unpleasantness if, without sufficient reason, he opposed a powerful feeling born in childhood, strengthened in adolescence, and fortified and purified in times of misfortune . . .

So after thinking it over for a long time and discussing the matter with his family, the old landowner presented himself one day at *Villa Inés*. As one may suppose, he caused the most welcome surprise. He embraced his nephew affectionately, asking a thousand pardons for past injustices . . . and so the wedding was on.

To human nature, happiness is much like misfortune. Both result from highly revolutionary, unforeseen accidents to which the fingerboard of feeling is not adjusted and the lazy rhythm of the heart is not attuned.

Julián offered living proof of this great, sad truth. His profound joy robbed him of sleep, took away his appetite, and made the ideas bubble in his brain until they bordered on delirium, threatening to lead to decadence and nervous prostration. But for this that little rogue Inés was partly responsible. In her loving exchanges with her fiancé, she was so radiant, so passionate, so divinely captivating and desirable, that Julián was forced to fall back on that highly accredited remedy, potassium bromide, in order to calm his shaken nerves a little . . .[34]

Once the emotional fervor of the first weeks had passed; once their deposit of sweet endearments was exhausted; once the long period of palpitations and arrhythmia had ended, their hearts resumed the peaceful rhythm of health. At last, having recovered the calm and attention necessary for the task, Inés and Julián could gather the fibers, feathers,

---

34. Potassium bromide was a commonly used sedative in the late nineteenth century.

and cottons for their comfortable, warm nest of love. In their own good time, they could choose the leafy branches and beautiful flowers that would offer the most pleasant shade, protection, and fragrance.

And they married . . . and were happy . . . and had strong, beautiful, intelligent children . . . And the loving couple made the long journey to old age without suffering any eclipses of their sweet, loyal feeling for one another, or of their serene joy . . . the joy that is an inexhaustible fountain of health and strength.

When Julián was old and alone, after he had lost the admirable companion to whom he owed all possible happiness in this lowly world, once his children had married and scattered themselves to the four winds, any time he felt his heart shaken by a gust of cold skepticism or his soul washed by an enervating wave of melancholy . . . he would open the old album where he kept that precious relic, that comforting scene of the nocturnal visit . . . For in that most tender, heartening episode, Inés had been filled with the fervor of love. Aflame with emotion and beauty, her face pale like a moonbeam and her eyes languid and faint, she had converted the whole, formidable charge of passion accumulated since adolescence into the purest essence of a kiss . . . At the sight of that sublime picture, Julián would feel the tears disappear from his eyes and the clouds vanish from his mind. And he would exclaim:

"Yes, life is good, and happiness exists . . . only . . . they last for such a short while!"

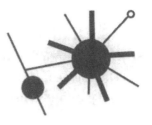

THE CORRECTED
PESSIMIST

Juan Fernández, the protagonist of this story, was a young
doctor of twenty-eight years: serious, studious, not lacking
in talent, but utterly pessimistic, with a misanthropic streak.
An orphan with no relatives, he lived a sullen, self-absorbed
life in the company of his family's old housekeeper.

In the period in which we find him, our hero was suffering
from a fresh wave of nausea toward life and indifference toward society. He was neglecting his practice and his relations
with his friends, who still saw him every once in a while, and
spending his time deeply absorbed in works whose melancholic tones matched the sentimental timbre of his spirit.

It always pleases an unhappy man to know that his misery
is not being played out for the first time, and that his decaying concept of the world and of life itself has also found a

home in strong, cultivated minds. You can certainly understand why Juan took solace and entertained himself by reading Schopenhauer and Hartmann; hateful, demented Nietzsche; and deep, gloomy Gracián.[1] The pride of knowing that his opinion coincided with those of such competent gentlemen produced some little whiffs of consolation. From time to time, he could feel their fleeting warmth thawing the frozen lake of his will, slightly relieving his painful lassitude of body and spirit.

For unhappy Fernández, life was a tasteless, endless bad joke that Nature was playing for no apparent reason or purpose. The human mind was a rudimentary calculating machine that fails in all arduous operations. Our knowledge was an old book full of slashes and gaps whose list of errors was longer than the original text. The senses were a crude, childish apparatus with neither range nor precision, good only for hiding the infinite palpitations of matter and the innumerable enemies of life. The heart was a fragile, undisciplined pump that grew painfully, inopportunely agitated at critical moments, clouding our intelligence and paralyzing our hands. And then, finally, there was the will, which was rather like an airborne thistle seed, fluctuating at the mercy of the lightest puff of wind and committing the foolish error of mistaking mobility for freedom . . .

With such ideas and feelings, it is hardly necessary to say that our doctor had few friends and even fewer hopes and illusions.

Still, he was not fully to blame, for his feelings did deserve some compassion. In the past two years he had lost his beloved father and mother: he, a victim of tuberculosis; she, carried off by infectious pneumonia. At that time, Juan himself was slowly recovering from a dangerous

---

1. German philosopher Arthur Schopenhauer (1788-1860) argued in *The World as Will and Representation* (1819) that the universe consisted of representations accessible to people and an unknown driving force or "will" that could never be understood. In *The Philosophy of the Unconscious* (1870), German philosopher Eduard von Hartmann (1842-1906) described the unconscious as an intermediary between rational and irrational thinking. Friedrich Nietzsche (1844-1900) developed Schopenhauer's idea of the will and challenged accepted moral beliefs. Spanish writer Baltasar Gracián (1601-58) developed the literary school of *conceptismo*, which stressed plain-spoken wit over classical references. Gracián's novel *El criticón* (1651), described society from a savage's perspective. According to Schopenhauer, it was one of the best books ever written.

bout of typhoid fever. Just days before falling sick, he had concluded—unsuccessfully but honorably—a hard-fought battle to win a certain academic chair at the University of Madrid.[2]

As if this dark cloud were not thick enough, even his fiancée, Elvira, a handsome, sensible girl who was the daughter of a rich, influential industrialist, had begun acting cold and disdainful. But in truth, she had more than sufficient reason for this.

Our sullen doctor had never pleased don Toribio (such was the girl's father's name). The old businessman recognized a good deal of intelligence and industriousness in his aspiring son-in-law and even saw a future for him in finance, but he found his taciturn character and his dark, unpleasant philosophical inclinations distasteful, simply intolerable. He had thus never looked favorably on his daughter's relations with Juan, who at the time was the family doctor (in particular the mother's, whose fits of hysteria he could repress quite skillfully). Still, don Toribio left the young lovers to guess that he would authorize the engagement once the studious doctor, who had long been preparing to compete for a university chair, actually acquired that coveted academic property.

As the reader will surmise, Juan's failure made that ambitious father's enmity even more acute. Poor Elvira, who had developed real affection for her fiancé—mainly because she had thought him so worthy of pity—battled painfully amidst her inflamed feelings, never daring to take a definite stance. To reject the man to whom she had promised to be faithful, and to reject him because of his recent academic slight, was an act of cruelty and indelicacy of which she felt incapable. But to accept him generously and unreservedly would mean rebelling openly against her father's authority, an undisciplined attitude which she, as a loving, submissive, well-educated daughter, did not dare to assume.

With all this going on, the balance of her feelings was inclining vis-

2. In late nineteenth-century Spain, candidates for academic jobs competed directly with each other in *oposiciones,* the word Cajal uses here. There is no English equivalent.

ibly against Juan. His fervent protestations of love in their brief, furtive exchanges could not counteract the powerful suggestion of coldness and aversion she was inhaling at home. These latter suggestions
were so much more effective that—as one might expect—our protagonist's moral character, once exalted and poetized by love, had shrunk
somewhat in the prudent young girl's eyes. Physically and intellectu-
ally, today's Juan was worth much less than yesterday's . . .

Don Toribio's daughter had a cold temperament, and her heart never disturbed the operations of her intelligence. When she saw the young
man's intellectual defeat, she began to perceive the weaknesses of a talent and education she had imagined insuperable. Studying her fiancé
with watchful, analytical eyes, she thought she saw the stigmata of a
physical degenerate in the languor and anemia following his illness and
the dark pessimism of his ideas. He seemed unable to mount any vigorous resistance against the crushing burden of work. Perhaps he was
destined to wither and decay before he could enjoy the sweet, supreme
sacrifices of fatherhood.

These great misfortunes and setbacks made Juan's character extremely bitter, especially since it was already darkened by morbid literature and disheartening philosophy. He felt as though his pessimistic concept of the world were shrinking his own personality. Gradually,
he was abandoning that consoling confidence in his own faculties that
pushes us to battle on valiantly. When we must face failures and disil-
lusionments, this confidence compassionately stimulates the imagination, the tireless forger of excuses for our faults and comforting
thoughts about our aching self-love.

Every lost battle needs a traitor, a Mephistopheles responsible for the
unforeseen disaster.[3] When there is none—as is generally the case—it
is necessary to invent one. Only this way can man, an animal given
to intense motor discharges, regain his calm and recover his self-confi-

3. Mephistopheles represents the devil in Goethe's *Faust* (1805, 1832). In the play, Faust and
Mephistopheles sign a pact saying that if Mephistopheles can offer Faust any worldly experience so pleasurable that Faust wants it to last, then the devil may have Faust's soul.

dence. To keep from breaking down inside, we have to break something outside of us. There are many ways to find relief. A frustrated Bismarck will hurl crockery to the floor and kick it furiously about.[4] A failed candidate for an academic chair must hurl the purported justice of the tribunal and the abilities of his opponents into the gutter—verbally, of course. This idiotic, consoling reaction frees us from so many evils, this wonderful conversion of spite into sarcasm known as the right to stamp one's feet with rage!

This salubrious swabbing of the cerebral decks leaves us feeling like new, leading us as though hypnotized to a fresh, clear state of mind full of vivifying hope. But to carry it out rapidly, we have to be a little optimistic. Our inhibitory motor pathways have to be a little loose and emotional; our concepts of justice and self-worth, a little unclear.

Unfortunately, Juan had a bilious temperament and an emotive, brooding, suspicious brain, as rich in neuronal *collaterals* as in melancholic images. Far from being egotistical or disdainful of other people's praise, he had a clear sense of his own mental deficiencies and incurable smallness. In his soliloquies, which were ever more frequent, he exclaimed with tones of infinite bitterness:

"I'm worth nothing . . . I know nothing! I feel defeated and prostrated in body and soul. Yes! I'm defeated in soul because during this last battle, my lack of self-possession, my enervating insomnia, and my invincible fatigue spoiled and diminished my work. I'm defeated in body, because during my recent sickness my defensive forces were on the point of abandoning me, leaving me to the ravages of the microbe . . . Even if I finally did save my honor in the intellectual fight and my life in the physical one, I've been left a pitiful ruin. My body has become a vile feeding trough for germs; my soul, a hatchery for sad thoughts and depressing feelings . . ."

---

4. Otto von Bismarck (1815–98), chancellor of the German Empire from 1871 to 1890, was largely responsible for provoking the Franco-Prussian War and unifying Germany with Prussia as nucleus.

2

Four more months passed by, and Juan's wounded self-love continued to bleed. His organic weakness and aversion toward life continued their crescendo. Sad, painful visions tormented his nights. With each passing day, he became more sullen and withdrawn. He abandoned his practice almost entirely and stopped seeing aloof, inconstant Elvira, whose detachment and coldness were exasperating him . . .

In this deplorable state of mind, he wrote a terribly pessimistic book called *The Blunders of Providence,* the fruit of his gloomy meditations. The book, which was rather like a late, systematized expression of the providential right to stamp one's feet with rage, sometimes gave him some consolation. The person who falls always likes to blame the horse for the rider's failings. But let us not criticize this injustice. It gives us the strength to persist in great undertakings! And it is so easy to change the bridle! . . .

With all of this happening, the day that Juan wrote the last page of his book, he fell into a deep depression. It was four o'clock on a lukewarm spring morning. The bells of a nearby clock sounded slowly, harshly, like a death rattle. Far away, a dog was barking plaintively. Every now and then, he could hear the happy aria with which a rooster announced the coming of the King Star, the spirit who triumphs over darkness and death. From time to time he perceived the loud rumbling of the early morning omnibuses, whose vibrations, communicated to his room, made his furniture shake, his lights flicker, and his sheets of paper tremble . . .

That awakening of Nature, eager for light and activity, that hot surge of bustling life painfully irritated the unhappy philosopher's sick sensibility. In a fit of supreme disillusionment, he seized the last pages of his book in his trembling hands and flung them into the fire.

"What's the use of writing? . . . Can I maybe change the course of the world, stop the stupid tide of protoplasm that's rushing blindly toward the abyss of pain and death? . . . Glory! What is it but oblivion deferred? Humanity, which arose from death, must end in death. The mechanisms of the Cosmos and the inevitable laws of *entropy* prove it to us with their iron formulas. Will my fruitless lamentations slow the rising of this unfeeling, habit-ridden star even a thousandth of a second, the star that is about to shed light (yielding the energy of its heat) on the same barbarous, desolating scenes in which the individual is implacably sacrificed to the species; the species, to the whole stream of life? Will I inspire pity in inexorable fate, incomprehensible Providence? Without distinguishing the genius from the microbe, they love to destroy life with life, as though the overwhelming burden of work, the piercing sense of our own impotence, and the insuperable tyranny of cosmic forces were not already enough to create human misery?"

With a gesture of wild, arrogant defiance, his blazing eyes burning into the shadows near the ceiling as though he were facing some unknown being, he exclaimed:

"Whoever you are, Prime Mover of the universe, implacable Spirit, inaccessible Principle, impassive Nature, tell me, why did you create the enemies of life, the cruel, insidious pathogenic bacteria? What need was there for them in the economy of the world? I admit that proud, tyrannical Alexander was struck down by the *Plasmodium malariae* in the greatest splendor of his glory. I understand that Napoleon, the conqueror of peoples and furious slasher of men's throats, fell on St. Helena with his stomach eaten by the still unknown germs of cancer. I know that Hegel, the prodigious sophist who paralyzed Kant's positive philosophical analysis with the toxin of the *Idea,* was poisoned by the cholera bacillus.[5] I can see, in sum, why the destiny of nations and the fate of civilization itself are at the mercy of a mosquito bite or the unlucky flight of a spore.

"But why do you also choose your victims among the humble and

5. Alexander I (1777–1825), emperor of Russia from 1801 to 1825, defeated Napoleon but fell victim to malaria (or pneumonia) after a campaign in the Crimea. Napoleon (1769–1821) developed stomach cancer in 1817 while living in exile. Georg Friedrich Hegel (1770–1831) left Berlin for the suburbs when cholera broke out in the summer of 1831. When he returned to teach for the fall semester, he caught cholera in November and died after only one day.

the good? Why do you let pathogenic bacteria capriciously sow death in the workshop, the temple of regenerative labor; in the laboratory, the sanctuary of science and magnificent podium for the divinity; and in the fruitful furrow where the worker—a sorcerer unaware of his marvelous alchemy—collects the sun's rays so that they may someday flash out in a genius's brain?

"If only you had compensated by granting us senses and intelligence strong enough to help us avoid these great dangers! If only, to save us from these threats, we had sufficient visual acuity to see these virulent germs! If only we had an olfactory sense that could protect us from odorless toxic gases, and a gustatory apparatus keen enough to reveal ptomaines and poisons in our food and drink! According to naive philosophers, our senses and intelligence are good because they reflect yours! Our eyes and ears are windows to the soul—opening out into a black abyss! . . . What physicist would boast about making crude instruments so deceptive that they impose qualities on us like rhythms? Their distorted, fragmented images are modified and disturbed by fatigue, the laws of relativity, and the unparallelism of excitation and reaction . . .

"When it comes to sensation and analysis, our senses are so feeble that they pick up only a paltry range of the immense variety of cosmic palpitations. They give us one chromatic octave, a few varieties of sounds, and a small, insignificant group of odors, flavors, and tactile impressions. They're so mendacious that the visual sense shows us stars as radiations instead of luminous points. It shrinks distant objects, presenting them indistinctly if they're more than thirty meters away, and it grows weary and clouds over before one reaches fifty, when one is still in the prime of one's mental virility. In brief, it suffers from so many stupid illusions that they alone can explain the crazy cosmogenic and religious systems mankind has created, systems that have retarded and perhaps forever prevented the definitive reign of science and truth.

"And what shall we say about the human mind and will? They're the rightful crown of a miserable freak, a pitiful mistake . . . Our intellect is so feeble that it's still debating the nature of matter and the criteria for certainty, as in the time of Xenophanes and Pyrrhon.[6] Our memory is so fragile that in critical moments, it's clouded over with emotion. On the other hand, though, during the hours designated for sleep, it sends its inopportune images parading by in an interminable procession. Our capacity for critical thinking is so weak and myopic that it mistakes kindness for truth, belief for demonstration. On every occasion, despite the dictates of reason, the flattering lure of desire goes on and on.

"But as grave and deplorable as our senses' and mind's deficiencies are, the defects of the will are even worse. How helpless and unprotected man is in the bloody struggle for life! Just look at him, all pale and trembling in the presence of danger! He's as weak and overwhelmed as some bird transfixed by a snake. To defend himself, he has eyes that observe the enemy and a protective instinct that dictates the motor reactions that will save his life. He has foresight, which orders him to throw all the coal into the furnace . . . But still, when the critical moment comes, he feels his heart beat painfully and tumultuously as if some bad angel were bewitching him. He feels a terrible pressure in his chest and sees with anguish that his arms go limp, his legs buckle, and his intelligence—the first weapon to be disabled—goes dim and surrenders. And this is the highly praised king of creation? This is the image of God on earth? What cruel sarcasm! What bloody irony!"

• • •

Just as he reached this point in his harangue, a roar of thunder resounded through the room. A purple cloud flooded the chamber with mysterious light, and from the midst of it, hesitant and floating, emerged the shadow of a venerable old man. He had a long beard and a com-

---

6. The Greek poet and philosopher Xenophanes (560–478 B.C.) thought that physical appearances were deceptive, concealing the fact that all things were really one. Pyrrhon of Elis (360–272 B.C.) founded the Skeptic movement. He taught that the quest for truth was vain since in any debate, equally valid arguments could be made for each side. He also believed that it was a waste of time to consider whether sensory impressions were valid.

manding gaze and expressed himself with calm, engaging words and gestures of supreme, overwhelming authority.

When Juan saw this fantastic apparition, he was terrified. Believing himself the victim of some terrible nightmare, he instinctively rubbed his sleepless eyes and shook his head, hoping, no doubt, that the spectral vision would melt away.

But the spirit advanced toward the frozen philosopher. After touching him gently on the head to reassure himself of his corporeality, he began speaking to him in sweet, soothing tones:

"Fear not, and let me ease the pains and worries of your aching heart. I am the spirit of science, sent by the Great Unknown to enlighten men's minds and sweeten the sad fate of every living creature, in gentle gradations. My names are many: the philosopher calls me *intuition;* the scientist, *fortunate coincidence;* the artist, *inspiration;* the merchant and politician, *luck.* I am the one in the scientist's laboratory or the scholar's study who suggests fruitful ideas, decisive experiments, inspired intuitions, and magnificent, triumphant syntheses. Thanks to the secrets that I whisper into geniuses' ears, the unhappy human race is slowly escaping the limbo of gross animality, and your pitiful cries of pain echo every day less insistently through the celestial spheres.

"Poor, deluded creatures! I understand the cause of your bitter complaints all too well. They come from two gross illusions which I am still not permitted to remove from human consciousness, except in a few select minds. You think that in the world order, impenetrable to your small intellects, you are the *ends*—or worse yet, the *sole end*—when you are merely the *means,* rude links in an endless chain, simple terms in an endless progression . . . In your childish mania, this false assumption has made you adjust the world's mechanism to the wretched model of your own personality. You attribute *laws and legislatures* to phenomena, *finality* to causes, and *morality* and intention to Nature. You ignore a postulate that has been demonstrated a thousand times by your sharpest, most enlightened thinkers, namely that the Cosmos is an ensemble of innumerable realities. By necessity, they evolve not toward what is *better*—according to your petty interests—but toward remote shores that will be forever unknown to man, even to those superior forms that will emerge from mankind as the butterfly emerges from the dull, sleepy caterpillar.

"Your second error is presuming that the Prime Mover should interfere with the noble course of evolution, suppressing evil with one blow, when really it is the spur of progress and stimulus of protoplasm. In your boundless egotism, you expect that this interference will bring fulfillment and the final reign of truth. What nonsense! It is sheer insanity to expect the Supreme Principle to exclude pain, for life is adjusted to it as a current is to a channel.

"And it is just as absurd to ask Him, with His infinite foresight, that He suddenly hurl the ultimate truth into the darkness of your knowledge when it would be incomprehensible even to the superman. If in some stupendous act of condescension the Unknown should rend the sublime veil of Isis from your eyes, my words would sound as strange to you as Kant's *Critique of Pure Reason* or Laplace's *System of the World* would to a fly.[7] If the most general truth were suddenly released, it would not destroy the universe, as one spiritual, paradoxical thinker has said. It would simply be as though nothing had been revealed.

"The Cosmos is a great system of hieroglyphics, of which scholars from each epoch will laboriously decipher only a few phrases: those corresponding to their own particular evolutionary stage of the human species. Positive progress means inspiring geniuses with only that part of the truth that can be assimilated without doing grave harm to life itself. Pride and impatience! These are two pernicious impulses you

---

7. Isis was an Egyptian goddess believed to protect people as a mother protects a child. She was also associated with healing. Immanuel Kant's *Critique of Pure Reason* (1781) tries to establish solid foundations for human knowledge and define the limits of what people can know. Pierre Simon de Laplace's *System of the World* (1830) uses higher mathematics to explain the mechanism of gravity and the movements of the solar system. Both are notoriously difficult to read.

must tear out of your heart if you want to climb the Calvary of existence without tears.

"Your misfortunes have inspired such deep compassion in me that they make me remind you of a few simple truths. These have been self-evident to a few thinkers free from prejudices and ridiculous excesses of pride, thinkers who have studied the mechanism of the Cosmos and the history of Nature.

"You should know, my son, that the study of humanity is not the highest, most perfect, complex ideal of which animal protoplasm is capable. It is only the best possible one under the current conditions offered by what you childishly, anthropomorphically call matter and force. You are worth a great deal, for just as the microbe is the seed of man, you are the germ of the superman. You are worth very little, on the other hand, because your intelligence and will are carefully adapted to the present conditions of the Cosmos, which are extraordinarily hostile to the sublimest displays of your intelligence and raptures of your sensibility.

"Your own egotism betrays you. What you see as bias and injustice, from your point of view, are really the greatest equity and highest justice. Like the nervous system, the vital principle sacrifices the happiness and freedom of each individual cell for the security and stability of the living hive. In the same way, the great Mover of evolution has resolved the contradictory desires of the whole and the parts, sacrificing individuals for species and low, rudimentary forms for those of higher organization.

"To the powerful retina of God, there are no distances, and the laws of perspective do not apply. The sea and the waves, the atoms and the stars are painted on it with equal clarity and distinctness. In his luminous vision, which is synthetic and analytic at once, individual lives are molecules perpetually renewed in a vast sea of protoplasm. In its foam and rushing waves, one can already glimpse the pure, winged forms of the future, the only humanity worthy of Him. For He knows how to draw back—at least in part—the densely woven curtain of Maya, and He can peer out into the unfathomable abyss of eternal realities without getting dizzy."[8]

"But," babbled Juan, recovering his composure, "if the Supreme Cause, in His infinite love, really cares for all of Nature, then how does He permit the bloody struggle for life, in which one obtains food by killing, and pain is the only response of weakness to superior force?"

"It is not my task to reveal the ultimate justifications of life's perennial conflicts, which must forever choose between murder and suicide. If you must satisfy your curiosity, then you should know that this misery results from the indomitable inertia of matter and the standard tendency of forms to stop developing and regress. To drive evolution, we had to institute pain and death, the only forces sufficiently powerful to stimulate the creative, adaptive potential of individual energy. In the Supreme Intelligence there is no room for the superfluous, for superfluity is always a mistake. And so He turned unavoidable death—or rather, the *dead*—into a stepping-stone for life, ordaining that the higher forms should feed on the lower.

"Do not ignore the glaring fact that there is a chemical evolution working in parallel with the morphological one, and that the extraordinarily complex cerebral *proteids,* the physical basis of thought, arise through the gradual transformation of simple albuminoids assembled by plants and lower animals.[9] Consciousness and reason are really transfigurations of lower life forms. It is because of this that the exquisite work of a genius is kneaded together with his own and other people's tears. In the scratching of a pen on paper or the hard blows of a chisel on marble, one hears the groans of pain and exhaustion of millions of lowly, sacrificed lives. Like a will o' the wisp, an idea represents the posthumous splendor of the dead."

"All this is clear and easy to understand," replied Juan. "I find it nat-

8. In Hindu philosophy, the maya is a divine force that makes people believe their illusory perceptions of reality represent what is actually there.

9. Proteids and albuminoids were terms used for proteins in Cajal's day.

ural that animals, who are essentially consumers, should live at the expense of plants, which are essentially producers. It also makes sense that carnivores, even man, feed on lower animals, winning refined coal for their machines like miners who tear it violently out of the earth's bowels. But it is also true that very often this wise law of chemodynamic progression is inverted, and the lower life forms feed on the higher."

"That's your pride talking again. I can see that in your mind, the infantile illusion man has created about the world has become an incurable obsession. You are just like one of those voracious caterpillars: when they find food and shelter in a piece of fruit, they presume that the gardener raised it especially for them . . . Give up this gross hallucination, and you will see once and for all that to the Absolute, there are neither chosen people nor aristocrats. Emergent and dying life forms are equally worthy of the attention and care of Infinite Love. The sounds of the living world reach the celestial heights without any differences in intensity, so that the cries of a microbe—the *ovule* of future forms of humanity—are heeded with the same mercy as the laments of *homo sapiens,* the lowly embryo of the remote *superman.*

"Your compassion, already sullied by human egotism, does not surpass the bounds of the human species. The compassion of God—pure, infinite, and inexhaustible—extends far beyond life, radiating outward into the darkest hollows of the molecular world . . . But you have to understand . . . We are talking about compassion a priori, as it was felt when the idea to organize matter and distribute energy first arose in the divine mind, creating the great possibilities of suns and nebulae.

"He does not touch up His work as a painter retouches his painting. In the beginning, the sublime Artist prepared the canvas and colors, brought the brushes to life, and then let the magic picture of the universe paint itself. When it came to the color black—the color of pain— He used just the right amount to stimulate thought and action, to counterbalance pleasure and make it desirable. Where the divine work ends, and the marvelous Eden (which your naive Bibles posit as the beginning of the world) emerges from the canvas with the supra-spiritual, winged beings sent to enjoy and understand it, the majestic Painter achieves his glories by seeing how each new form on the interminable canvas confirms the foresight of His supreme Intelligence."

"But what about bacteria?" repeated Juan.

"These bacteria that you hate so much play a momentous role in the economy of Nature. They dissolve the remains of plants and animals, sending the oxygen, carbon, and nitrogen sequestered by organic matter back into the environment. Thanks to their ability to grow in weak, degenerate organisms, they correct dissonance, imperfection, and incongruence in higher forms and keep animal evolution from trailing off into degradation and impotence.

"He made microbes invisible not out of treachery, as you so irreverently imagine, but out of charity. Filled with kindness toward man, Supreme Providence made them extremely small, so that the presence of these harsh executors of divine justice would not disturb your reason, ruin your pleasures, or make your existence loathsome. It is true that science, in an apparent act of rebellion, has invented the microscope to take these minuscule enemies by surprise. But this in itself is an intellectual benefit of the microbe. Still, you would do poorly to take too much pride in this crude instrument. As of yet, it's a very imperfect toy.

"Millions of tiny, ultramicroscopic lives still elude your resolving power: the bacteria of the bacteria, the impalpable dust of myriad beings dispersed throughout the land, water, and air. You don't know about the imperceptible intracellular colonies, little symbiotic federations, which are only now beginning to appear—as the most daring conjectures—in your most audacious scientists' minds. Someday, perhaps, you will be able to discover the morphology and habits of these minuscule, ultramicroscopic organisms, which border on nothingness and are quite distinct from even the crudest molecular structures. But to do this, you will have to abandon the simplistic principles of amplificatory optics. These are based on the banal refraction of visible light waves, coarse oscillations which are only affected by particles greater than a few tenths of a micrometer. You must look instead to the invisible radiation of imponderable matter, which is infinitely more delicate and still unknown.

"Once and for all, you must realize that science can never exhaust the dominion of life. The invisible, which is infinitely more important than the visible, will always envelop you. Each age must have its inaccessible enemies, for the stallion of progress gallops only when goaded by the spurs of death.

"But," replied Juan, regaining life by degrees, "if it's true that the lower life forms that destroy man descend stepwise into nothingness and elude the instruments invented by science; if, according to what I've just heard, divine mercy and foresight are infinite, then how much trouble would it have been for the sublime Modeler of the brain and retina—the two most precious jewels in creation—to have increased the analytical capacity of our senses, especially vision, so that the invention of the microscope would have been superfluous?"

"Because," answered the spirit, "as I've already told you, one of the greatest skills of the supreme Intelligence is to work with a spirit of exquisite foresight, but at the same time, with the neatest and strictest economy. It would be impossible to amplify your visual acuity so greatly during this phase of your morphological development. To do this, we would have to break the great chain of causes taught and respected by God. It would be a dangerous superfluity, and in Nature, what is superfluous always does harm."

"Still," Juan dared to insist, "I can't understand how it would hurt anything to increase the analytical power of my retina . . ."

"You poor, unfortunate creature! What would be the point of producing such a monstrous, graceless thing? Even if your senses were to gain power and impressionability, what good would they do you? How could they broaden your understanding of life and the world if you lacked—as you now lack—a brain sufficiently well organized to register and combine these new inputs? It is much more likely that this

exceptional privilege would turn you into a monster, an isolated being. With your sensibility, it would cause only conflicts and unhappiness.

"Once and for all, you are going to lose your innocent illusions. The
Unknown has invested me with the power to vary the forms of life, and
for your sake, I am going to bring about a prodigious transformation.
As of tomorrow morning, when your eyes first behold the light of day,
you will see all objects within your normal focal range as though they
had been amplified a thousand times. Since I have no intention of
exhausting your patience or ruining your life, you should know that
this extraordinary gift will last only a year."

• • •

Once he had said this, the spirit of science disappeared, and Juan fell
into a deep sleep.

3

When Juan awoke, the morning was already well advanced. An unusual phenomenon called his attention. Although the windows were her-
metically closed, the light from the balcony seemed to enter as though
there were no obstacles, filtering in through the slits in the shutters.
In these golden bands, endless corpuscles of various sizes and colors
were fluttering in dizzying whirls.

Some were black, opaque, and angular like coal; others seemed long,
transparent, and brilliant like crystalline threads (filaments of cotton
and wool). Many had spherical or ovoid forms and perfect diaphaneity, so that they looked like mold spores considerably amplified by a
microscope. All of these floating particles were rising and falling, and
crowding together with impetuous movements. In an endless motion,
they passed from the light to the shadows, leaping over the furniture
and catching themselves in the bedclothes and whiskers of the astounded philosopher. When they collided with his nose and mouth,
they rushed threateningly into his lungs with each inspired breath.

Believing himself to be the victim of some bizarre dream, Juan quickly got out of bed. But when he crossed one of the shining curtains of light, he saw, stupefied, that his nightshirt had been converted into a coarse mat woven with brilliant, white crystalline cylinders. His hands, rough and traversed by deep canals, had been changed into a kind of giant honeycomb, interspersed with drill holes and bristling with transparent yellow penises (the holes of the glands, and the hair).

When he looked toward the bed, which was licked here and there by little tongues of light, he discovered a complex lattice of coral bars on the quilt. Finally, when he picked up a piece of paper from the floor, he saw it had been converted into an intricate pattern of icicles (filaments of compressed cotton). It was enough to drive one mad! This monstrous transformation of his body and the objects around him filled him with profound terror. What did it mean?

Then, suddenly, he remembered his vision of the night before and realized what the cause of this stupendous phenomenon must be. The spirit had not deceived him.

His eyes had been turned into microscopes, though not by changing the optical dioptrics. This would have been impossible, except by altering the form and size of his visual apparatus. Instead, the spirit had somehow refined his retinal organization and optic pathways and heightened the exquisite sensibility of the photogenic substances in his visual corpuscles. Each cone or impressionable cell of the *fovea centralis* had been decomposed into hundreds of individually excitable filaments, and a corresponding multiplication of conducting pathways had occurred in the optic nerves and visual centers of the brain. Really Juan was not seeing objects as larger, but as more detailed. The visual angle was the same as it had always been, but as a result of this multiplication of the impressionable units, the sensitive membrane of the optic globe now had the precious ability to discriminate and differentiate objects and colors at almost infinitesimal fractions of an angle.

As a result of this extraordinary perfection, our protagonist perceived things as though they were laid out on the stage of a powerful micro-scope (as long as they fell within his normal visual range). In order to see the way everyone else did—that is to say, without minute details—he had to distance himself considerably from objects, which grew pro-gressively smaller according to the known laws of aerial perspective and the dioptrics of letters.

When our hero began testing his eyes' marvelous perspicacity, his satisfaction and joy knew no bounds. He felt a flash of that same sub-lime, profound astonishment a butterfly must feel when he abandons the mask of his sleep-inducing chrysalis. Touched by the spirit of sci-ence's magic rod, the gloomy, pessimistic philosopher had been trans-formed into an extraordinary being, a portentous genius. The spell that had been cast over his visual system was now broken, and Nature was going to manifest herself exactly as she was, not as unlucky blind men—the rest of his species—imagined her to be. What priceless ad-vantages this sublime privilege would bring! What astonishing, ex-traordinary discoveries awaited him!

At last, Juan was freed from this state of enchantment by the unpleas-ant voice of his old servant and the rough scrape of the door. When it opened abruptly, it sent a gale wind full of dust and indefinable rub-bish into the philosopher's face.

"Does the young gentleman want his chocolate? . . . It's already nine!" exclaimed his housekeeper. Without asking permission, she entered the room and immediately opened the balcony window.

"Close that, for God's sake!" cried Juan, his retinas dazzled by the powerful brightness of the sun. He sensed his body being enveloped in a sweeping current of brilliant particles that threatened to clog up his lungs.

They were all the detritus of life high and low, the foul emanations of the gutter. They were the invisible, winged scraps of millions of beings which, like snakes, shed their skin and cast it off as pieces of film into the blue cloaca of the atmosphere. They were all the endless carbon blocks launched like projectiles from the chimney-canons of houses and factories, and the countless filaments of silk, wool, and cotton snatched out of men's clothes by the wind. They were, in sum, the indefinable microscopic shavings with which workshops pollute the environment, converting it into a chaotic *pandemonium* where shapeless particles of stone, dye, metal, and wood mix in desperate confusion.

Poor Juan believed himself to have fallen into a pestilential swamp, or to be witnessing the dissolution of a world whose elements had regressed to their primordial state of chaos. Although he knew perfectly well that an organism has defenses against this furious inundation of floating corpuscles, he could not suppress the disproportionate reactions of his instinct, which told him unceasingly to shut his mouth and nostrils and protect his eyes with his hand. He was terrified that some gigantic carbon block would damage his ocular cornea, impairing the mechanisms of his surprising analytical instrument.

One must confess that this struggle between the new reality and an organism disposed and reconciled to a whole different range of visual impressions was beginning to be quite taxing, even mortifying.

Still, Juan's curiosity was stronger than the irritation of his nerves. Maintaining control, he dressed himself rapidly without looking at his clothes, drank his chocolate without studying its composition, pulled on his rigid, smoky spectacles to preserve his overexcited eyes, and rushed headlong out into the street.

There the spectacle that met his eyes seemed like the dream of some delirious naturalist. The *mosaic world* and the *crystal world:* these two phrases sum up the odd, disconcerting sensations Juan felt when he found himself in the whirlwind of the street of Alcalá and began regarding the sidewalks, buildings, trees, and people.

All his simple impressions had become compound impressions; continuity had become discontinuity.

No longer did he see any rich, uniform colors, fused together through gentle transitions. There were no smooth, unified surfaces. Instead, anywhere that he saw objects, he saw mosaics: conglomerations of colored particles and aggregates of filaments and cells. Gray masses, even those that appeared white to ordinary vision, exhibited hailstorms of specks and spots of gaudy color that no one would have suspected they contained.

At the same time, stones, marble surfaces, clothes, trees, etc., revealed a foundation resembling some kind of wax or crystal covered with cavities, stalactites, ridges, facets, and fissures. Decomposing itself in the light, it produced bright, coruscating, and extremely varied reflections.

Let us describe some of our philosopher's surprising observations in detail. In his increasing wonder, he was imagining he had suddenly been transported to another planet.

On the trees, the leaves seemed to consist of innumerable opaline, translucent, polyhedral components. In their dense substance, he could see irregular accumulations of green spheres, probably grains of chlorophyll, and some other corpuscles that lacked it.

A florist's bouquet had turned into an object so strange and surprising that it took Juan some time to identify it. The petals on the geranium looked like open pomegranates, whose red grains were covered with soft tulle. The calyces of the roses resembled the white honeycombs of bees, swollen with pink, fragrant nectars. Finally, the leaves of the lily resembled giant, crystalline tulips surrounding a splendid jewel of topaz and diamond. The marvels of light added even more to this beautiful work of nature, sprinkling the infinite curves and ridges of the artistic, diaphanous mosaic with moving stars like tiny, trembling jewels.

But what most surprised our philosopher was the strange, unpleasant appearance of the faces of passers-by. Along with the false enchantment that had allowed him to see the color, smoothness, and uniformity of the skin, all beauty had vanished. Always he saw the same wretched mosaic, disrupting surfaces and decomposing hues! Here again was the hailstorm of sharp, infinitesimal reflections spattering the rough contours with dazzling sparks! The soft, fleeting transition of light into shadow had given way to a rough granulousness, the wild, coarse ruggedness of an epidermis that, when seen from afar, looked something like a hedgehog's hide and not unlike the scaly skin of a crocodile.

On even the smoothest, finest cheeks, he discovered with horror that there were shapeless masses of waxy membranes, maybe semidetached epidermal cells. He could see black holes indicating the fetid apertures of glands. Finally, he spied some schools of stout whales, pieces of skin whose frayed borders—garnished with filth and bacteria—were swinging threateningly in the air. Here and there, the complex furrows and sculpted precipices of the yellowish epidermis highlighted the boundaries of these strange organic constructions even more strongly. In Juan's fantasy, they evoked the gigantic monsters of fables or the huge, thick-skinned animals of the antediluvian fauna. With each respiratory movement, they stirred and cracked like some terrain shaken by an earthquake. The labial folds, nostrils, and imposing talons of these human monsters were spraying turbid fumes into the atmosphere, in which gelatinous strings of mucous, fused leukocytes, detached epidermal layers, and infinite numbers of bacteria were glittering in the sunlight.

Their eyes, above all, gave him a strange impression, a mixture of terror and surprise. Surrounded by two mobile curtains of vibrating bamboo poles (the eyelashes), the cornea revealed itself as a curvilinear, crystalline mosaic. Behind it, one could see the velvety, polychrome tapestry of the iris. Finally, way at the back, was the purple mantle of the retina, embroidered with red by vascular ramifications and perpetually shaken by the rhythmic beat of the blood's corpuscles.

A distressing uniformity marked those human faces, from which all differences of lineage, profession, and race had disappeared as if by magic. Essentially democratic, this new coarseness had standardized the female faces to such a degree that up close, our disoriented observer could not distinguish ugliness from beauty or youth from maturity.

But then, what difference did it make—as far as aesthetic appreciation was concerned—whether those cutaneous wasp-nests, deserts, and brushlands ended in this place or that? What did it matter how many branching capillaries or spots of pigment there were in each macaroon of flesh? What difference would it make to the moon if someone were to take away some of its craters or shrink some of its mountain ranges?

One must realize that for poor, disillusioned Juan, all the women resembled each other as they do in the darkness: they all seemed to be pockmarked by the same horrible, variolous scars. Luckily, our hero had a temperament that does not easily take flame. Had he wished to emulate the glories of don Juan, he would have to have regarded his potential conquests from at least 100 meters away in order to keep his erotic enthusiasm from cooling. On the scale of seductive efficacy, this inane amatory proceeding would have been about as useful as sweet-talking the stars through a telescope.

Ever more surprised and disillusioned, our sharp-sighted observer continued on his way. Confused and troubled by the dust that carriages and streetcars were raising, he protected his mouth with an antiseptic handkerchief. Finally, he reached the Puerta del Sol, the vent of all human exhalations and main duct of the capital's airborne detritus. He had just entered the street of Carretas and crossed the whirlwind of insane emanations emitted by the poor, unkempt flesh crammed like sausage meat into the Cuatro Caminos tramway, when suddenly, he felt a jet of wet particles hitting his face. A man with tuberculosis who was standing on the sidewalk outside the government buildings had coughed and spat in our curious explorer's vicinity.

How horrible! Receiving this unexpected volley and seeing the endless corpuscles floating in the repugnant spatters on his handkerchief filled his soul with terror and his stomach with nausea. Thanks to his exquisite retinal sensitivity, which let him discriminate diaphanous particles that were normally only perceptible in micrographs and stained preparations, he recognized all kinds of cells in the sputum, though not without some difficulty.[10] First, he saw orange disks (red blood cells), and transparent, gelatinous spheres that trembled on contact with the air (leukocytes). Then there were diaphanous films, epithelial cells from the mouth and fauces. At the same time, he could see elastic fibers like snapping whips, and vibrating corpuscles from the trachea whose velvety, threadlike appendices were rippling rhythmically like blades in a field of wheat. Numerous microbes wriggled their flagella as they struggled to keep from drying out. Finally, he saw the terrible tuberculosis bacteria, mounted threateningly on the viscous, transparent globules of pus.

And the people were calmly breathing in this snow pulsating with death! The germs in the pus, the germs of grippe and pneumonia, were leaping from mouth to mouth in such a way that their innocent victims never offered the slightest defense. They were not even aware of the terrible guests to whom they were giving such a comfortable refuge in their insides!

Something in this sad, lamentable scene seized our hero's attention, keeping him there in his observatory. I am referring to the open-hearted, basically egalitarian nature of the microbe. To pathogenic bacteria, men and animals, rich and poor, are all just fields to cultivate. They are all equally advantageous and desirable lodgings.

One had to see how unconsciously a highborn woman breathed in the flu bacillus expelled from the chest of a ragged, brazen tramp. As an arrogant, haughty ex-minister stepped out of a luxurious coach and prepared to enter the Department of the Interior, one could see him inhale—with pleasure—the tuberculosis bacillus just vented from the ulcerated lung of a furious anarchist. A few swindlers and police inspectors were politely trading pus-dwelling micrococci the way people ex-

---

10. To curtail the reader's astonishment, let us recall that besides having extraordinary analytical power, Juan's visual organ was exquisitely sensitive to the most delicate contrasts of light. Because of this remarkable property, he could see cells, microbes, and other microscopic bodies with a refraction index barely different from that of their medium with the most perfect clarity (Cajal).

change paper snakes at carnival time. It was a great pity to see how a repugnant ringworm germ (*Achorion schoenleinii*) found a safe, warm bed in a sweet, overgroomed young woman's splendid head of hair, after detaching itself from the filthy, half-scraped hide of a beggar. Finally, when two young ladies kissed each other on the cheeks, they inoculated each other with the microbes of scurvy and erysipelas.[11]

What a desolating spectacle! In the face of invisible enemies everywhere, the only weapons were the most absolute indolence, indifference, and defenselessness. To think that men could dream up lightning rods to protect themselves against storms, and rifles to protect themselves against thieves and outlaws—against remote risks and threats, the most unlikely contingencies! Yet they have been unable to invent anything sufficiently powerful to protect us from the aggression of these artful, microscopic poisoners. They still lie in wait in their invisible realm, claiming thousands of victims in each nation each day!

Distressed by these painful thoughts, our philosopher was making his way toward the Prado in search of a purer, less-dangerous environment. Suddenly, when he reached the Neptune Fountain, he had the unfortunate idea of visiting the Fine Arts Museum.

If only he hadn't done it! What a terrible disillusionment! The magic spell of color and outline had been completely dissolved. In its place, the loathsome *mosaic* revealed itself in all of its terrible nudity, the same image that had been following him like an hallucinatory obsession.

First, he saw furrows, hills, and valleys formed by irregular deposits of amber varnish, all broken by cracks like the ones the summer sun makes in dried-out mud. Every contour of this angry, congealed sea emitted lively reflections like myriads of stars, disrupting the color

11. Erysipelas is an inflammation of the skin caused by the bacteria *Streptococcus pyogenes*. Its victims develop red, hardened skin, facial swelling, and a high fever. Ringworm is an inflammation of the skin caused by fungi or mold. Ringworm of the scalp, the kind referred to here, is caused by the fungus *Microsporon audouini* and is highly contagious. People develop scurvy due to a vitamin C deficiency, not an invasive microbe. It is odd that Cajal would include it here, since it had been known for some time that scurvy could be prevented with a diet containing fresh fruits and vegetables. Since so many diseases were being attributed to microorganisms at the time, physicians may have thought that a limited diet merely weakened people, leaving them vulnerable to a scurvy "microbe."

atrociously. Through the turbid varnish, he glimpsed ravines and sandy riverbeds and polychromatic pebbles, all scrambled and heaped together in the most nauseating confusion. These were the impressions received by Juan's astonished eyes when he regarded the sweet, pasty flesh of Murillo's virgins or the strong, honest, precise brushstrokes of Velázquez's paintings.

Aside from the appearance of an immense, dried-out mudhole that was conferred by the varnish, what might properly be called the paintings had been transformed into a coarse mosaic. Each one consisted of millions of fragments of simple colors that were harsh and impossible to combine. Nowhere could he see those compound blends, those infinite, sweet gradations of light and shadow that give pictorial art its charm and fascination. Standing there before those canvases, Juan was like some yokel at St. Peter's in Rome, trying to examine the famous mosaics from the distance of distinct vision (thirty-three centimeters).

No matter how inartistic the reader may be, he will easily understand how these unbearable incongruities and dissonances of color, perspective, and pattern must have been shocking our hero. On some canvases, the chromatic palette seemed so incomplete that they might have been attributed to an artist suffering from some strange daltonism.[12] In vain he searched them for important shades like green, orange, and violet. It is a known fact that compound colors are formed on the palette by mixing simple tints: red and blue make violet, and so on. When such mixtures are broken down by analytical techniques, it becomes clear that the complementary tints have been shining even though we could not perceive them. For as is well known, what we see represents the effects of distance and our confused vision of the very small.

As one may presume, those paintings also lacked the unexpected vigor and intonation achieved by good colorists. Boldly, they stroke their subjects' heads with rays of green, purple, and orange, knowing

12. British chemist and physicist John Dalton (1766–1844) proposed that all matter consisted of atoms. He was by no means the first to do so, however. The Greek philosopher Democritus (460–370 B.C.) and Roman philosopher Lucretius (of the first century A.D.) had envisioned matter much the same way.

that the observer's retina—when placed at the right distance—will blend and harmonize the image.[13]

Still, our disoriented visitor would have been able to receive a normal aesthetic impression from the paintings, but only from a sufficiently distant point of view. Unfortunately, the rooms of the museum were much too small for that, and one could hardly ask the State to construct a building of two square kilometers for the exclusive convenience of this one odd guest.

From these aesthetic perceptions and anatomical observations, Juan deduced that art resists analysis less successfully than Nature. When the retina's power is exhausted, Nature still offers infinitesimal forms that are often as beautiful as those available to ordinary vision. But art—a mere copy of crude sensory impressions—works with rough, amorphous elements. In order to maintain the aesthetic illusion, they must hide themselves in the dark dominion of the invisible.

In the hidden depths of life, there is always palpitating life, but in the depths of artworks, ugliness and death quickly appear. Whoever the spectator may be—man, eagle, or insect—the tableau of organic nature will always maintain its mysterious fascination for him, a certain organization and inaccessible consciousness. In contrast, the pictorial work—so closely adapted to our lowly optical perception—lacks profundity and universality, for it will never be perceptible to all beings in the same way. It will lose its charms the minute our chromatic capacity and retinal differentiation make the slightest advancement.

When Juan left the Prado Museum, he encountered a spectacle as unforeseen as it was surprising. During his visit to our wonderful picture gallery, a cold, wet north wind had begun to blow, and the sky had suddenly turned overcast. Just as our hero reached the street of Alcalá, drops of water began to fall that were mixed with delicate flakes of ice.

Somewhat vexed, Juan looked around him and suddenly found him-

13. We will remind those laymen uninformed about pictorial physics that when three rays of bright colors are placed very close together and viewed from a distance—green, orange, and violet, for example—they give rise (through retinal synthesis) to a sensation of white or gray because they are all affecting a single retinal cone (Cajal).

self enveloped in a curtain of gigantic icicles. Depriving him of his sight, they forced him to walk gropingly, as though he were caught in a dense darkness. Thanks to his exquisite ability to perceive the contrasts between refraction indices, the contours of raindrops, multiform crystals, and air bubbles in the snowflakes were outlining themselves on his retina with unaccustomed vigor. One might say that the water from the sky had lost its ordinary diaphaneity and had turned into foam.

Moving from surprise to surprise, our hero was already beginning to lose his fear. But he could not suppress a certain trembling when he saw how those huge conglomerates of capricious, elegant stars disintegrated on colliding with his face and clothes. The air pockets lodged in them exploded like soap bubbles, sending their last, twinkling reflections up into the sky.

What a pity Juan's hearing did not match his sight! The spectacle would have been even more surprising. The sound of huge water drops splashing onto the ground, the zooming of flakes rushing through the air, and the explosions of bursting bubbles would have produced an infernal uproar in his ears, a truly deafening concert.

What strange things, those waterdrops! Juan had thought that he knew what a liquid was. They had explained it to him in physics class, where they had spoken of *surface tension.* He had learned about the cohesive force by virtue of which a drop maintains its spherical form and unified personality, rejecting all *hydrophobic* substances, that is, all those that cannot be humidified. With simple sight, this phenomenon is hard to verify and is thus unlikely to create a profound impression. Now, however, it revealed itself before Juan's watchful, telescopic eyes with matchless clarity and proportions.

In order to understand our observer's wonder and amazement, the reader should picture a collection of huge rubber bladders, like the balls that give children so much amusement. Imagine some of them attached to filaments of wool from people's clothes, like balloons caught in the branches of trees. Now suppose that with the least shock, these giant balloons divide as though they were living beings to form smaller, equally spherical balloons . . . Picture all the strange transitional forms (stalactites, question marks, et cetera) that the liquid cells will assume before yielding to the law of gravity and abandoning their desired resting places. Finally, imagine the brilliant image of the sky painted onto the curved mirrors of these thick, proteiform, crystalline cloaks, and you will have some idea of what our hero must have felt when he observed the unexplored realm of the waterdrop, the liquid cell.

Juan's curiosity and wonder reached their peak when he spied an unlucky animalcule—a microbe, perhaps—caught in one of these formidable drops. Struggling desperately, it was trying to escape this liquid element whose crystalline borders, impervious to its anxious flailing, must have seemed more impregnable than the Great Wall of China. Finally, a rude blow from a flake of ice knocked the waterdrop to the ground. Thanks to the granite's *absorbability* and the consequent dissipation of the liquid, the surface tension was conquered, and the aggrieved castaway was finally liberated.

But this was not the only dramatic transformation produced by the water. By washing façades and sidewalks, statues and protruding sculptures, by expelling the superficial air from objects and varnishing and polishing the whole city, the downpour gave a new, more prestigious, sympathetic face to the lowly inorganic world. Through the watery varnish, the marble wall sculptures looked like splendid works of gold encrusted with diamonds, from whose facets the light drew magical, sparkling reflections. The ordinary almond pattern of the granite came alive with unexpected splendor. In a thousand different combinations, it displayed the greenish and bluish tones of the mica, the pearly tints of the feldspar, and the diamondlike brilliance of the quartz. For greater glory and splendor, the light added a delicate iridescence and vivid spectral colors to these beautiful streams, when the luminous waves interfered with subtle cloaks of air in the mica. And these magical rainbows, invisible to common eyes, were flashing and eclipsing like showers of stars with each change of the spectator's position. There was a whole world of beauty buried and hidden in the infinitely small!

Who would have thought it! Even the gutter had been ennobled. Struck obliquely by the sun which shone out for a moment from between the clouds, crystals of calcium carbonate were sparkling in the muck. He could see silvery, multicolored filaments of silk; strands of wool like the trunks of palms; pieces of paper like huge slabs of granite; green, polyhedral plant cells; brilliant, spherical spores; and finally, the elegant, whimsical shells of protozoans (the organic forms of chalk).

From the preceding passages, it must have become apparent that under the influence of Juan's exceptional eyes, the living world—particularly the animal one—had lost its enchantment. But the inorganic one, in contrast, was revealing inexpressible, unimagined marvels. As a result of these discoveries, a new conception of beauty and ugliness was slowly crystallizing in our hero's mind. In the order of the inorganic, he thought, the ugly, the gray, the amorphous, everything that neither attracts our glances nor speaks to our will, is really a confused, disordered mixture of crystalline elements. All are beautiful in themselves, but normally they're inaccessible to our senses. In the organic world, in contrast, the impression of ugliness and repugnance comes from our inopportune looks at its constitutive elements (cells, fibers, membranes, appendices, etc.). For these are infinitely less regular, colorful, and brilliant than the components of mineral formations.

"In conclusion," our philosopher reflected, "if analysis discovers hidden marvels in the kingdom of rocks, then in the kingdom of life (and in its imitation, the work of art), it dissolves beauty. For beauty is an effect of our synthetic vision and our naive ignorance of the mysterious threads of the vital tapestry. From this, one can see that in all things, there is something beautiful and attractive. It's all a question of placing yourself at the right point of view, of moving in close with a microscope or distancing yourself with a telescope."

"Maybe," Juan hypothesized, "if Nature has created beings with senses less acute than ours, then many of the objects we find unpleasant, jarring, or indifferent would be pleasant to them, even beautiful.

Who knows whether the insect finds flowers much more beautiful than we do, or sees colors, forms, and proportions in the sands and stars that are unavailable to our senses! What must a sunset look like to a bird? . . .

4

Not long after the exploration we have just described, our protagonist was already growing used to the splendors of light and the extravagances and surprises of a world as real as it was unrealistic. One day, it occurred to him to attend a performance at the Royal Theater.

His passion for music brought him to that aristocratic coliseum. He knew that from the boxes and galleries, the scenery would have a deplorable effect, as would the faces and costumes of the singers. He thus resolved to take no notice of visual impressions and instead attend solely to acoustical ones, which luckily were absolutely normal. To accomplish this, he could think of no better course than to sit in the darkest, most forgotten corner of that paradise.

The first act of *Carmen* was just drawing to a close, and the noisy applause of the claque was still resounding through the hall when our dilettante spotted his former intended in one of the boxes. Unable to contain the impulses of his heart (for he still loved her), determined to submit his ex-fiancée to the implacable dissection of micrographic analysis, he left his corner and went down to greet her.

This act could not possibly have bothered don Toribio's family. Our hero had renounced his position as Elvira's official intended, and this circumstance gave him a certain freedom to chat with the disdainful young lady. In reality, the ex-fiancés had never quarreled, nor had there ever been any reason to. It was just that the thermometer of love, which in Elvira's heart had never reached the temperature of vehement passion, was sinking insensibly toward zero. Little by little their souls had moved apart, and the romance of love, which grew less and less spirited, had stopped resounding in the ungrateful girl's ear when her heart had refused to keep time to it.

Well, as we were saying, Juan entered don Toribio's box, where Elvira and her mother were sitting. All jovial, powdered, and elaborately dressed, they were showing off elegant dresses, expensive jewels, and splendid coiffures.

If the protagonist of this story meant to erase the seductive images he had retained of this serene, reasoning woman; if he yearned to destroy the artistic vision of a ponderous, solid, healthy beauty around which his imagination and feeling had raised an illusory dream of love, then one must confess that he succeeded entirely.

Juan's illusion melted completely away. Various circumstances contributed to this thawing. As is generally known, woman—who is mistress of the art of pleasing—has still not learned the science of illumination. At gatherings of friends[14] or in the theater, she chooses her seat as God wills it, never considering that there are lights that coarsen the skin, disrupt the harmonies of line and color, and add ten years to one's age.

This is just what happened to poor Elvira. Without the least misgiving, she sat down right next to an electric light that harshly and obliquely illuminated her features. Exaggerating the incipient, almost imperceptible wrinkles of her twenty-seven-year-old face, it cruelly highlighted the slightest irregularities and defects of her skin. To crown her misfortune, our heroine's face these days no longer offered the springlike freshness and luxuriance of former times. It had been tarnished considerably by the lingering effects of erysipelas and by the irritating effects of the winter cold (that dreadful enemy of delicate constitutions and fine skin). Contrary to her custom, the poor girl had fallen back on the use—and even abuse—of cosmetics.

Seized by the greatest amazement, Juan searched in vain for any possible correspondence between that incredible lump of feminine flesh bristling with warts, little penises, encrustations, and scales, and the poetic image of the graceful girl stored in the shrine of his memory. What a disillusionment! Her head had been turned into an impenetra-

---

14. Here Cajal again uses the word "tertulia," a group of friends who meet regularly to discuss issues of interest.

ble thicket of waxy brown bamboo poles spotted with dandruff, puddles of perfume, and colonies of microscopic fungi. Under the electric light, he could see an uneven pavement of red and white grains on her lips and cheeks, a shining carpet of carmine and white bismuth particles. The fine skin of her cheeks and forehead was covered with stratifications and stalactites of rice powder (starch globules) clotted and compressed by *cold cream*. Here and there, among the clearings of the starchy skin and hairy thicket, he could see upright monoliths: vast, translucent epidermal films with curling edges. On these lay the crouching, wriggling strings of the erysipelas streptococcus. Finally, to complete this hideous picture, let us mention the sooty debris on her eyelids, huge pieces of charcoal that gave her eyes the grotesque look of a clown. In some viscous saliva on her lips, whole hatcheries of bacteria were swimming and gesticulating with the greatest gusto and pleasure.

This spectacle looked nothing like the angelic companion of man. On the contrary, it suggested some filthy, gigantic pachyderm, some unknown antediluvian animal that could inspire only pity and repugnance. What a terrible disillusionment!

"So this," thought Juan to himself, "is what that famous feminine beauty amounts to at bottom. This is the immortal Helen, subjugator of man and cause of so many foolish errors, mad acts, and crimes! And all to receive this nauseating wave of salival microbes on our desiring lips, as if it were a supreme prize! All to feel the rude contact of a molting epidermis and a yielding pig's brush against our skin! . . ."

Trying to conceal the infinite disenchantment in his heart, Juan offered some polite commonplaces to the women in the box, then stood up to take his leave. "Until we meet again, Juan," intoned Elvira in a sweet, caressing voice. But as these words left her smiling lips, a few microscopic drops of saliva from her adorable mouth sprinkled our protagonist's face and clean shirt front. Heedless of the discourtesy he was committing, he quickly cleaned his face and hands, as though some corrosive liquid had fallen upon them.

For in the shower of his beloved's breath, once inhaled with such pleasure, he thought he had seen the *capsules of Fränkel's diplococcus*. There, lurking like some threatening shadows, were the terrible infectious agents that cause pneumonia.[15]

That rude gesture shocked haughty Elvira, and spitefully, she resolved never to forget it.

5

With each passing day, poor Juan's life was becoming more difficult.

Certainly his prodigious clear-sightedness was letting him avoid microbes, but this new advantage had not affected his sensibility, which was growing ever more touchy. The trouble was that it was accustomed, *ab initio,*[16] to a whole different range of visual sensations.

Because of this disharmony between excitations and reactions, he was repulsed by wine, water, meat, . . . basically by everything. He experienced the greatest difficulties when it came time to eat, for even though he personally intervened in the culinary tasks, sterilizing, filtering, analyzing, and cleaning the primary materials, he often discovered bacteria or ugly little bugs in his food and drink that turned his stomach and took away his appetite. Due to a psychological phenomenon that is difficult to explain, even the cleanest, most nourishing blancmanges[17] caused hesitation and repugnance.

For to his eyes, meat was no longer meat, but packets of red, contractile worms (striated muscle fibers). Bacon looked like a mound of huge globules, boxes of bonbons filled with oily liquid and starlike crystallizations (adipose cells and margarine crystals). Bread appeared as a conglomerate of starchy granules embedded in transparent bedrock (gluten) where one could easily see every kind of filth. Cheese struck him as a disgusting breeding ground for microbes, a sort of Noah's Ark palpitating with dirty life, a nauseating carrion that would turn the

---

15. The reader should recall that pneumonia germs often inhabit the mouth, fauces, and nasal passages of healthy individuals (Cajal). The pneumonia *diplococcus* was discovered by bacteriologist Albert Fränkel (1848–1916).

16. *ab initio,* from the outset

17. *blancmanges,* dishes made from cornstarch and milk, usually with some sort of sweetener

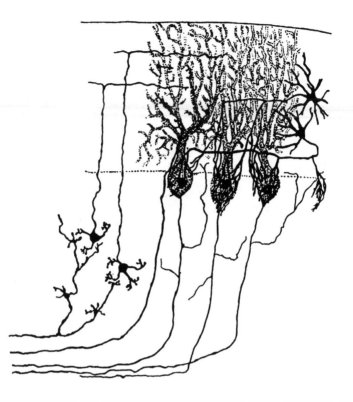

Figure 3. A schematic representation of the connections of Purkinje cells in the cerebellum (1894)

stomach of a corpse. At times, when he found himself in the dining room surrounded by appetizing dishes, he imagined that he was in a histological laboratory and, driven by some strange aberration, was about to devour a bunch of microscopic preparations. Brains, in particular, filled him with superstitious dread.

"Who," he exclaimed, "would dare eat a nerve cell raising its supplicating arms, which still seem to be vibrating from the pain of the butcher's mortal blow?"

Of course, he also hated fresh water, where the insidious typhoid bacillus and *Bacillus coli communis* were swarming, along with other germs. He was disgusted by wine, which was frequently contaminated with *Mycoderma aceti* and *Torula cerevisae,* and by milk, which was teeming with tuberculosis bacilli, not to mention the middling bacteria that cause fermentation. In the end, he consented to drink only boiled water that had been previously sterilized with a Chamberland burner.[18] With all of these misgivings, Juan took infinite precautions with the cleaning and sterilization of plates, glasses, bottles, tablecloths, knives, and forks. Considering his eccentricities and meticulous scruples, one can imagine the mood of the unhappy cook. She simply thought that her master had taken leave of his senses.

In fact, our protagonist was not at all far from losing his reason. Before his astonished eyes, the spell that had governed his life had vanished away. Those thin, rosy veils were disintegrating, the ones with which merciful Nature disguises the sharp bitterness of things and the crude structure of the world.

If he wanted disorder and disagreeable impressions, he had only to go out into the city and countryside. When our hero wandered through the outskirts of the city, he was surrounded by a lively swarm of fine particles. Imposing themselves on the foreground according to size, they stole his view of the remote blue distances.

When he ventured into the traffic and din of the city, he experienced an even greater torture. The extreme impurity of the environment left him lost and disoriented, and he struggled in vain to focus on remote objects (or at least, those that would have been remote had his eyes afforded normal images of objects): buildings and monuments, carriages and people. But a curtain of undefinable impurities, continually shaken by the wind, even by the palpitations of sound, softened the contours of things and exaggerated the distances in the background. Like a traveler surprised in the countryside by a furious snowstorm, he could glimpse the horizon only in very brief intervals.

18. The fungi *Mycoderma aceti* cause the fermentation that produces vinegar. *Torula cerevisae,* now known as *Cryptococcus,* are a genus of yeastlike fungi with round cells. Bacteriologist Charles E. Chamberland worked with Louis Pasteur and helped to prepare the rabies vaccine. He was known as a superb technician.

Only when the day was waning, when the light from the sky bathed the land in a sweet, wan clarity, did the dizzying, untimely atmospheric dust begin to settle, granting Juan some relief from the painful fatigue of his eyes.

For this reason, he could often be seen at sunset, wandering alone in the hidden paths of the Retiro, absorbed in his own reflections under the dark branches of the pines. There, freed from the turbulent rush of daily sensations, he could think and recover his self-possession, swimming in the restless sea of his memories . . . But ah! He needed to go back very far, to traverse almost the entire record of his youth, to stumble on some pleasant memory that would compensate for the bitter present and comfort him in his despair.

6

Eventually Juan tired of these strange, disheartening explorations, and his mind felt ready for more virile, serious enterprises. One day he said to himself:

"I still have six months left of this marvelous clear-sightedness. Let's put it to work for the good of humanity—let's contribute to science and illuminate the hidden secrets of life. In my hands, the microscope and telescope will extend their ranges enormously, yielding amplifications of which physicists have never dreamed. What portentous discoveries I'll make! My glory will be sublime! Present and future generations will be amazed by my supreme conquests! No doubt I will pass as an extraordinary genius, an analytical demon, a monster of penetration, intuition, and logic . . .

So, filled with ardent enthusiasm, he set right to work.

He began by seeking recommendations from the scientists at the astronomical observatory. He developed a friendship with its kind, courteous director, who let him scan the fathomless abysses of the heavens with a powerful telescope on clear summer nights. He had the good fortune to discover stars whose existence had never even been suspected, comets which until then had been invisible, and nebulae whose pale flame lit up the unexplored blackness of space. Along the way, he quickly resolved the most arduous problems of planetary physics, chemistry, and biology: the atmosphere of the moon, the habitability of Jupiter, the question of the Martian canals, the chemical composition of the stars, etc.[19] For one must realize that to his eyes, the luminous band of the stellar spectrum revealed chromatic and absorptive rays absolutely invisible to all other astronomers.

Not content with these stupendous revelations, he set up a micrographic and bacteriological laboratory in his own home. Multiplying the microscope's power with the marvelous acuity of his eyes, he tenaciously studied diseases of unknown origin and had the good fortune to reveal the ultramicroscopic germs of cowpox, smallpox, measles, syphilis, tumors . . . who knows what all![20]

He published the valuable fruits of this productive labor in singular, surprising, extremely lucid monographs, revealing the world of the great and of the very small. His researches reformed scientific thought and opened up splendid horizons for future investigation . . .

But ah! These admirable findings ran into one minor obstacle . . . No one believed them.

Unsettled in their solemn dignity as official authorities, the astronomers asked:

19. In 1877, Italian astronomer Giovanni Schiaparelli observed *canali* (grooves) on the surface of mars. When this word was mistranslated as "canals," it caused a sensation, since people took the structures for signs of intelligent life. The Martian canals were still a subject of debate at the time Cajal published these stories.

20. Cowpox, smallpox, and measles are caused by viruses, not bacteria. Although British physician Edward Jenner had demonstrated in 1796 that inoculation with cowpox prevented smallpox, neither virus had been identified in 1905. Syphilis is associated with a spirochete, *Treponoma pallidum,* which is extremely difficult to see and could be observed easily only in 1906 after the invention of the ultramicroscope. Although *Treponoma pallidum* was identified in 1905, its discovery may not have been announced until after the *Vacation Stories* went to press. Tumors (Cajal probably means cancer) are not caused by any known microorganism. In 1905, considering the speed with which diseases were being attributed to microbes, it seemed reasonable to speculate that cowpox, smallpox, measles, syphilis, and cancer were caused by microorganisms too small to be observed. With the first four diseases, Cajal guessed right. We are still investigating the causes of cancer.

"How can we take seriously a dreamer who swears he can see the satellites of Uranus, the lands and clouds of Jupiter, and stars of the sixteenth magnitude, all with the naked eye?"[21]

For their part, the histologists and bacteriologists exclaimed:

"How much faith can we put in the descriptions of some fool who brags he can see blood corpuscles and the tuberculosis bacillus with the naked eye, a man whose strange findings no one has been able to confirm?"

• • •

This universal skepticism, so cruelly mortifying to his self-love; the increasing coldness of his friends, who took him for a raving lunatic; and his growing dislike of people and things sent our philosopher into a state of dark desperation. The wonderful, superhuman gift that had seemed like a herald of glory and happiness had turned into an inexhaustible source of bitterness and disillusionment. As so often happens, the blind were judging the seer. The one who should have felt pity was the one who was pitied. Once again, genius was taken for dementia and, in return for its humanitarian, self-denying effort, received only ignominy and ingratitude.

7

One warm, tranquil autumn afternoon, Juan was strolling through the shady paths of the Retiro, not far from the arbor of the *Fallen Angel*. Yielding mechanically to the reflexes of his muscles, he sat down next to a hedge under the gigantic pines. Just in front of him was an opening in the branches, a sort of locutory through which he could hear the vigorous grinding of carriage wheels, the vibrant conversations of men, and the silvery laughter of girls.

The sun was slowly setting, reddening the tops of the trees, gilding

21. The magnitude of a star indicates its brightness and distance. Those of the first magnitude are brightest and closest, and a star five orders of magnitude lower than another is a hundred times as bright. Stars up to the sixth order of magnitude can be seen with the naked eye; those of seventh or higher, only with a telescope.

and spiritualizing the women's faces. Little by little, he sensed the arrival of that sweet, melancholy hour in which Nature darkens and ideas take light; in which the magnificent foliage of the woods, momentarily adorned by the sun, exchanges its greenish-orange tone for one of blue-violet; in which light suddenly abandons us as if the world were falling into a deep cavern. From the serene, unchanging atmospheric heights, an august silence descended that seemed to dampen the murmur of leaves and the harsh rattle of carriages. From time to time, bats beat the air with their dark, silent wings, like souls in pain.

Exquisitely sensitive to the faintness of living things, Juan's spirit merged with his surroundings, and he felt himself penetrated by that terrible melancholy that plants seem to give off when they are abandoned by the sun, their force and their God.

After glancing absentmindedly at the horizon, which was visible in places between the trunks of trees, our hero fixed his eyes on the western sky, which was discolored by a long brushstroke of soot. It was the smoke from an electric plant that was about to illuminate the city.

"This black smoke," exclaimed Juan, "is associated with light just as pain is with thought. I, too, have desired light, a great deal of light . . . and I succeeded, no doubt, in illuminating my intelligence. But ah! The smoke from that flame darkened my heart and dulled the sky of my happiness . . ."

Soon after this, the evening star appeared in the east, as red and threatening as a tragic specter. Juan looked at it obstinately. Once more he regarded its dried-up seas; its bare, craggy mountains; its empty, inert craters; its gigantic fissures . . .

"Here," he said to himself, "we have a faithful image of our sad fate! Once the pale moon, too, had a heart full of molten lava and lived a life overflowing with force and activity. Once it was adorned by splendid vegetation, animated by rushing rivers, wrapped closely in the cerulean tulle of an atmosphere, and crowned with a golden diadem of clouds. But by some inevitable law of evolution, beautiful Diana has become no more than the fleshless skull of a world. Her gigantic orbits are turned toward the earth, on whose strength and vitality they cast their last, envious looks. In the same way, our empty orbits will some-day be turned toward the stars, but ah! They will never be touched by the golden brush of light . . ."

When he reached this point in his brooding, Juan fell into a deep prostration. Sad thoughts always lead to more sadness. A throng of painful memories rushed into his mind: the premature death of his parents, his lost dreams of glory, his love without hope. This upwelling of intense, agonizing emotion was followed by a subconscious state in which perceptions and images flared up momentarily like flames about to extinguish themselves. Making a powerful effort, struggling to rekindle the light of his thought, he continued:

"I see blackness, and I feel nothing but cold. It's as if a dark wave of stellar night has penetrated my soul, and the icy temperature of interplanetary space is saturating me like a wandering meteorite. I feel as if all the cells of my body are fighting to scatter themselves like a swarm of mad bees . . . What a shame that death suspends consciousness without transferring it from the brain to the cells, and from these to the molecules! What a happy moment it must be for the carbon and nitrogen atoms trapped in the albuminoids of protoplasm, that moment of ultimate liberation when they escape into the free dominions of the atmosphere. What a great pleasure it would be to feel oneself dissolve into nothingness, to hide oneself from the light, fluttering soundlessly like a bat that takes refuge in a cavern. To fall into the abyss like a ship that capsizes in the darkness, producing no froth or visible eddies! To leave no bitterness in anyone's heart!

• • •

Cold, sticky sweat bathed Juan's face. His thoughts and words ceased. His skin trembled with that intense shivering that accompanies dark, dreadful, undefinable sensations. His heart was beating rapidly and immoderately, and his blood, fleeing his cold periphery, focused its heat on his most noble, vital organs. The thread of conscious perception, which had been growing ever thinner, now threatened to break altogether. In this agonizing moment, as though bidding a final farewell to an ungrateful world, Juan extended one last, faint look at the happy, boisterous beings just a few steps away. They were expressing the powerful, obstinate current of ordinary life, which was equally indifferent to pain and glory . . . And, oh, what cruel irony! In that procession of soulless bodies he thought that he saw—or actually did see—the disdainful, insensitive Elvira.

Yes . . . it was she! She was riding in a luxurious carriage, her head outlined against the light, her hair gilded as though ignited by the last red tinges in the sky. Her face was serene, ennobled by blue reflections from the east, but her black eyes were burning and inflaming. Her lips, like geranium petals, were curled into a spiritual smile. She was displaying her adorably feminine figure with its graceful, youthful, round curves, enjoying the men's sensual curiosity and the women's malicious looks. This impeccable statue was adorned with a magnificent dress of dark green velvet. Besides giving her body the look of a cocoon, it provided a wise artistic contrast, bringing a bewitching flush to her pearly, goddess's throat and her irreproachable ivory hands.

Yes . . . there could be no doubt! It was the old Elvira . . . that strong, well-balanced, self-possessed virgin who months before, on that fateful day, had been dissected and vilified by the implacable scalpel of analysis. But when regarded now from the appropriate distance—the distance necessary to maintain an illusion—when brushed gently by this soft, harmonious light, she was raised upon the crystalline pedestal of space, which makes suns lose their spots and moons, their craters.

This supernatural apparition reduced our near-expiring philosopher to speechless stupor. But fixing his eyes on this radiant star, he caught one of her ardent glances, and suddenly he felt a wave of hot blood inundate his brain. Taking comfort, his heart began to beat with the solemn, vigorous rhythm of health. One might have said that the cells of his living hive, once anxious for free expansion, were reknitting their nexus of solidarity and organic synergy. With the return of hope, life now seemed worth living, misery and all. And this stupendous resurrection occurred within a tenth of a second, the exact time it took for him to feel himself regarded by merciful, subjugating eyes full of nuptial promises . . .

8

At last, the term promised by the spirit came to an end. One day, after a lethargic, restoring sleep, the afflicted philosopher's eyes and brain recovered their normal way of seeing. When he first saw living beings with continuous skin tones and veiled structures, after a year of ruthless analysis; when he found the air, water, foods, and clothes free from disgusting detritus and threatening bacteria, he believed that he had been set down on a new planet ruled by some kindly, paternal, merciful God.

Gradually, our protagonist recovered his old, ingenuous equanimity and was cured of his pessimism and rebelliousness. The harsh lesson he had learned made him fairer with his fellow men and much stricter with himself. A great light began to shine in his mind, and as a result of these new reflections, he vowed to alter his conduct radically.

First and foremost, he resolved to adjust his thoughts and actions strictly to the invincible laws of intellectual and moral evolution, without opposing them in the least. Rather than resisting them, he drew his principles of individual and social conduct straight from these evolutionary laws. His motto became that of Epictetus: "O Nature! I want what you want!"[22]

Of course, he gave up his satanic mania of blaming Providence for physical and moral evil, seeing them instead as an unavoidable consequence of the brain's weakness and imperfection. He understood that pain and misfortune are irremediable, for they originate in the very essence and structure of the organic machine. Because of this, they can only be alleviated by instilling altruistic love for the collec-

22. The Greek vase-painter Epictetus (fl. 520–500 B.C.) was famous for his style and craftsmanship.

tive organism. People must be inspired with the firm conviction that they are all sister cells in a great living unity, Nation or State, whose prosperity and happiness depend on all their individual sacrifices.

He became tolerant of errors, especially religious and philosophical ones. For when they were ennobled and sanctified by sincerity, they now seemed like idealistic reactions to compensate for misfortune. They were merely consoling legends, bringing sweet, idealistic air to the desert of a mind without concepts or the emptiness of a heart without love. And when the error had to be corrected, because it didn't engage people's sensibility or merge with a system of ideas based on painful reality, he would erase it with the same gentleness, sweetness, and care with which one removes a spot from some precious, delicate silk.

Even his own misfortunes now appeared in a new, singularly encouraging light. In them, he was beginning to discern a providential warning about the growing weakness of his race and the pressing need to invigorate it physically and morally.

Mankind was on the way to justice and sincerity, and when the insults and intentional injustices of men were viewed in light of that higher goal, they contained a great living essence of wisdom and social foresight. What looked like cruelty to one selfish individual became generous charity when regarded from the serene heights of collective utility.

In this way, Juan was gradually converted to the fervent cult of the species. He became merciful and indulgent with his adversaries, for he saw that when most human impulses are calmly and carefully analyzed, the same ones that seem egotistical and repugnant are really sacred, controlling drives crucial for the continuity and prosperity of the race.

"My judges did well," he said, "to reject a candidate who was studious and smart enough, but also hot-headed, bitter, and disorganized. My friends were right to scorn a pedantic, affected man who prided himself on destroying the optimism and faith necessary for survival and happiness with his dark, desolating philosophy. And Elvira was no less reasonable and prudent when she broke off relations with a man who was weak and sickly, and strange and ill-humored to boot.

"In her cold rebukes, which were once unbearable to my ego, the spirit of the species was speaking. As irreverent as it may seem to advocates of militant individualism, one must realize that in the contract of love, future humanity is a witness with a right to be heard. If the presumed outcome of the conjugal union would oppose the sacrosanct laws of evolution, then the coming generation must always offer its veto. This forced witness often speaks out in women from the depths of their unconscious minds. Worried about the stability of form and the progress of intelligence, this voice must have transmitted the dumb protest of thousands of immature germ cells straight to Elvira's consciousness. Fearing that they would never see the light of day, they let out the ominous wail of a whole future humanity threatened with death on the vine, or maybe a downward slide into the ignominy of degeneration or madness.

9

Two more years had passed, and Juan was now a new man. Once his psychology was altered and his conduct corrected, the rewards were not long in coming.

After another competition, he won a post at the Provincial Charity Hospital. His patients, always more abundant, brought him substantial benefits. His friends, now more numerous and sincere, surrounded him with love and praised his kindness, discretion, and talent, even his lovable weaknesses and defects. Gracián warns us, "be sure to have some small faults and defects so that envy will feed on them and never dare touch the better part of you." Heeding this advice, Juan became lighthearted, incorrect, and careless for the first time in his life, abandoning the solemn rigidity in his diction and gestures. He lost that stingy, meticulous care of his syntax which, besides giving him an air of annoying pedantry, was robbing his words of their spontaneity and grace—the affability, familiarity, beauty, and enchantment of every-day conversation.

No one remembered his old folly and madness, which people kindly attributed to the great moral shock produced by the death of his beloved parents.

And since a healthy, tranquil brain and heart make the best nutritional tonics, our enlightened philosopher also improved physically. At that time, he was a handsome young man of thirty-two, tall, robust, and elegant, with a kindly, intelligent air.

Elvira, well-balanced and serious Elvira, still had not married. Don Toribio wanted to unite her with a rich, mercantile friend of his who was young and very much in love, but who lacked refinement and talent. As always, the prudent young woman would not let her arm be twisted so easily. The suitor fell far short of the intellectual type she envisioned, a man of firm will and obvious talent who would be her guide and refuge in her life and rein in her feminine nervousness. The awaited Lohengrin[23] had to have all the qualities a celebrated author has deemed indispensable for the man of genius: the idealistic spirit, refinement, and altruism of Don Quixote; and the self-possession, robustness, and positive outlook of Sancho. So far, the watchman in her heart had still not glimpsed that mysterious, enchanted bark.

Luckily, prudent Elvira ran into her former fiancé one day, the mad, long-suffering Juan. She remembered him as a pale young man with dark rings under his eyes whom she had surprised more than once making his melancholy way through the shady paths of the Retiro. But when she saw him this time, she was most pleasantly surprised; more than surprised, she was subjugated. A powerful knocking in her heart told the exultant young woman that, at last, she had set foot on the promised land.

Certainly she had heard about her old lover's triumph and prosperi-

23. In German legends, Lohengrin is a knight who arrives in a swan-shaped boat to rescue a noblewoman in distress. His origins are mysterious, and he refuses ever to reveal them.

ty, but she would never have suspected the wonderful transfiguration of his physique. There was a new expression of seraphic sweetness in his gaze, and an enchanting peace and cheerfulness in his spirit. Smiling with satisfaction, the spirit of the species withdrew all his old omens.

Elvira was approaching thirty, so it made no sense to waste time with rhetorical approaches. Since Juan rightfully took offense at them, the brave young woman resolved to take bolder steps to reduce the distance between them. With an impetuous wave of fiery blood, she would melt the ice once and for all. One day, Juan received the following brief, expressive epistle:

"Forget the past, and attend to the present. The present is that you are the man of my dreams, and I love you. Please don't ask me why I have changed, or lose yourself in long psychological speeches. I couldn't tell you myself. My heart has spoken: that's all there is to it. Do you want to know what it's saying? I'll be waiting for you tonight at the Royal Theater."

"A good sign!" exclaimed Juan when he received this expressive epistle. "The spirit of the species has made amends with me."

Not for a single moment did he feel the wretched temptation to throw Elvira's old rebukes back in her face. Instead, he rushed to the appointed place and resumed their interrupted relations with more hope and affection than ever.

And they married, and were happy. And they say that the spirit of the species never regretted his deed when, years later, he saw their beautiful, robust progeny.

THE NATURAL MAN
AND THE ARTIFICIAL MAN

The following conversation, of interest for many reasons, took place in Paris in the spring, unfolding on the lively Boulevard Montmartre in the free expanse of an open-air café.

At a small table under a protective polychrome canopy sat a gentleman of about thirty-four years, tall and dark with an unfurrowed brow and alert, intelligent eyes. Between sips of coffee, he was distractedly reading a daily paper, casting furtive glances at the open part of the *trottoir* from time to time. There before him, in a endless, colorful procession, filed hustlers, lazy flaneurs, graceful women, and neat, well-dressed girls.[1] To satisfy our reader's natural curiosity, let us say straight off that the person in question was don Jaime

1. *trottoir,* sidewalk; *flaneur,* a person strolling through a city for pure pleasure

Miralta, a Spanish expatriate. A celebrated engineer, he directed an important, highly accredited manufactory of electrical devices.

Suddenly, through a random glance, his attention was drawn from his newspaper to a severely dressed man at a nearby table. The stranger had a grave, solemn air about him and was wearing Spanish mourning clothes.

"I know this man," thought Jaime. After running through his memories, he recognized the newcomer as his old classmate and opponent at the Athenaeum, don Esperaindeo Carcabuey, the baron of Vellocino.[2] After returning his old companion's look, his neighbor suddenly rose from his seat and rushed over to greet him effusively, exclaiming:

"What? . . . You, here? What a pleasant surprise! Tell me . . . What's happening in your life? Six years without any news! I knew that as a result of the persecution you'd been subjected to, you had left the country . . . but I thought you were in America . . ."

"Well, as you can see, my dear Esperaindeo, I'm now living in Paris, and I'm living extremely well. I've become a brand-new industrialist, profiting from several patents I hold for the invention of some electrical devices and a few million francs I've earned in a fair fight. But what the devil brings you to Paris all by yourself? I thought you'd become some grandee, delegate, or conservative senator in Madrid, the flower and ornament of aristocratic salons and charitable organizations, the staunchest advocate of governmental authority aligned with social order and religion . . ."

"Look, don't try to get back at me with irony, things really couldn't be any worse! Ah, if you only knew! I'm so unhappy, so terribly unhappy!"

---

2. An athenaeum is an association where controversial scientific and literary issues are discussed. It is worth noting that in all of Cajal's stories, the characters' names have a particular resonance. Here "Miralta" sounds like "looks high," whereas Carcabuey suggests "ox-head," or worse, "caca de buey," "bullshit." "Esperaindeo" suggests "esperanza," Spanish for "hope," and "in deo," Latin for "in God." Taken together, the first and last names imply that it is foolish to place all of one's hope in God rather than taking active measures to solve one's own problems. For Cajal, though, individual initiative and religious faith were not mutually exclusive.

"What? You, unhappy? A young man like you, an only child, heir to a substantial fortune, the model of Christian virtues and image of gentleness and humility, and married to perhaps the saintliest, most devoted daughter of the Church . . ."

"Don't talk about my gentleness, for God's sake! It's cost me everything . . . Look . . . You have no idea how happy I am that I've run into you. You're catching me in the midst of a real psychological crisis. In my mind, a lot of things are starting to come apart that I'd thought were fixed and axiomatic. And you're going to help me . . . yes . . . because only a self-made man like you, created by his own efforts, blessed with powerful individuality and invincible energy, can give me the help that I need . . ."

"My good man, you've got me on tenterhooks! What's wrong? Tell me . . . you can trust me. You know very well that, despite our differences of temperament and intellectual taste, I've always regarded you as a good friend . . . Even more than that: I've always seen you as a man who had a heart of gold, but whose noble impulses couldn't overcome the errors of education or the poison of religious dogma. I'll never forget the generosity and zeal you showed, working to acquit me in that wretched trial when I was accused of violating the censure laws . . .

"So sit down . . . tell me everything. I don't have anything I need to do this afternoon . . . and even if I did . . . It's so wonderful to hear about our own country and friends after so many years away from it all!"

"I really appreciate your kindness. I expected no less of you. Even though your radical politics and freethinking made my family dislike you, I always respected and admired you . . . Maybe it's because I saw in your moral foundation so much of what I lacked in my own: an honest, enlightened mind and an honorable will dedicated to the cult of goodness and truth . . . Jaime, my friend, I want to tell you everything . . . to confess all the weaknesses and memories that until now I've never had a chance to express.

"My life is a clinical case history that you should hear and think over as a doctor and psychologist, to see whether you can't offer some saving remedy. I'm a poor victim of a bad education who has had his eyes opened by misfortune . . . eyes that had never before seen the reality of things. When I think now about my ideas and feelings, I realize that I'm not a person acting under his own free will who has come into this world to contribute something to our common culture and social welfare. I'm just a puppet whose strings are being pulled by the living and the dead, just one more repeated, interchangeable copy of that great edition of the human book written by tradition and printed and published by habit. I'm not—well, I'm not an *I*. I'm everything but that, the *not-I* of the philosophers.

"I am just a lowly article manipulated by all hands but my own. I am just soft wax, on which suggestion, authority, and education have printed whatever they wished, for the feeble elasticity of the raw material was never strong enough to erase those deformative marks or generate one original, spontaneous fold. God knows, if my life has been a failure, it's not my fault. Other people loaded the cannon; I, a mere inert ball, could only follow the trajectory they calculated. But the seditious, skillful gunners aimed wrong, and instead of sending my body into the Paradise I had dreamed of, they smashed me into a rock. And in the meantime, the damned teachers have been so contented, so satisfied! But let's not digress, here, let's get to the point. And don't you smile at me if you find some very realistic detail in the story I'm about to tell."

After looking up at the sky for a moment, as though to illuminate his blurry childhood memories, Esperaindeo continued:

"Well, sir . . . my sad fate affected even the act of my conception. My mother, who had been sterile up to age fifty, was determined to have a child. Seeing that the saints were not about to grant her this privilege, she consulted a famous doctor, a specialist in reproductive disorders. With my father's approval, he proposed artificial insemination. So I'm really the son of my mother and a syringe.

"To prevent a miscarriage of this almost miraculous fetus, my mother swallowed no end of medicinal concoctions and heard God knows how many Masses, sermons, rosaries, and prayers. But despite all this divine help, it took the violence of the forceps and ergot to pull me into this world.[3] I can only hope that no lasting impressions have been made on my head any more deforming and severe than those of that obstetric instrument!

"During my first months, they bundled me up in tight, heavy warm clothes that restricted my movements. They bottle-fed me and raised me on milky wheat paste, and my mother, totally devoted to her son's care, refused to let me breathe any fresh air during my first three years for fear of the cold and the germs. The only exceptions were the day of my baptism, when I got a splendid case of typhus, and my confirmation, when I caught diphtheria.

"As soon as I started walking and talking for myself, the people around me filled my imagination with abstract concepts and images of invisible beings who lived up above, rather than awakening my sleepy mind with some clear, basic facts about the reality down here below. Between prayers, they exhausted my memory by telling me absurd fables, stories of demons, and the lives of the saints . . . tales essentially contrary to the principles of natural causality, and much more likely to make a child think that the laws of the world can be suspended at the whim of some celestial being.

"By the time I was ten, I was a pale, weak, sickly little boy, rather like a plant that's been raised in a cellar. To protect me from diseases and bad company, they never let me run and play with other boys my own age. I remained in this state of mental and moral virginity until I was eleven, my memory filled with ghosts and mystical concepts that eluded my understanding. I never possessed one single, distinct image of the world, which seemed to me like a vague, mysterious dreamland full of terrifying nightmares.

"At this point, they decided I was ready to begin my secondary education at a Jesuit school. There I learned to read Latin and Greek, the

---

3. The hallucinogenic fungus ergot was used in the nineteenth century to induce uterine contractions.

languages of the dead, and to look down on French and German, the languages of the living and vehicles of modern culture. In those classrooms full of mysticism and the odor of snuff, I acquired an attitude of aristocratic disdain toward the secular sciences: toward mathematics, physics, natural science, and biology, the source of people's wealth and well being. At the same time, I developed an exclusive, fanatical passion for rhetoric and the humanities, especially theology, which Donoso Cortés has called the "first and most noble of the sciences, the universal science par excellence, the one that contains and embraces all disciplines, human and divine." To tell the truth, I never saw very far into my professors' ingenious arguments, which were based principally on Saint Thomas's philosophy.[4] But I considered them excellent and irrefutable, for who would ever have suspected that such learned men of such unblemished virtue could deceive me and themselves?

"Besides, with my personality as a pasty-faced, artificial man, open to any sort of suggestion, I never saw the need to question them. My head became a kind of carafe that unconsciously admitted anything my attention funneled into it. The concept of natural law was completely alien to me, and I looked at the world as one endless miracle, swallowing all the tales they told me of supernatural events without the least touch of indigestion. Bitter experience has shown me that we scorn or detest what we don't know or practice enough. And I, who had never used my reason, ended up hating it, even more so once I learned of the infinite errors and ungodly acts men had committed when attacked by the insane desire to think. In the end, why think? I asked myself. It's so much easier just to believe . . . and besides, it's so much quicker, so much more sparing of cerebral fuel!

"I had a good memory, and they developed it even more through

---

4. Spanish orator and politician Juan Donoso Cortés (1809–53) was a descendant of the sixteenth-century explorer of Mexico. Saint Thomas Aquinas (1224–74), an Italian monk of the Dominican order, systematized Catholic theology. He developed Scholasticism by trying to reconcile Catholic beliefs with Aristotle's philosophy, which he defended as valuable to Catholics.

continuous exercise. One must admit that my teachers were rigorously logical. Given their far-reaching concept of life—a preparation for death—didn't it open the way to heresy and compromise men's eternal salvation to develop a spirit of independence or a critical sense in their pupils? And didn't it protect men from attacks of doubt and willful errors to wear down philosophical personalities by constantly suggesting how weak and inappropriate individual judgments are, as sources of metaphysical truth? And to compensate, didn't it help to fill pupils' minds with pious doctrines, showing the norms and precepts of Christian morality? Wouldn't it guarantee them inalterable calm in this life, and everlasting bliss in the next?

"Since the guiding light of revelation and Christian philosophy had completely cleared up all essential questions about cosmic mechanisms and man's nature and purpose, it seemed that engulfing myself in the analysis and contemplation of worldly, perishable things was sheer frivolity, a crazy desire to scorch myself in the flames of hell. Naturally, I had no desire to get scorched. Not for nothing did I have a Christian father and mother; learned, zealous spiritual guides; and an income of eight thousand duros a year!

"Without too much trouble, you'll be able to guess what remarkable progress I made in rhetoric, history, religion, and scholastic psychology, and what middling—or nonexistent—progress I made in physics, chemistry, physiology, and natural history. These latter sciences were taught by two reverend Jesuits who interpreted the Bible so shrewdly and ingeniously, they could prove that microbes, X rays, and the circulation of the blood had all been faithfully foreseen in the stories of Genesis and the flashes of revelation to Saint John, though in an esoteric form that could be understood only by geniuses.

"In my desire to show off my memory and lay in a stock of weapons for my future eloquence, I would spend my vacations immersed in the writings of the Church Fathers, mystics, and Christian apologists. I guzzled down all the anthologies of their sayings, their images and metaphors describing the heroism of the martyrs, the miracles of faith, the perpetuity and civilizing mission of the Church, and the profundity and supreme clear-sightedness of ecclesiastical philosophy. I used to spew out these phrases in continuous, flowing streams, declaiming them in emphatic, resounding tones. Knowing my childish love for pompous, turgid speeches, my teachers chose me to speak for my fellow students at the solemn academic and religious festivals in honor of Saint Ignatius, which were attended by the cream of the school's aristocratic clientele.

"I can still remember the wild enthusiasm I produced one evening when we were celebrating the Sacred Heart of Jesus. In less than half an hour, I unloaded on those people the whole, undigested cargo of ratty flowers crammed into my memory. It was madness! When my speech was over, one of the haughtiest upper-class women was seized by mystic fervor and began devouring me with kisses, calling me a *pillar of the Church,* a *chosen vessel,* and a *hope for the good cause.* The truth is that when it came to recitations, I was a genius. My inventiveness was like a gift from God!

"Once I turned seventeen and passed my preparatory courses, I began studying law at the university. Law put even more distance between me and Nature. To my belief in a *miracle-world,* I now added the fetishism of written law. Each legal precept struck me as something real and immanent, something that transcended human conventions and the material interests of the masses. When viewed through the pages of codes and laws formulated by pedantic theorists in their ivory towers of subjectivity, the image of real man, with his impulses, interests, and passions, grew so dim that it almost disappeared. Naturally, with my traditionalist feelings, I felt that human laws were simple, practical interpretations of divine ones, and I regarded legislators and judges as mere delegates of the Church. I believed they should formulate laws and administer justice in its name, not in that of the people or the king.

"Once I had finished my studies, the whole world seemed to smile upon me. My powerful vocation and passion for glory sent me flying into battles of words. At first, as long as I restricted myself to lectures at the Luises and other ultramontane strongholds, I found my path strewn with roses.[5] But unfortunately, my teachers at the Jesuit school and university believed they had found a vigorous defender of the faith and a fierce, magnetic orator. With the best intentions, they urged me to defend the principles of the *Syllabus* and scholastic philosophy against the militant rationalism of academies and athenaea.

"Normally, my memory would have gotten me through this arduous task. My speeches were a mosaic of fragments skillfully glued together so as to hide the joints. In them I interwove entire sentences I had taken from Bonald, de Maistre, Raulica, and Donoso Cortés with phrases from Balmes, Ortí y Lara, Brunetière, Pidal, Mir, Fajarnes, and Polo Peyrolón.[6] I learned by heart all the arguments that these writers wielded against desolating positivism, bearing in mind all the reasons and allegations proving the reality of biblical revelation, the divine origin of life and mankind, the supernatural character of language, and the redeeming mission of the Church.

"To accommodate myself to my role models and the predominating taste of our Catholic polemicists, I feigned unspeakable hatred and disdain for Büchner, Draper, Moleschott, Vogt, Darwin, Haeckel, Bain, Herbert Spencer, Wundt, etc., who struck me as materialists and athe-

5. "Ultramontane strongholds" were intellectual discussion groups dominated by political and religious conservatives, strong defenders of papal authority.

6. Here Esperaindeo lists prominent French and Spanish theologians known for their rhetorical skill: French writer Raymond Bonald (1600–1653); French philosopher and politician Joseph Marie de Maistre (1753–1821); Italian philosopher and rhetorician Joaquín Ventura de Raulica (1792–1861), a Jesuit priest; Spanish philosopher Jaime Luciano Balmes (1810–48); Spanish philosopher and publicist Juan Manuel Ortí y Lara (1826–1904), known for his arguments against positivism; French Academician Fernand Brunetière (1849–1906), the editor of *Revue des deux Mondes;* Spanish orator and politician Alejandro Pidal y Mon (1846–1913), a lawyer who used his rhetorical skill to defend Saint Thomas Aquinas's teachings; Spanish writer Miguel Mir y Noguera (1841–1912), a formidable orator and devout Catholic; and Spanish philosopher Manuel Polo Peyrolón (1846–1918), who promoted Catholic beliefs and attacked evolutionary theory.

ists in disguise.[7] To chastise them as they deserved and my grandiloquent oratorical skills demanded, I diligently accumulated the most
appropriate adjectives, like *perverse, base, vile, crude, fetid, nauseating,
repugnant, concupiscent, low, sensual, execrable, abominable* . . . Nor did
I have to look very hard for correspondingly pious and humble words.
I found them in the gentle, beatific homilies of our bishops and the
polemical speeches of our Thomists.[8]

"But a strange thing happened. No matter how hard I tried to scrape
up some epithets of this type in the works of foreign neo-Thomists
(writers from Lovaina's school, for example), my efforts were fruitless.
From this I gathered that in matters of faith and intolerance, our Christian polemicists are far more advanced than in matters of courtesy and
politeness. I have to admit that at that time, there was a current of real
hatred pulsing under this Christian student's rhetorical indignation,
which was so highly celebrated in the gallery.

"It was impossible for me to conceive of a materialist or freethinker
as anything but a low, crafty, sensual being capable of any sort of crime,
a perpetual candidate for a prison or penitentiary. They had taught me

7. Esperaindeo now lists the best-known nineteenth-century materialists and positivists.
Materialists believed that eventually physical laws would explain human consciousness so
that there was no need to invoke an unknowable "soul." Positivists believed that increasing
scientific knowledge would steadily improve people and societies, leading them toward a
higher moral state. German physician and philosopher Ludwig Büchner (1824–99), one of the
greatest advocates of materialism, created great controversy with his atheistic book *Force and
Matter* (1855). British naturalist John William Draper (1811–82), who studied light and photography, was antireligious and offended many Catholics with his *History of the Conflict between Religion and Science* (1875). Physiologist and philosopher Jacob Moleschott (1822–93)
argued in *The Circuit of Life* (1852) that thought and emotion had a material basis. Norwegian
novelist Nils Collet Vogt (1864–1937) wrote novels severely criticizing the social order. British naturalist Charles Darwin (1809–82) argued in *The Origin of Species* (1859) that species had
evolved by natural selection. German embryologist Ernst Haeckel (1834–1919) was the main
disseminator of Darwin's ideas in Germany and proposed that all organisms had descended
from a single unicellular ancestor. Scottish psychologist and philosopher Alexander Bain
(1818–1903) hoped to ground psychology in neurophysiology. British philosopher and sociologist Herbert Spencer (1820–1903) tried to unite biology, psychology, and sociology into a
single body of knowledge. German psychologist Wilhelm Wundt (1832–1920), author of the
influential *Principles of Physiological Psychology* (1873–74), founded the first European laboratory for experimental psychology in 1879. All of these men's ideas would have been offensive
to someone who believed people were endowed with immortal souls whose workings science
could never explain.

8. Thomists are followers of Saint Thomas Aquinas.

that in heretics and unbelievers, virtues are vices, flashes of pride or hypocrisy or long-term effects of their old Christian upbringing, and I believed it in good faith. Still, before long, experience showed me that individual behavior depends upon character. It says much more about the quality of one's education and the balance of one's passions than about one's religious creed. To sum up the moral physiognomy of this innocent defender of the faith at the Athenaeum, I would have to say that I was Catholic by habit and suggestion; ultramontane by imposition; imprudent and immoderate by imitation; and a flowery, rhetoric-loving orator by prescription.

"Well, as I've been telling you, it was no bed of roses. My debates at the Athenaeum brought me my first real troubles and disappointments. And you, despite the restrained, exquisitely courteous way you treated me, you really put the screws on me with your cold, steely, robust criticism."

"Bah! When I was there, I was just as scared as you were. Just let me tell you—"

"You know that whole part of my life perfectly well. If you remember, an essay called 'The Absurdity of Positivism and Evolutionary Theory' was proposed for discussion in the Division of Political and Moral Sciences, and I was its willing, arrogant defender. If only I hadn't done it! That essay was an outpouring of animosity, sectarian rage, and unspeakably violent language. A threatening cloud of individualists, rationalists, materialists, positivists, Kantians, anarchists, socialists, even opportunists and conservative-liberals clamored for the floor, berating me and yelling like maniacs. Once they had it, they took turns attacking all the weak points of my speech: the paradisiacal innocence, the intentional omissions, the scientific and philosophical deficiencies, even the presumptuousness and audacity of its form . . . They reduced my brand-new, artificial rhetoric factory to rubble, and in passing lavished the most scornful irony and contemptuous allusions on the defender.

"Unfortunately, those bitter words were directed at me for good reason. As always seems to happen, they were going a little beyond the level of the attack, responding to a series of imprudent challenges and sharp invectives I had been leveling at freethinkers and Masons in general and materialists in particular.[9] I am not a cool, self-possessed person, and burning with holy indignation, I responded furiously, using all the beautiful phrases and commonplaces stored up in my memory. But unluckily, my stockpile gave out on me. I had to fall back on rehashed arguments, while the arsenals of my adversaries seemed always replenished and replete. As is often the case, since I lacked good arguments and substantive knowledge, I tried to get out of the fix I was in by resorting to outbursts of feeling and terrifying jeremiads.

"One day, with a heroic attitude and a tragic face, I drew myself up in the chair and strung together all the prepared phrases I could remember. I declared that positivistic and evolutionary doctrines mock and degrade man, lowering him to the condition of a brute, and that they dry up our noble thirst for the ideal, the guiding star of our existence. I said that they kill the hope of the poor and unfortunate and that they exalt clever wickedness, the most hateful kind of wickedness there is. I said that they destroy the roots of morality, which lie not in the low ground of utility, but in the higher ground of obedience to the Ten Commandments. And I said that finally, once they were established as the norms of practical life, they would lead to a general overflow of antisocial passions, a total anarchy of willfulness, a state of abject savagery from which our faith in God and the living light of the Gospels redeemed us centuries ago . . .

"My ratty rhetorical flowers, upbraidings, and arrogant phrases were warmly applauded by traditionalists and supporters of the Church. But ah! Their applause did not convince me. Despite my eloquence and the enthusiasm of these co-believers, one fact was plainly apparent. As the anarchists, materialists, and Darwinists challenged the authority of the

9. Descended from medieval associations of itinerant stoneworkers, modern Masons have retained the system of secret signs by which members have traditionally recognized one another. Because of their secrecy, the Masons have been accused of being antireligious and being involved in endless conspiracies. Masonic lodges, however, exist only to promote brotherhood among their members.

Bible, the divinity of Jesus, the infallibility of the pope and the Church, the superiority of Christian morality to that of other religions, the harmony of science and revelation, the proclamation of charity as the only solution to social problems, etc., most of their objections remained strong or were only very weakly or loosely refuted. My natural candor, stronger than any feelings of self-love, would not let me create any illusions. Because I had been forbidden to do any spontaneous critical thinking and had prepared myself with pure philosophical, defensive erudition, my intervention in these debates turned into a complete fiasco. Once the heat of battle had passed, some of my most loyal friends, whose sincere, robust faith had not eclipsed their reason, must have realized it as well.

"Defenders of dogma are notorious for knowing less about science than freethinkers do about religion. What a great variety of strategies they had for their attacks, and what a vast wealth of arguments! I would never have believed that the destructive force of modern philosophy had penetrated so far and so deeply. For each controversial objection that our beloved texts had foreseen, they had a thousand original rebuttals from the ever-renewed fields of geology, physics, and sociology, even contemporary metaphysics and psychology.

"For example, we denied that life could have developed the sublime instrument of language of its own accord, through a process of evolution. But they cut us off, citing the existence of rudimentary phonetic languages in apes, dogs, and many other animals. They showed us the transitional steps between the systems of expression of civilized men and savages and told us about human tribes so crude and degraded that they lack abstract words, they can't count past five or six, and their lexicon consists of only a few sounds. We arrogantly proclaimed the universality of the belief in God and the immortality of the spirit, and they gave us an infinite number of strange names of primitive peoples in Africa or America who led a purely vegetative life, lacked even a shadow of religion, and were besotted by the most abject fetishism.

"We sang fervent hymns to the infinite wisdom of the Creator and the inexpressible harmony and beauty of Nature, and they mentioned I don't know how many animals that had been simplified through parasitism or adaptation: eyes that don't see, muscles that don't work, incredible monstrosities, bizarre cases of atavism. Finally, they talked to us about tapeworms and microbes, whose sad mission is to sacrifice the King of Creation, after inflicting the most cruel tortures upon him.

"Solemnly we denied evolution, demanding that the Darwinists and Haeckelians show us the morphological transitions between the species living today. We asked to see the transitional form between a reptile and a bird, for instance, or between an orangutan and man. Well, they responded by throwing our ignorance right back in our faces, describing a strange, ugly-looking fossilized animal, the *Archaeopterix macrurus,* a sort of lizard with feathers that combined the features of birds and reptiles. Then there was the ape-man of Java, with a cranium halfway between that of an orangutan and a Malayan man.[10]

"We defended the unity of consciousness and the doctrine of free will, and they overwhelmed us, describing a vast number of cases of hysteria involving double or triple personalities. They cited a whole legion of physiologists and philosophers whose experiments demonstrated the sovereign power of hypnotic suggestion and the possibility of completely abolishing the free exercise of the will.

"Finally, we proposed that universal remedy for social ills and inequities, the charity of the rich and the resignation of the poor. But they told us that remedies that had failed for eighteen hundred years were not remedies, but jokes, and that the real panacea was not piety, but justice . . ."

"As a matter of fact, I remember very clearly all the trouble you had defending yourselves against adversaries you didn't respect. But let me

10. The *Pithecanthropus erectus,* a fossilized ape, was discovered in 1849 by Dubois (Cajal). Eugene DuBois (1858–1940) found the fossilized hominid *Pithecanthropus erectus* in Java not in 1849, but in 1891 (translator). The *Archaeopterix macrurus* is the oldest known fossilized bird. It has a long, reptilian tail and was cited by Darwin in *The Origin of Species.*

tell you something: your defeat wasn't caused so much by the weakness of your dogmatic position, as by the erroneous tactics you used. Who would ever have thought of fighting Darwinists and positivists with arguments from Saint Thomas?

"In a debate, as soon as your opponents discard revealed texts and reject tradition as a sure way of illuminating scientific problems, you, too, have to leave the ground of scholasticism and enter the arena of biological research. Scientific theses can only be fought with facts or scientific induction. If you'd adopted a more graceful attitude, arming yourselves from the inexhaustible arsenal of paleontological, zoological, embryological, and physiological facts, you couldn't have helped but win. There one finds weapons for all arguments and tastes, to fit the most contradictory theories . . ."

"Unfortunately, though, I couldn't enter that new ground, for it was completely unknown to me. To know how to scrutinize Nature and perceive its revelations, you have to love it, and my mental outlook—ruined by education—inclined me to do exactly the opposite. In those unforgettable debates, I showed everyone I knew my classics by heart, and could effortlessly recite the eloquent prose of Father Mir or Bishop Cámara.[11] But frankly, I think it's an arduous task, even for a solidly built, original, well-organized mind, to refute evolution, a doctrine that has inspired the thought of almost every scientist today and transformed every field from geology to sociology . . ."

"You're certainly right about that, and I would hasten to add that the task will get harder each day. Science has been cultivated by thousands of lofty, independent spirits. Its volume of positive facts keeps growing unceasingly, and with them its means of doing battle. Faith, on the other hand, has kept to its rigid old formulas. It has remained stationary, still brandishing the battered sword of Aristotelian and scholastical logic, a kind of Bernardian sword that modern scientists and thinkers regard with Olympian disdain, if not poorly concealed

---

11. Spanish theologian Tomás Jenaro Cámara y Castro (1847–1904) attacked the materialist arguments in Draper's *History of the Conflicts between Science and Religion.*

amusement . . . But please keep on with your story, and forgive my interruptions . . ."

"Well, as I was saying, I wasn't terribly satisfied with playing Saint Thomas's apostle, a task far beyond my scant efforts. So, lacking the motivation to discover any new levels of polemics, I hurled myself into the arena of contemporary politics. Naturally, I sided with the ultramontane contingent, and they didn't receive me at all badly. My reputation as a champion of the ideal and my old-school Christianity—minted with the original stamp and free from any liberal rust or defects—opened the doors of many clerical discussion groups.

"With these credentials, I was able to enter the mansion of a highborn, eloquent man, at whose soirées benevolent funds were apportioned, districts were assigned, and bishops were appointed. This character, who was certainly no fool, must have sized up my natural candor and gentle, submissive air right away. Thinking, no doubt, of making me his tool, he got me appointed as the representative of a rural district. This generous mentorship made me that political boss's puppet. It was God's own fault that I knew nothing but tutelage and texts. Until now, I had cobbled my speeches together with passages from Fray Ceferino and Padre Cámara, but now I had to take my boss's words as scripture.[12] He deigned to plan the most minute details of my speeches, extending his generosity so far as to compose rotund, grandiloquent sentences; manipulative, Machiavellian phrases; even clever personal references, all expressly for me.

"As you'll remember, my campaigns in Congress constituted a whole new kind of error. I was a solemn expounder of pompous phrases and rigid structures, and I knew nothing about men and their petty snares and passions. I was thus incapable of adapting myself to the cunning twists of parliamentary tactics. Now that we've lost our faith in great ideals, our parliamentary battles are no longer about social utility or

12. Fray Ceferino (198–217), an early Roman pope, may have been tortured for refusing to renounce his faith.

national advancement. Instead, they are driven by egotists who want to enrich themselves and their political parties.

"For a speaker from the opposition—the hindrance and stumbling block of parliamentary governments—the immediate objective is to discredit the ministers, whoever they may be. By doing so, he hopes to win some advantage over the ministerial *leader.* In the ensuing uproar among the majority, he couldn't care less if the tournament degenerates into an all-out fight and noble foils are replaced by ragpickers' penknives.

"This is just what happened the day I made my first political speech in Congress, supporting the government policy and parliamentary faction directed by my boss. The democratic speakers, who must have recalled my uncompromisingness at the Athenaeum and distinctly clerical slant, made me the target of their bloodthirsty attacks. Their objective was to rattle me and make me lose control by using biting invective, taunting insults, even systematic, obstructive interruptions. In vain the president rang his bell to restrain the disrupters and keep my faltering, loudly accompanied speech afloat! . . . But I lost my patience and ruined everything. At last, red-faced with emotion, shaking and stammering with rage, and completely discomposed, I sat back down on the bench. I was not even able to hurl some poisoned dart at my interrupters or adopt the graceful pose of a fallen gladiator. From then on, I lost my enthusiasm for politics. I rarely joined in the debates, and when I did, it was always with fear. In the end I dropped out entirely."

"But again, you suffered that defeat not because of any lack of oratorical aptitude on your part, but because you had only navigated the still waters of dogmatic exposition. You had never seen oceans troubled by the tumultuous waves of human passion or the clash of opposing forces. You knew nothing about man with all his intrigues, wiles, and low appetites, and then, suddenly, without any moral preparation whatever, you found yourself facing the professional politician, one of the most pernicious products of European civilization. In that parliamentary storm, you were like a hunter who, without ever having ventured into the jungle or seen any wild animals except those painted in children's books, suddenly throws himself into a fight with a ferocious tiger with no weapon but a slender cane. You'll have to agree that the essentially prophylactic method of your education, a method based on systematic abstention from knowledge of the world's bitterness and treachery, was not the most suitable one for a political orator.

"With a few very rare exceptions, the men who usually prevail in parliamentary disputes are those who have been training themselves for verbal battles since adolescence. Since their youth, they have purposely sought opposition and hostility, not to persuade people to do things, but to develop mental agility and hone their diction and creative thinking. At the same time, they've been learning how to shut down that deadly, inborn emotion that restricts our field of thought, disorders and incapacitates our best efforts to think and remember, and reduces us, in the gravest, most critical moments, to a purely reflexive animal like a decapitated frog. Only by contradicting and enduring the contradictions of others from a very young age do great polemicists acquire that flexibility of mind and expression that lets them adapt themselves quickly to the thousand little incidents and phases of a debate. They learn how to improvise a brilliant response to an inopportune phrase loosed by an impatient adversary, disconcerting him with their clever, explosive replies. Like a good pilot, a true political orator must keep his presence of mind when facing the angry waves. Like a hunter, he has to know how to shoot the bird on the wing in an instant, without ever stopping to take aim. In sum: it's all a matter of practice and adaptation. You apparently felt so out of place in that cauldron of treachery and concupiscence that you never wanted to adapt and persevere . . ."

"No, Jaime . . . I firmly believe that I would never have succeeded in politics. In the arrogance and forwardness of a political orator, there is something innate. You have to be superior to feel superior. Art and education undoubtedly play some part in guiding and taming the force of an overflowing personality, that commanding, almost satanic will of a leader of men. But they can't create one iota of moral energy. Besides . . . only microbes can refresh themselves in infested media. I was ashamed of my pitiful status as a political puppet, and my delicate sensibility was repulsed by the pleasures, flattery, and indignities with which one buys personal advancement in the lowly market of parliamentarism.

"Well, to continue with my story, after my unfortunate venture into parliament, my family suffered some severe reverses. Our wealth had already been considerably diminished by generous contributions to charitable foundations, and my father now lost most of the remainder on the stock market. Months later, to crown our misfortune, a manager in whom we had placed all our trust ran off to South America with the deed to a profitable farm, the only one that remained to us. Possessing powers of attorney that authorized him to sell it, the scoundrel delivered the fatal blow while my parents were away. At that time, they were off on a fervent pilgrimage to Lourdes, busily begging the Virgin for shelter and protection in our time of tribulation.

"That disaster completely ruined us. My father, who was sickly and old, simply succumbed to the unpleasantness. My mother, torn apart by the pain, sought comfort in religion. And I, unexpectedly converted into head of household and overwhelmed by the burden of family responsibilities, found myself obliged to work, something that had never even occurred to me. Since I had a degree as a doctor of law, the best thing to do seemed to be to set myself up in private practice and dedicate myself to the tasks of the bar."

"Well done. And I suppose your friends, for the most part rich and influential people, offered their kind protection and sent a few cases your way?"

"Oh, no, my friend! Those duchesses who had applauded me so warmly at the Luises, those wealthy co-believers who had celebrated my spirited campaigns against the socialists and freethinkers, they all stopped visiting me once they knew about our financial ruin. To all my pleas for protection, they simply shrugged their shoulders and went back to their petitions, cases, and suits against the detested, roguish liberals: Salmerón, Canalejas, Montero Ríos, Maura, Dato, Silvela, and any others of the legal profession.[13] Even the most recalcitrant ultramontane lawyers chose to conduct their business before the tribunals of ex-ministers or influential political bosses in hope of being appointed advisors to the Crown.

"In vain, then, I enrolled myself in the legal college and immersed myself in the works of Alcubilla, Sánchez Román, Pacheco, Mittermaier, Martínez del Campos, etc.[14] It was useless to take on the defense of who knows how many poor devils, or to plead for them passionately and ask for their protection under the principles of the bar and the law. No, there was nothing! . . . Not even one lousy suit to bring in some bread and butter money or one miserable consultation so that I could keep plugging along! I was getting desperate! Certainly I never lacked enthusiastic supporters among my friends, people who were apparently quite sincere and praised the brilliant style of my defenses and the doctrinal richness of my presentations. They raved about the classical quotations with which I embellished my speeches, which were always well seasoned with Saint Thomas's definitions and the council's decrees. They also spoke highly of the rectitude and wisdom with which I interpreted the appropriate legal texts and applied them to the

13. Esperaindeo is referring to some of the most prominent nineteenth-century Spanish politicians: Nicolás Salmerón y Alonso (1838–1908); José Canalejas y Méndez (1854–1909), who once served as president of the Athenaeum; Eugenio Montero Ríos (1832–1914), an advocate of religious freedom; Antonio Maura y Montaner (1853–1925); Eduardo Dato e Iradier (1856–1921), who promoted the study of criminology; and Francisco Silvela (1845–1905).

14. Esperaindeo now names some well-known nineteenth-century legal scholars: Marcelo Martínez Alcubilla (1820–1900), famous for his studies of the Spanish administrative system; Felipe Sánchez Román (1850–1916); Francisco de Asís Pacheco (1852–97), who wrote on international law and women's suffrage; German lawyer and politician Karl Joseph Mittermaier (1787–1867), a liberal who represented the district of Heidelberg; and General Arsenio Martínez de Campos (1831–1900), who was active in politics.

cases at hand. But real success, the kind that is rewarded with fat hon-oraria and a well-established reputation . . . that always eluded me.

"I honestly think that here, too, my education led me astray. Aside from his talent—as far as his professional life is concerned—a smart lawyer is essentially an amoral being who couldn't care less about the ethical status of his defendants. If his client turns out to be a scoundrel, fine; if he's innocent, so much the better. But I, who was raised to hate or ignore everything sinful and blameworthy, was horribly disgusted by having to defend rash, low-life clients. I lacked the freshness, the *sans façon,* the theatrical touch needed to depict an outlaw as an an-gel of innocence and goodness. Besides that, I lacked the spontaneity, flexibility, and cunning indispensable for exploiting those thousand little incidents that arise unexpectedly in an interrogation. I didn't know how to take advantage of all the ambiguities and contradictions in the experts' testimonies so that they will work in the defendant's favor. Therefore, so as not to offend my inherent sense of righteousness or upset my meticulous orthodoxy, I defended only innocent men, or at worst, petty criminals favored by extenuating circumstances. Under these conditions, my emotional oratory—delivered in pathetic, lyrical tones—would sometimes achieve some results."

"That's so funny! . . . couldn't you see that by acting that way, you were distancing yourself even further from reality and heading for a sure fall? What would you say to a doctor who only treated curable patients? You have to take things as they are, not as they should be. In the most critical moments of life, you should remember this max-im of Feuerbach's: 'Accept the world that is given to us.'[15]

"Often, the world demands that the practice of law be either fiction or theater. So let's either become actors or give up the profession alto-gether. A man who can't see the shades of gray and complicate his

---

15. German philosopher Ludwig Feuerbach (1804–72) argued that God, as traditionally understood, was only a projection and an illusion. He attacked the idea that the soul was immortal.

moral psychology should be a pastor of souls, not a defender of criminals. In a lawyer's spirit there must be something of the fox's cunning, the sphex's insidiousness, and the lion's impetuosity and nobility. There's a reason why there are no lawyers in the book of saints, except maybe for the patron saint of the Plague . . .

"Besides, in this profession, as in all things, the prestige of the art makes up for its faults. There is real glory and supreme pleasure in transforming error into proof through a stroke of genius, or casting deep shadows over the facts of a criminal case. There's even glory in disrupting the cautious prudence of judges and juries with showy plays on words. Like a doctor, a lawyer should see his supreme goal as reintegrating a disturbed life into society, without stopping to see whether there's a criminal or an innocent man behind it. I remember the wisdom of Aristotle's words. When they called him names for giving money to a scoundrel, he replied: "I am giving it to humanity, not to this particular man." The defender of a criminal can also say, "I am defending unfortunate humanity, not a particular man, who may or may not be a criminal."

"You're right, no doubt, but I was an innocent man, a character without junctures, shadows, or hidden folds. The ongoing fictions and impersonality of the forensic ministry were extremely distasteful to me. An incorrigible idealist, I wanted to develop only the noble, generous aspect of the lawyer's mission, doing all those beautiful things that Castro writes about in his *Critical Discourse on Law:* "They [the lawyers] are the ones whose righteous decisions extinguish the fire of flaming discords, the ones who stand watch so that the public may rest peacefully. They bring consolation to the unfortunate. Through their authority, poor widows and orphans find relief from their troubles. Their houses are temples where justice is worshipped; their studies are sanctuaries of peace, etc."[16]

"Yes, of course, but Castro, who after all was a lawyer himself, is for-

---

16. Esperaindeo is citing Galician jurist Francisco de Castro's (b. 1730) *Critical Discourse on Laws and their Interpretations* (1765).

getting about the other side of the coin. He's expressing himself more as a poet than someone writing a real definition. Using the same line of thought, you could just turn your praises around, saying: 'They are the ones whose *crooked* decisions *turn flaming discords into bonfires,* the ones who stand watch so that the public may rest *uneasily.* They bring *despair* to the unfortunate, etc.'"

"Well, yes, exactly, but school regulations never required our professors to reveal the truth about the goals of our profession."

"I couldn't tell you whether it's because of some exaggerated accommodation to reality, or some mental remnant of Hegelianism that has resisted the buffeting of positive science, but I'm constantly trying to see some real, useful purpose in even the most defective, imperfect products of Nature and the spirit. This is what happens when I think about the social utility of lawyers.

"It seems to me that the mission of lawyers is to *separate things into their component parts,* like the microbes that cause fermentation. Thanks to their weakening, dissolving action, the most stubborn, badly amassed fortunes are broken down in the interest of the collective good. Because of this mission, the fierce *homo sapiens,* an ex-anthropoid who is essentially an *aggressor* like the gorilla, has abandoned the sword for the sealed document and converted his bloody battles into the subtlest disputes. Now that they've been tamed by these skillful trainers, the simpleminded litigants rush onto the field not to exchange deadly shots, but to flash banknotes, which their protectors quite naturally snap up. Among other beneficial effects, this process gives apoplectics a good, wholesome bleeding and imposes Christian humility on arrogant people. At the same time, it redirects the flow of money so that it passes from dull-witted, inattentive people into the pockets of those who are sharp and wide awake. One must realize that this is a great, Providential, equalizing task for which our wise Civil Codes provide ample opportunities and abundant weapons! Designed by lawyers, these codes naturally work to their advantage.

"Yes! In the treetops of this impenetrable legal jungle, where the exuberant branches overlap, intertwine, and oppose each other in a thousand ways, those lawyers gnaw away like caterpillars in cabbages. It'll be too bad for them if logic and common sense heed the voice of Nature and try to correct and simplify our laws! But keep on with your story, my dear Esperaindeo, and pardon me once again for my impertinent thoughts."

"Well, I'm now ready to tell you about the most painful thing . . . the shameful event that has led to our unexpected meeting . . . Forgive me if, in describing it, I conceal certain details of this disgraceful insult, whose memory upsets and inflames the most intimate fibers of my being . . .

"Disappointed by the long deferral of my legal success, and hard-pressed at times by unsatisfied material needs, my poor mother resolved to marry me to a rich heiress. I hardly need to tell you that I, a virgin in the exercise of electoral rights, saw no need to go outside the social register to choose a wife who suited my taste. So I married a woman who was an ugly, capricious, hysterical orphan, but who was also the owner of a substantial dowry in government bonds. This brilliant match was arranged for us by Father Zahorí, a counselor to my mother and my fiancée's spiritual advisor.

"But my mother and I were soon disenchanted. In that house, which was never ours, we lived like guests. Not a single cent was at our disposal. My wife's considerable income was consumed by her little luxuries, whims, and charitable donations. Raised in a convent and related to the most pious families at court, my wife spent her time performing acts of devotion, attending religious services and festivals, directing charitable organizations, and visiting monasteries and convents. Once in a while we would see each other at home.

"My poor mother was tormented by the bitter deception to which we had fallen victim, but when she gently admonished my wife for her extravagance and unjust disdain for me, her hysteria burst out uncontrollably. Without the least delicacy, she threw our poverty in our faces and ended by saying she was "spending her own money." I should have taken charge of the situation, making myself the effective head of household and administrator of my wife's estate, but my mild personality and some remnant of poorly understood dignity held me back.

"Magdalena—for such was my wife's name—valued me as one values a good painting or a well-bred horse. At church services and on walks, she showed me off like a trophy. But of any true feeling there was not a trace. Her heart, seemingly saturated with divine love, was incapable of feeling worldly love. In our intimate chats and domestic quarrels, I could sense a virile will quivering behind that frivolous soul, hostile to the interests of our home and determined to oppose all our counsels and plans.

"Hoping to restrain her haughtiness and extravagance, I appealed to the decisive authority of Father Zahorí. But he refused to have anything to do with the matter, saying he didn't want to intervene in domestic disputes or affairs of conscience. My poor mother was desperate: the loving, diligent daughter-in-law of whom she had dreamed, the one who was to care for her and ease her troubles in her sorrowful old age, had turned out to be an ungrateful egotist!

"And now for the awful, painful conclusion to my tale. Just when I least expected it, just when we had pretty much reconciled our differences, my mystical wife Magdalena, the paragon of Christian virtue, abandoned her home and fled abroad. And under what repugnant, odious circumstances! Taking advantage of one of my absences, that disloyal, treacherous woman cashed in the bonds that comprised our entire fortune, took all her jewels, and left Madrid with a little romantic dandy, a long-haired poet and enthusiastic member of the Society of Saint Vincent de Paul.[17]

• • •

17. Saint Vincent de Paul (1581–1660) dedicated his life to organizing charitable societies through which well-to-do people—especially women—could help the poor.

"And so now I find myself here in Paris, miserable and dishonored, my heart still bleeding from the recent loss of my mother. I'm here in search of that adulteress, whose whereabouts I must ascertain in order bring my divorce suit and claim—how shameful to have to say it!—that portion of her income that belongs to me. It's vile, dishonorable money, and having to ask for it does infinite harm to my self-love . . .

"I would proudly reject it if I just knew how to do something . . . if I could only work for my own success and win that economic independence without which dignity, self-respect, and satisfaction of one's self-esteem are just vain words . . . But I'm good for nothing . . . My memory is crammed with beautiful phrases, formulas, definitions, and classifications: words, words, and more words! In modern society, you don't prosper with rhetorical figures. They don't pay you for the beautiful things you can say, but for the useful things you can do.

"And the saddest thing of all is that I don't even have my faith left to console me. It has all but capsized as a result of my friends' and co-believers' devastating rejection, the poorly masked contempt of my confessors, and the general indifference of society. To crown my bitterness and disenchantment, certain facts about life and miracles recently unearthed by the Reverend Father Zahorí lead me to believe (God pardon my suspicions!) that his intimacy with my wife was not strictly limited to the spiritual realm . . .

"Thus ends my tale. With all my soul, I beg you to help me. As I've told you, I'm in the midst of an ideological crisis, a real emotional meltdown. Take advantage of this favorable disposition of my mind, if you think it's still possible to regenerate a brain that has never thought or wanted anything on its own. Help me dismantle the suggestions of pride, the fantastic constructs erected in my soul by tradition, example, and education. Make me a worker, a useful modern man. I can still feel something alive in me . . . something protesting the triple yoke of philosophical dogma, class privilege, and ritualistic thinking. Believe me . . . The puppet longs to move by itself and is about to avenge itself against all the Maestros who once pulled its strings, controlling its actions and will."

"You've been a victim," responded Jaime, "of the artificial nature of education. But luckily, there's a cure for your disease. The apt criticism with which you've judged the causes of your failures and misfortunes shows that, by some extraordinary miracle, the damage has not compromised the most intimate, vital parts of your thinking machine. Heads, like mills, grind out whatever they're given. They fed you fiction, and you manufactured ghosts. Until today you've lived in darkness, like the men in Plato's cave, exiled from the dominion of truth.[18] You only began to see reality when it started knocking vigorously on the doors of your conscience. Direct experience of the world, stronger than all the conventions of education, has swept all the ivory castles of tradition and painted scenery of faith out of your soul.

"The religious ideal is so beautiful and sublime! One might compare it to those *threads of the Virgin,* those infinitely fine silver fibers with which spiders, in autumn, connect the trunks and branches along pathways and lanes. The artist stops, enchanted, before this delicate obstacle and studies the way these bright, quivering, crystalline threads snatch golden flashes from the setting sun's rays. When regarded through this magic, luminous tulle, the mountains and trees grow soft and dim. But ah! Suddenly the rolling automobile of progress comes along, and the shining curtain falls forever. Despite all the effort exerted to raise it, it disappears in an instant, mercilessly disclosing the bare, implacable reality . . .

"Anyway, I applaud your misfortunes. Without them, you would still be asleep. And considering that your critical faculties have not been wrecked, I'll find a way to strengthen them. On the day you become a

18. In *The Republic,* Plato (428–348 B.C.) uses an allegory to explain how people are transformed by the truth. He compares ordinary people to men watching the shadows of puppets in a cave by firelight. According to Plato, achieving enlightenment is like stepping outside of the cave and seeing the sun for the first time. After this experience, the shadows in the cave lose all meaning.

man, you'll forever abandon parasitism and error, two tyrants that seem like good friends to our sensibility, but in reality are its most insidious enemies. Then you'll see what supreme, noble enjoyment you can feel! When you let your personality and talents develop freely . . . when all your brain cells, numb from disuse, join their vibrant expansions and sing a clamorous hymn to redeeming work . . . then you'll understand the sublime pride and supreme ecstasy in this profoundly religious phrase: 'I am free, I live by my own work, and thanks to my labor, humanity will have a little more pleasure and a little less pain . . .'

2

"But before describing the regimen you need, I'm going to tell you about my own life, as I offered to do a short time ago. You know nothing about it except for a few episodes. If you think about it honestly, you may find in it a lesson and a pathway to follow.

"I was born in a village in the Pyrenees to very poor parents, small farmers who could give their children no education but that offered by the public school. As soon as I learned to read and write, dire necessity forced my father (who had six other children) to offer me as a shepherd to a wealthy rancher in our neighborhood. Imagine a young boy of barely eleven years, who in school had glimpsed a great, shining Heaven of knowledge, reduced to the lowly calling of guiding a flock of almost three hundred sheep through the mountain passes and common pastures. Meanwhile, his father and brothers were sweating away, working in the fields and orchards to earn their bread.

"From that time on, my life and thought were modeled after untamed nature. What little I learned in school—some notions of arithmetic, geography, history, and literature—was enough to keep the passion for knowledge alive in my spirit, a longing for infinite truth about the world and its causes. In my heart, I resolved that my lowly condition there was only temporary and that, sooner or later, with persistent labor and hard work, I would free myself from brutality and ignorance, those terrible evils that come with poverty.

"Luckily, the schoolteacher often comforted and helped me, encouraging my hopes and ambitions for an intellectual life that better suited my taste. He was an excellent man, an indefatigable hunter. When he met me on the mountain, he would give me some book and tell me: 'Jaime, you know that I respect you, and I've always had the highest hopes for you. Look . . . for God's sake, don't ever lose the habit of reading. Don't fall into that drowsy, bestial state in which you can no longer see the wonder of things, like your poor companions down there in the fold. Keep in mind that you were born—I am absolutely sure of it—to be something more than an ignorant shepherd. Very soon I'll be able to find someone—in the end I know I'll find someone—who will take an interest in you and pay for your education. So please wait patiently, and in the meantime, keep working.

"'Living out here among rocks and trees doesn't mean living alone. All around you is the infinite, eternal reality with all its endless wonders. Explore this little world, even though at first you may fall victim to the crudest illusions. The key thing is that you acquire the habit of looking and listening, of paying attention and thinking abstractly, of seeing the great in the small and ascribing effects to their causes.'

"Oh, what an excellent friend and teacher! Oh, the tears that come to my eyes when I think of that beautiful, righteous heart, that wonderful man who brought human statues to life! Without his encouraging words, I might have just vegetated, turned into a crude, miserable farmhand amidst those rocky crags! Luckily, his kind admonitions fell on an awakened, ambitious soul. And so I earnestly promised him never to let my newborn mind grow moldy and to dedicate my free time to the observation of Nature.

"To record my daily impressions, I bought a whole lot of pencils and paper with my first year's earnings, and I made myself three thick notebooks. As my teacher had told me, an open field is a museum and library at once, where one can find pleasant occupations and noble tasks for all the faculties of the spirit. My setting was a high valley framed by jagged mountain peaks that were crowned with perpetual snows. Up above, the dark blue sky was divided, cut into narrow wedges along the horizon by the undulations of gigantic mountain peaks. Down below, in the inhabited world, the river unleashed its rushing torrents, fertilizing pastures and orchards and lapping against the poor, dull brown houses of that damp place.

"I've just said that my peaceful high valley was a museum-library, and I'll add that it consisted of three shelves, each painted a different color. The highest, or blue shelf, held books and maps that dealt with the sky, the clouds, and atmospheric phenomena, along with the stars and their orbits. The brown, or middle shelf, represented by the mountains, revealed the composition and properties of rocks and fossils and the form and origin of glaciers, lakes, and mountain streams. One could read it all in the gigantic layers of the murals along the mountainsides. Finally, the green or lower level spread polychrome pictures before my eyes. There one could observe living woods and meadows, fields and villages, the soft, mysterious charm of plant life, the magic of aromatic flowers, the impetuous whirling of birds and butterflies. And then there was man, with his instincts and passions, his reason and intelligence.

"Of the things that offered themselves to my attention, some were moving, and others were not. The latter were the rocks, crystals, and fossils, to which I dedicated my smallest notebook. The pictures on the highest and lowest shelves, in contrast, the pictures of the sky and of life, were constantly changing and forced me to record their strange metamorphoses day by day. I filled two thick notebooks with my rudimentary observations of the rising and setting of stars, the times of flowering and fructification of plants, and the developmental phases and curious instincts of insects, quadrupeds, and birds.

"Little by little, that sovereign law of the eternal rotation of things began to take root in my spirit. I became aware of the perpetual coming and going of the stars in their orbits, of the endless roaming of life, which condenses and hides itself in germ cells when cosmic conditions are adverse, and dilates and expands itself in showy, marvelous constructions when the warm breath of spring melts the snow and frees the land from its winter numbness.

"As a result of these crude but insistent observations, I began to acquire an appreciation of Nature. I began to develop an ordered, logical memory, and with it a capacity for critical thinking. Because they were a faithful reflection of living, palpitating reality, my perceptions and ideas associated and organized themselves according to the normal relations between objects in the outside world. Phenomena that were linked in the real world through unchanging laws of succession and coexistence were also connected in my brain (as ideas) and interwoven via neural pathways so strong that nothing could break them. Because I was so busy inspecting and cultivating the material world, I never felt that vague need, that indefinable longing for metaphysical dreams that is so disruptive to legitimate associations between ideas.

"This endless work of observation, along with the excitement of the objective concepts it produced, allowed a simple logic to develop in my brain. It was one-sided, no doubt, but strong and secure in its powers. When I thought inductively, it never occurred to me to ponder causal laws in themselves, converting efficient causes into final ones.[19] In the flower, I saw an obligatory precursor of the fruit; in the egg, an unavoidable condition for the development and *éclosion* of the chick.[20] To explain these phenomena or, better said, to conceive of their explanation as something possible rather than falling back on some special power or entity distinct from organic nature, I found it much simpler to presume the existence of internal, material forces in living matter. In time, science would shed light on these mysterious forces, just as it has shed light on the admirable mechanism of planetary motions, reducing it to geometrical laws.

"Only in moral matters, when I faced the difficult problem of free will, did the human spirit strike me as a plausible or at least reasonable

19. Jaime is referring here to Aristotle's classification of causes. Efficient causes explain how something happens; final causes explain why it happens.
20. *Éclosion* is the French term for hatching.

hypothesis. Anyway, if people had souls, I felt obliged to admit animals must have them as well. The crude, simple men I saw every day were still so little removed from pure animal reflexivity that any essential difference in the classificatory scheme descending from the *primum movens* seemed like an unjustifiable privilege.[21]

"The fruits I gathered in those innocent, primitive explorations of Nature later persuaded me of a truth advocated by many great educators. There is only one way to teach: to make the student contemplate reality directly, guiding him along the same path followed by the historical evolution of science (except for some abbreviations and simplifications required due to time pressure). As I see it, only reality produces brilliant ideas, fruitful ideas that can give rise to actions.

"Then there's that other indispensable factor, the teacher who develops a student's ability to observe and knows how to give him the illusion he's discovered some small detail that escaped the eyes of the first explorers. How often the innocent error of adding a new star to the heaven of knowledge has turned amateurs and dilettantes into respected scholars! When the young observer learns through bibliographic searches or tips from his teacher that his supposed conquests are really the work of an eminent past genius, he will not get discouraged. On the contrary, he will gain confidence in his own powers. He might think about it this way: 'if I've confirmed a past investigator's results today, maybe other contemporary or future investigators will someday confirm mine. So let's get to work! The field is vast, and the labor is infinite. There's plenty for everyone. Through the power of our own wills, we can convert today's clouds into tomorrow's constellations.'

"I'm sure you can see that don Enrique Fernández, that wonderful teacher I told you about, was the gentle, tireless instigator of all my adolescent ideas and feelings. Because he was an orphan with no mon-

---

21. The *primum movens,* or prime mover, was the ultimate cause of all movement in Aristotle's universe. It has since been interpreted as a divine force. Jaime refers here to a traditional scheme for classifying life, a "Great Chain of Being" descending from God and the angels down through people and animals.

ey to pursue a degree in science, that noble philosopher was instead forced to qualify as a teacher and bury himself in a small town. But he developed a great deal of love for his spiritual calling, and he practiced it as if it were the holiest sacrament. 'Since I couldn't be a great scholar myself,' he used to tell us, 'I want to make great scholars.'

"Impressed by my seriousness and the interest and profound attention I gave to my lessons, he developed an affection for me that was more than paternal. At least every two weeks, under the pretext of hunting rabbits or mountain goats, he would come and visit me in my wild retreat. When he looked through my notebooks and saw that his favorite pupil was developing a true reverence for Nature and a taste for precise, well-ordered observations, my intellectual progenitor's satisfaction was very great. He marveled that a shepherd boy could have learned to draw so accurately with no teachers but light and no models but natural objects. Encouraging me to follow this fruitful path, he would tell me, 'to draw is to analyze, to discipline your wandering attention, to observe by correcting and meditating.'

"I'm always so moved when I remember his last visit to my mountain pasture. He had just won a chair as professor at the Teachers' College in the provincial capital, having performed brilliantly in the intense competition. He was going to have to leave me, perhaps forever. We were seated on the highest part of a granite overhang, from which we could see the whole misty valley laid out before us. There in the remote purple distance was the Gratal range that separates the cold, green region of the Pyrenees from the warm, golden plains where the grapevines grow and the fig trees bear their fruit. My teacher's eyes were clouded by a shadow of that solemn, mysterious sadness that arises when things draw to a close and two hearts must unavoidably be separated.

"'My son,' he began, taking one of my hands paternally into his own and speaking with tones of infinite tenderness, 'I am going to the city to gather the fruits of my labors, but I am not abandoning you. From there I'm going to keep looking out for your education, sending you scientific books and working to free you from this distressing situation. You can probably imagine how enthusiastically I've recommended you to the mayor and the doctor, and I've tried to awaken our congressman's interest on your behalf. It will be a miracle if, among all those potential patrons, we don't find one to make a man of you, so that your life and your calling can harmonize at last.

"'Meanwhile, don't waste any time! The darkness in which you're now vegetating isn't the kind of darkness that atrophies the soul's eyes. It's the blackness of the earth in which the tree of intelligence silently extends and nourishes its roots, storing sap so that it may later push its highest branches up toward the sky. Keep studying, and study for your own sake. Pay attention to what your books tell you, but pay more attention to what Nature tells you, since it is the model for your books.

"'Keep in mind that your future depends on the degree of independence and originality with which you judge reality and the world. In the social machine, you have to be a motor, not a wheel; a personality, not just a person. Be *yourself*, not *everyone else*. Never believe too much, and get all the devils, goblins, legends, and fables out of your mind. When it comes time to think or argue, remember that the strongest position is always that of the skeptic. Don't accept theories from books as pure gold. The time for theorizing will come later, when your judgment has grown strong, developed its critical wings, and lost its youthful vulnerability to suggestion. With one voice, Nature and logic demand that knowledge be acquired in this order: first, the facts, the recording of perceptions so as to maintain the relations between them when they reached consciousness. Then you can develop general empirical laws, and finally, hypotheses and theories.

"'Your isolation here won't last much longer. But if, against all my expectations, it continues for several more years, you'll run two serious risks about which I want to warn you: verbal clumsiness, due to lack of practice; and wild, selfish individualism. To minimize the first risk, I would urge you to hold monologues without trepidation, to read aloud, and finally, to create fictional conversations, conferences, and polemics. Imagine that your herd is a big audience, and this rocky overhang is the lectern from which you're directing your words to them, explaining your observations and findings in the natural and physical sciences. Don't be afraid to talk and argue with your friends in the fold or with the smugglers and customs officers who frequent this lonely place. Even foolish contradictions and ignorant stubbornness can suggest brilliant ideas. Man is a social creature, and to get aroused, his intelligence needs the buzzing of the hive. There is no creature more solitary or individualistic than the infusorium, but even an infusorium has to conjugate with another of its species from time to time, or it will perish. Minds are the same way: if they don't conjugate, they languish and die.

"'Finally, write to me often, not just to tell me your doubts, but to practice your compositional skills and loosen up your syntax. Don't forget that in the city, fortune and power go to the one who speaks and writes the best. The respect we earn depends less on what we know than on our ability to persuade. You have to speak well to be well liked, and above all, to win people's confidence. A man who's too quiet, when he isn't taken for a fool, always spreads mistrust. In his enigmatic silence, we see the threatening stillness of a viper or a deceptive mirage of peaceful waters.

"'The second risk you run is that you may develop an unpleasant, antisocial individualism, a very disagreeable sort of pride. You must fight that tendency as you would your worst enemy. Never forget that your talents are worthless except for your society's sake and your society's utility. Keep in mind that, despite your apparent isolation, you're a cell in a national organism that sustains, educates, enlightens, and protects you. Your current estrangement from higher, civilized life is a critical stage in your spiritual development. You're a larva weaving the intricate cocoon of a thinking brain so that tomorrow you can fly through the open air of science and action.

"'When you really think about it, you're not in exile from society. Like a diver submerged in the ocean depths, you have an ample tube connecting you with the region of light and air. Through it you receive the oxygen of paternal love, the splendor of culture, and some throbs of human warmth, among which mine are certainly not the least comforting and inspiring.

"'Here I will end, my son, stressing my main point just one more time. You're unlucky; you came into this world when the whole planet was already apportioned. But don't get discouraged. If you're really worth something, if you really have some of that energy of a leader of peoples or an inspirer of souls, there will be no shortage of people to cultivate lands, weave tapestries, and build palaces for you. Like Napoleon's soldiers, you, too, carry the general's sash in your knapsack. But for society to emboss you on its shield, you'll have to create something great and incontrovertible; you'll have to struggle and conquer.

"'But before you turn your weapons against the world, try using them on yourself as sculptor's tools. Sculpt your own brain, the only treasure you possess. You lack fields to till and gardens to enjoy, so work the field of your own mind and decorate and embellish the garden of your fantasy. These are riches that human greed can never take away from you. So try to become a Croesus of ideas.[22] There will be more than enough people who will want to buy them from you. If interested, industrious men don't ask for them, then foolish men of leisure will, for men are never content to look like what they are. Well, everything I've told you here should be enough for now. Good-bye, my son.'

"In a fit of paternal tenderness, that noble old man kissed me on the forehead, and after wiping away a furtive tear, he disappeared down the steep mountain path. With all the emotion I was feeling, it seemed as though my teacher's head acquired a halo of light as it moved further and further away from me, sinking down toward the horizon like the evening star. As soon as his image disappeared, I wrote his advice indelibly into my memory, recording it with the greatest enthusiasm. That's why I can still remember it so perfectly today . . ."

"The way you describe him, your teacher is such a touching, sympathetic figure. Such an old-fashioned soul, but such a modern way of

22. Croesus, king of Lydia in the sixth century B.C., was famous for his wealth.

teaching! You certainly profited from his wise lessons! From a mile away anyone can see that your early education, carried out amidst nature under the warm sun of that careful arouser of intelligence, molded and tempered the mind of a future investigator. It created a strong, healthy sense of logic and an energetic, perseverant will."

"I don't want to gloat over your kind remarks, which I can see are motivated by friendship, but I agree that that brilliant teaching was decisive for my future. Thanks to my mentor's inspiring precepts, I was able to develop a certain intuition or critical sense, along with an aversion to supernatural hypotheses. Because of him I was able to liberate my brain, so that all through my childhood and adolescence, that time of mad, powerful suggestions, I could distinguish true, proven concepts from rhetorical disguises that looked like the truth. Almost at first sight, I could spot the distilled, artificial allegations of school prejudice, sordid self-interest, and naive sentimentalism. Unlike you, I studied things first, then books, so that the books illustrated things for me without implanting suggestions and distorting my way of seeing. When it came time to study scientific or philosophical systems, everything happened just as my teacher had predicted. Because my sense of reason was strong and well prepared, it could react consciously either for or against these systems.

"It is well known that when red or slave-holding ants take to the field, they raid the anthills of their black counterparts, capturing and kidnapping their unfortunate larva. Later, when these larva develop in the foreign nest, they find themselves enslaved without ever even suspecting that they were born free. I have my good fortune and my teachers to thank for letting me be what Nature wanted me to be, saving my will from the captivity imposed on mental life, now by the red ants, now by the black ants . . ."

"What a wonderful comparison! I'm so ignorant about even the most basic elements of the natural sciences, it would never even have occurred to me!"

"The more I think about the problem of education, the more I'm persuaded that the human brain isn't made to adjust itself to books, but to things. When a child focuses his attention on a faint copy of the world printed on a piece of paper, he retains very little and understands only poorly. This is because his attention, which seizes ideas and fixes them in his mind, has never worked with the living splendor of direct perception, only the pale light of symbols and abstract formulas. When you look at the world through other people's heads you see only man, not the objective reality of the Cosmos. For me, there's an even bigger difference between living concepts—which emerge automatically and gracefully in the mind through the direct contemplation of phenomena—and concepts called forth by the pale, mutilated descriptions of professors or texts, than there is between a photograph of nature and a photograph of a photograph. Once the cerebral machine loses contact with Nature, it works only with echoes and shadows, and its constructions come out false, weak, and colorless.

"If I weren't afraid of abusing our right to make comparisons, I would gladly compare the brain to a legislative assembly in which each congressman—each nerve cell or group of nerve cells—represents one district in the cosmos. In well-constructed, well-administered heads, as Spencer would say, the coordination between external and internal relations is lawfully established. Each representative knows the desires and interests of his district and expresses them very faithfully. But in poorly educated heads, as in corrupt parliaments full of members chosen in rigged elections, the representatives or *neurons* are all ignorant puppets elected through political influence. They know nothing about the districts they represent, nothing about political or social science except for what is written in their boss's or patron's policies, the living texts to which they owe their parliamentary seats. Because of this, when these bishops *in partibus* believe they're advocating the real desires and needs of their people, they're only furthering the ambition, greed, and personal prosperity of their political bosses.[23] But enough

23. Bishops *in partibus* are bishops living in countries of unbelievers.

of these annoying similes. With your permission, I'd like to continue my story.

"I was just about fourteen when one day my master came to visit his corrals and herds. Noticing his young shepherd's strange hobbies, he looked through my notebooks when I wasn't around and was surprised to see so many descriptions and drawings. When I came back down from the mountain, he gestured toward the bulky notebooks and asked me, 'My boy, who taught you these things?'

"'Mainly my teacher, but I also got some things from books and a little from experience.'

"'But how did you develop this curiosity, so unsuited to your age and calling?'

"'What? Don't you think skies and mountains, trees and flowers were made to be admired and known? When I'm alone up there in the mountains, they seem to look at me like someone who wants to be questioned, and I question them. By studying them very patiently, I've gotten to know a little of their language and gestures and have been able to look through the pages of their wonderful old history book . . .'

"In the end my master took me out of the fold. At that time he was mayor of that place, and he had already been contacted by my beloved teacher. Not long after that, he brought me and my parents great joy by getting the town council to pay for my education in arts and letters. I wanted to study engineering or medicine, but unfortunately for me, maternal love—which can be just as jealous as it is great and self-sacrificing—intervened and turned my vocation another way.

"My mother was longing for filial affection. At that time she was forced to share her sons' love with several daughters-in-law, for my brothers had married. She wanted her Benjamin to remain forever celibate—that is, to become a priest—so that she could live in his company and monopolize his heart.[24] And so, to appease her, I changed my course and entered the conciliar seminary in Huesca. I did it with

24. In Genesis, Benjamin is Jacob's youngest and best-loved son.

every outward appearance of submission, since there was no way in the world I would have offered my protectors the sad spectacle of filial rebellion. Still, I cherished hopes of freeing myself later on, as soon as a favorable opportunity arose.

"What joy I felt when I held books of natural history, physics, chemistry, and mathematics right there in my hands! And what noble, well-earned pride I felt when I found my rudimentary observations fully confirmed in their pages! In those books, I saw a thousand interesting problems that had been inaccessible to my inexpert intelligence, all of them admirably resolved. There was a whole, shining legion of illustrious dead men who had left their tombs to come talk to me, centuries of thinking people who had come to grant me the precious fruits of their meditations with their generous hands . . . What a delightful feast for the spirit, those three years in which I feverishly, emotionally assimilated all those wonderful astronomical, physical, chemical, and biological facts, laws, and theories!

"But I was never content with textbooks alone, even though they were generally very succinct. I also devoured masters theses, which gave me a reason to frequent the seminary library and the copious one at the Provincial Institute. Mercilessly, I plundered the theses my comrades had written over the past few years, especially the bibliography of my teacher, my dearest friend and spiritual confidant.

"But my enthusiasm for works of theology, sacred history, and dogmatic philosophy was much less vivid. Certainly I found in them some excellent moral doctrines, some passages with captivating eloquence, some truly ingenious dialectical artifices to reconcile the postulates of experience with revealed truths. There were some sublime outbursts of mystic love that scorned the earth and reached, like flowers, toward the light of heaven. But I was also surprised by ideas and tendencies that poorly matched my spirit's intellectual and emotional inclinations. It seemed as though most Christian philosophers and moralists had little love for life and the world and regarded the facts and conclusions of the physical and natural sciences with aristocratic scorn.

"Although I was familiar with the profound altruistic feeling it could inspire, Saint Paul's phrase, 'knowledge swells your pride, but charity brings you to life,' sounded bad to my ears. Nor was I pleased by a certain doctrine of Saint Augustine's. In his mystic fervor, he reproached man's desire for glory, which he said was 'like an impurity that keeps us from being like God.'[25] As if the Supreme Maker hadn't created the world for His own glory, and as if art and science—the greatest, most brilliant things the world has to offer—weren't the work of those who love fame, the worthiest sacrifice rendered to divine wisdom!

"I was filled with confusion by the dogmatists' notorious—though unadmitted—disdain for scientific truth, along with their excessive mistrust of the powers of individual reason. Why be suspicious of science, the logical, human interpretation of God's works, and mistrust man's intelligence, a reflection of the divine? In the end, logic, too, is a revelation of the Exalted. It's an innate, universal Bible, the alpha and omega of all Bibles . . ."

"Yes, but you'll have to agree that this Bible can be quite difficult and dangerous to read . . ."

"That's true, but I, who loved that incomparable moral system proposed in the Gospels, was then nourishing the naive illusion that I could ground it in the firm soil of science. But I was quickly disenchanted . . . My professors were right: God's work, when interpreted by reason, is irreconcilable with the dogma proclaimed by the Church . . . My spirit, which grew more troubled each day, became a stage for terrible battles in which light flashed out like thunderbolts in a tempest. Gradually, this intermittent, fleeting spark became a resplendent, burning torch, and a desolating conviction arose in my soul. I came

25. Saint Paul (A.D. 10–67), known as Saul of Tarsus before he became an apostle, traveled widely and spread the Christian faith. African bishop Saint Augustine (354–430) was the most important early Christian theologian, recording his beliefs in his *Confessions* and *City of God*.

to believe that the fundamental fact on which the whole, shining fortress of Christianity is based—the divine inspiration of the Holy Scriptures—is a formidable error. It is caused by an innate tendency in man: his definitive, utilitarian instinct to persist and survive.

"Once I had experienced this sober awakening, all the great religions assumed the same philosophical and ethical worth in my eyes. They all looked to me like laudable but premature efforts to clear up the terrible enigmas of life and the world. Born when science and logic were still in their infancy, how could they possibly have found the solutions to such well-kept secrets?

"But you must have been glad to free your reason from the chains of faith."

"No, on the contrary . . . When I felt the shock of that unexpected revelation, a great sadness took hold of me. I had become another man, a separate being, because it was impossible for me to share other people's illusions and hopes. In an emotional state like this, I would have heard Voltaire's sardonic laughter as a cruel profanation, something like the grotesque guffaw of a clown at a funeral. I saw myself as worthless, fallen, exiled from Heaven, abandoned to death and nothingness. I felt as if all those mysterious, golden threads had been broken, the ones that—according to our ingenuous faith—link all creatures to the infinitely merciful heart of God . . . Can there be any greater sorrow than that?

"After that I wandered alone in long, melancholy walks along the banks of the Isuela, living in the solitude of my heart like a castaway on some inhospitable desert island. Did I have the right to rob my innocent comrades of their pleasant, heartening illusion, to interrupt their rosy dreams of eternal bliss with a cruel, brutal awakening? But my tears flowed not just because of my humiliated pride or my lost illusion of another existence. I cried, above all, for the miserable smallness of frail human reason, which despite the clairvoyance of genius and the brilliant artfulness of logic, has been—and for many centuries will continue to be—a victim of the grossest illusions . . . Poor humanity, incapable of living in peace without hoping for immortality, or enduring this world's bitterness without dreaming of the raptures of a better one!

"Gradually, the strongest, healthiest aspects of my mental being reacted against all this enervating, depressing brooding. My grave psychological crisis began to subside . . . When I began to love life again, I ended up seeing in these great mirages of religion and philosophy a certain profound logic, *the logic of the necessary error, the educating error.* Nature, I told myself, cultivates, imposes, and beautifies error. Our brains incubate it even more lovingly than truth; our hearts light cheerful lamps before it; our social conscience consecrates and honors it. A deep feeling palpitates in this strange *consensus unus* of nature and the spirit, the senses and the intelligence.[26] It would be a very strange thing if this profound tendency, rooted in the very depths of our instinct, were not serving some useful end.

"'Who knows?' I thought. 'Maybe illogical hypotheses are like those rudimentary organs that have now almost disappeared but which once performed advantageous, highly important functions in the economies of organisms!' When one thinks about our future full of stupendous discoveries and unexpected corrections, the man of today seems like an innocent boy for whom illusion is an indispensable food. If one were suddenly to deprive him of his pretty toys and replace his wet nurse's magical tales with the severe maxims of science, wouldn't that mean disrupting his magnificent development later on? If the Ephemera suspected its imminent old age, would it still joyously celebrate its abundant nuptial rituals in the sun?[27]

"When everything is said and done, what do we know—poor creatures—about the purpose of life? Where is it heading, this current of protoplasm sprinkled with bits of curdled foam—the cells—in which man is the hindmost latecomer? Is its course the work of intelligence or chance? Are we moving toward truth, or toward happiness? Are we ends in ourselves, or just instruments? Who knows!

26. A *consensus unus* is a perfect agreement.
27. The Ephemera is an insect that lives for only one day.

"Luckily, as vast and dense as the clouds of philosophy may be, they don't usually descend from our brains to our hands. When it comes time to think, we may have doubts, but when it comes time to act, we feel very distinctly that whatever the ruling Principle of the Universe and life may be, this Principle can't abhor His work. He can't stop looking with favorable eyes on the way it's moving toward love, progress, and peace. From this we can conclude that loving other men, forgiving and understanding their mistakes, and enlightening one's intelligence means supporting the thought of the Unknown, wanting what God wants . . .

"When I started thinking about this beautiful, redeeming task, I soon noticed that the religious hypothesis still had a great mission to complete: to found a democracy based on the unlikely but reassuring assumption of the existence and essential equality of spirits. Religion must console the unfortunate until those happy days of human justice arrive. It must dissipate the dark terrors of death with the beautiful illusion of a splendid, final dawn. With constant suggestions of charitable, altruistic behavior, it must gradually tame the fierce impulses man has inherited from the lowest forms of animal life. Finally, it must keep life strong, cheerful, and serene until those happy days when goodness becomes an infallible instinct and justice, truth, and sublime poetry and beauty become innate tendencies . . ."

"I am truly amazed that you, aided only by the powers of reason, came to doubt revealed truths when renowned philosophers like Renan needed many years of historical, archaeological, and linguistic studies . . ."

"My dear friend, there's nothing extraordinary about my precocious rationalistic thinking. It was a simple effect of mental hygiene. If I had done what that illustrious French writer did, inhaling the incense of churches and convents all through my childhood and adolescence instead of the wild, pungent aroma of free Nature, I would never have been able to scrape all the rainbowlike crystallizations of religious ideals or the carboniferous deposits of dogma off of my brain. By the time I escaped from my high cliffs and fell into the Church, my sense of logic was already too strong and resistant, as my teacher had surmised, to be poured into the bullet mold of tradition.

"But even with this lucky circumstance and my mentor's undeniable role in creating it, there are simply some instinctively refractory natures, personalities with very little inclination toward the supernatural. I don't mean to brag that I belong to that special group of strong, stubborn minds that are resistant to suggestion and always looking toward the earth. The thing is, though, ever since my childhood I've felt a strange repugnance toward doctrines that contradict the teachings of the senses and the dictates of experience. As proof of this, I can tell you that when I was ten years old, I laughed at the idea of witches and devils. When my friends, the village boys, praised the efficacy of prayers for appeasing the anger of the elements, or extolled the marvelous virtues of Saint Osoria of Jaca for removing demons from the bodies of hysterics, it was impossible for me to suppress my expressions of incredulity. It was even less use trying to explain to me why the poor villagers have such a profound fear of divine wrath. If the Absolute rules the world according to invariable physical laws, as traditional philosophy would have it, then fear of the law is a useless, unfortunate derivation of feeling and reactive energy that could be put to much better use in a valiant, penetrating analysis of the law."

"According to what you've just said, you're rejecting the cult—the very spirit—of religion, which in spite of all represents a moral bond between man and his Creator. What's the use of praying, if the pre-established course of things isn't going to change one iota? Imploring God for something would mean vainly asking for a violation of a universal law . . ."

"Of course! That's exactly why I think that, given the presence of invariable laws, our role should be limited to studying them and fulfilling them with the least harm to evolution and life. As I've just told you, we have to blend our personal efforts compassionately into the common current of Nature, converting ourselves from the lowly beggars we've been into sublime collaborators with divine thought. In any case, let's bear the truth bravely, for only this kind of valor will bring tolerance and tranquillity, strength of body and serenity of spirit. Only through active, courageous optimism will man one day succeed in mastering those two tremendous fatalities of cosmic evolution: individual death and world ruin . . .

"If the comparison weren't so common and crude, I would gladly compare human beings to horseflies, buzzing restlessly over the skin of the soliped who nourishes them. You have to understand that the insect, which is incapable of thought, flees frightened and bewildered from one spot to another instead of calmly studying the laws governing its host's muscular reflexes so that it can foresee the lashes of its tail. And man behaves just the same way! . . .

"Well, as I was telling you—I'll return now to my story—my faith, which had never been *fired in the furnace,* decayed completely once I discovered the oddities, contradictions, and errors in the holy books. It was not helped by studying the ingenious but hopeless efforts of Saint Thomas to reconcile religious dogma with the principles of Aristotelian philosophy and the laws of natural reason. Feeling an intense patriotism as a wild, untamed Celtiberian, I followed our people's traditional practice and questioned all religions imposed by exotic peoples. I always thought that as long as we're condemned to err perpetually in philosophical matters, a national lie is better than a foreign one. We are affirmed and uplifted by the eloquence of Saint John Chrysostom or the philosophical talent of Saint Augustine.[28]

"Besides, I found the theodicy and morality of the Jewish people crude, primitive, and essentially materialistic. This race's claim that they were God's chosen people seemed even more intolerable and repugnant to me, along with their fickleness and apostasies, their haughty disdain for other nations, their barbarous hatred of Egyptian and Greek culture, and to top it all off, their lack of love and compassion . . . How is it possible, I asked myself, that in an age when the spiritual

---

28. Saint John Chrysostom (347–407), the archbishop of Constantinople, was known for his powerful use of language and his clear, direct sermons to the common people.

Egyptian, Jewish, and Greek civilizations were flourishing, harsh Jehovah chose such a crazy, furious, inhumane people as the vehicle for his word and the pedestal of his glory? And to think that we Europeans have copied from this horde of maladapted neurotics in such a servile way—the Aryan people, the intellectual one par excellence, the one that invented logic and critical thinking, discovered the planet, and created the arts and sciences. The Aryans generously redeemed us from every kind of slavery, from the crudest myths and legends, forging from them a norm for our conduct, an ideal for our spirits, and a consolation for our hearts! . . ."[29]

"Your words surprise me . . . I had assumed that like all rationalists, you were enthusiastic about the Jews and admired their knowledge."

"You couldn't be more wrong. I greatly respect those learned Jews who have freed themselves from the synagogue and incorporated themselves morally and materially into the countries in which they live, the ones who collaborate in the great enterprise of mastering natural forces and examining the deep secrets of life . . . But as for the others . . . the ones who still consider themselves a superior people and keep waiting for an avenging Messiah, the ones who are hostile toward the society of which they are a part, who put up with it exclusively so that they can be its managers and cashiers, its fearless, big-bellied bourgeois . . . those . . . As far as those are concerned, I consider them the leprosy of the European nations."

"You mean you approve of their old expulsion from Spanish territory?"

"I think that if the greedy, sordid, selfish, anti-patriotic acts of which they were accused were actually true, their banishment was a prudent,

29. In the nineteenth century, philologists decided that Sanskrit, Persian, Greek, Latin, and Germanic languages were all descended from a single ancestral language, the "Aryan" language. During the Romantic period, ethnologists invented an Aryan people (or "race") to go with this language. The French aristocrat Count Gobineau (1816–82), a racial determinist, associated the Aryan race with Germanic peoples and maintained that the white or Aryan race was superior to others. In the twentieth century, Gobineau's ideas were adopted by the German Nazi party, who agreed with him that racial mixing would undermine national strength. Jaime is paraphrasing Gobineau's ideas here. At the time, they were widely accepted. Historically, however, there is no evidence of there ever having been an ancestral Aryan race.

appropriate social measure. Still, we committed an inexcusable error with grave economic consequences when we failed to encourage pure-bred Spaniards to develop an ardor for business and the industries that were then monopolized by the Jews. Because of this, a whole cloud of Flemish, Genoese, and French merchants, bankers, and smugglers fell upon our nation, taking advantage of our stupid pride as spendthrift noblemen and leaving us without a penny . . .

"Well, as I was telling you, the state of my soul gradually became irreconcilable with the clerical profession. My conscience was repulsed by those fictions which are excused only by sincerity, so that the error is almost appealing. In the darkness of dogmatic theology, where every predicate contains a hopeless contradiction, my sense of reason, whose wings had already been clipped, was choking to death. I felt some of that terrible oppression a fish must feel when it is used to light and oxygen and then accidentally falls into the black ocean depths without the deep-sea fauna's saving phosphorescence or the habits of living at high pressures. To navigate safely in that dark sea of dogma, I needed the beacon of faith and the docility that makes one receptive to great moral impulses.

"For this reason, after I had finished my fourth year of Latin and philosophy, I bravely resolved to nip my clerical career on the bud. I went about it very quietly, avoiding any bothersome polemics or displays of rebellious, petulant unbelief. I hid my intentions from all of them, sadly taking my leave of those comrades who had been so good and kind to me. I bade farewell to my venerable professors, who, in their ingenuous kindness, must have seen a future preacher and ardent catechist in my zealous hard work and passion for philosophy.

"Naturally my parents, who were filled with anger, loudly condemned my resolution. In vain I tried to convince them that hardworking, honest doctors, engineers, and lawyers tend to earn substantially more than an obscure village priest and can thus be more liberal and generous to their families. Not even a heartfelt letter from my old mentor and teacher was enough to placate that paternal wrath, although my teacher justified my change of direction with a thousand persuasive arguments and offered the brightest predictions for the future.

"Still, my conviction never wavered; it was more powerful than the suggestions of feeling. And so, determined not to waste any time with vain disputes, I transferred to the institute at the end of that summer, making sure that I received credit for the courses I had taken at the seminary. Taking advantage of their open curriculum, I earned a bachelor's degree.

"In the meantime, though, a grave misfortune occurred. The mayor, who had been my generous patron and the sole arbiter of that municipality, suddenly died. Under the pretext that I was a troublemaker and ne'er-do-well, the stingy city council took away my scholarship. But my course was already laid out. Equipped with a letter of recommendation from my teacher and exactly enough money for the trip, I headed for Madrid, determined—God willing—to study science or engineering. And so I ended up in the City of the Bear, absolute master of myself and about thirty reales left over from the trip.[30] At last, after a good deal of pain and struggle, I had freed myself forever from the suggestions enslaving me to my family and patrons. From here on I was going to be what the English call a *self-made man, a man who makes himself, by himself.*

"But as it's impossible to sculpt souls without feeding bodies, my immediate concern was how to nourish my own. When I arrived, I found myself lost in the whirlwind of the Puerta del Sol, looking astonished at that sea of bustling, indifferent human beings. It was the human desert that Descartes saw in Holland.[31] To them, my insignificant figure was like an inorganic body, some loose block of stone that had

30. A real is worth about a quarter of a peseta.

31. French philosopher René Descartes (1596–1650) first went to Holland in 1618, serving for about a year in the peacetime army while studying mathematics and architecture. He then returned to Holland in 1628 and stayed until 1649, writing most of his major works in that country. Descartes, a Catholic, may have left France for Holland because he preferred the greater religious freedom of the Protestant country. Before Descartes left France in 1628, Cardinal de Bérulle was aggressively lobbying him to use his talents to promote Catholicism.

somehow fallen into the current. They parted around me with greater indifference than a wave, except that waves at least lick and caress the stones along their way. When people bumped into me, they looked at me—if, indeed, that was looking—with the peripheral region of the retina on which we register indifferent, fleeting images, impressions condemned to be eternally forgotten. Happy are they who, on reaching their desired haven, feel themselves targeted by the *fovea centralis* of the visual membrane, that magnificent, luminous portal to attention and love! . . .

"But I had no right to look down on these rude, bustling people. Maybe some of the ones who were disdainfully avoiding my provincial coat and old-fashioned hat were carrying the two precious pesetas I needed to survive for one day. I had to make contact with that human wave, where despite the apparent calm and coldness, there might well be some human warmth and compassion.

"Needless to say, I wanted to work, to live a great life, a noble life, one that generously repays its bread with the noisy vibration of muscles or quiet whispering of thought. Certainly I deserved protection and shelter, for I was not entering the common field of work like some parasitic microbe. I was more like a humble seed borne by the caprices of the wind, a seed that was begging those thousands of human plants monopolizing the soil and light for one little piece of free ground where it could let its cotyledons swell, one narrow little opening where it could look up to the sky and raise the modest flower of its soul . . .

"My mentor's letter of recommendation had some very good effects. Unfortunately, the director of the college for first- and second-year instruction, to whom it was addressed, already had as many teachers as he could use. He could only offer me a very modest post as a companion to day pupils from wealthy families and some tutoring that gave me just enough to survive. I had to look elsewhere for the money I needed to pay tuition and buy textbooks. By exploring and making some inquiries, after enduring months of real anguish, I finally ran across a modest industrialist who needed a simple bookkeeper. I agreed to work for him for the reasonable salary of eight duros a month, but only under the condition that I work at night, when I had fulfilled my other obligations.

"During my second year, things really started to move along at full sail. Because I passed my preparatory courses with honors, I saved the money I would have spent on tuition for the next ones. Gradually my earnings increased. My studiousness and deference pleased the director of the college, who appointed me temporary professor of mathematics and physics at a twenty-five duros a month. Not long after this, I entered the competition at the university and won a modest but very useful post as a teaching assistant for laboratory classes.

"Why go on with the details? It's enough to tell you that after six years in Madrid, I had earned two degrees, one in engineering and the other in science, and I had received excellent grades. I had also had the good fortune to win the respect of my professors, who raved about my enthusiasm for observation and my undeniable passion for teaching. I was already labeled as one of the teachers of our future generations and a real hope in the area of scientific research.

"I should have followed the course laid out for me by my vocation and aptitudes. Using my own mental powers, I should have tried to study and resolve the most difficult problems of mechanics, physics, and chemistry, especially in their relation to industry, that well-known goddess to whom the great nations owe their wealth and power. But ah! The irresistible attractions of social life destroyed my focus, diverting me from the healthy, useful, regenerative path of scientific and industrial productivity. Among these were our mania to approach problems encyclopedically, and the sensual cult of woman, an essentially Spanish disease almost unknown among the cold, hard-working men of the North.

"Once I had stabilized my economic situation by obtaining that respectable faculty post, my first concern was to complete my education by studying modern philosophy, especially English positivism and evolutionary theory. These readings did me a great deal of good, even though they distracted me from my daily work, for they refined and strengthened my ability to think critically. The bad part was that they gave me certain ideas, and as often happens, I developed a ridiculous passion to inoculate other people with them. To accomplish this, I initiated the stormiest polemics in journals, political discussion groups, and Athenaea.

"Some very officious friends of mine contributed heavily to these propaganda campaigns, deploring or pretending to deplore the fact that such a spirited, talented speaker with such outstanding oratorical gifts—in their judgment, of course—was vegetating in obscurity amidst books, swan-neck flasks, and laboratory equipment. 'Scientists,' they told me, 'should reach out to the public at large and perform some work of great social importance.' I was foolish enough to listen to them. As a result, I went to the Athenaeum to discuss that infamous essay you alluded to earlier, "The Absurdity of Positivism and Evolutionary Theory." There I declared myself the staunchest advocate of positivistic criticism and Spencer's evolutionary theories.

"It would have been best for me if I'd failed from the start in those memorable debates that received so much attention from the press. But against all my expectations and best interest, I made a big impression on the public and—why deny it?—deeply satisfied my self-love. Who isn't intoxicated by the exaggerated praise of friendly journalists and heated applause from the gallery?"

"But all modesty aside, you have to admit that you achieved great triumphs in those days as a speaker and polemicist. Your responses really stung your opponents, for they were as hard and cold as steel, yet flexible and well-suited to the style of each challenger . . ."

"Bah! I may have been momentarily stunned by the applause, flattery, and friendship of that coterie, but as soon as I could think coolly again, I was quickly disillusioned. I could see just how vain and fruitless those showy oratorical tournaments were."

"Even you! . . . the formidable debater!"

"Yes . . . I've always been a very serious, honest person. As a professional physicist, I mourn the scattering and waste of cosmic energy, and as a man, I hate the fruitless scattering of intellectual energy. The truth is that at that time, I still harbored the innocent hope that I could convince the irresolute, move and indoctrinate the undecided, and expose the vacuity and impotence of the recalcitrants. But believe me, even before I was through with those heated polemics, I had lost all my illusions as a propagandist. Why try to hide it? The real victory, the one that matters, is measured by new endorsements won and old alliances broken, and that had been absolutely nil. When the president concluded those debates with his official summary and his golden key, the speakers from the center, the right, and the left were all still sitting stiffly and solemnly on their respective benches without having changed their opinions one iota."

"I think you're right."

"For the first time, I felt my spirit painfully hurt by a sorrowful phenomenon: the human mind's impenetrability to the truth. That's when I realized that our beliefs, like physiological phenomena, are not dynamic processes that can be altered by the buffeting of scientific logic. On the contrary, they are something static and organic, some type of strong, rigid cerebral construction erected in youth and supplied with such vast tracts and powerful wheelworks that no one and nothing can move them. To block out any sort of renovating suggestion, self-interest and emotion work closely with this fatal organic structure, erecting ramparts and walls all around the preconceived system. Unfortunately, that daring phrase of the anarchists, 'tell me how much money you have, and I'll tell you what your ideas are,' is a sad, profound truth. From this you can see that to improve daily life, the only useful—or at any rate possible—thing to do is not to transform the minds of grown men. Instead, we have to explore and learn about their intellectual, affective, and muscular reactions so that we can get around them and use them in our own best interest."

"Still, in those famous debates, it seemed to me and the other speakers on the right that the impartial people in the audience were moved by your eloquent speeches, especially the people in the gallery."

"Oh, no! . . . Don't tell me that you believe, perchance, in the impartiality and neutrality of the general public! My dear Esperaindeo, I am sorry to rob you of this illusion. There is only one educable, transformable public . . . that of each particular school. The grave, noble elders who make up congresses and academies are a bunch of limestone crystals who emerged from their maternal waters a long time ago. Their facets can be broken, but never remodeled. Besides, what we call "the general public" is really a very uneven mixture of elements with highly diverse anthropological values. A preliminary analysis reveals the following psychological types:

"First, there's the *curious type,* that is to say, the man who simply wants to be entertained and amuse himself listening to all the debaters' crazy ideas. He especially likes it when, in the heat of battle, they descend to the low ground of personal attacks. This renowned dilettante prides himself on knowing and dealing with the leaders of each faction and sect, whom he enthusiastically congratulates in the hallways. In exactly the same way, he boasts of knowing and saying 'tu' to the comedians, and visiting the actors' boudoirs in the theater.[32] Aside from this, he is incapable of thinking; he has acquired all his opinions without ever really noticing it.

"Second, we have the *silent sectarian,* the man who seems tolerant and impartial because he never talks or comments on the speakers' phrases in the hallways. In reality, though, he has a stiff-jointed political or philosophical creed protected by a triple barrier of prejudices. When he comes to the debates, his main goal is to take pride and delight in seeing how eminent, talented people support and defend his common, ordinary ideas. This, of course, greatly flatters his self-love.

"Third, we have the *officious, ingratiating friend* (perhaps the most

32. Spanish has two words for the English "you": the informal "tu," which is used for friends, family, and children, and the formal "usted," which is used for adults one does not know well.

common, well-known type). This man certainly loses no sleep over the endless disputes between scientists or the chimeras of philosophy. His desire for personal gain, however, obliges him to applaud these budding grandees as future dispensers of political favors.

"Fourth, and finally, we have the rarest type, one who is almost always missing from the solemn auditoriums of Athenaea and intellectual discussion groups. This is the *indecisive thinker.* Driven by his love of truth, he attends these doctrinal discussions looking for arguments that will incline the balance of his thinking decisively one way or the other. Sometimes he's in the honeymoon stage of the recent convert, and he's asking the champions of his school to strengthen and support his new faith, which is still quite timid and fragile.

"And this, my friend Esperaindeo, is the pitiful harvest for which an honest polemicist can hope! . . . You'll have to agree that it's not an especially glorious task to convince people who are already convinced, or to convert obscure loners whose traditional beliefs have been slowly eroded by autodidacticism and the destructive pick of critical thinking. Although it may hurt our pride as witty, wordy orators, we have to admit that in philosophical, religious, and political matters, when dealing with mature audiences, the famous triumphs of grandiloquent speakers amount to no more than this: in the minds of a few, well-prepared listeners, they replace the pale light of suspicion, of vague, hazy conjecture, with the bright, purifying torch of true belief.

"Another issue that made me so weary of these fruitless battles of words was the professional orators' habitual, irremediable dishonesty. Contrary to what I had expected, an orator is neither a thinker nor a scientist, but a lawyer. On his lips, God and the soul, matter and force, evolution and regression, error and truth are mere cases to be won at all cost. Only to poor charity-boys like us would it occur to fight honestly and get really angry with these exploitive people. How incredibly silly, to shout oneself hoarse and get all worked up yelling insults, when everyone knew that the leaders of each school were just playing out some ridiculous farce! For in that parody of a council definitor, the shameless, self-serving speakers—that's what most of them were—never meant to do anything but show off their wit and eloquence.[33] In passing, they would ask the grave political patriarchs (who deigned to smile at the squabbling youngsters from their benches) for some desirable position at court or some fat sinecure."

"Well, yes, of course, but that house of learning has ended up suffering for its own sin. It's precisely because of this excessive exhibitionism and *posing* that no political party today ever recruits its speakers from the Athenaeum."

"In my view, the evil we're speaking of doesn't just afflict literary and political institutions: it's much deeper and more widespread. Despite centuries of refined culture, man—especially intellectual, modern man—still maintains the boorish psychological state of his predatory mammalian ancestors. He longs for his old life as a savage hunter and instinctively opposes any steady hard work. Generally he realizes that in almost all social acts, the *intellectual hunter* seeks primarily to assert and display his personality, only secondarily to investigate the truth and proclaim it in good faith. In the process—with a good deal of strutting and rhetorical flourishes—he informs the long-suffering public that from here on in, they will have to deal with one more parasite. If they support him well, he will be pleasant and harmless, but if they fail to respect him or force him to endure the exhaustion and tedium of intense, everyday work, he will turn pathogenic and deadly."

"As far as I'm concerned, I can only say that I share your opinion. In those doctrinal debates, nothing drove me crazier than that perpetual sleight of hand by which the original question magically disappeared, and that academic bullfighting, through which the audience's attention was skillfully diverted from argumentative weaknesses with the red cape of sentimental rhetoric."

"That useful tactic, so indispensable to people sustaining false the-

33. A council definitor is a meeting of the high officers of a monastic order to discuss disciplinary matters.

ses, reminds me of those ridiculous proofs invoked in our so-called *affairs of honor.* 'I am not certain,' says the outraged husband to the seducer, don Juan, 'about whether you have overcome my wife's virtue, but there is one way to resolve all doubts and settle the question. And that is to prove, in front of four imbeciles, that I am as courageous as you, and that I am as capable of dying of a hemorrhage or paralysis in the open air as the most savage of men.' In exactly the same way, when the grandiloquent orator has been disarmed by the bull of logic, he seems to say: 'I don't know whether the facts underlying such-and-such a theory are true or false, but I know one sure way to clear up my uncertainty, along with that of the public. And that is to show that I am extremely eloquent, that I can pull the strings of people's feelings most adroitly, and that I've memorized lots of beautiful phrases that have absolutely nothing to do with the question. Someday, these phrases will get me to the red benches of Congress, or to some useful position as undersecretary.'

"But to take up the thread of my story, which has already been broken so many times, I will tell you that a year after my disenchantment with oratory, my attention—which has always been naturally restless and fickle—was keenly attracted by something much more serious and worthy than metaphors and synecdoches. I am referring to the spectacle of pain and misery suffered by the impoverished classes. Feverishly, deeply moved, I read through the eloquent books by the apostles of social justice: K. Marx, Lassalle, Kropotkin, Bakunin, Reclus, Grave, etc.[34] As I read, my spirit underwent a harsh shock comparable only to the one I had received from my readings back at the seminary.

"In the contradictions of philosophy, I had discovered the poverty of the human mind, which is doomed to lose itself in the clouds. In these spirited, fiery vindications of the oppressed, what struck me

34. Jaime was reading the best-known nineteenth-century socialists, communists, and anarchists: German economic theorist Karl Marx (1818–83); German socialist Ferdinand Lassalle (1825–64); Russian anarchist and geographer Pyotr Alekseyevich Kropotkin (1842–1921); Russian anarchist Mikhail Aleksandrovich Bakunin (1814–76); French anarchist and geographer Jean Jacques Reclus (1830–1905); and French anarchist writer Jean Grave.

was the insuperable dryness and selfishness of powerful men's hearts. With deep sorrow, I realized that just as two thousand years of free philosophical meditation have failed to free us from the tyranny of simpleminded religious myths, several centuries of liberal political programs and serious sociological studies have not been powerful enough to save us from injustice. For the first time, my reason—which was normally quite dull—saw through the decorous appearance of a democratic, altruistic social organization and discovered the cruelty and treachery of inherited barbarism. I saw crude, anarchic individualism, by virtue of which each person's will fought selfishly to satisfy its own most ignoble appetites. No one had any regard for the weak and helpless, and no one stopped for a moment to think about social happiness and harmony.

"The strong man and the rich man are not like cells in a higher organism. In the social body, they are much more like microbes, parasites more burdensome than any described by zoology. The actual microbes, which don't want to give their hosts too much trouble, restrict themselves to destroying a few useless organs (the apparatus for crawling, chewing, protecting, etc.). The human tapeworm, on the other hand, denies itself nothing and seizes and devours everyone with equal zeal . . .

"I'm not going to describe this part of my life in detail, since you already know it as well as I do. As you'll recall, that's when I waged my socialist propaganda campaigns at political meetings and working men's societies, and my political, anti-individualist campaigns in the press. Nor will you forget that right after our national setbacks and misfortunes, I founded a regenerative newspaper. Nobody wanted to be regenerated, though, because they all measured their moral health according to their economic prosperity or their indifference to their country, among other things. And so my poor daily paper died, but not before arousing the wrath of doctrinaire liberals who could not forgive my harsh, bloodthirsty attacks on individualism. In his passionate fervor, one insolent one even wrote that 'the only thing I was trying to regenerate was my own wallet.'

"Once again I had made a terrible mistake! . . . There's no point trying to arouse people who take pleasure in just dragging themselves along. The most serious sign of decadence in a people is not in their defeats. It's in the innocent calm with which most of their statesmen take pustules for beauty spots and soft lymphatism for muscular turgor . . .

"At any rate, with the kind of passion and immoderacy I was showing at that time, I was heading for a very bad end. As you'll recall, the authorities' intense irritation with me and my newspaper's lively commentaries on the cruel repression of a strike landed me in jail, where I would have rotted if it hadn't been for your kindness and the generosity of a minister who came to my aid."

"It certainly struck me then that the liberal grandees at the university, who were supposed to be your friends, maintained the utmost indifference, leaving you in the lurch, as they say."

"That should come as no surprise . . . I've always been persona non grata in those resolute literary circles where they cultivate the freedom of thought . . . of their leaders. I've always respected and looked up to learned men of a certain kind, the ones who devote themselves to free philosophical speculation in times of obscurantism. Even when these men believed in some fantastic doctrine, some premature, false synthesis, they had the unusual merit to combine critical thinking very closely with righteousness and moral strength. But in the end, these thinkers would constitute a school, and like any other organized living thing, a school loves only its own children. I had the misfortune to grow up far removed from their teachings, coming to the world of ideas when the bright new system of deductive thinking was already melting away. Besides, the illustrious teachers of that brotherhood professed an absolute, dogmatic, unquestioned individualism, just like the standard-bearers of militant democracy. They could never have looked favorably on

my protests—which were perhaps a little too vehement and passionate—against exaggerations of the democratic principle. But in my view,
these exaggerations led to the predominance of clericalism."

"Well, you really did take a wrong turn when you tried to win over
the brand-new, authoritarian defenders of Spanish democracy. Driv-
en by some compulsion to imitate, or maybe by the bitter lessons of
exile, they always chose individualistic England as their political and
economic model. Just about the time that you made your arrogant
appearance in the arena, the free-traders and autonomists down at the
Athenaeum were commenting and chewing delectably on the dense,
specious arguments of a book by Demoulins. Blinded by his hatred of
Germany (a land undermined, in his opinion, by its functionalism
and socialism), he attributed the triumph and prosperity of Albion
solely to the pronounced individualistic, particularistic character of
the Anglo-Saxon people."

"Now here, my friend, is a book that seems to have been written *ex
professo* to keep the French and Spanish from carefully examining the
real causes of the problem.[35] Certainly no one will deny that an education bent on forging strong, well-rounded personalities that will
energetically take the initiative has been an important factor contributing to the superiority of the northern peoples. But we can't be so
fond of simple formulas as to underestimate or ignore other, much
more decisive causes. Among these, I wouldn't hesitate to mention
national *solidarity,* the fanatical cult of the hive. Unfortunately for us,
this powerful drive to organize and preserve is weak and hesitant in the
fickle, anarchistic, noisy Latin countries.

"It's a great thing to be able to develop the human personality in all
possible directions, thanks to an integral, supra-intensive culture. This
way it becomes self-sufficient and can free itself from the moral and
economic guardianship of the state. But if the fifty-armed giant Bri-

35. *Ex professo* means "professedly" or "by profession." In this context, its meaning is closer to "expressly" or "specifically."

areus[36] doesn't dedicate some of his appendages to the service and defense of his country; if no individual feels for the collective whole the same intense love that he feels for himself, then his race of *learned titans* will always be shamefully routed by legions of patriotic pygmies or heroic barbarians. This is what happened to refined, individualistic, skeptical Greece when it ran up against Roman patriotism. And just recently, it's been happening to England itself, to that cultured, patriotic, liberal land of Albion, in its fight with the semibarbaric but formidable, heroic, and synergistic Boer people.[37] History is full of other such examples."

"So are you saying that in your opinion, the intellectual and political supremacy of the Anglo-Saxon people is due mainly to their cult of national solidarity, and that all other anthropological and geographical factors should be relegated to the background?"

"Exactly. What would England be today without the courage and self-sacrifice of its great warriors, explorers, and scientists? The glorious triumph of Nelson and Wellington over Napoleon—was that due to individualism, or to patriotism?[38] Quite possibly there's no people more individualistic, more particularistic, more *cabalistic* than ours. You already know how things look around here. In social mechanics, as in physical mechanics, no useful work ever comes of forces that are widely dispersed. It results only from energy that is channeled and directed toward a foreseen end."

"If that's the case—and your reasoning seems impeccable to me—how do you explain this *functionalism* or *employomania,* the incurable disease of the Mediterranean peoples?"

"As far as the *functionalism* is concerned, I don't think it's related to

36. Briareus, a giant from Greek mythology, was said to have a hundred hands.

37. In the Boer War (1899–1902), British troops fought Dutch Boer settlers for control of South Africa. Although badly outnumbered, the Boers, who had lived in Africa for much longer than the British and knew the terrain, repeatedly frustrated the British army.

38. Sir Horatio Nelson (1758–1805) defeated Napoleon at sea in the Battle of Trafalgar (1803), preventing him from attacking England. Arthur Wellesley, duke of Wellington (1769–1852) defeated Napoleon on land.

any socialistic or individualistic tendency of the particular peoples involved. It's simply the sad result of national poverty, the bitter fruit of our lack of education and culture.

"Some may argue that the physical and mental hypertrophy of the individual citizen leads inevitably to respect for the flock and heroic, unselfish civic-mindedness. It seems natural that realizing the greatest productive potential of each individual should increase the capacity of the stream into which they all feed. But does this kind of economic prosperity really create the aptitude for self-sacrifice? If a people's life is perfectly pleasant and easy, doesn't that lead, on the contrary, to cowardice, laziness, and political indifference? Will a man who can do without the state sacrifice himself for the state? Will a people who know how to live so well know how to die? . . .

"This is one of the most difficult problems any educational system must face: not just to create great producers, but to create patriotic producers. When we're intensively educating the *human animal,* we've got to instill a vivid feeling of love for his country and the intellectual and moral patrimony of his people. As we're encouraging the free expansion of our young people's activities, we've got to impose the religion of duty and discipline—something of that communistic feeling so distasteful to our democrats—as a wise and prudent counterweight. I'm sure that if we don't, we may produce a plentiful harvest of learned men, political and scientific dilettanti, and wholesome, big-bellied bourgeois, but nothing like that robust, synergistic social body we need, one that can respond manfully and triumphantly to any sort of external aggression.

"In conclusion: the greatness and splendor of a people is the magnificent synthesis of all of their individual sacrifices and heroic acts, the sublime flowering of a plant so delicate and demanding that it can only flourish when it's watered with the blood of heroes and illuminated by the minds of scientists. The most powerful countries arise and reach their high points in history just as islands of coral emerge from the seas, crowning a strong pedestal that is shaped daily by innumerable sacrificed existences."

"Your thoughts suggest an explanation for a phenomenon I've never been able to understand fully: the meager success of our scientists and scholars in the field of personal investigation. They know how to think, but they tire so quickly. Doubtless they must lack that powerful nourishment that creates saintly perseverance: the desire for glory and the love of one's country. For I would claim—and here I call upon your experience—that when it comes to spiritual endowments, our scholars can compete with the most eminent European scientists."

"And you would do very well to make this claim. You can take the word of someone who, for professional reasons, has had the opportunity to talk intimately with a great many international scientific luminaries. You should know, my friend, that Spanish intellectuals are just as *smart* as—no, what am I saying? *much smarter* than—their counterparts north of the Pyrenees. If you can believe it, I would even go so far as to say that they gather so few laurels in the garden of investigation because they're too keen-sighted and *practical*.

"My studies of the psychology of scientists have convinced me that to devote one's existence to one great idea and triumph in the disputes of civilization, one has to be clever and shrewd enough to smell out the new facts and then determine their laws. At the same time, though, one has to be innocent and naive enough to sacrifice one's existence, pursuing things as vain and chimerical as the fine mist of glory and the gratitude of men. This unique mixture of idealism and childlike innocence, sagacity and vanity that characterizes the purebred scientific conquistador is almost unknown among our professors, who—if you'll pardon the crudeness of my diagnosis—are either too shrewd or too simpleminded."

"I suppose our excess of imagination hurts us as well."

"No, I think we're too prudent and well-balanced for madness to take much hold on us. Even if we did surpass foreigners in imagination—something highly unlikely, considering that we see the greatest creations of literature and philosophy as imported goods—this excess of imagination, in itself, would not hurt us. What's hurting us is the poor use we make of it, employing it to weave pompous phrases instead of forging fruitful hypotheses. Imagination is so crucial to scientists that people are right to keep repeating a truth I'm sure you've heard too many times already: when you're studying Nature, you find only what you're looking for. And *what you're looking for* is almost always an anticipated vision of the truth, a luminous image of your constructive imagination to which the facts end up adjusting themselves.

"Not even the worship of beauty obstructs the religion of truth. The scientist, like the lark, has to know how to fly and sing . . . Yes . . . he must fly very high and far in order to discover new horizons. Unfortunately, our talent here in Spain is much more like that of the pheasant, a bird with a graceful carriage but a very limited capacity for flight . . . But, dragged along by automatic associations of ideas, I've strayed from my path once again, and I should really go back to it."

"I'm the main one to blame here, for I've been interrupting your tale with all sorts of annoying, inopportune questions. Please pardon my indiscreet curiosity . . . Go on."

"Well, as I was telling you, because my socialist program was so helpful, harmless, and cheap, it antagonized the liberal groups who were then sharing power. My final, most bitter campaign involved freedom of education. You must remember it, for it gave you a chance to strike a gallant blow for the Church."

"Yes, I remember now . . . That article that provoked such bitter responses in the daily papers."

"Even now, I still think I was right, at least when it comes to defending the liberal State. I claimed that in a democratic system, all liberties are sacred except for one: the right to deny liberty. All collective actions are legitimate except for this one: the suicide of the ruling class. Everyone knows that social communities, like individuals, contain two personalities: the present one, endowed with certain rights and duties, and the *potential* one, like that of a future person who has only rights. In romantic terms, this means that just as a nation—personified by its ruling class—guarantees the rights of its contemporary citizens, it must show the same honesty and care in guaranteeing the rights of its future citizens, in whose name it exercises a godly, inalienable tutelage.

"All right, I thought. In the process of evolution, the most sacred duty one has toward one's young is to teach respect for the process of evolution itself. One must ensure that during the ontogenetic process, the child's brain and mental energies are not submitted to disturbing suggestions of dogmatism so that in the end, they can freely achieve their maximum critical efficacy and productive potential. Can we fulfill this pedagogical goal by putting our people's education into the hands of a single political faction, precisely the one that boasts it is already in possession of the truth and thus denies our right to free examination, imposing invariable norms on our abilities to think? Just show me the dog that abandons its pups to the wolves."

"Still, my dear Jaime, I must admit that in that debate, it seemed to me your opponents were in the right. In my view, your arguments would have been impeccable if religious institutions had demanded an exclusive right to educate and indoctrinate the young. But isn't the field open to lay competition? Who can prevent the creation of private schools run by laymen or liberal Catholic teachers? If, as you claim, the vast majority of all fathers are Catholic, I don't see how they can avoid entrusting their children's education to religious organizations without falling into the violent excesses of a Jacobinism against democratic principles."

"There the democrats and the clericalists think rightly, and in a highly significant partnership. But if, at some point, we want to come to an understanding about educational freedom, we first have to clear up one ambiguous issue. In Spain, despite all the fuss and pretensions of people who talk constantly of the *national Christian conscience* and the *neutral conservative classes,* the liberal outlook predominates. Let's be clear about this: jointly, the united liberal parties represent a great improvement over reactionaries of any kind. But when they want to bring about some social action or merely further their educative ends, they can't muster that powerful army that can be mobilized in an instant by the

233

traditionalists and the clergy in conjunction with women—who for well-known reasons represent a formidable clerical force. It would be a shameful oversight for the liberal government to ignore this dangerous moral alliance, whose goal is clearly to create generations blindly dedicated to the cult of the past and hostile to all modern freedoms.

"Women's spiritual dominance would be plausible if their educational deficiencies didn't put them a full two centuries behind men. Religious training combines with this inappreciable aid from our better halves to create economic advantages that prevent official schools from offering competent instruction. These advantages show themselves in the facilities and privileges of conventional life and in the fair sex's inexhaustible generosity toward religious institutions. Let's face it: as long as wives continue to act as priests' ambassadors in the bosom of the family; as long as the regular clergy are not subject to the same moral sacrifices and material needs as the rest of the country; as long as the liberal and democratic parties fail to prevent the absolute freedom of widows and spinsters crazed by fear of purgatory to make their wills as they see fit, they will be committing the most terrible blunder. By yielding generously and submissively to this female-clerical alliance, they are allowing them to teach our youth political views devoid of the strength and conviction one needs to govern and civilize. In their deliberations of the big issues, the innocent democrats are held back by their nunlike scruples. They should keep in mind that there is something more important than all their laws and principles, something in whose name even tyranny is justifiable: the interest and prosperity of the State, and the development and intellectual flowering of the people.

"Needless to say, my political campaigns were as vain and fruitless as my philosophical ones. It's a formidable task, fighting prejudices and demagnetizing heads stubbornly oriented toward a star that disappeared from the heaven of reason long ago, but whose influence helped create great communities and powerful institutions. Once people were stripped of their last defenses, my naive reformism only persuaded them—for it was certainly time—that this lowly world, which is barely ready for philosophy, is not yet ready for justice. Despite the most eloquent, flattering propaganda, we're still going to have to pass through centuries of selfish individualism and unmitigated parasitism. No matter how altruistic and powerful a man is, how can one man's actions transform an entire collective psychology?

"Well, as you can see, if I didn't want to destroy my life completely, I was going to have to take an entirely different course. There was still time: I had all the aggressiveness of a twenty-seven-year-old, and I was burning up with desire for glory. I wanted to do something significant, something decisive, something that would outlast the ravages of time and the whims of fashion and taste.

"Clearly, ambitious desires like these can only be fully satisfied in the sciences. And so, with the patience of a Benedictine and the strength and ardor of a willing hero, I dedicated myself to scientific work. As I told you, I've always had a knack for experimental physics. Its truths enchant me not just for the brilliance and precision of their mathematical form, but for the wonderful, fruitful ways they can be used to promote life, making it easier and more spiritual for us.

"Besides, I was so sick of the endless controversies to which social and moral truths are always subject, by some incontrovertible law. I wanted to work on neutral ground, where any mental conquests—if I were lucky enough to make any—would have to be accepted by everyone, even the uneducated masses. Who argues about the telephone, special analysis, the dynamo, or the locomotive? Who haggles with their discoverers about the tribute and admiration they should be paid? Luckily for physicists and chemists, they differ from philosophers and artists in that they never have to rely on the erratic, arbitrary judgment of posterity. Only for them does Apollo spur on his swift chargers, crowning the happy victor with glory before the chill of old age and fear of impending death pull the golden cup of fame from their thirsty lips . . .

"And so finally, after two years of intense mental labor and persistent work in the laboratory, I had the indescribable joy of discovering some new facts in the inexhaustible domain of electricity and radiology. Fortunately, they proved highly valuable for industry. When we tested my apparatus on a small scale, I was satisfied, for the models we'd built clearly confirmed the exactness of my predictions. But these tests quickly exhausted the resources of a humble professor living on the meager salary of a public official.

"So I had to apply for help from the government to build my electrical and radiographic machines on a grand, definitive scale. But as often occurs in such cases, I only got caught up in an endless tangle of red tape and lost valuable time and patience. Not even a flattering report from a learned academy and the vote of confidence of a famous engineer were enough to win me official support. Maybe the memory of my inept socialist campaigns contributed to this ministerial indifference and these administrative delays. But then again, patriotism and generosity in Spain have always been oriented toward war. To loosen our purse strings and inflame our hearts, you have to invent deadly machines that can blow up a city or sink a battleship. My poor contrivances were certainly good for the transmission and transformation of energy, but unfortunately, they offered no immediate sensational opportunities for killing people on a grand scale . . .

"With my hopes withering and my resources drying up, I was forced to emigrate, seeking warmth and shelter for my projects in foreign lands. After swallowing endless slights and insults because of the fact I was a Spaniard—everyone took me for a dreamer a priori—I finally settled in Paris, whose renowned Academy of Sciences studied my inventions and then gladly accepted them. At last, my Palm Sunday had arrived. Encouraged by this academic *exequatur*[39] and helped by a good-hearted woman who is now my wife, I achieved my goal of building the real models and showing everyone their originality and utility. Soon I had the money I needed to convert my fantasies into strong, prolific industrial creatures, a testament to their creator's hard work and intellectual honesty.

39. An *exequatur* is an official letter from a government authorizing a commercial agent to act.

"And so I built a huge factory, installing the most powerful motors and best-equipped workshops. I tried out new kinds of dynamos, storage batteries, Geiger counters, and radioactive generators on the international market. Today, they're making their way triumphantly around the world, building a reputation for the company and bringing in fat returns. Rather than subsiding, the importance and prosperity of my business are increasing every day. Now that the output of the original factory has tripled, a whole multitude of little white buildings has sprung up around my laboratory. In them work a noisy, cheerful army of laborers who feed on my intelligence and ideas as a forest feeds on the sun's rays. I'm happy, because I've fulfilled the great dream of my life. If the world of knowledge is a polyhedron with an infinite number of sides, I've polished and decorated one tiny facet of it in my own, personal style. That's where a grateful posterity will carve out my modest epitaph."

"Jaime, my friend, that's wonderful! . . . I am truly amazed . . . Certainly I've never doubted the keenness or the depth of your talent. But there's something in your sublime victory that saddens me as a Spaniard, and it wouldn't be very loyal or honest of me to conceal it . . . It hurts me to think that in order to find recognition of your merits and a pedestal for your glory, you felt forced to leave the country. Tell me, in the happy exile in which you now live, have you lost your love of your country?"

"No, never . . . Despite all the time I've spent in France, it's never even occurred to me to give up my Spanish citizenship. Besides, what are all my humble inventions but the fruits of fiery, heartfelt patriotism? Some men sacrifice themselves on the altar of their *alma mater* as victims of war or international hate; the poets praise them with passionate, high-sounding hymns. The best thing I can give is my scientific creations, and so, as a kind of mystical incense, I offer up my own brain, quivering and exhausted from intense thought; burned and consumed by powerful desire . . .

"Don't think that the voluntary exile in which I now find myself has even slightly diminished my intense feeling of Spanishness. In the nostalgic eyes of its absent son, the beloved image of our homeland doesn't shrink as the distance increases. On the contrary, it expands and grows ever more beautiful. It's like those drab, ordinary mountains: when you look at them from afar, their peaks rise up gracefully and take on all the colors of the sky."

"Bravo, Jaime! Your eloquent tones comfort and inspire me. In my ear, they sound like the *jota* or the verses of the long-forgotten *March of Cádiz*.[40] They're reaching my soul at just the right time, too, for right now everything—even the things I've held most sacred—is falling to pieces as a result of my misfortune. Just now, in a moment of emotional indulgence I greatly appreciated, you were talking about your longing for immortality . . . about your fervent desire to leave a shining star for posterity. And because of an inevitable association of ideas, your generous impulse has brought me a feeling of deep melancholy . . ."

Esperaindeo paused briefly, held back by indecision. Then he continued:

"There's a troublesome thought bubbling in my mind that I probably shouldn't reveal to you. If I did, I'd be committing a great disrespect, maybe even an outright indiscretion."

"Speak freely . . . I'll respond as best I can."

"Well, all right. Since I have your permission, I'll be so bold as to express this doubt. Tell me, how do you reconcile your high hopes for glory with your strong belief in individual death and the inevitable end of life and the world?"

"What would you say if I were to tell you—with the greatest intellectual humility, of course—that apart from my patriotic feeling, the most powerful factor contributing to my scientific and industrial success has been my sad conviction that there's no life after death? What would you think of my intellect if I said that when things are going badly in the lab, I take heart from this simple saying: 'If my soul is condemned to die, then let's at least save the ideas. Let's work to cre-

40. The *jota* is a popular dance performed in Aragón and Navarre, Cajal's native region.

ate something living and lasting, some germinal concept that will be like a flame of life spreading from generation to generation, feeding and growing endlessly at the expense of the human brain.'"

"I must confess, I don't understand how the echo of posthumous applause can produce a pleasant sensation in an empty skull."

"Here, my friend, we're facing one of life's many paradoxes and contradictions: our instinct imposes a desire to live forever, but reason denies mad illusions like this. Still, we have to keep ourselves from analyzing these impulses too deeply, for—like many others that are no less absurd—they're designed more for the good of the species than for the prosperity of the individual. We should restrict ourselves to feeling and cultivating them, for only that way will our work be advantageous for humanity. Only that way will we achieve all the happiness that's possible in this lowly world once we know the truth.

"So that posterity won't forget us, let's hurry up and conquer the present. Let's get these fields plowed while we're still young, before the coldness of our years dampens our vigor and deadens our enthusiasm. The important thing is to make men's lives easier and more pleasant, to clear out a corner in the books and souls where our ideas can joyously flutter their wings. To do this, you have to emerge from the anonymous mass, that poor flock where people are counted by millions, and with your own merits enter the brilliant legion where people are counted by ones. The work is hard, and the disappointments and sorrows of the struggle are very great, but the victory is so beautiful, so gratifying! How exhilarating, the first time you feel yourself targeted by thousands of curious, adoring eyes from below! . . . And then there are a thousand other pleasures that follow in consequence, the results of the scientific and social value of your work. There's the gratitude of people you've rescued from poverty, and the supreme pride of knowing that when you came into this world, they didn't wear out the forge of Nature in vain . . ."

"Keep going! Don't stop, for God's sake! Your enthusiasm is the best possible medicine for me."

"If you could only see what a great pleasure it is to use your own creativity to transform a pure, abstract idea into a teeming hatchery of humanity, a spiritual archipelago overflowing with life and glowing with well-being! Ah, how little the unfortunate nations would regret the loss of their colonies if their sons, burning with holy patriotism, would try to broaden the moral horizons of their peoples. If only they could develop the radiant islands of their intelligence, sanctified by peace and hard work and inaccessible to conquerors or deserters! . . .

"But enough of this endless, irritating lyricism. I am finished, my friend, with my long-winded tale. In it, I've tried to give you a reflection of my life just as if I were a clear mirror. Now it's up to you to decide whether you want to follow this example or keep wandering the bleak moors of theology and politics."

"Oh, that's already decided. Your sound, vivifying arguments have already made a new man of me. I absolutely renounce this parasitic life under my wife's shameful, humiliating protection. I am at your service."

"Well then, as of this moment, consider yourself my private secretary, at ten thousand francs a year. You have to start somewhere . . ."

In an outburst of intense gratitude, good-hearted Esperaindeo threw his arms around Jaime. As he embraced him warmly and tenderly, he exclaimed:

"You are such a good friend . . . you always have been! May God repay you for this generosity!"

"No, stop! Don't mention it! . . . I would much rather have given you a job as manager, a much more important, high-paying position, but that job has already been filled by a person to whom I owe everything, except the very fact of my existence. Can you guess?"

"Your wonderful teacher?"

"Yes, the very same: don Enrique Fernández. Despite his advanced age and his reluctance to leave his beloved native soil, he finally consented to trade in his paltry ten thousand reales as a professor for the twenty thousand francs I can give him here. All I'm doing is discharging a sacred debt, but at the same time, the assistance of a man like that is invaluable to me in directing the complex mechanisms of the factory."

"By giving him that job, you showed your common sense as well as the goodness of your heart."

"Well, my dear Esperaindeo . . . while we've been engaged in this pleasant conversation, the hours have been slipping quickly by. It's very late. Let's go down to the factory. It's not very far . . . just a twenty-minute omnibus ride, which will take us as far as the Stock Exchange, and then fifteen minutes on a metropolitan train. When we get there, I'll introduce you to my family. You can get to know the *maestro,* and I'll tell you about your duties, which won't be very complicated or burdensome for the time being."

Minutes later, the two friends were climbing into an omnibus. Gradually, the fatigue following that profusion of words put an end to their animated conversation. A feeling of sweet serenity bathed the weary soul of each interlocutor. While Jaime leaned his arm against the window and looked absentmindedly out at the bustling pedestrians and swiftly passing carriages, his companion was studying the scientist's leonine head. The last red-tinted clouds of the evening were outlining his noble profile with gold, emphasizing his look of an energetic warrior. Esperaindeo was struck by memories of Jaime in other days, evoked by the contrast between the present and the past . . . He recalled his wise but vehement speeches at the Athenaeum, the redeeming, humanitarian harangues of a scientific apostle. What a terrible loss of a great leader! he thought. There are so few like Jaime, and poor Spain needs energetic men like him so badly, manly politicians and patriots! Finally, yielding to the tension of his ideas and feelings struggling to come out, he broke the solemn silence and exclaimed:

"Jaime, my friend, if they could see you now! . . . Who would ever have thought that you, the invincible champion of logic, resourceful orator, selfless advocate of the poor and unfortunate, future leader full of noble ambition, would end up on the peaceful shore of science and industry?"

"You shouldn't be surprised . . . As I was telling you, the world is not yet ready for philosophy or justice. It's a sad fact to face . . . but the thing is, despite the self-proclaimed tolerance of modern times, they only let you use your common sense in the tranquil field of science. So let's work there, since it's the only place they'll let us think freely. The apostles of justice will be heard later on, when omnipotent science has lit up all the caverns and dark corners of Nature and the spirit.

BIBLIOGRAPHY

Works by and about Ramón y Cajal and His Contemporaries

Benítez, Ruben. "La novela científica en España: Ramón y Cajal y el Conde de Gimeno." *Revista de estudios hispánicos* [Puerto Rico] 6 (1979): 25–39.

Brock, Thomas. *Robert Koch: A Life in Medicine and Bacteriology.* Madison, Wis.: Science Tech Publishers; Berlin: Springer, 1988.

Dictionary of Scientific Biography. Edited by Charles Coulston Gillispie. New York: Scribner, 1970–80.

Doyle, Arthur Conan. *The History of Spiritualism.* 2 vols. [1926]. New York: Arno Press, 1975.

Dubos, René. *Louis Pasteur: Free Lance of Science.* New York: DaCapo, 1960.

Granjel, Luis S. *Baroja y otras figuras del noventiocho.* Madrid: Guadarrama, 1960.

Haynes, Roslynn D. *From Faust to Strangelove: Representations of the Scientist in Western Literature.* Baltimore: Johns Hopkins University Press, 1994.

Koch, Robert. *Essays of Robert Koch.* Translated by K. Codell Carter. Contributions in Medical Studies, no. 20. Westport, Conn.: Greenwood Press, 1987.

de Kruif, Paul. *Microbe Hunters.* New York: Harcourt, Brace, and World, 1953.

Laín Entralgo, Pedro. "Estudios y apuntes sobre Ramón y Cajal." In *España como problema.* Madrid: Aguilar, 1957.

Larsen, Kevin. *La ciencia aplicada: Gabriel Miró y la traducción científica.* Madrid: Alpuerto, 1997.

———. "La ciencia y la literatura en *Nada menos que todo un hombre.*" *Anales de la Sociedad Científica Argentina* 229 (1999).

———. "Gabriel Miró y la individualidad endocrina." *Asclepio* 1 (1990): 335–46.

LaRubia Prado, Francisco. "'La aldea perdida' de Palacio Valdés: Tecnología y la cuestión del género literario." *Letras peninsulares* (2000).

Latour, Bruno. *The Pasteurization of France.* Translated by Alan Sheridan and John Law. Cambridge: Harvard University Press, 1988.

Lewy Rodríguez, Enriqueta. *El Madrid de Cajal.* Madrid: Artes Gráficas Municipales, 1985.

Loewy, Arthur D. "Ramón y Cajal and Methods of Neuroanatomical Research." *Perspectives in Biology and Medicine* 15 (1979): 7–36.

López Piñero, José María. *Las publicaciones valencianas de Cajal.* Valencia: Secretariado de Publicaciones, Universidad de Valencia, 1983.

Marañón, Gregorio. *Cajal: Su tiempo y el nuestro.* 2d ed. Santander: Zuñiga, 1950.

Mellizo, Carlos. "David Hume escribe a un médico: O La 'enfermedad de los doctos.'" *Revista de occidente* 148 (1993): 5–20.

———. "De Cajal a Martín Santos." *España Contemporánea* 2 (1989).

O'Connor, D. J. "Science, Literature, and Self-Censorship: Ramón y Cajal's *Cuentos de Vacaciones.*" *Ideologies and Literature* 1, no. 3 (1985): 98–122.

Perrín, Tomas G. "Cajal como Español." *Abside* 22 (1958): 191–216.

Pratt, Dale. "Literary Images of Spanish Science since 1868." Ph.D. diss., Cornell University, 1995.

———. "Sex, Science, and the Origins of Culture in Emilia Pardo Bazán." *Mujer, sexo, y poder en la literatura feminina iberoamericana del siglo XIX.* Edited by Joanna Courteau. *Siglo XIX* (1999): 39–49.

———. *Signs of Science: Literature, Science, and Spanish Modernity.* Purdue Studies in Romance Literature. West Lafayette, Ind.: Purdue University Press, 2001.

Santiago Ramón y Cajal (1852–1934) was a Spanish neurohistologist who produced beautiful, highly accurate drawings of nerve cells. In 1906, he won the Nobel Prize for medicine for proving that neurons were independent cells, not parts of a physically continuous nerve net. Because his microscopic studies of neurons led to our current understanding of nerve impulse transmission, many scientists consider him the founder of modern neurobiology. Early in his career, Ramón y Cajal wrote stories and novels featuring the most controversial scientific issues of his time. He waited twenty years to publish his fiction, however, probably because he feared jeopardizing his scientific career—either because of the stories' political content, or because a person known as a fiction writer would no longer be taken seriously as a scientist.

Laura Otis is an associate professor of English at Hofstra University. Trained in biochemistry and neurobiology, she compares the ways that scientists and creative writers develop their ideas. Otis is the author of *Organic Memory* (1994), *Membranes* (1999), and a forthcoming book, *Networking* (2001), which juxtaposes technological communications systems with those in living bodies. With a Ph.D. in comparative literature, she explores fiction and scientific essays in English, Spanish, German, and French. Otis was recently awarded a MacArthur Fellowship and an Alexander von Humboldt Fellowship for her studies of literature and science and is currently working as a guest scholar at the Max Planck Institute for the History of Science in Berlin.

———. "Stimulants of the Spirit: Metaphors and the Science of Ramón y Cajal." Unpublished manuscript, 1993.

Ramón y Cajal, Santiago. *Advice for a Young Investigator.* Translated by Neely Swanson and Larry W. Swanson. Cambridge: MIT Press, 1999.

———. *Cuentos de vacaciones.* 5th ed. Madrid: Espasa-Calpe, 1964.

———. *Degeneration and Regeneration of the Nervous System.* 2 vols. Translated by Raoul M. May. 1913. Reprint. New York: Hafner, 1959.

———. *Histology of the Nervous System of Man and Vertebrates.* 2 vols. Translated by Neely Swanson and Larry W. Swanson. New York; Oxford: Oxford University Press, 1995.

———. *Recollections of My Life.* Translated by E. Horne Craigie. Cambridge: MIT Press, 1989.

Simmer, Hans H. "Santiago Ramón y Cajal und die Typologie des Wissenschaftlers." *Medizinhistorisches Journal* 16 (1981): 414–23.

Tzitsikas, Helene. *Santiago Ramón y Cajal: Obra literaria.* Colección studium, no. 53. México: De Andrea, 1965.